# Cagaster

K[illegible]u Hashimoto



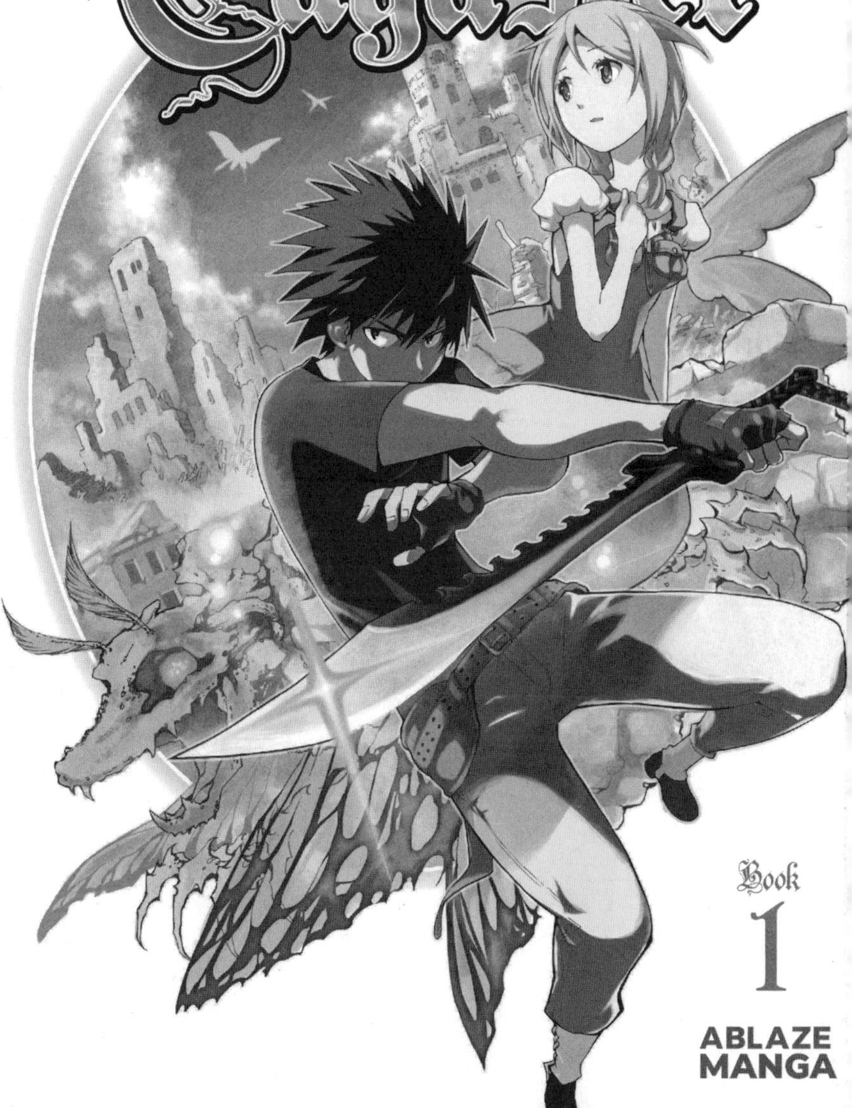

Book

1

ABLAZE
MANGA

# Cagaster

Kachou Hashimoto

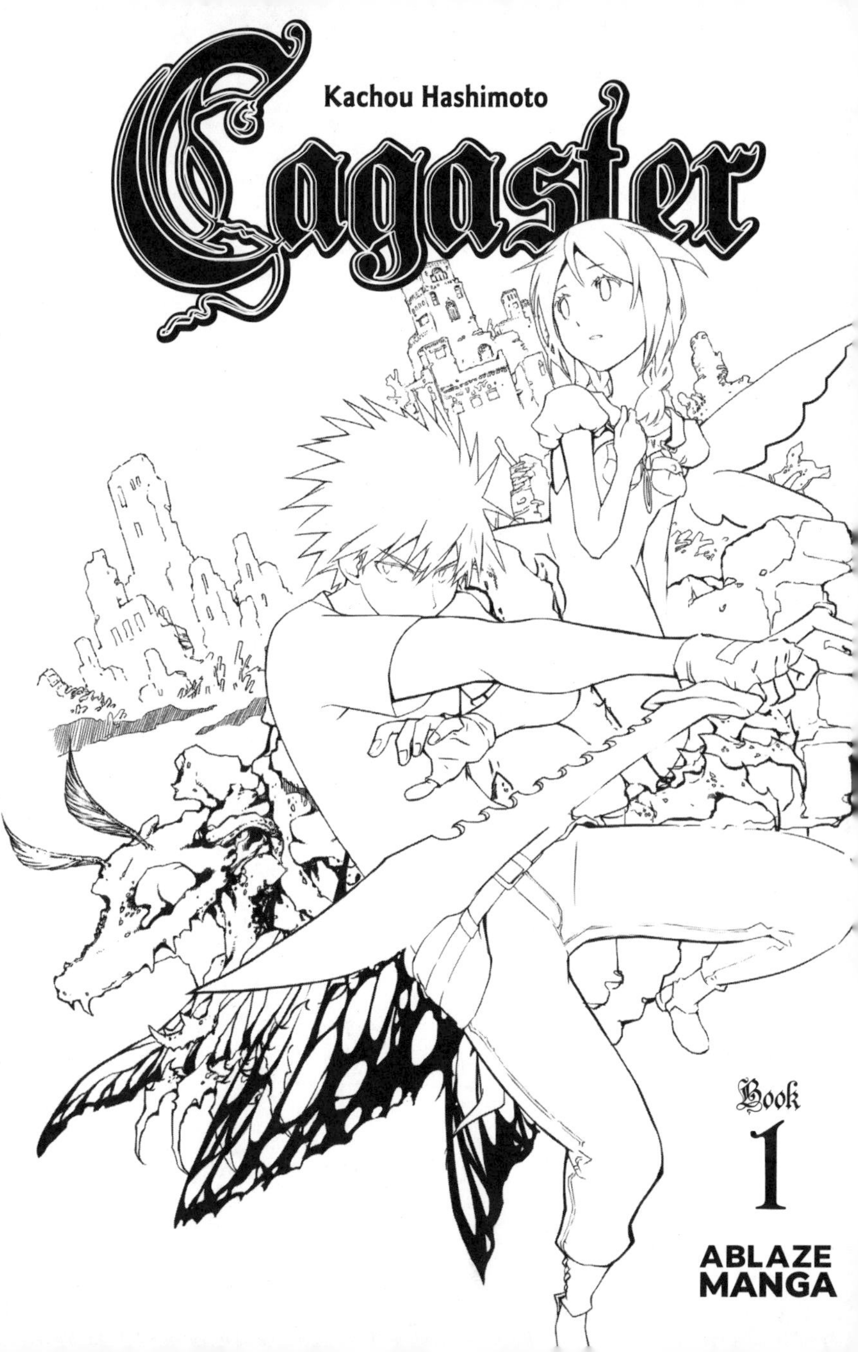

Book 1

ABLAZE MANGA

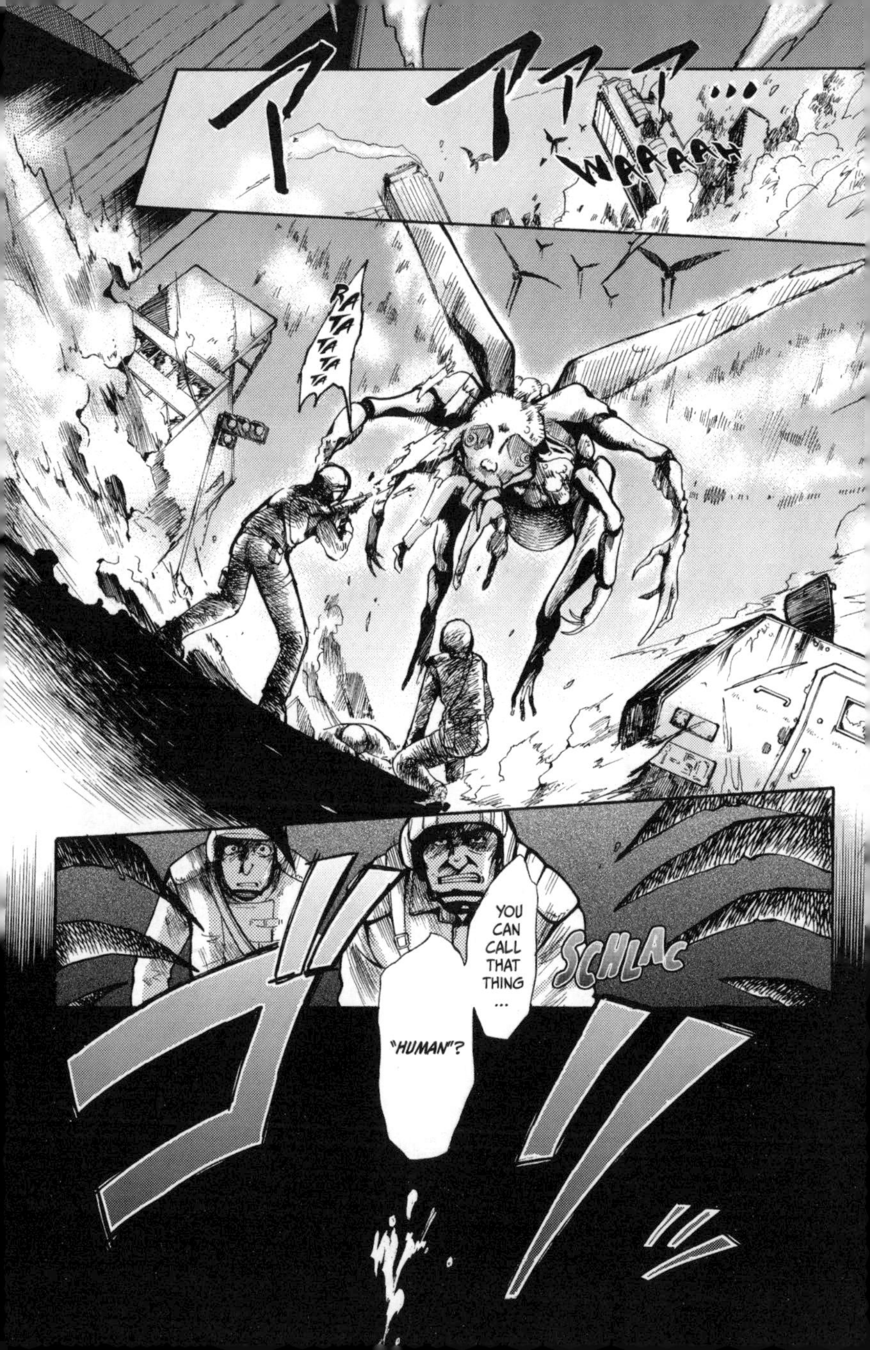
アアア…
WAAAAAH
RATATATATATA
SCHLAC
YOU CAN CALL THAT THING ...
"HUMAN"?

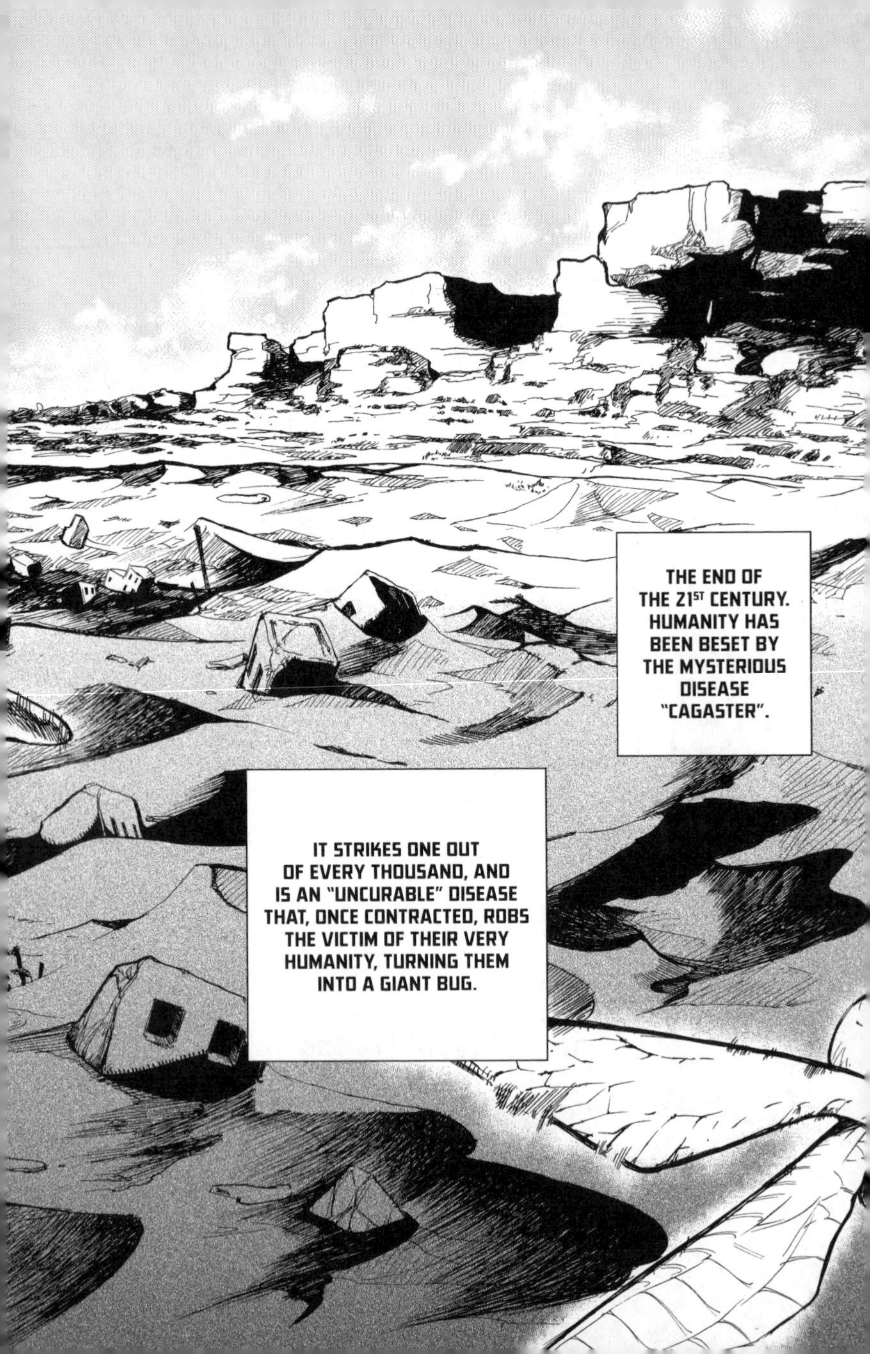
THE END OF THE 21ST CENTURY. HUMANITY HAS BEEN BESET BY THE MYSTERIOUS DISEASE "CAGASTER".
IT STRIKES ONE OUT OF EVERY THOUSAND, AND IS AN "UNCURABLE" DISEASE THAT, ONCE CONTRACTED, ROBS THE VICTIM OF THEIR VERY HUMANITY, TURNING THEM INTO A GIANT BUG.

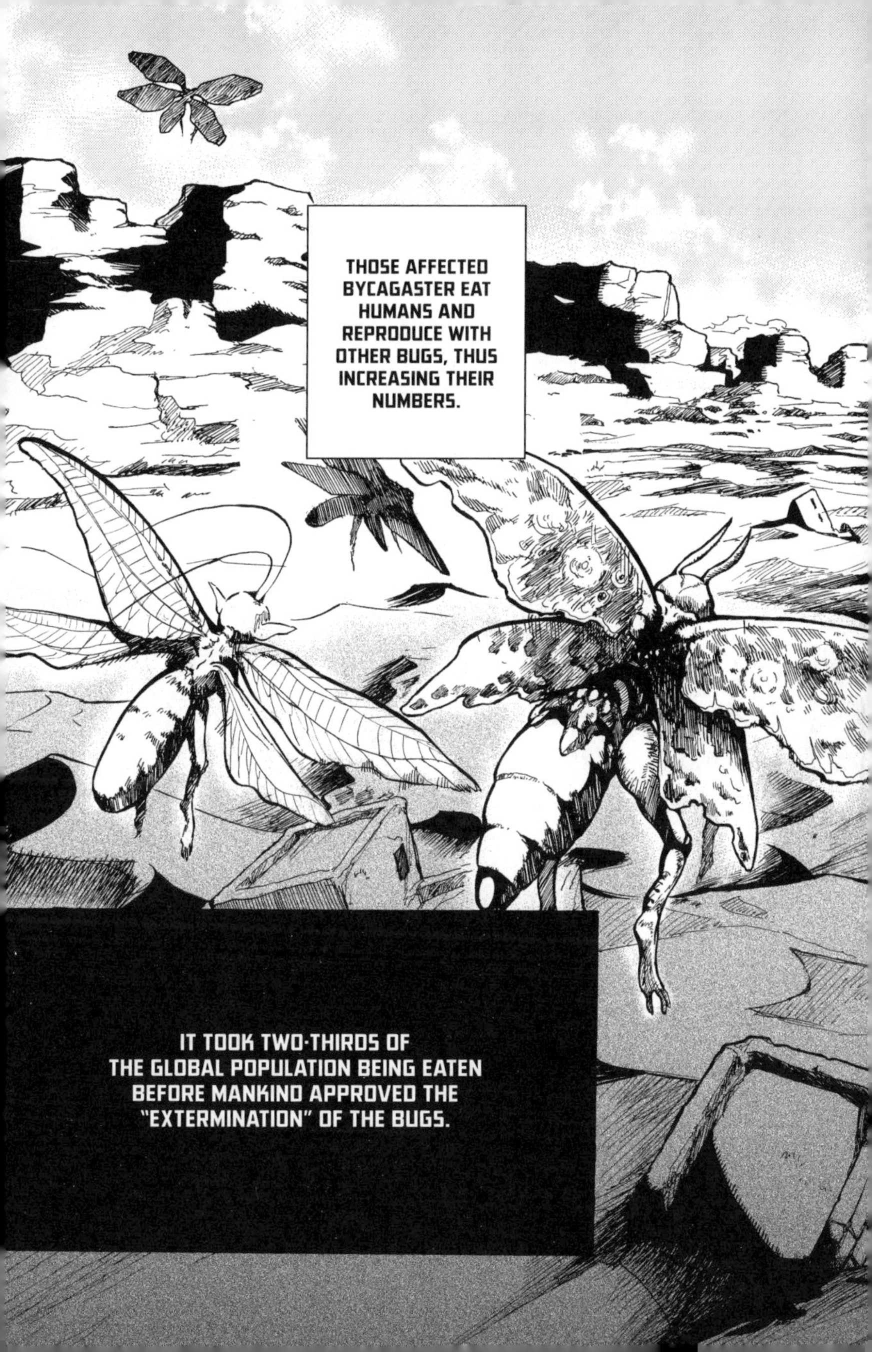
THOSE AFFECTED BYCAGASTER EAT HUMANS AND REPRODUCE WITH OTHER BUGS, THUS INCREASING THEIR NUMBERS.
IT TOOK TWO-THIRDS OF THE GLOBAL POPULATION BEING EATEN BEFORE MANKIND APPROVED THE "EXTERMINATION" OF THE BUGS.

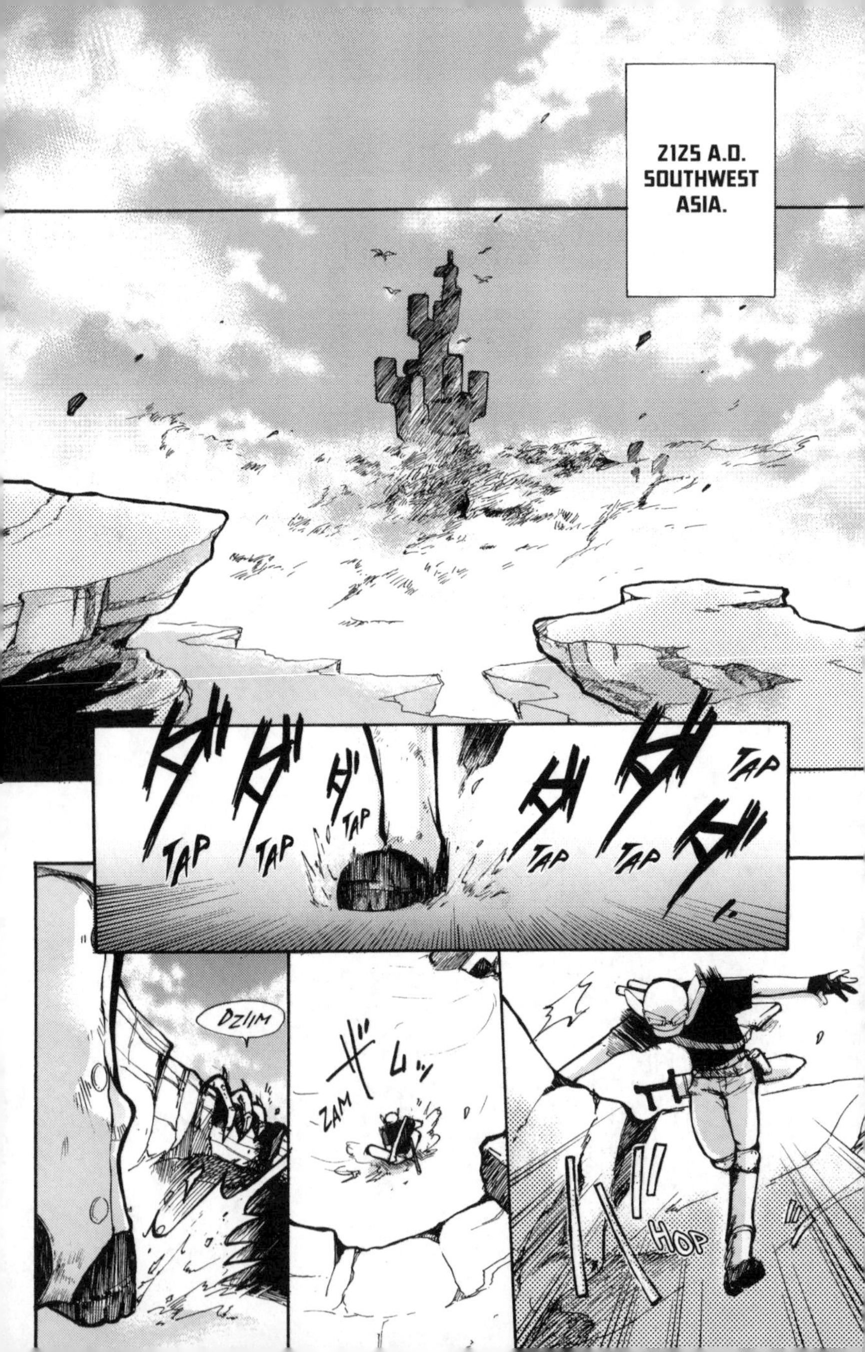
2125 A.D.
SOUTHWEST
ASIA.
TAP
TAP
TAP
TAP
TAP
TAP
HOP
ZAM
DZIIM

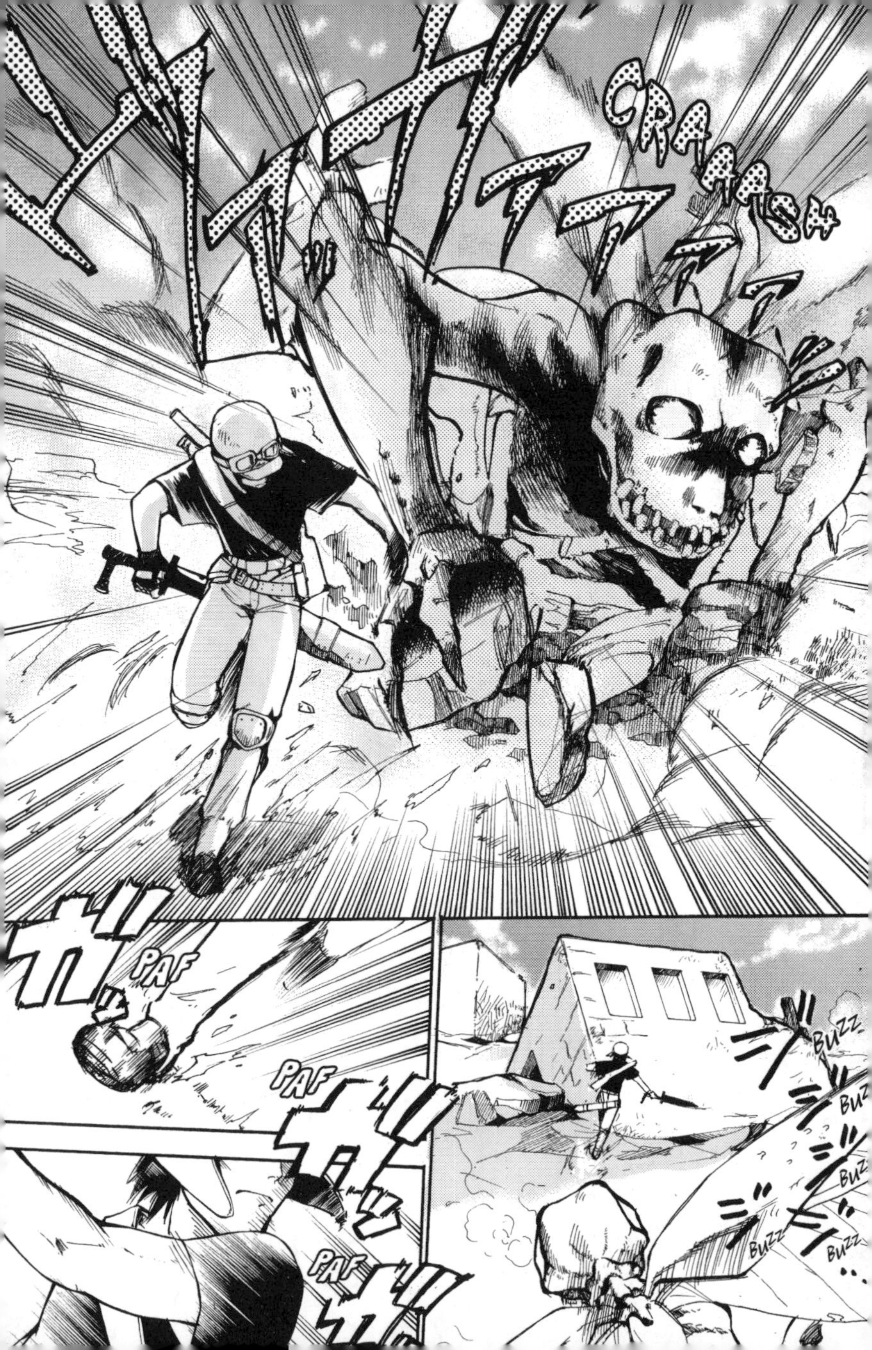
CRAAASH
BUZZ
BUZZ
BUZZ
BUZZ
BUZZ...
PAF
PAF
PAF

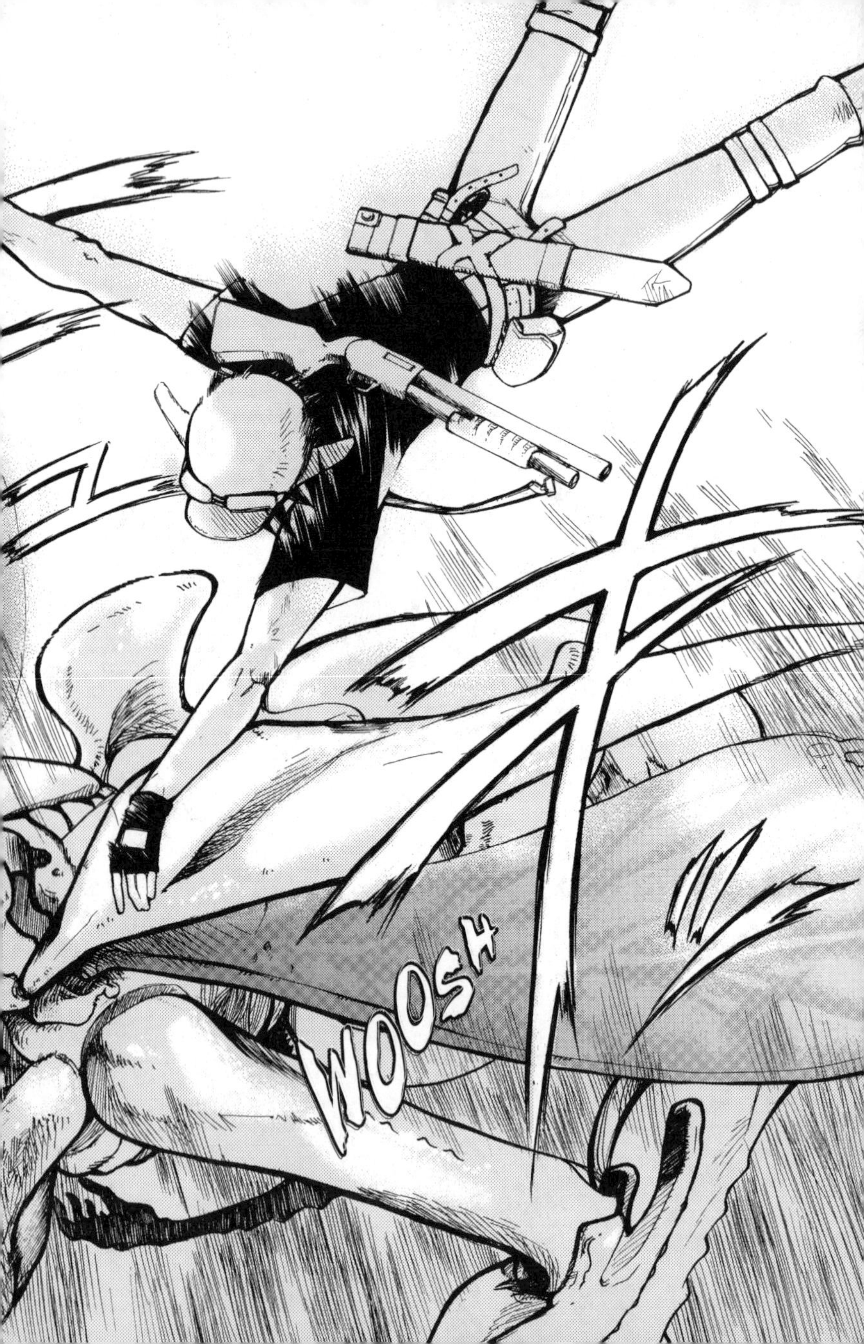
WOOSH

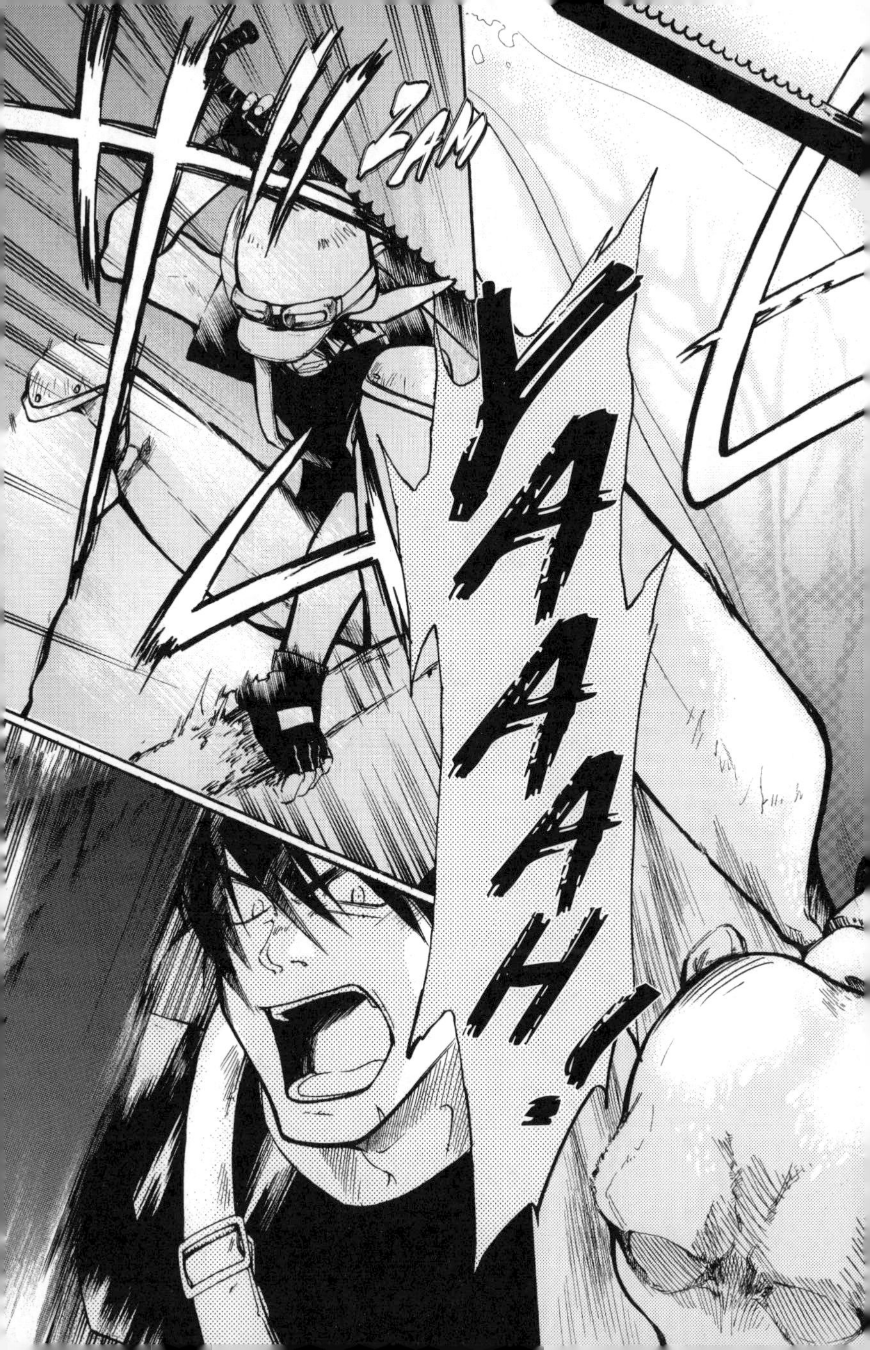
ZAM
YAAAAH!!

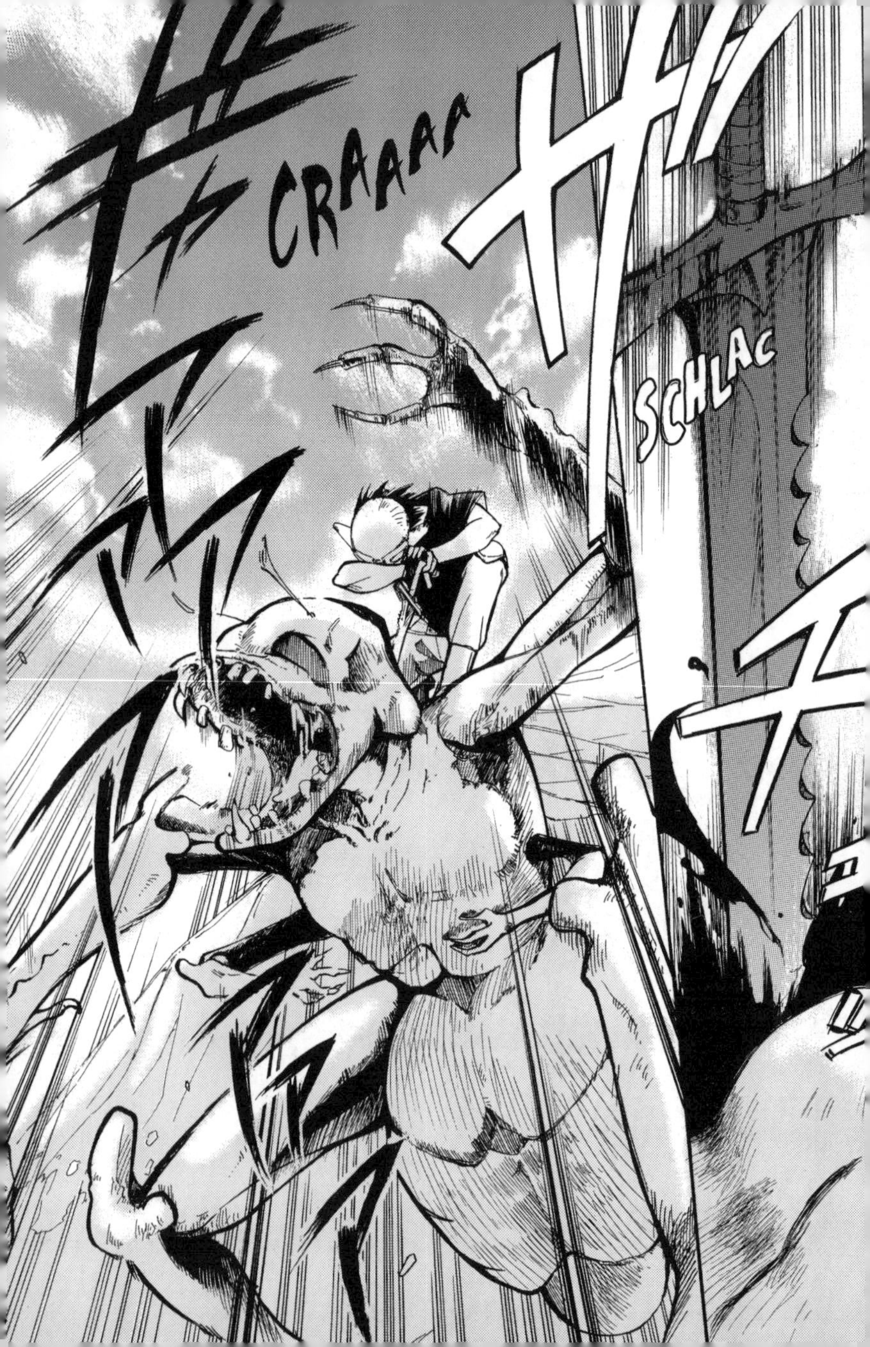
CRAAAA
SCHLAC

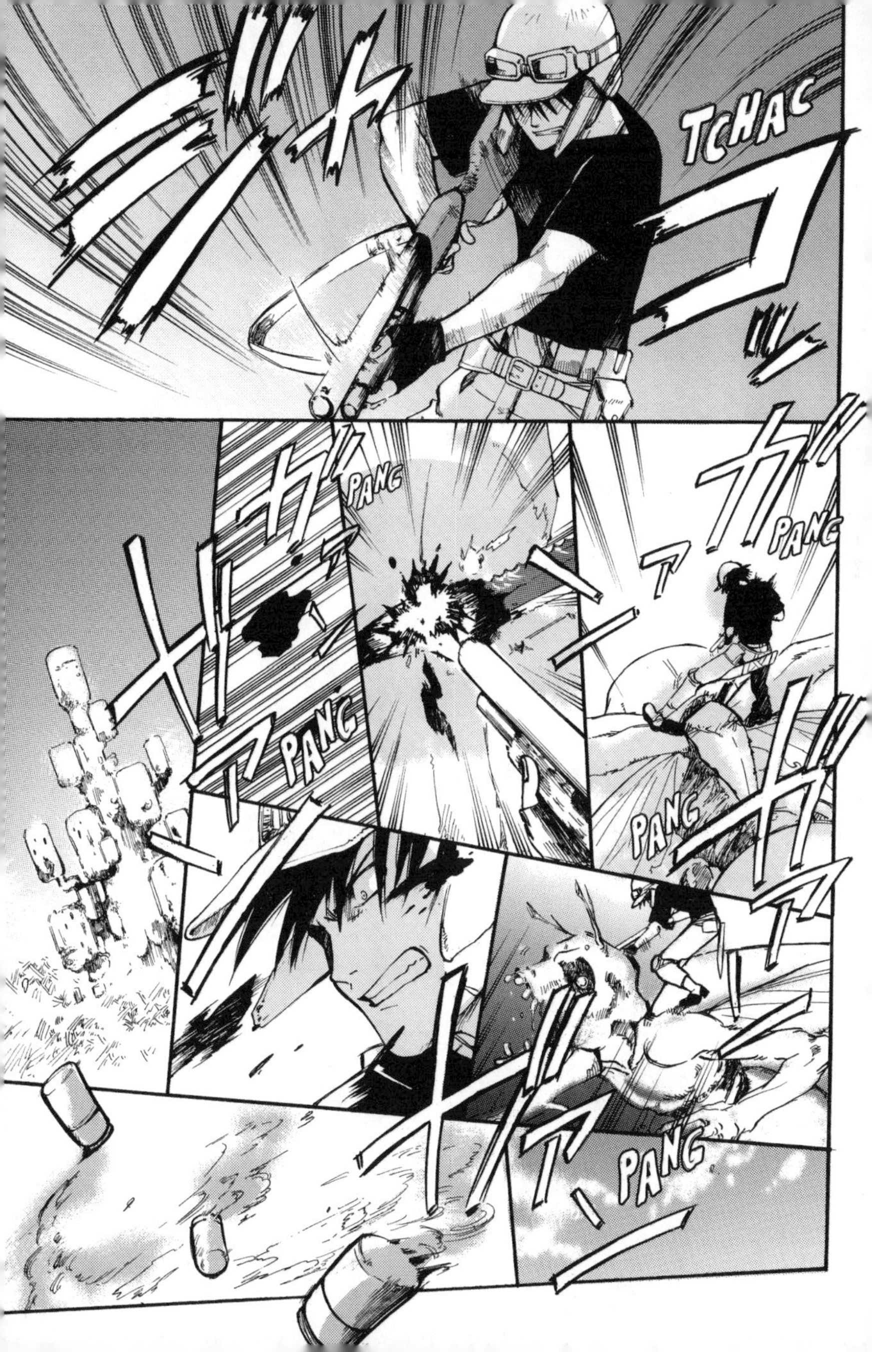
TCHAC
PANG
PANG
PANG
PANG
PANG
PANG

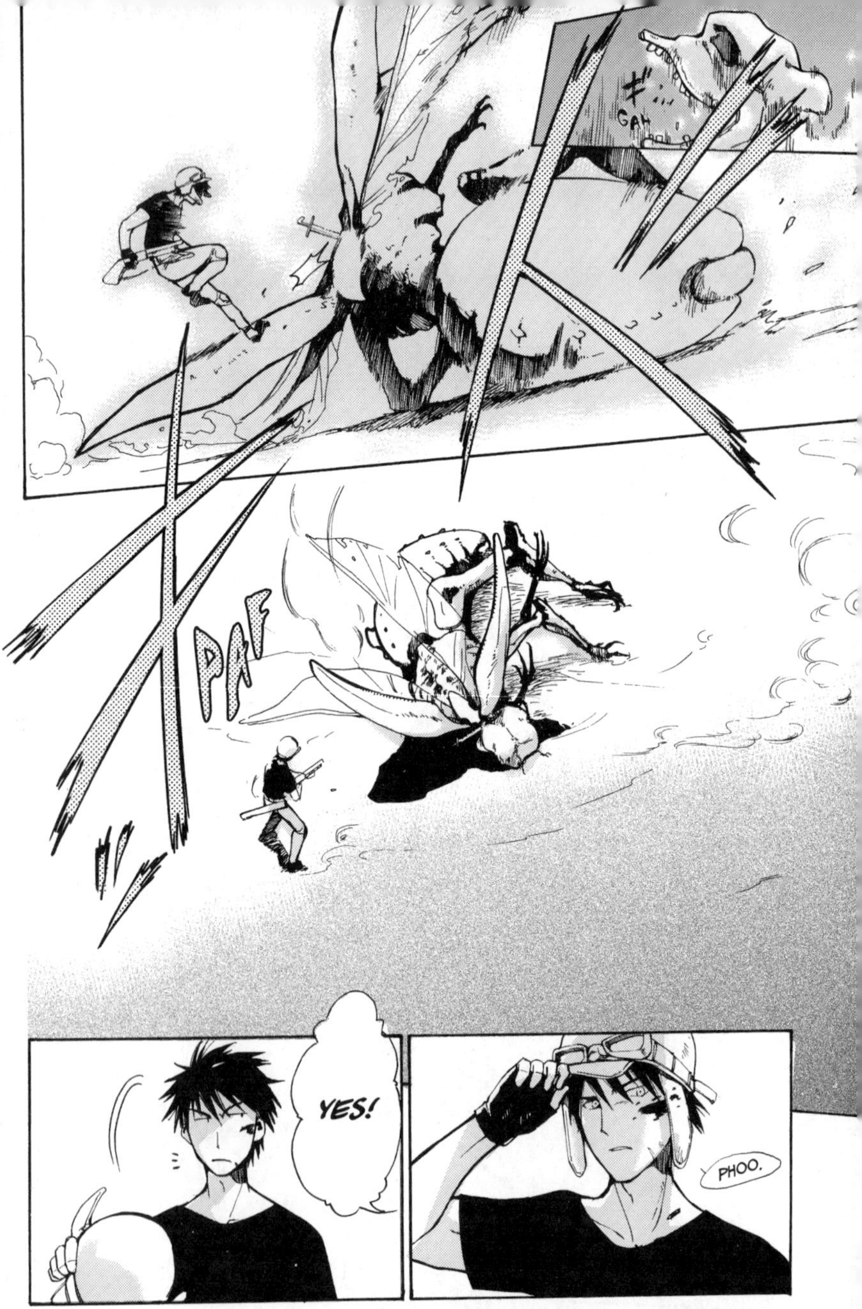
ギ…
GAH
PAF
PHOO.
YES!

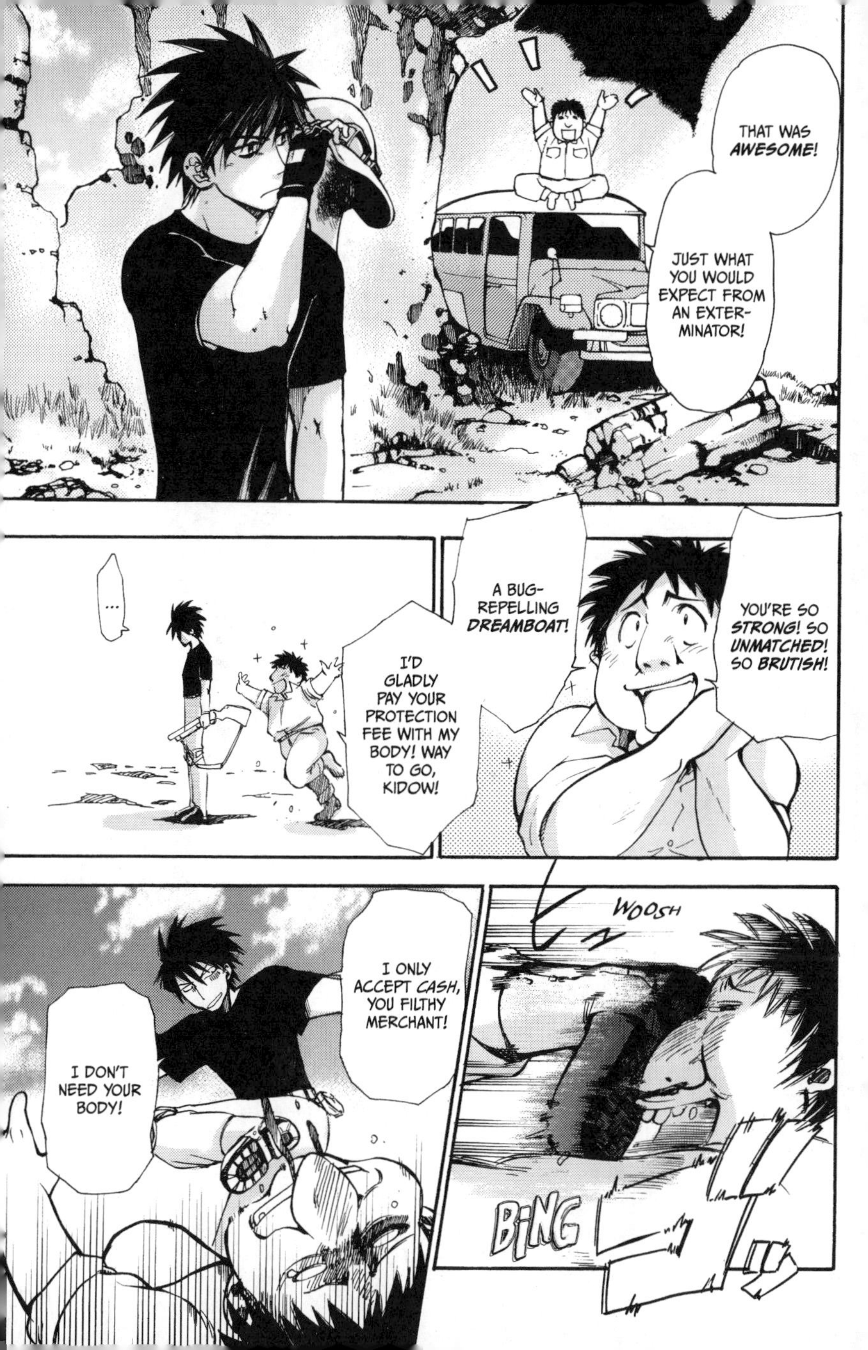
THAT WAS AWESOME!
JUST WHAT YOU WOULD EXPECT FROM AN EXTER- MINATOR!
YOU'RE SO STRONG! SO UNMATCHED! SO BRUTISH!
A BUG- REPELLING DREAMBOAT!
I'D GLADLY PAY YOUR PROTECTION FEE WITH MY BODY! WAY TO GO, KIDOW!
...
WOOSH
BING
I ONLY ACCEPT CASH, YOU FILTHY MERCHANT!
I DON'T NEED YOUR BODY!

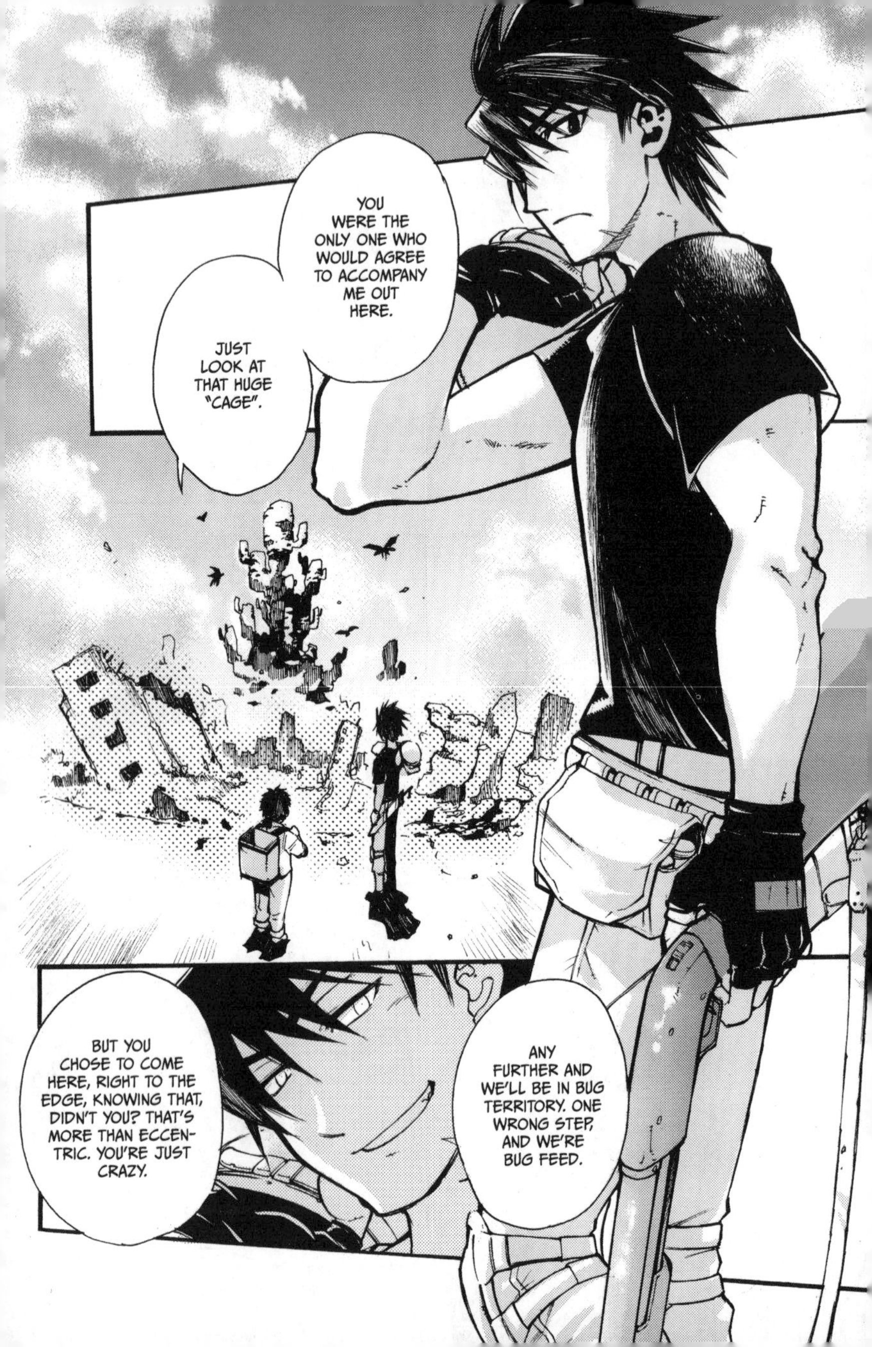
YOU WERE THE ONLY ONE WHO WOULD AGREE TO ACCOMPANY ME OUT HERE.
JUST LOOK AT THAT HUGE "CAGE".
ANY FURTHER AND WE'LL BE IN BUG TERRITORY. ONE WRONG STEP, AND WE'RE BUG FEED.
BUT YOU CHOSE TO COME HERE, RIGHT TO THE EDGE, KNOWING THAT, DIDN'T YOU? THAT'S MORE THAN ECCENTRIC. YOU'RE JUST CRAZY.

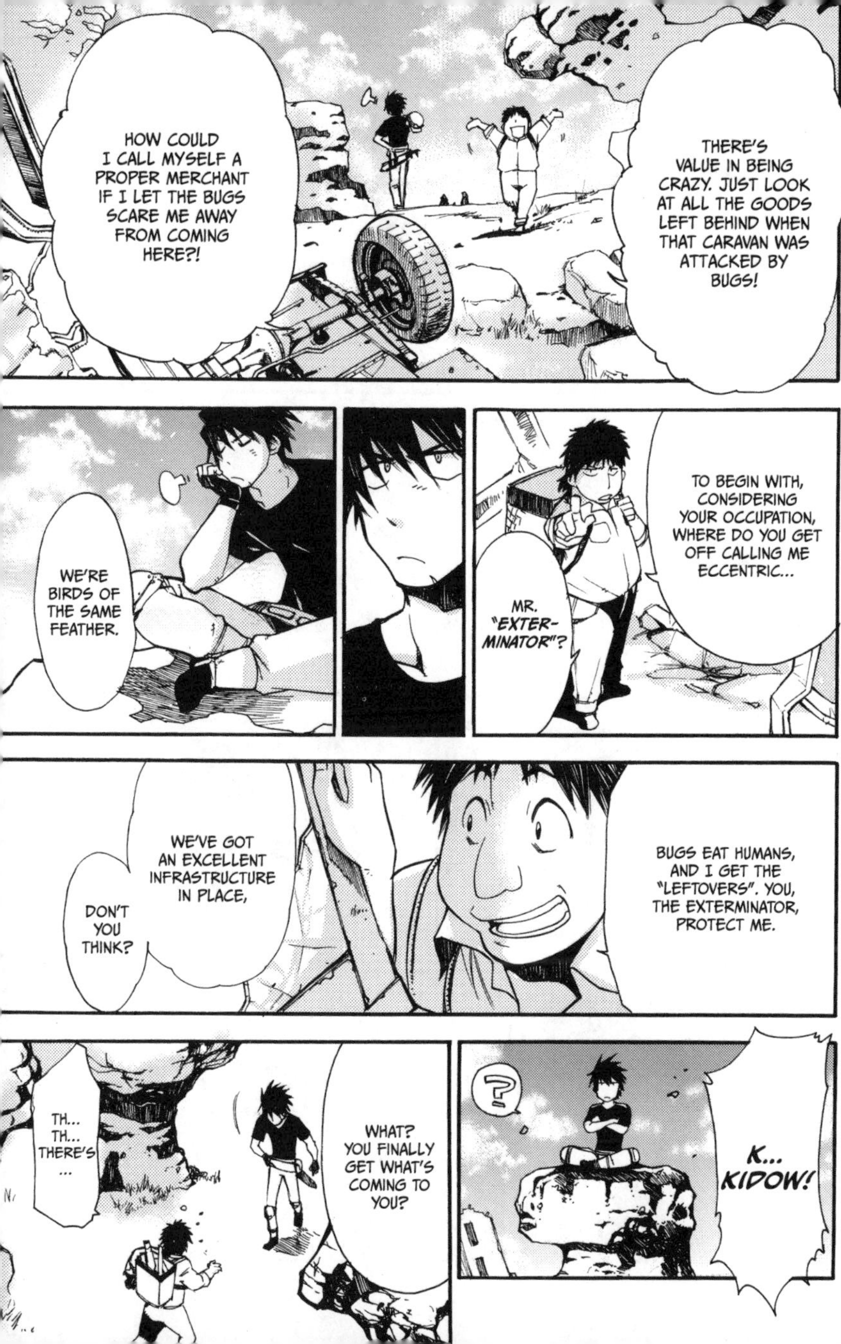
THERE'S VALUE IN BEING CRAZY. JUST LOOK AT ALL THE GOODS LEFT BEHIND WHEN THAT CARAVAN WAS ATTACKED BY BUGS!
HOW COULD I CALL MYSELF A PROPER MERCHANT IF I LET THE BUGS SCARE ME AWAY FROM COMING HERE?!
TO BEGIN WITH, CONSIDERING YOUR OCCUPATION, WHERE DO YOU GET OFF CALLING ME ECCENTRIC...
MR. "EXTERMINATOR"?
WE'RE BIRDS OF THE SAME FEATHER.
BUGS EAT HUMANS, AND I GET THE "LEFTOVERS". YOU, THE EXTERMINATOR, PROTECT ME.
WE'VE GOT AN EXCELLENT INFRASTRUCTURE IN PLACE,
DON'T YOU THINK?
K... KIDOW!
?
WHAT? YOU FINALLY GET WHAT'S COMING TO YOU?
TH... TH... THERE'S ...

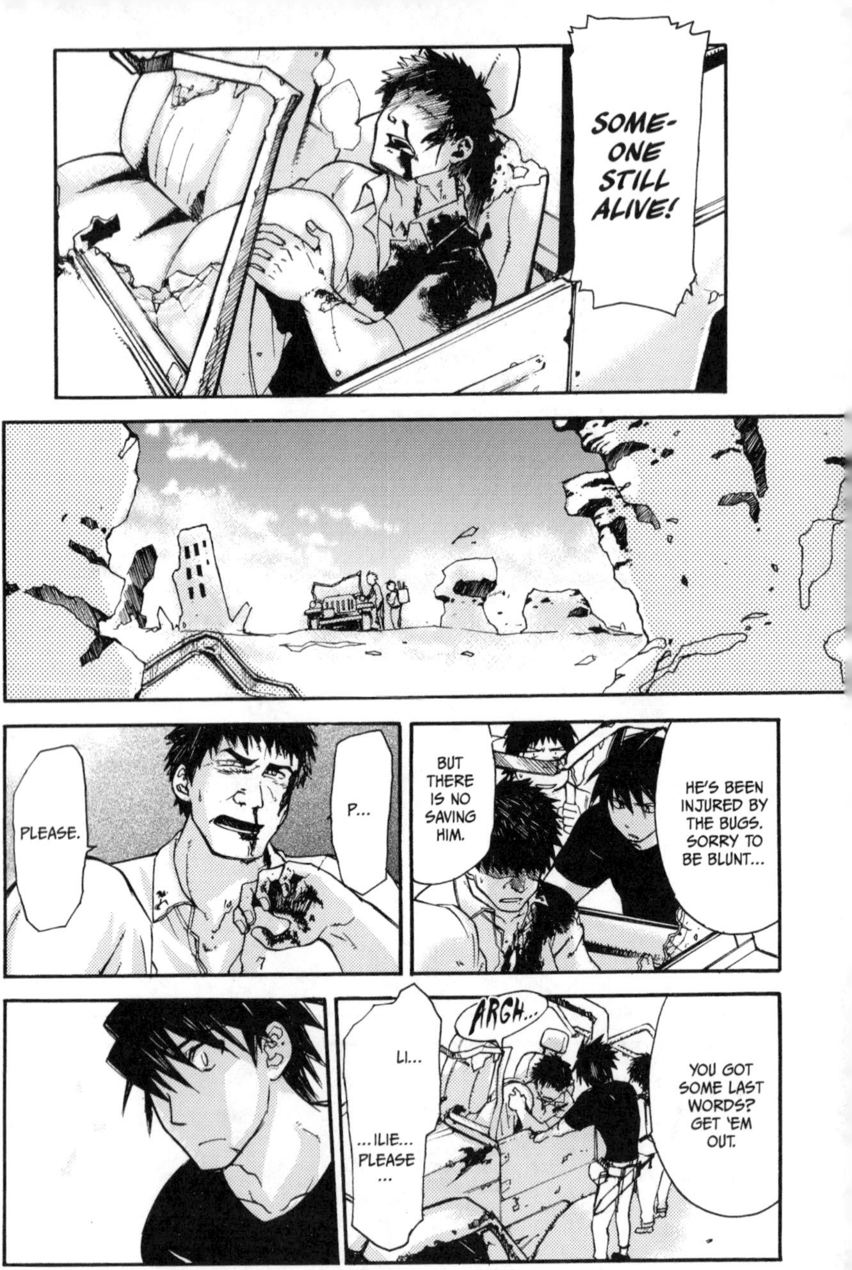
SOME-ONE STILL ALIVE!
HE'S BEEN INJURED BY THE BUGS. SORRY TO BE BLUNT...
BUT THERE IS NO SAVING HIM.
P...
PLEASE.
YOU GOT SOME LAST WORDS? GET 'EM OUT.
ARGH...
LI...
...ILIE... PLEASE ...

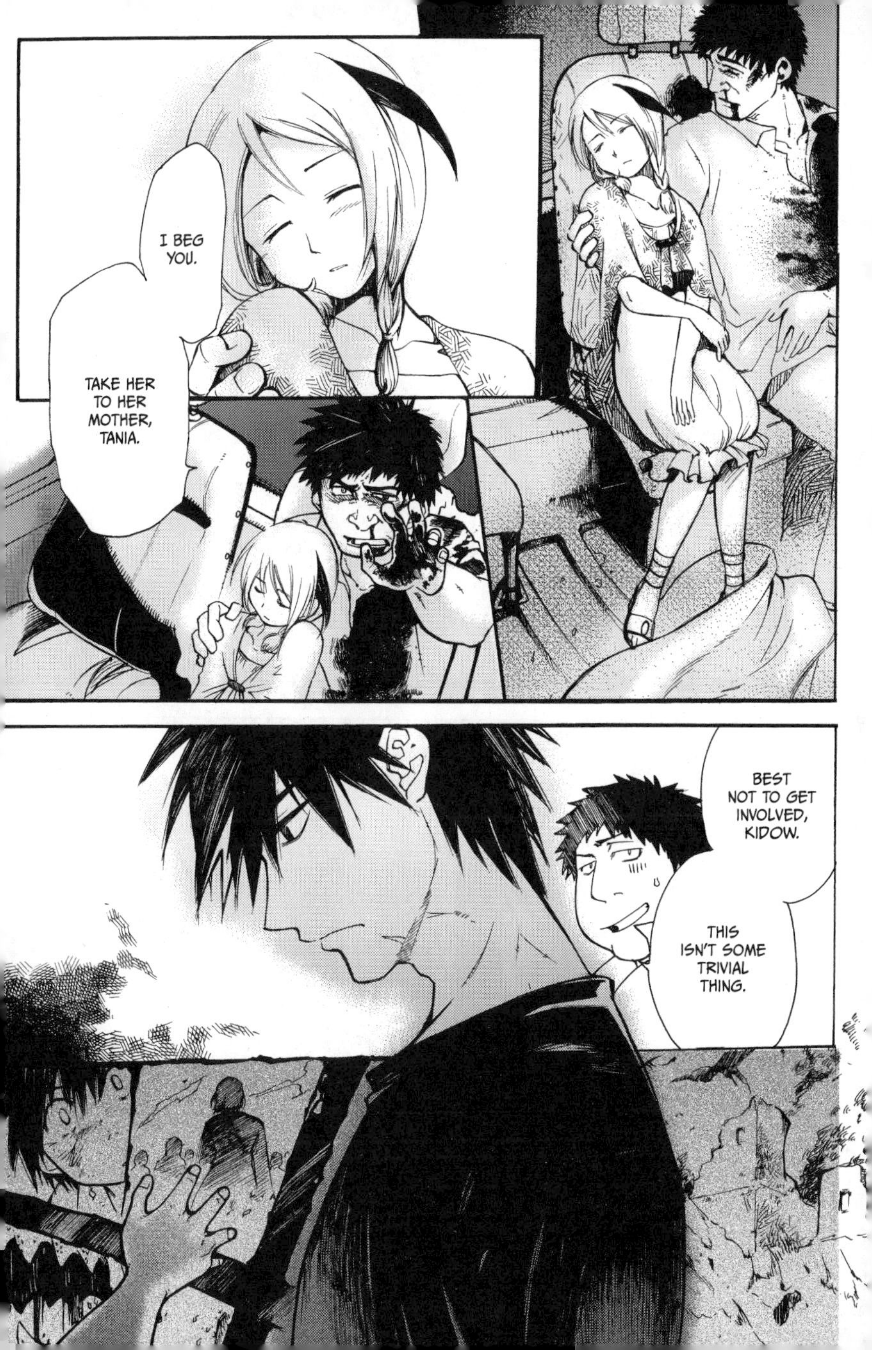
I BEG YOU.
TAKE HER TO HER MOTHER, TANIA.
BEST NOT TO GET INVOLVED, KIDOW.
THIS ISN'T SOME TRIVIAL THING.

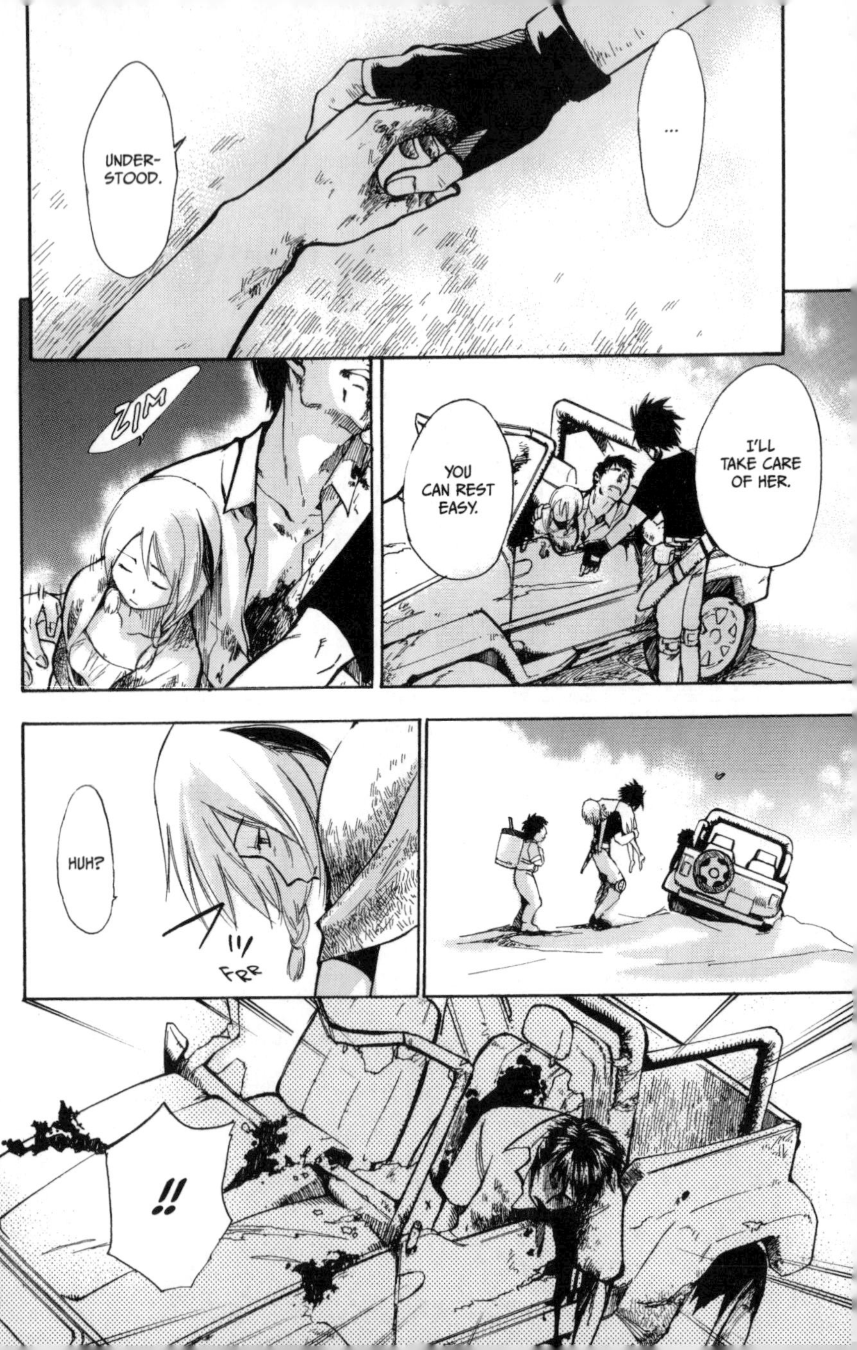
...
UNDER-
STOOD.
I'LL TAKE CARE OF HER.
YOU CAN REST EASY.
ZIM
HUH?
FRR
!!

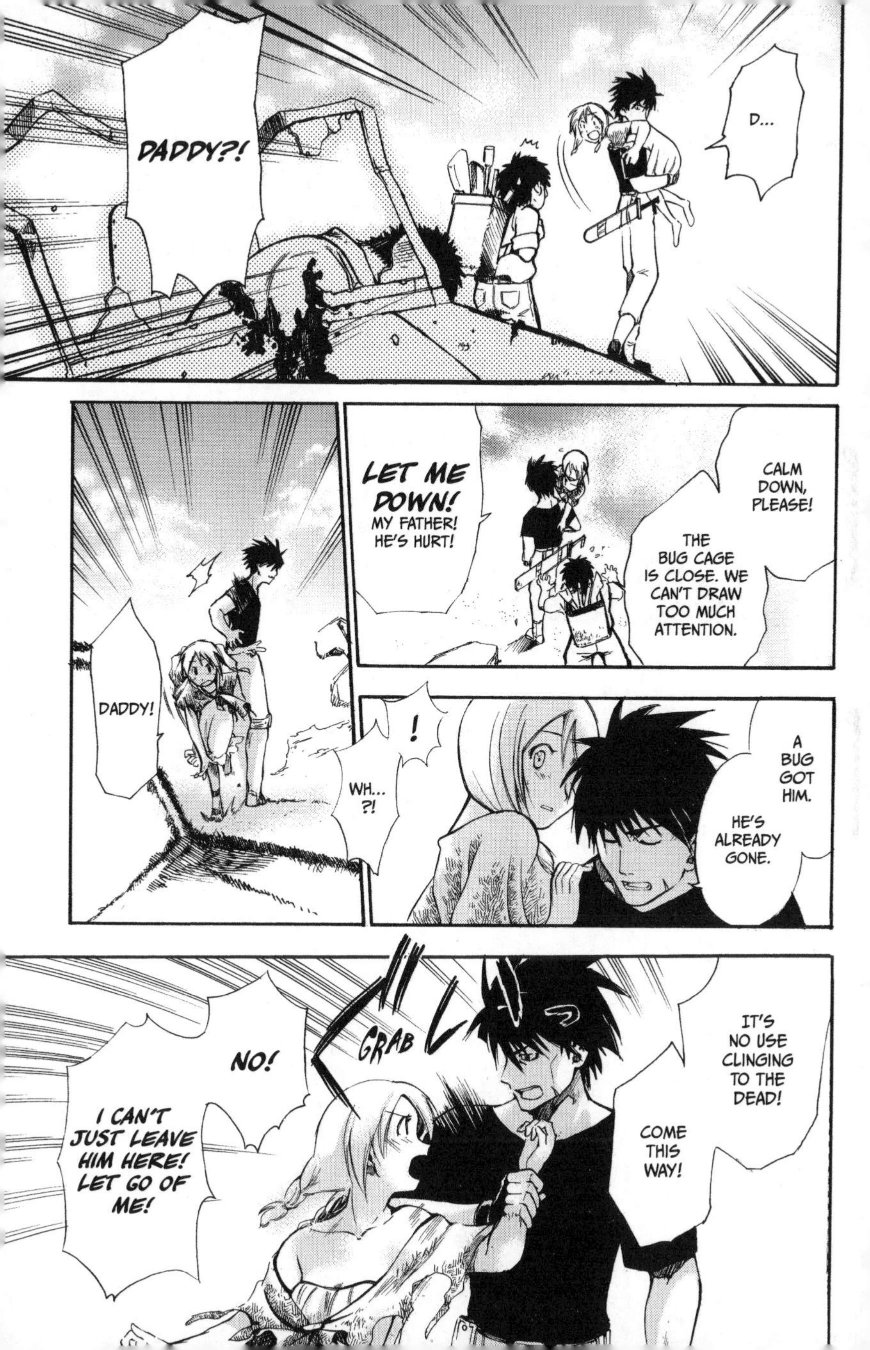
D...
DADDY?!
CALM DOWN, PLEASE!
THE BUG CAGE IS CLOSE. WE CAN'T DRAW TOO MUCH ATTENTION.
LET ME DOWN! MY FATHER! HE'S HURT!
A BUG GOT HIM.
HE'S ALREADY GONE.
!
WH... ?!
DADDY!
IT'S NO USE CLINGING TO THE DEAD!
COME THIS WAY!
GRAB
NO!
I CAN'T JUST LEAVE HIM HERE! LET GO OF ME!

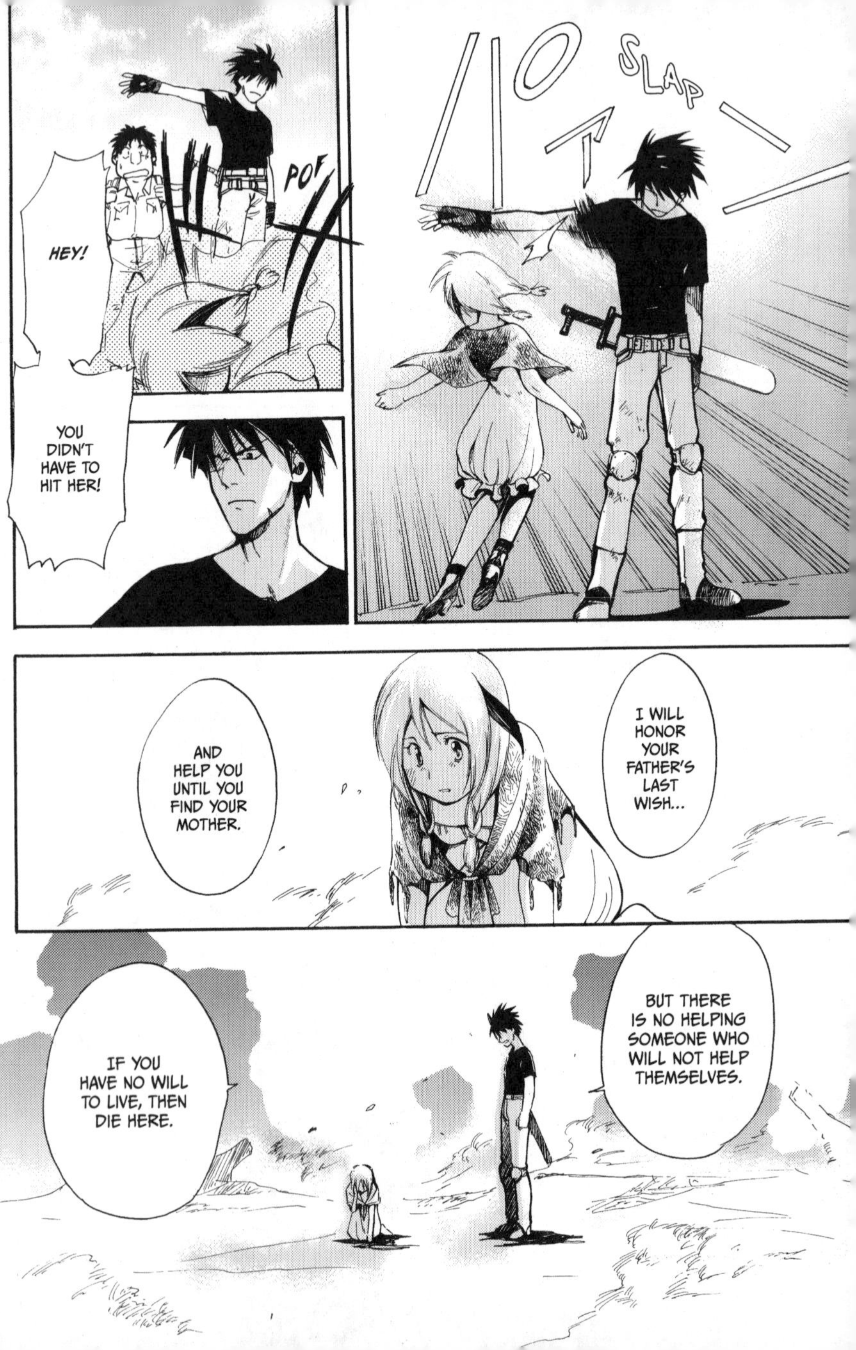
SLAP
POF
HEY!
YOU DIDN'T HAVE TO HIT HER!
I WILL HONOR YOUR FATHER'S LAST WISH...
AND HELP YOU UNTIL YOU FIND YOUR MOTHER.
BUT THERE IS NO HELPING SOMEONE WHO WILL NOT HELP THEMSELVES.
IF YOU HAVE NO WILL TO LIVE, THEN DIE HERE.

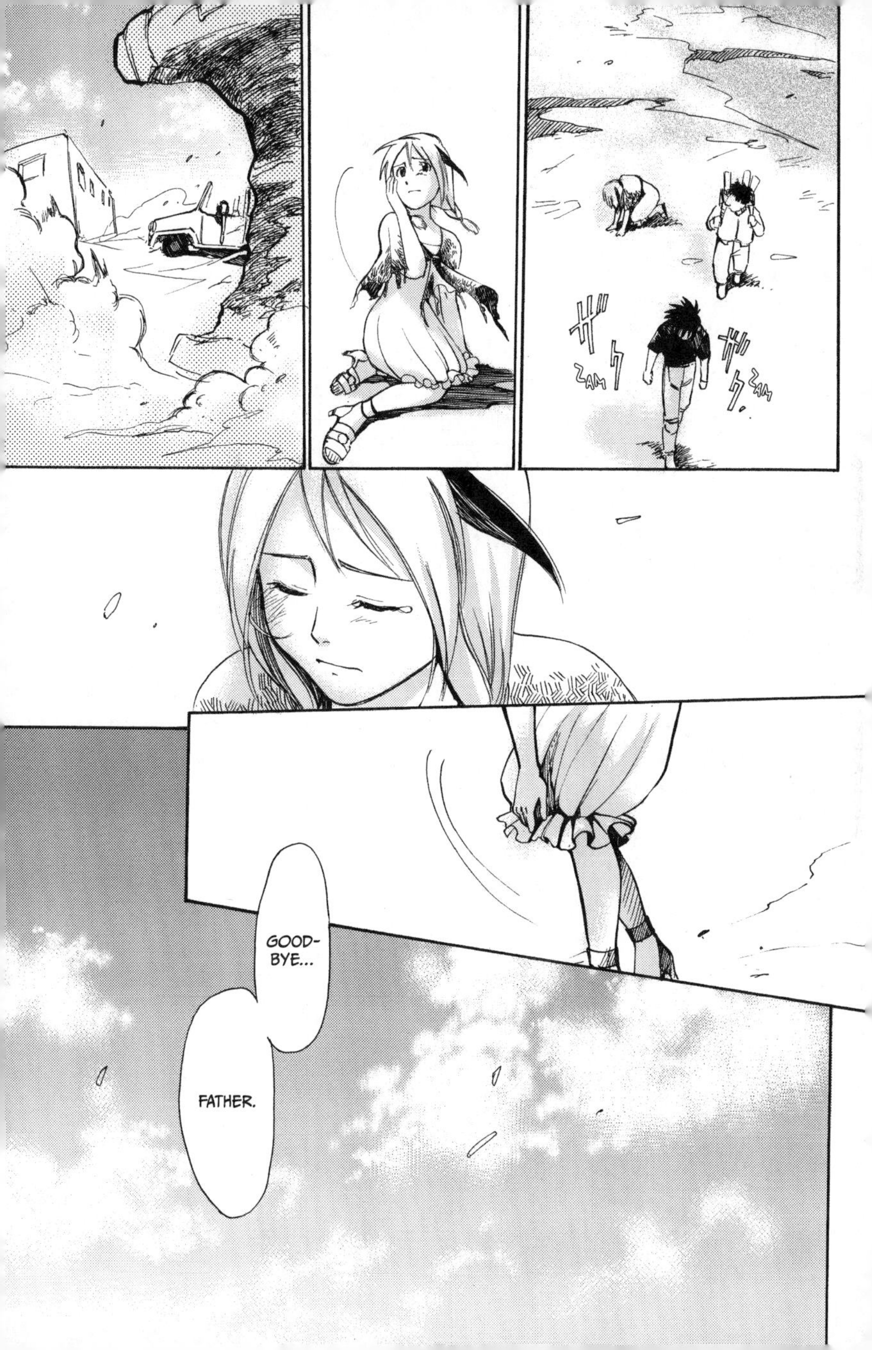
ザッ ZAM
ザッ ZAM
GOOD-BYE...
FATHER.

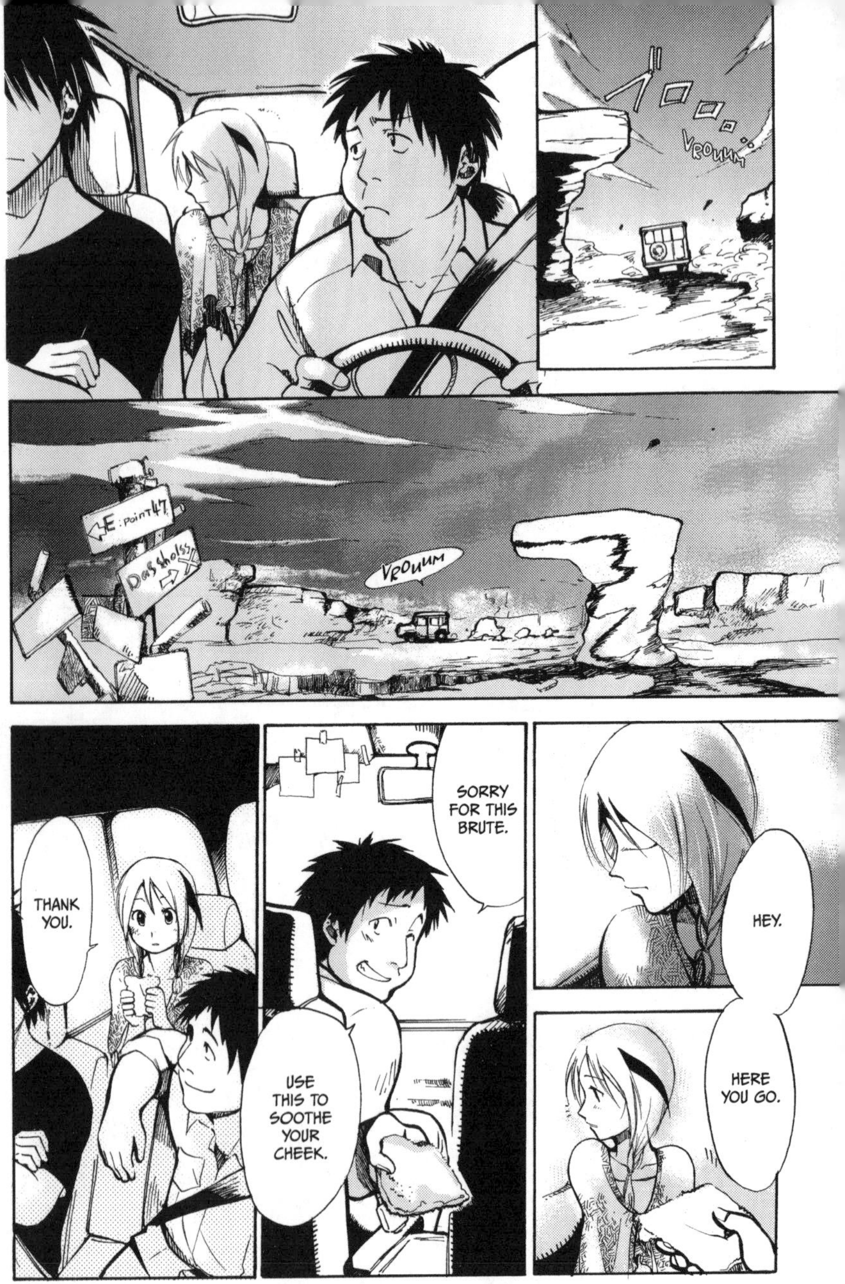
ベロロロ
VROUUM
E: point 47
VROUUM
HEY.
HERE YOU GO.
SORRY FOR THIS BRUTE.
USE THIS TO SOOTHE YOUR CHEEK.
THANK YOU.

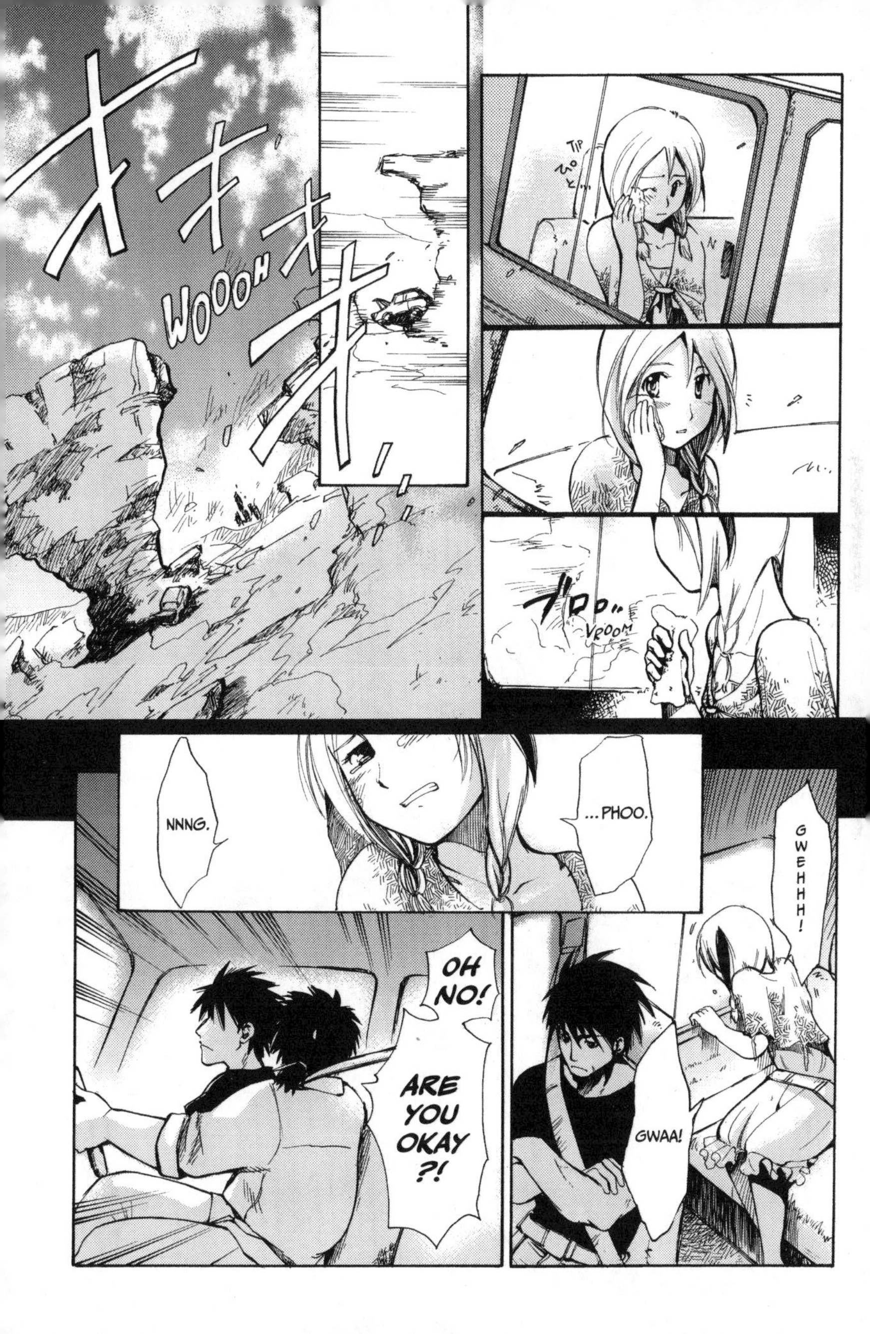
TIP
VROOM
WOOOH
...PHOO.
NNNG.
GWEHHH!
GWAA!
OH NO!
ARE YOU OKAY?!

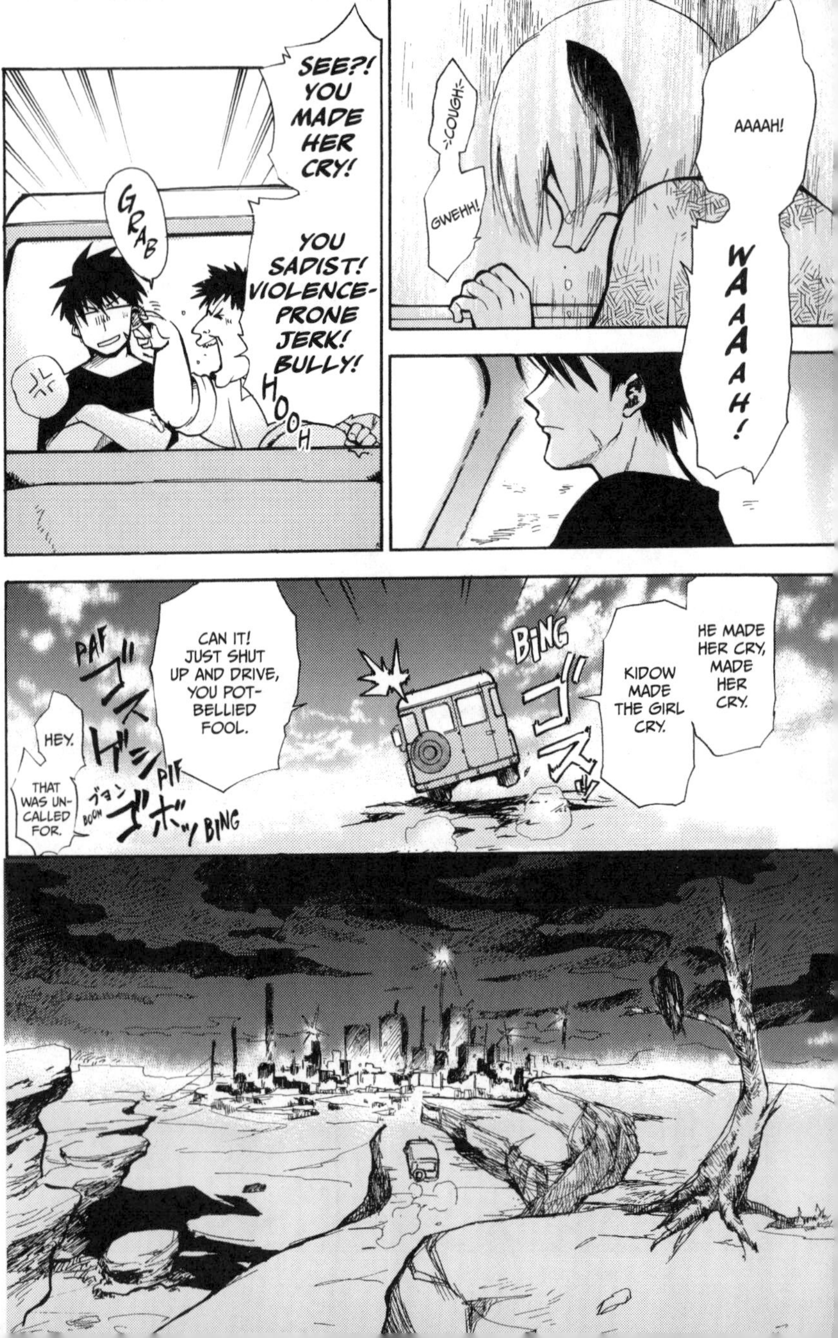
AAAAH!
WAAAAAH!
COUGH
GWEHH!
SEE?! YOU MADE HER CRY!
GRAB
YOU SADIST! VIOLENCE-PRONE JERK! BULLY!
HOOH
HE MADE HER CRY, MADE HER CRY.
KIDOW MADE THE GIRL CRY.
BING
CAN IT! JUST SHUT UP AND DRIVE, YOU POT-BELLIED FOOL.
PAF
PIF
HEY.
THAT WAS UN-CALLED FOR.
BOOM
BING

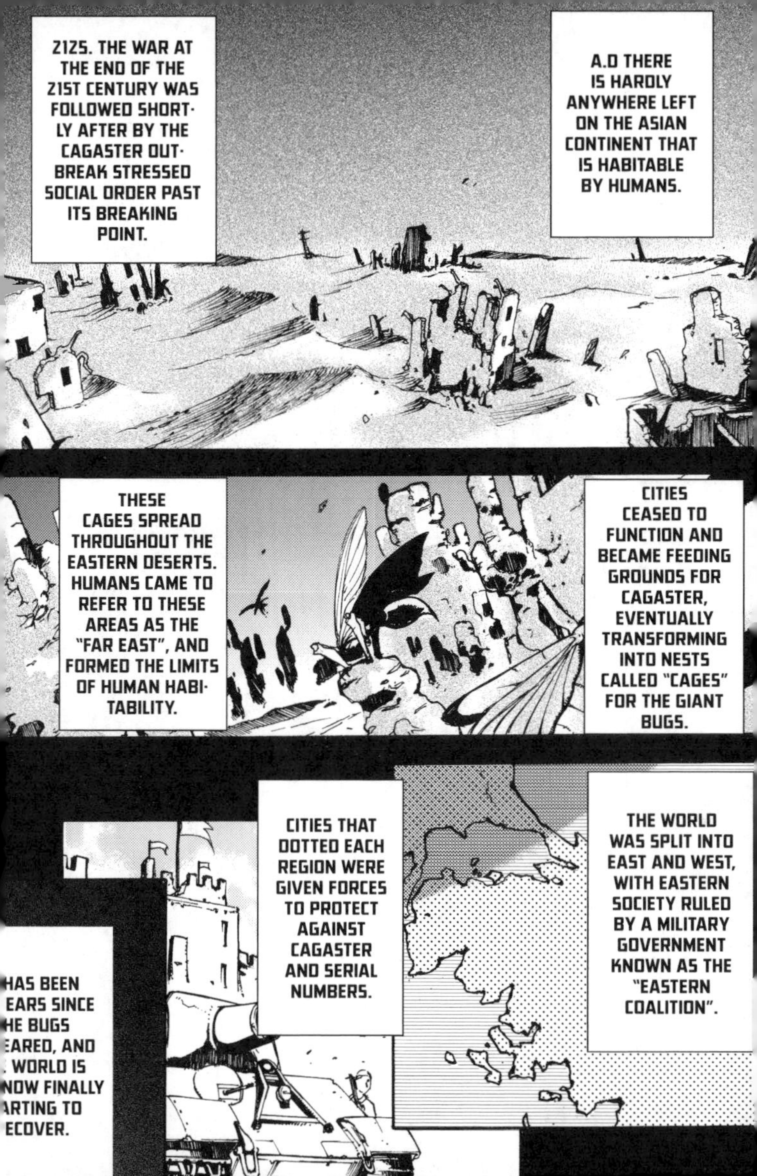
A.D THERE IS HARDLY ANYWHERE LEFT ON THE ASIAN CONTINENT THAT IS HABITABLE BY HUMANS.
2125. THE WAR AT THE END OF THE 21ST CENTURY WAS FOLLOWED SHORT-LY AFTER BY THE CAGASTER OUT-BREAK STRESSED SOCIAL ORDER PAST ITS BREAKING POINT.
CITIES CEASED TO FUNCTION AND BECAME FEEDING GROUNDS FOR CAGASTER, EVENTUALLY TRANSFORMING INTO NESTS CALLED "CAGES" FOR THE GIANT BUGS.
THESE CAGES SPREAD THROUGHOUT THE EASTERN DESERTS. HUMANS CAME TO REFER TO THESE AREAS AS THE "FAR EAST", AND FORMED THE LIMITS OF HUMAN HABI-TABILITY.
THE WORLD WAS SPLIT INTO EAST AND WEST, WITH EASTERN SOCIETY RULED BY A MILITARY GOVERNMENT KNOWN AS THE "EASTERN COALITION".
CITIES THAT DOTTED EACH REGION WERE GIVEN FORCES TO PROTECT AGAINST CAGASTER AND SERIAL NUMBERS.
HAS BEEN EARS SINCE HE BUGS EARED, AND WORLD IS NOW FINALLY ARTING TO ECOVER.

E·05, A CITY OF TRADE.

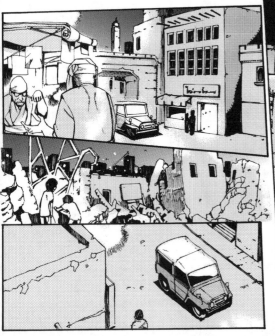

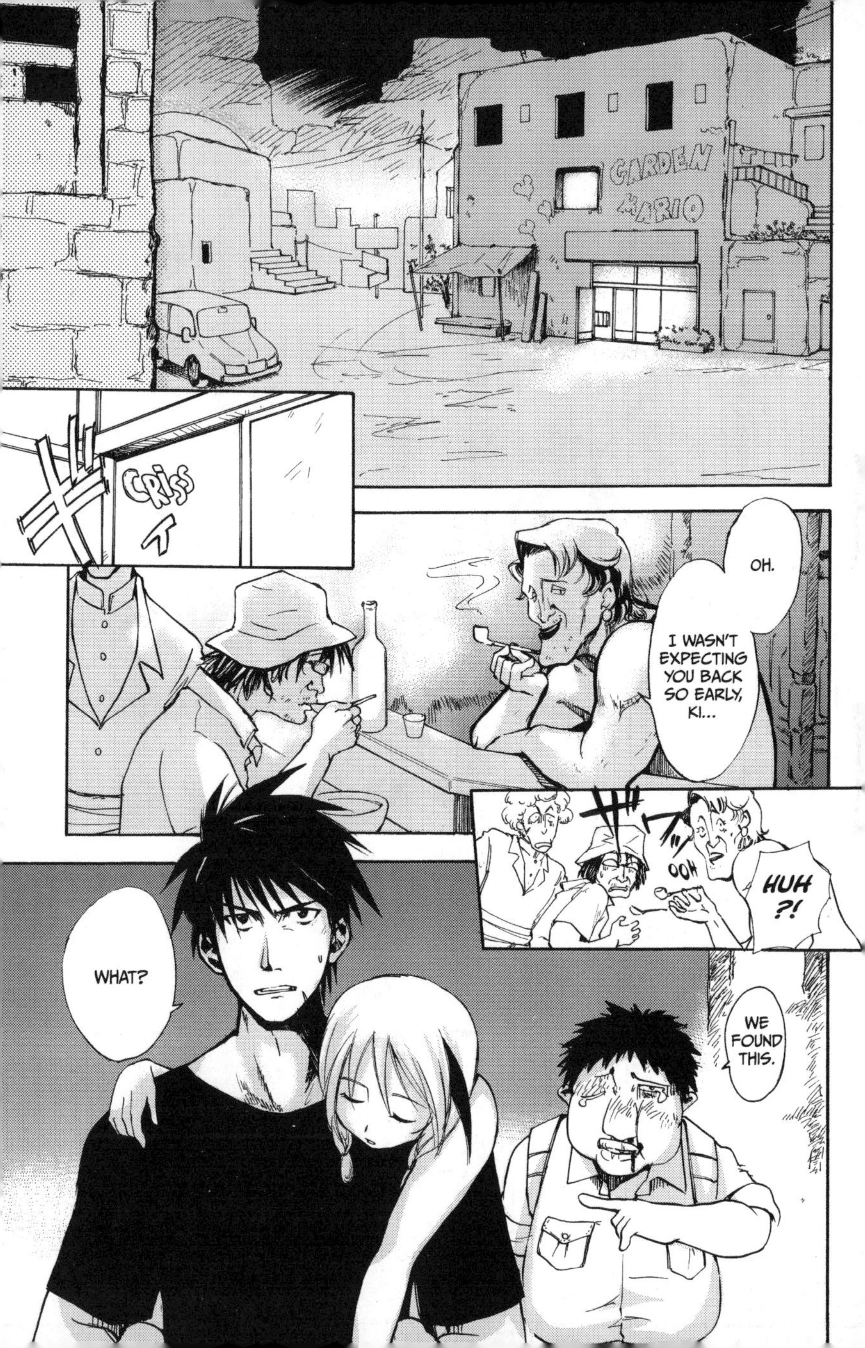

GARDEN MARIO
CRISS
OH.
I WASN'T EXPECTING YOU BACK SO EARLY, KI...
HUH ?!
OOH
WHAT?
WE FOUND THIS.

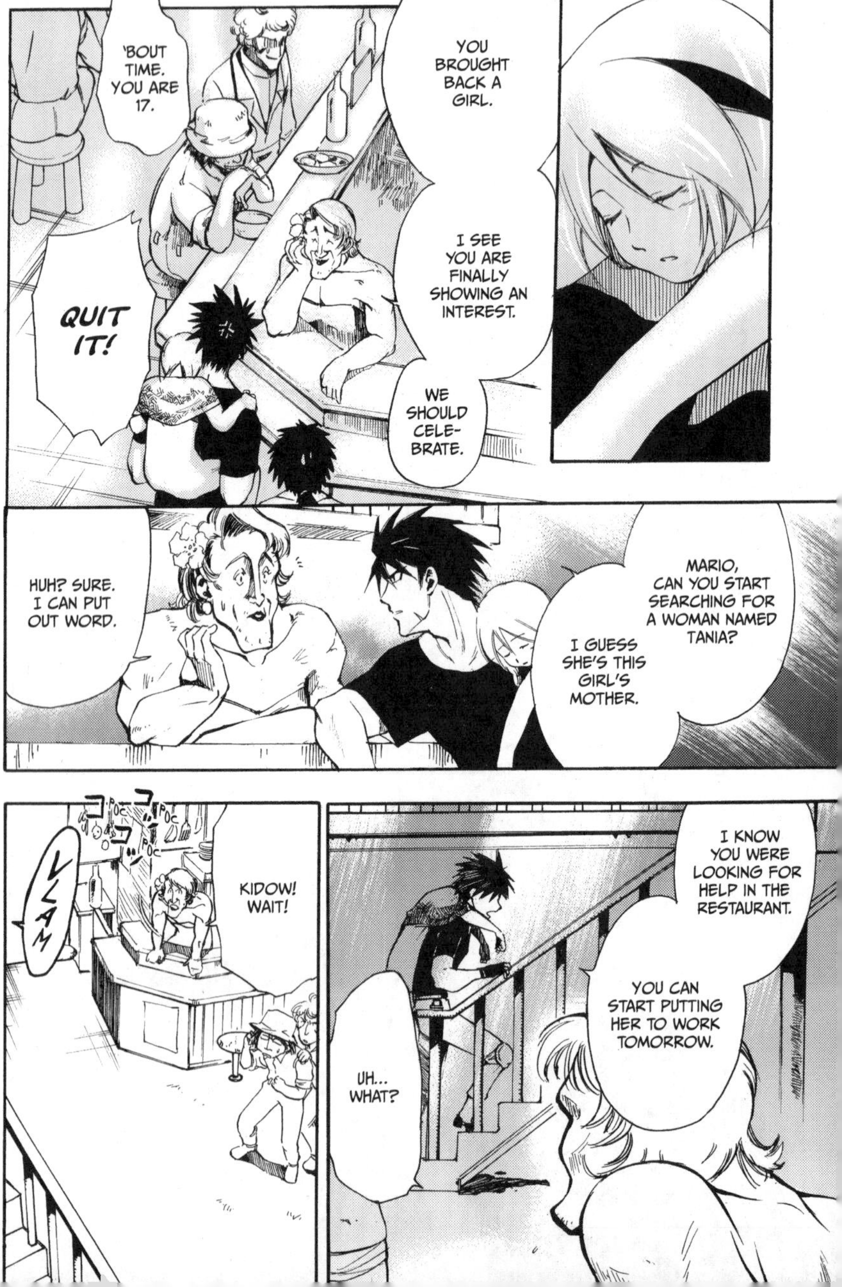
YOU BROUGHT BACK A GIRL.
I SEE YOU ARE FINALLY SHOWING AN INTEREST.
WE SHOULD CELE-BRATE.
'BOUT TIME. YOU ARE 17.
QUIT IT!
MARIO, CAN YOU START SEARCHING FOR A WOMAN NAMED TANIA?
I GUESS SHE'S THIS GIRL'S MOTHER.
HUH? SURE. I CAN PUT OUT WORD.
I KNOW YOU WERE LOOKING FOR HELP IN THE RESTAURANT.
YOU CAN START PUTTING HER TO WORK TOMORROW.
UH... WHAT?
KIDOW! WAIT!
VLAM
POC
POC
POC

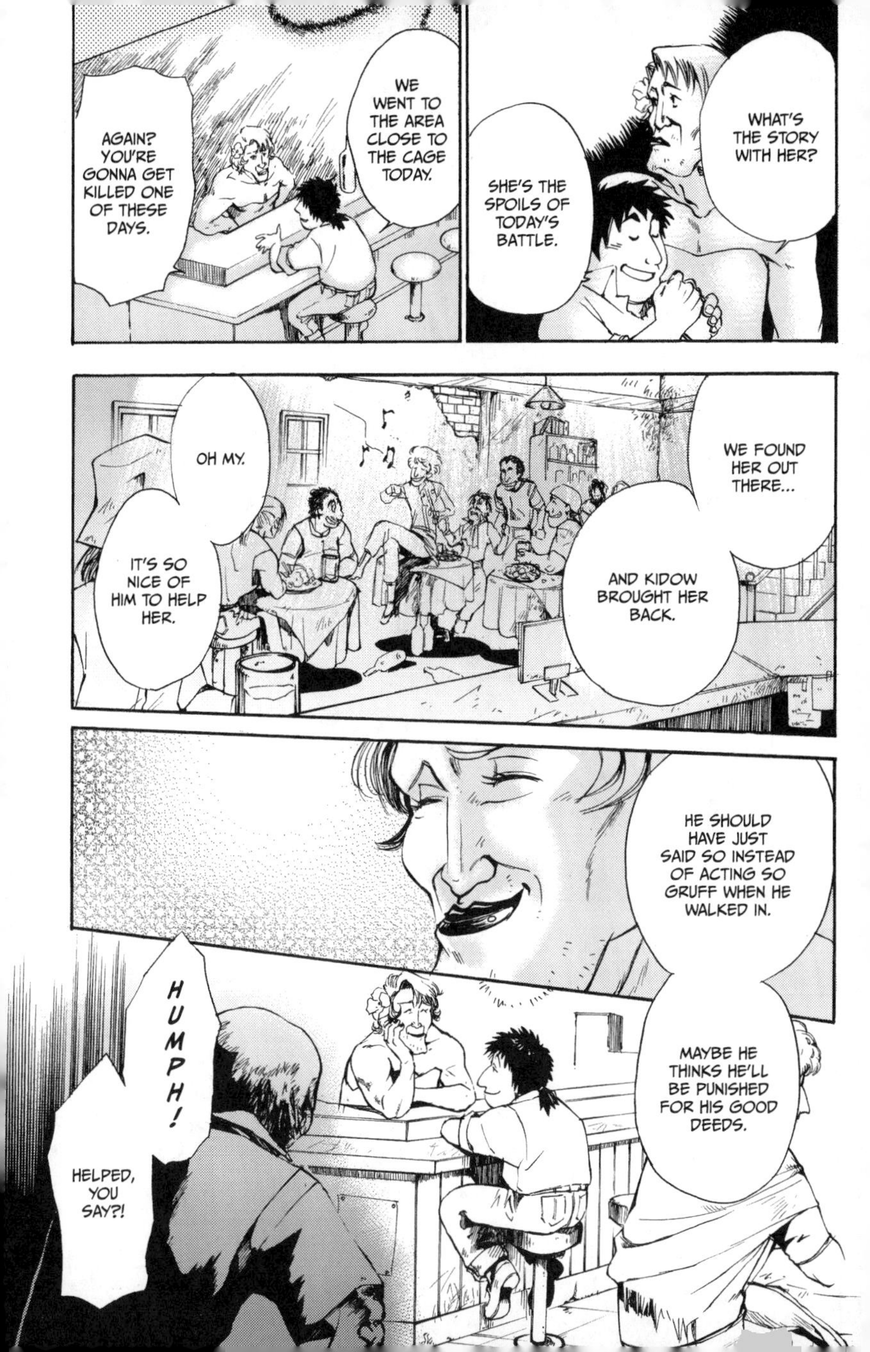
WHAT'S THE STORY WITH HER?
SHE'S THE SPOILS OF TODAY'S BATTLE.
WE WENT TO THE AREA CLOSE TO THE CAGE TODAY.
AGAIN? YOU'RE GONNA GET KILLED ONE OF THESE DAYS.
WE FOUND HER OUT THERE...
AND KIDOW BROUGHT HER BACK.
OH MY.
IT'S SO NICE OF HIM TO HELP HER.
HE SHOULD HAVE JUST SAID SO INSTEAD OF ACTING SO GRUFF WHEN HE WALKED IN.
MAYBE HE THINKS HE'LL BE PUNISHED FOR HIS GOOD DEEDS.
HUMPH!
HELPED, YOU SAY?!

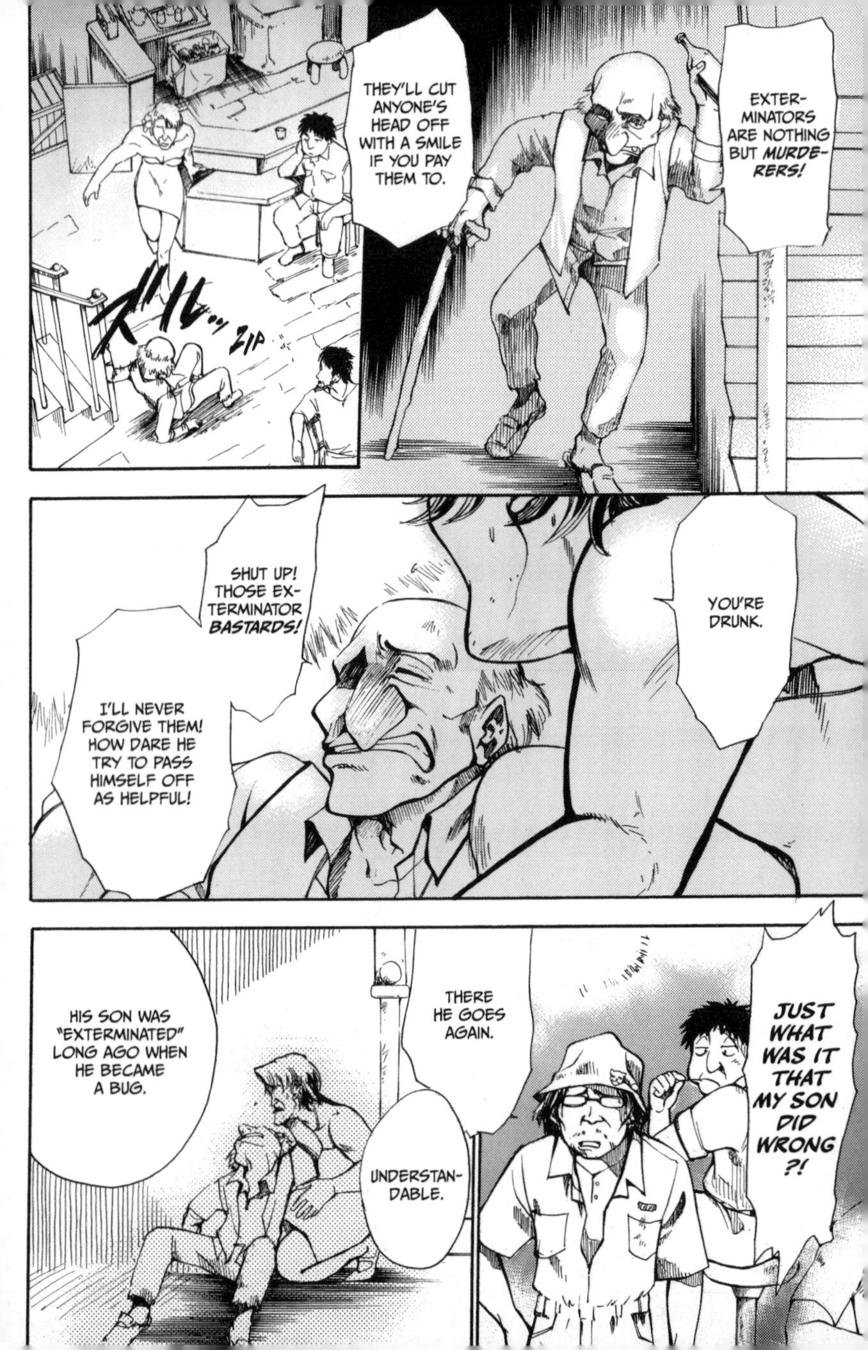
EXTER-MINATORS ARE NOTHING BUT *MURDE-RERS!*
THEY'LL CUT ANYONE'S HEAD OFF WITH A SMILE IF YOU PAY THEM TO.
ZIP
YOU'RE DRUNK.
SHUT UP! THOSE EX-TERMINATOR ***BASTARDS!***
I'LL NEVER FORGIVE THEM! HOW DARE HE TRY TO PASS HIMSELF OFF AS HELPFUL!
***JUST WHAT WAS IT THAT MY SON DID WRONG?!***
THERE HE GOES AGAIN.
HIS SON WAS "EXTERMINATED" LONG AGO WHEN HE BECAME A BUG.
UNDERSTAN-DABLE.

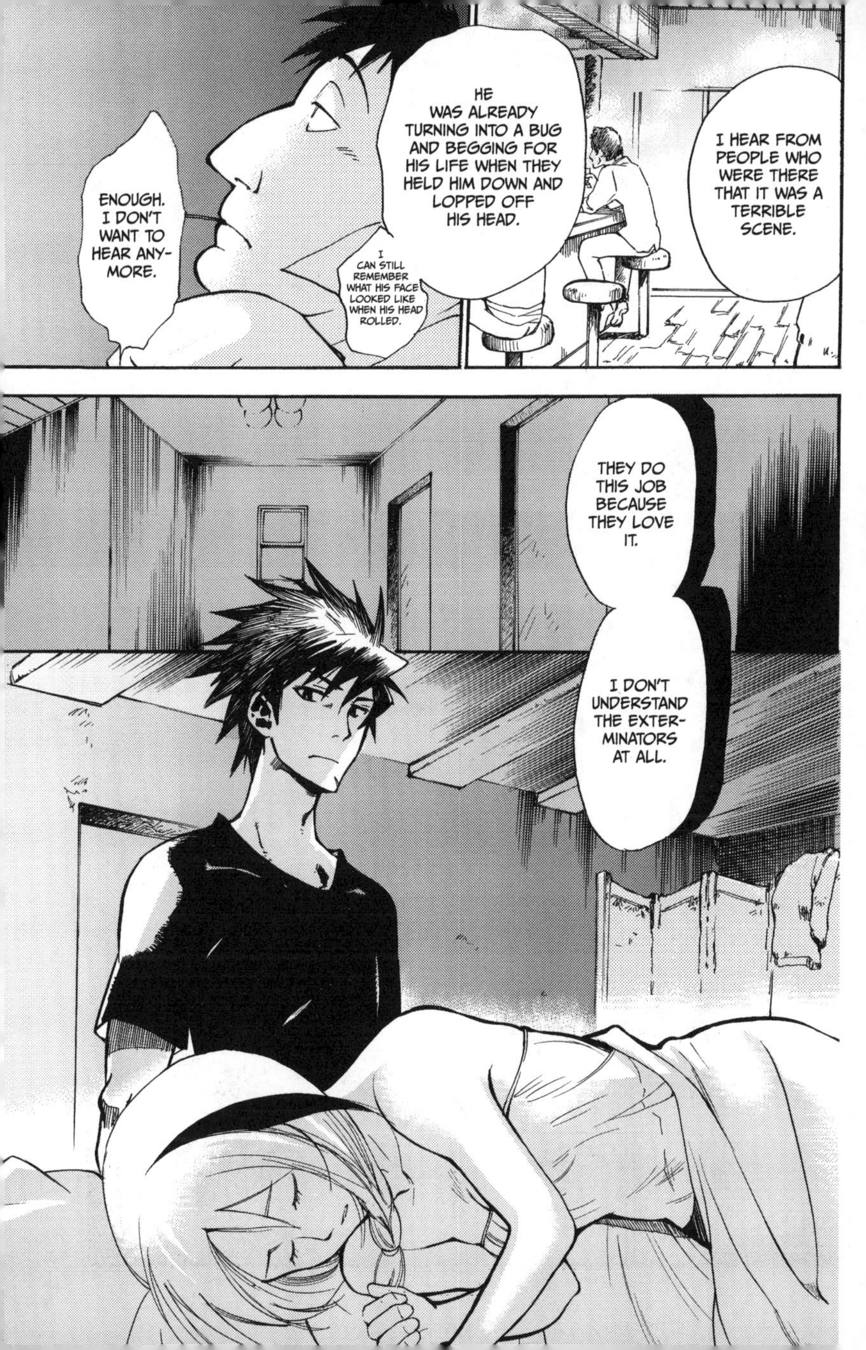
I HEAR FROM PEOPLE WHO WERE THERE THAT IT WAS A TERRIBLE SCENE.
HE WAS ALREADY TURNING INTO A BUG AND BEGGING FOR HIS LIFE WHEN THEY HELD HIM DOWN AND LOPPED OFF HIS HEAD.
I CAN STILL REMEMBER WHAT HIS FACE LOOKED LIKE WHEN HIS HEAD ROLLED.
ENOUGH. I DON'T WANT TO HEAR ANYMORE.
THEY DO THIS JOB BECAUSE THEY LOVE IT.
I DON'T UNDERSTAND THE EXTERMINATORS AT ALL.

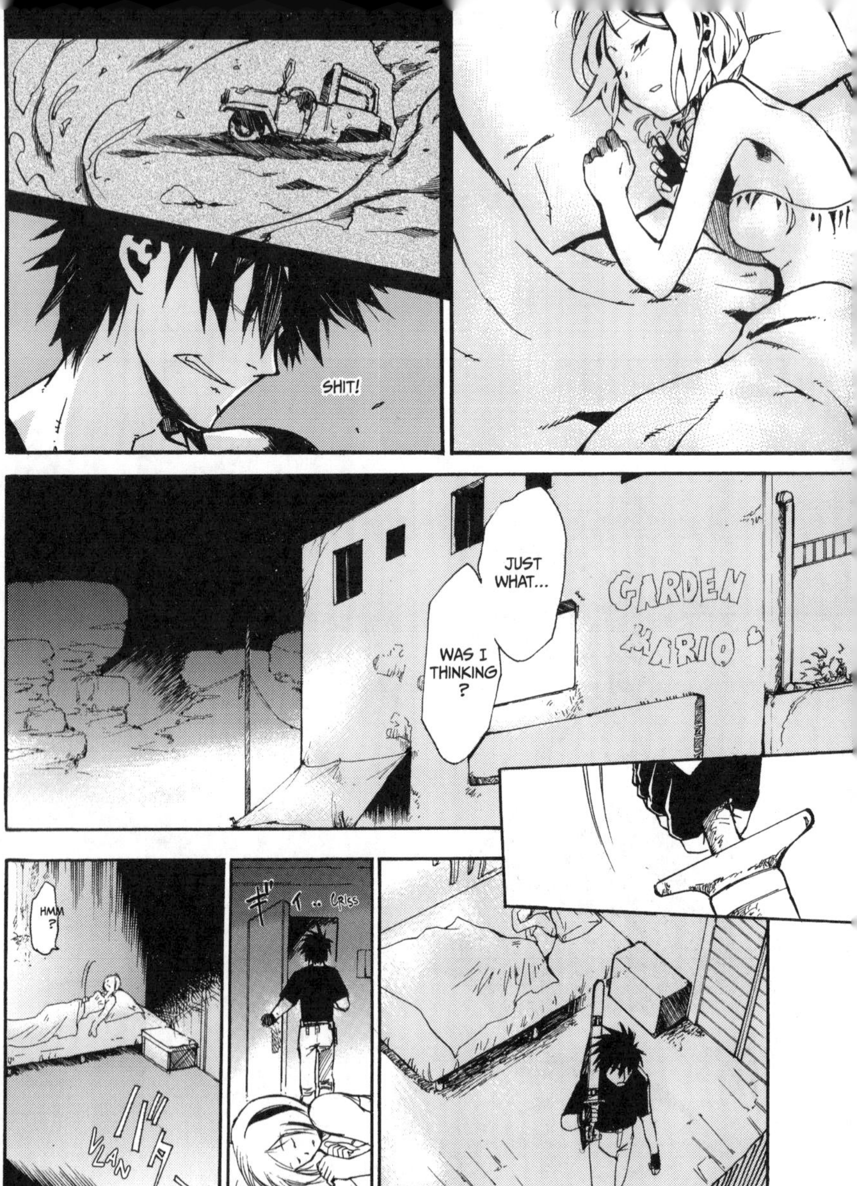
SHIT!
JUST WHAT...
WAS I THINKING ?
GARDEN MARIO
ギイ.. CRISS
HMM ?
バタン VLAN

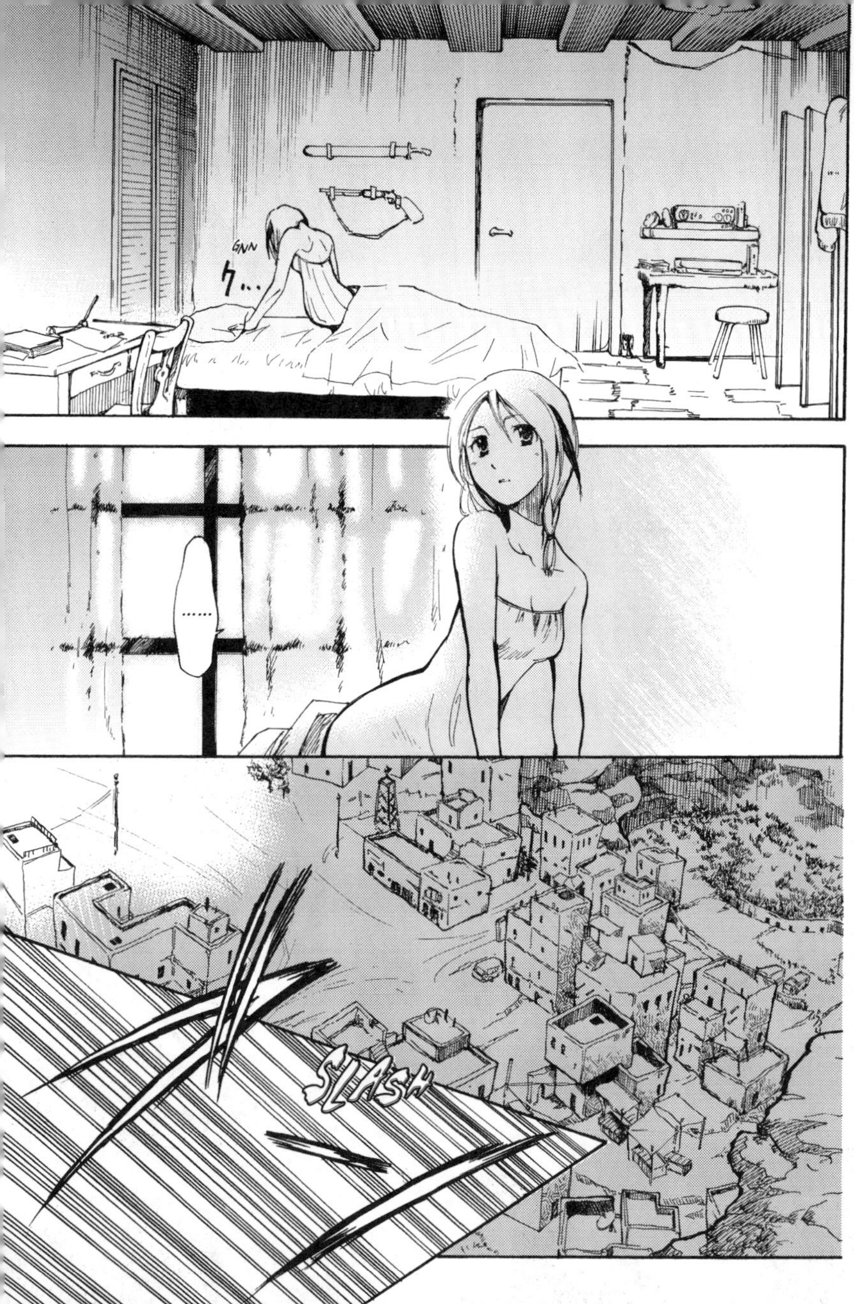
GNN
ク...
......
SLASH

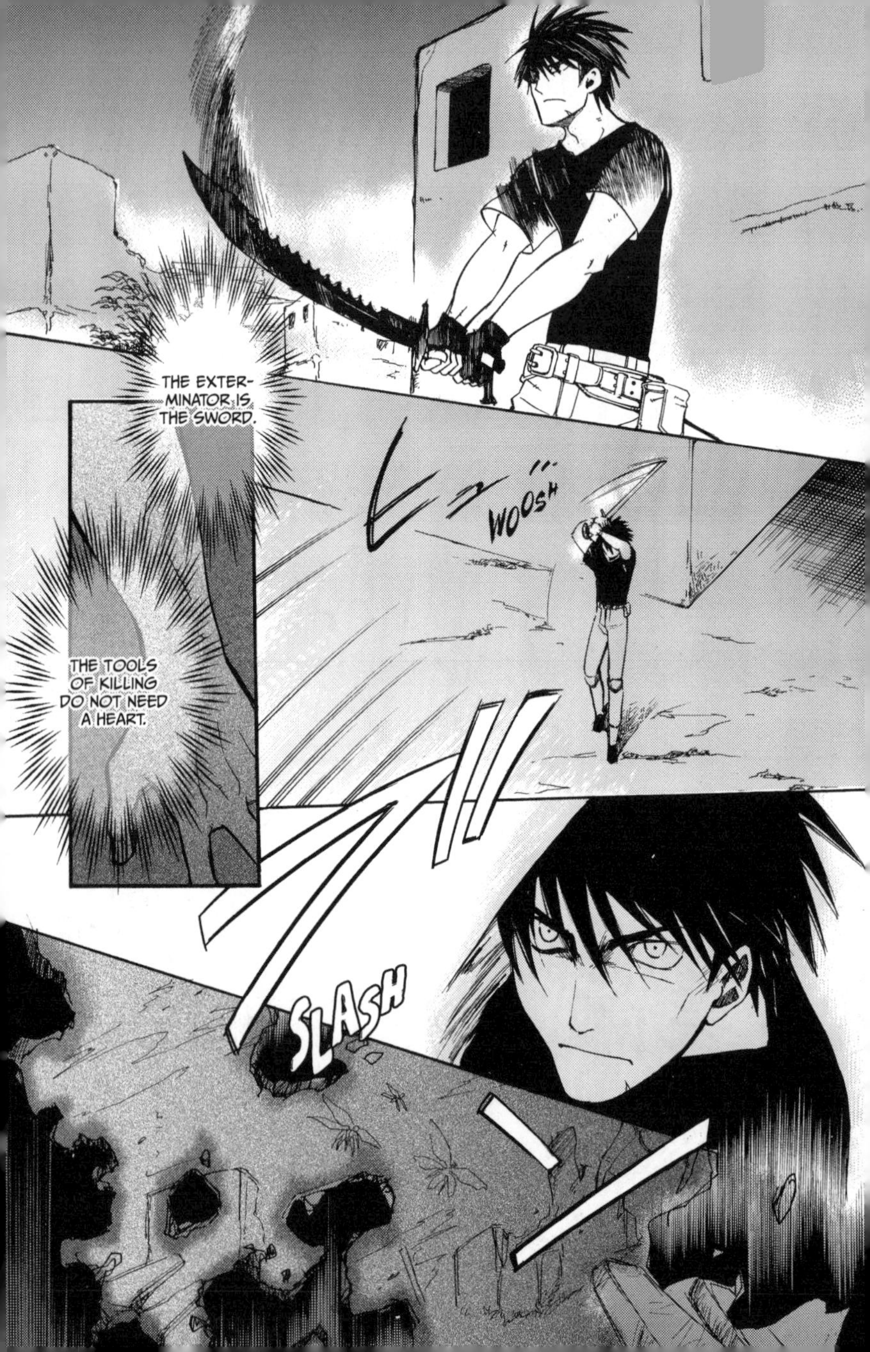
THE EXTER-MINATOR IS THE SWORD.
WOOSH
THE TOOLS OF KILLING DO NOT NEED A HEART.
SLASH

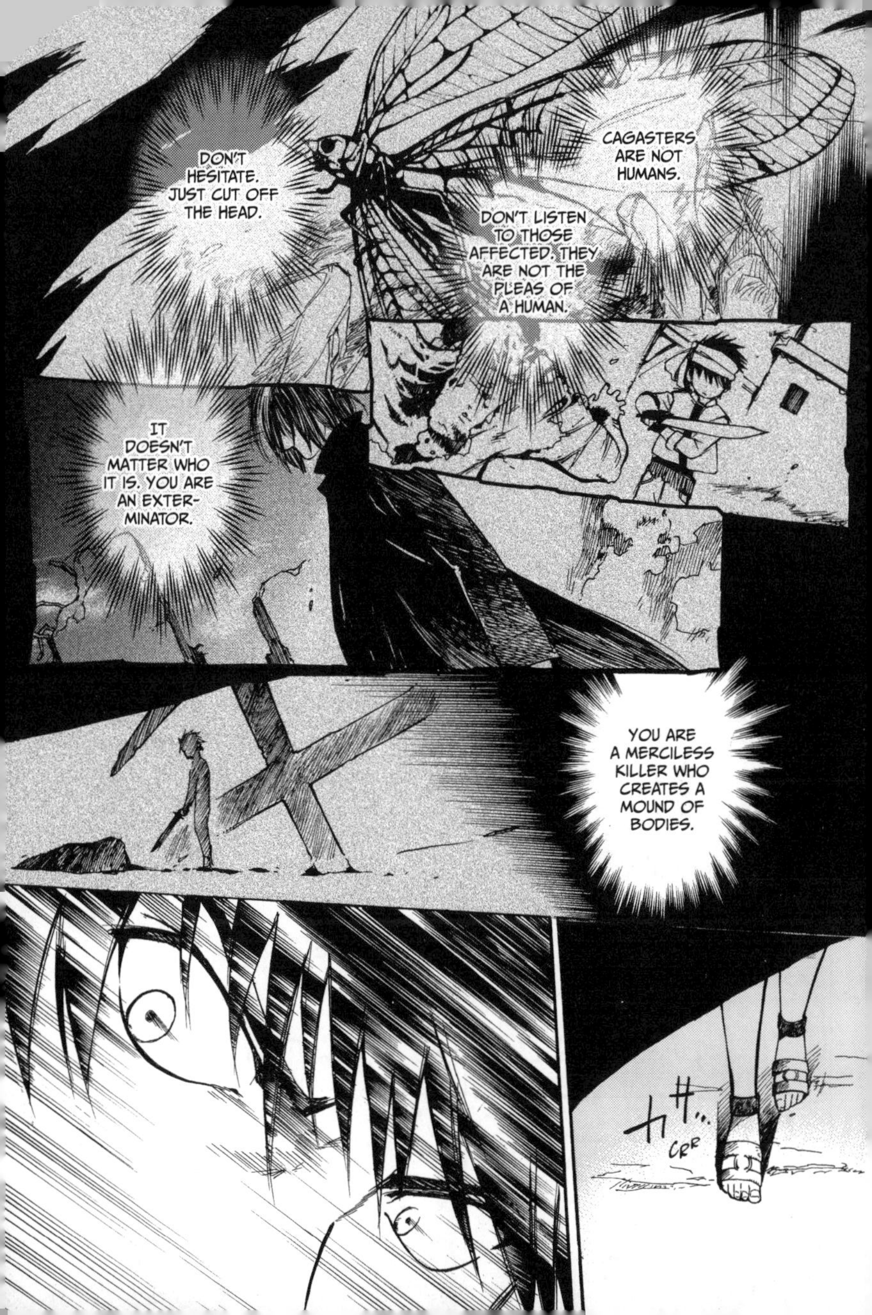
CAGASTERS ARE NOT HUMANS.
DON'T LISTEN TO THOSE AFFECTED. THEY ARE NOT THE PLEAS OF A HUMAN.
DON'T HESITATE. JUST CUT OFF THE HEAD.
IT DOESN'T MATTER WHO IT IS. YOU ARE AN EXTERMINATOR.
YOU ARE A MERCILESS KILLER WHO CREATES A MOUND OF BODIES.
CRR

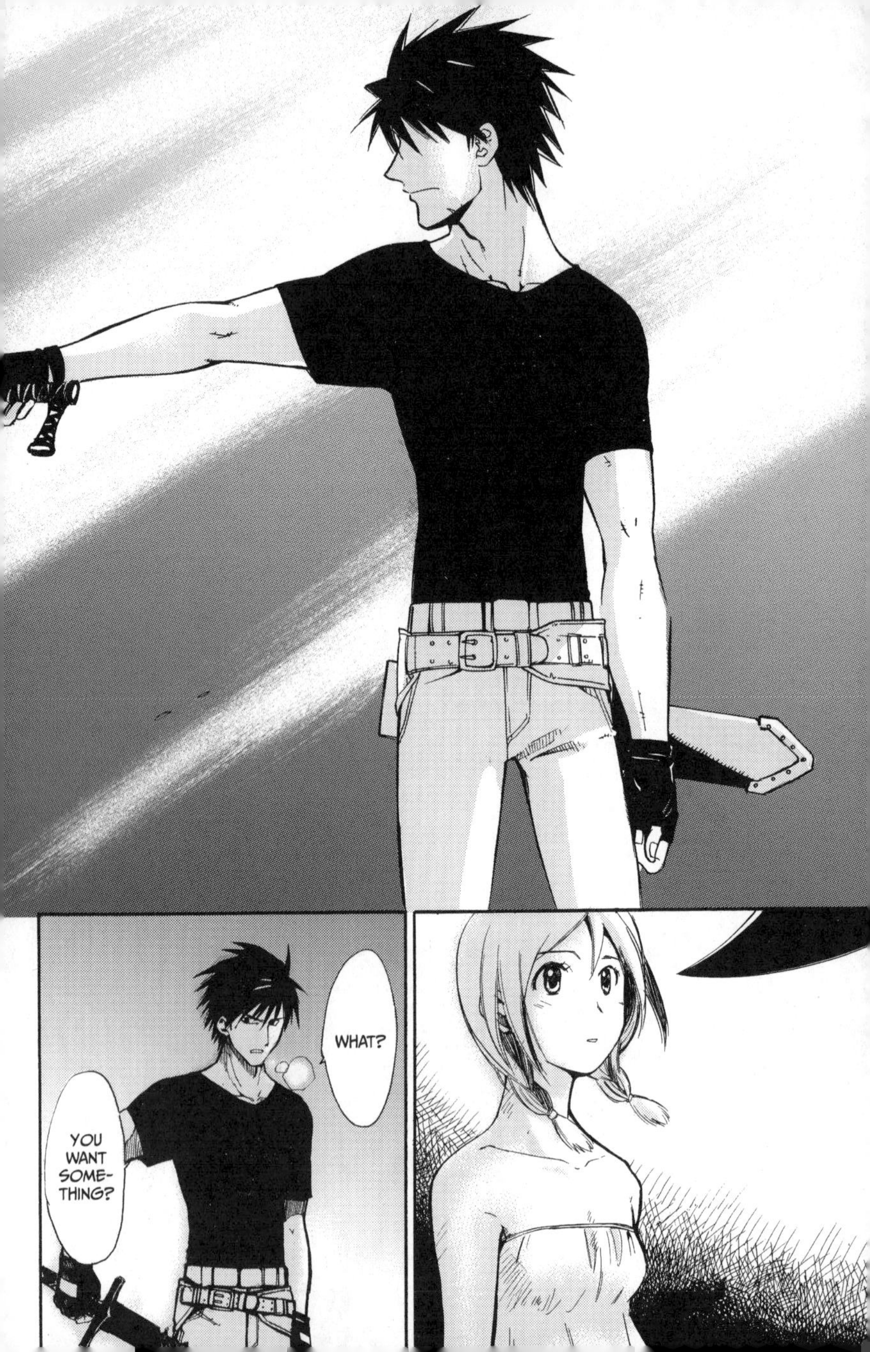
WHAT?
YOU WANT SOMETHING?

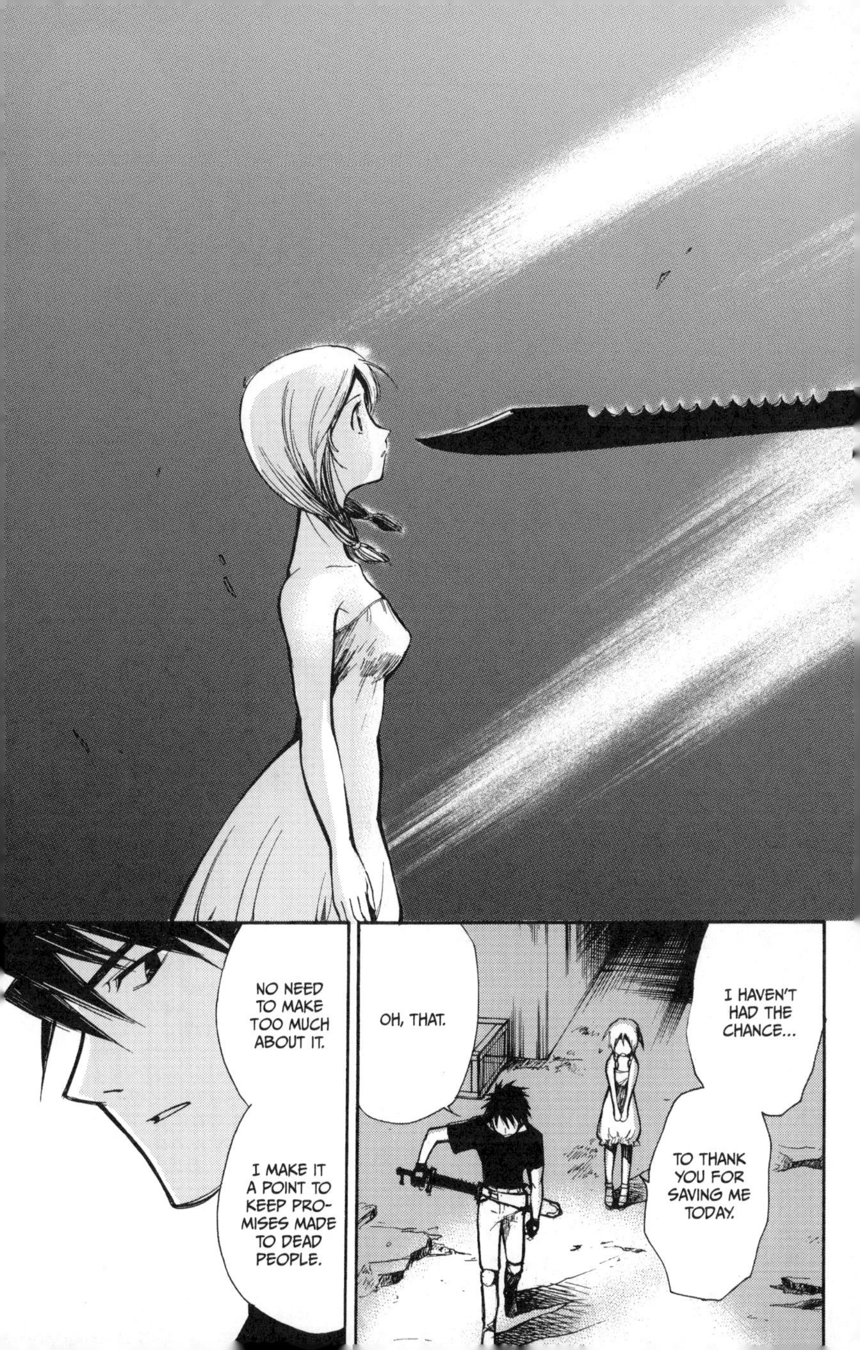
I HAVEN'T HAD THE CHANCE...
TO THANK YOU FOR SAVING ME TODAY.
OH, THAT.
NO NEED TO MAKE TOO MUCH ABOUT IT.
I MAKE IT A POINT TO KEEP PRO-MISES MADE TO DEAD PEOPLE.

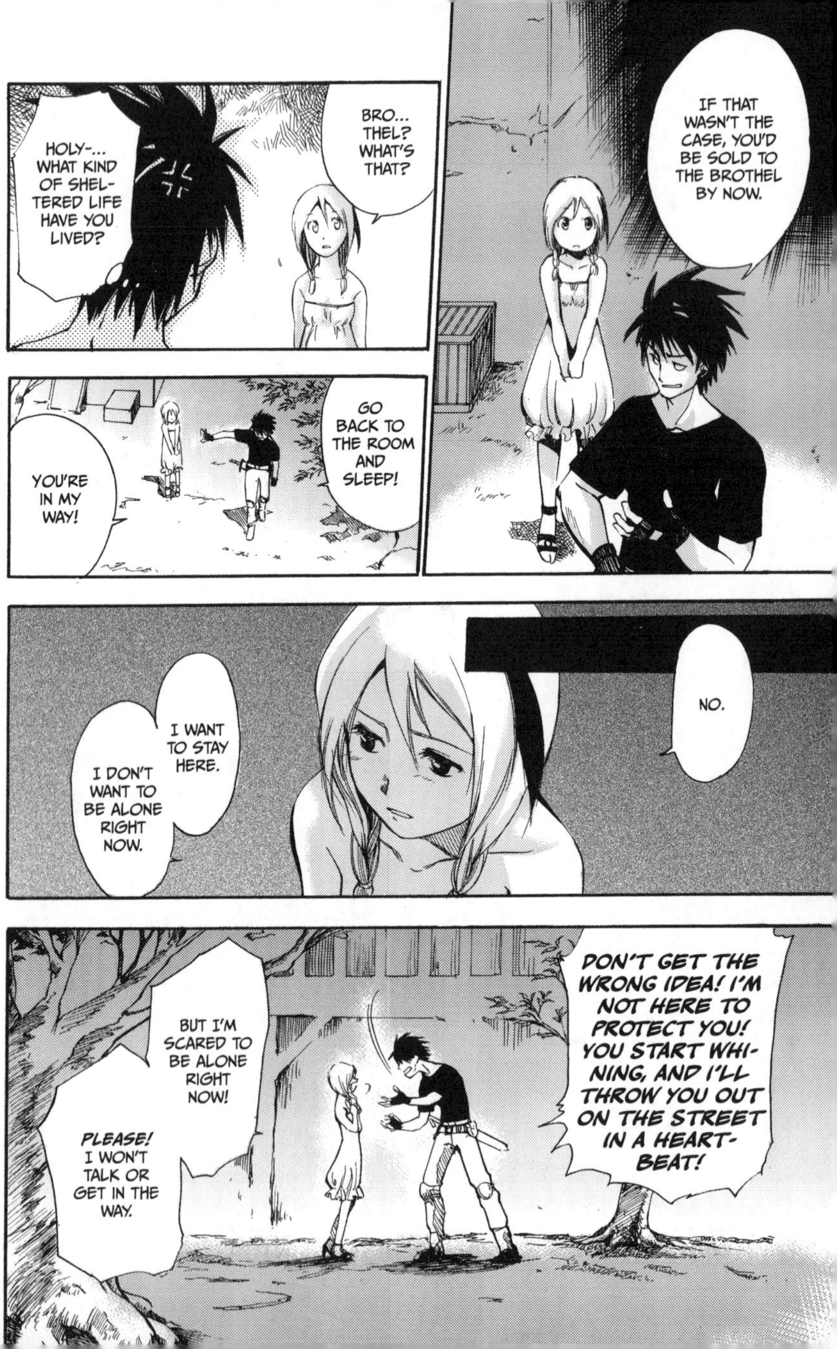
IF THAT WASN'T THE CASE, YOU'D BE SOLD TO THE BROTHEL BY NOW.
BRO... THEL? WHAT'S THAT?
HOLY-... WHAT KIND OF SHEL-TERED LIFE HAVE YOU LIVED?
GO BACK TO THE ROOM AND SLEEP!
YOU'RE IN MY WAY!
NO.
I WANT TO STAY HERE.
I DON'T WANT TO BE ALONE RIGHT NOW.
DON'T GET THE WRONG IDEA! I'M NOT HERE TO PROTECT YOU! YOU START WHI-NING, AND I'LL THROW YOU OUT ON THE STREET IN A HEART-BEAT!
BUT I'M SCARED TO BE ALONE RIGHT NOW!
PLEASE! I WON'T TALK OR GET IN THE WAY.

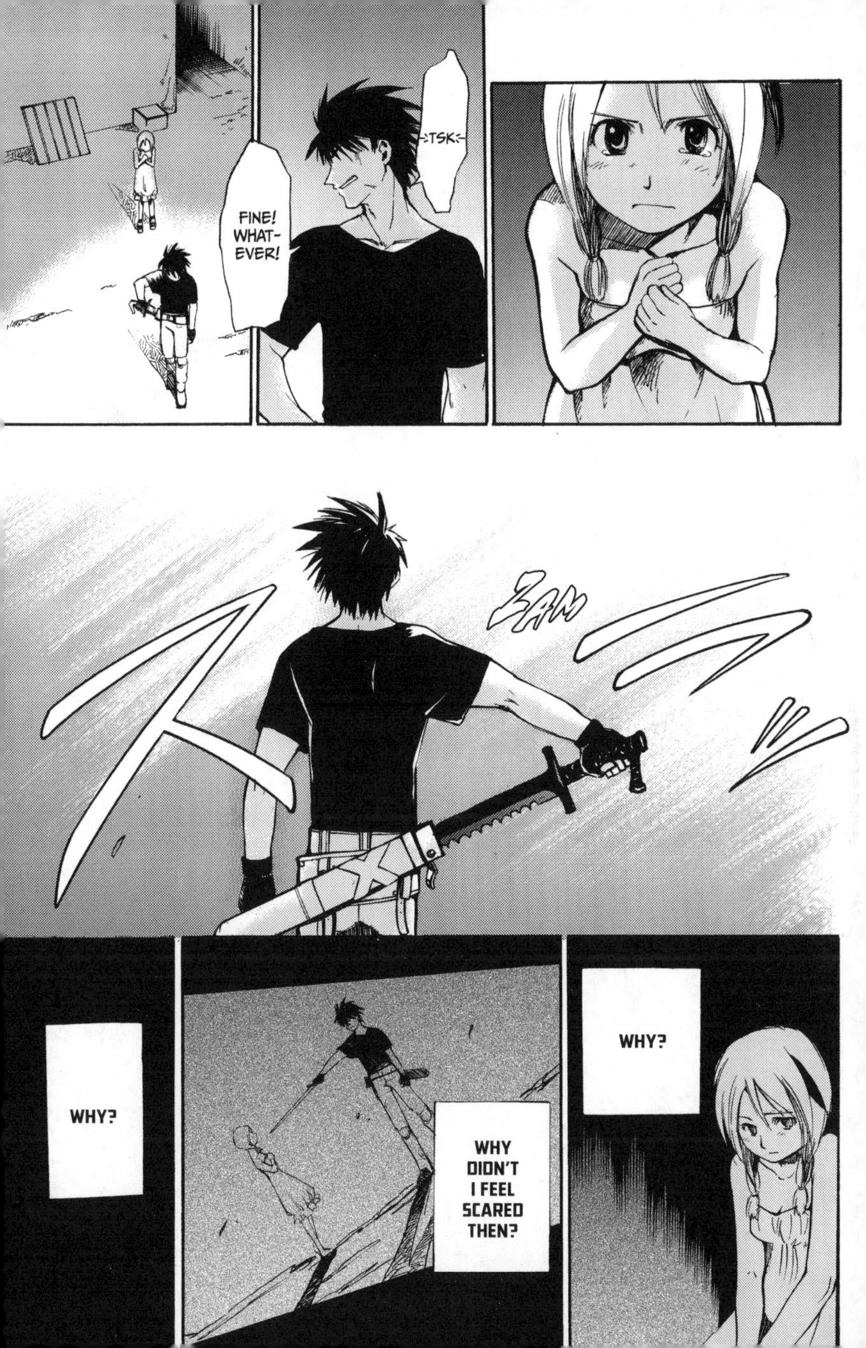
-:TSK:-
FINE! WHAT-EVER!
ZAM
WHY?
WHY DIDN'T I FEEL SCARED THEN?
WHY?

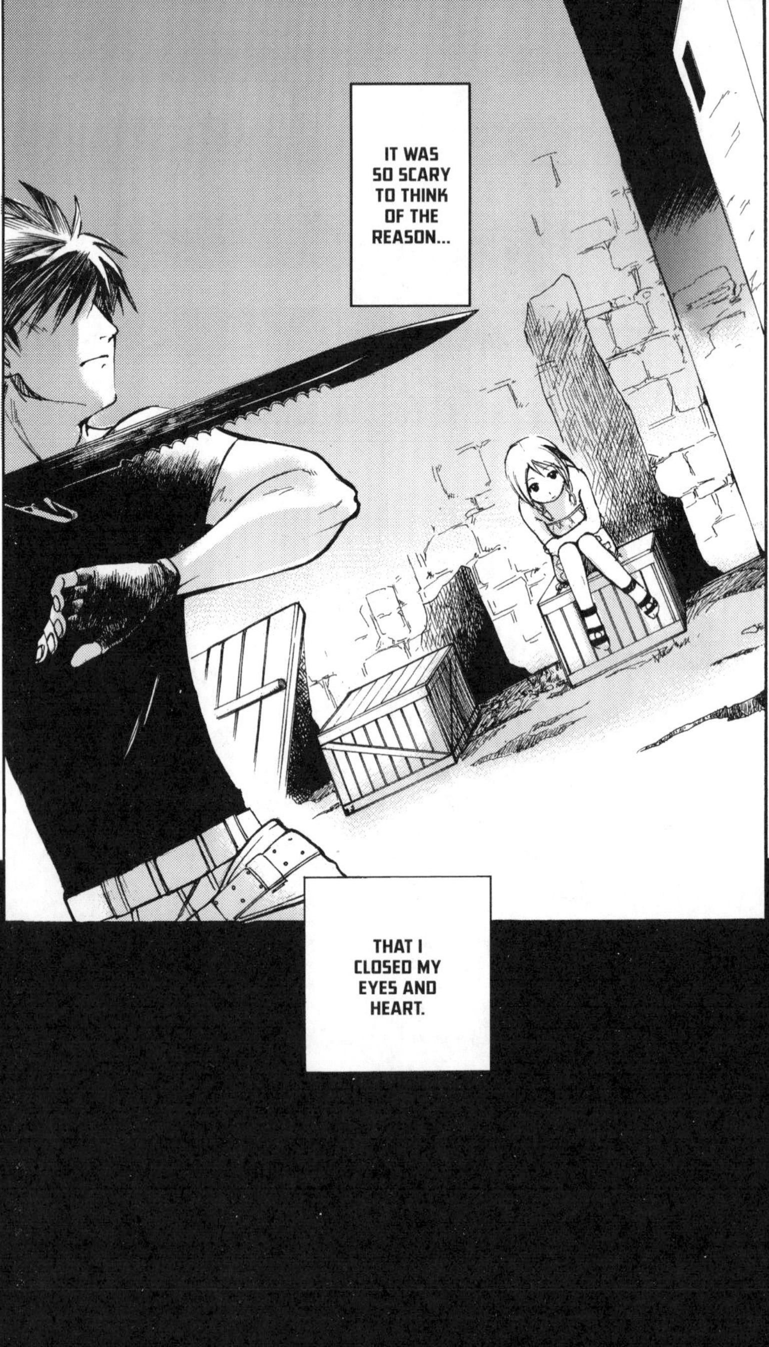
IT WAS SO SCARY TO THINK OF THE REASON...
THAT I CLOSED MY EYES AND HEART.

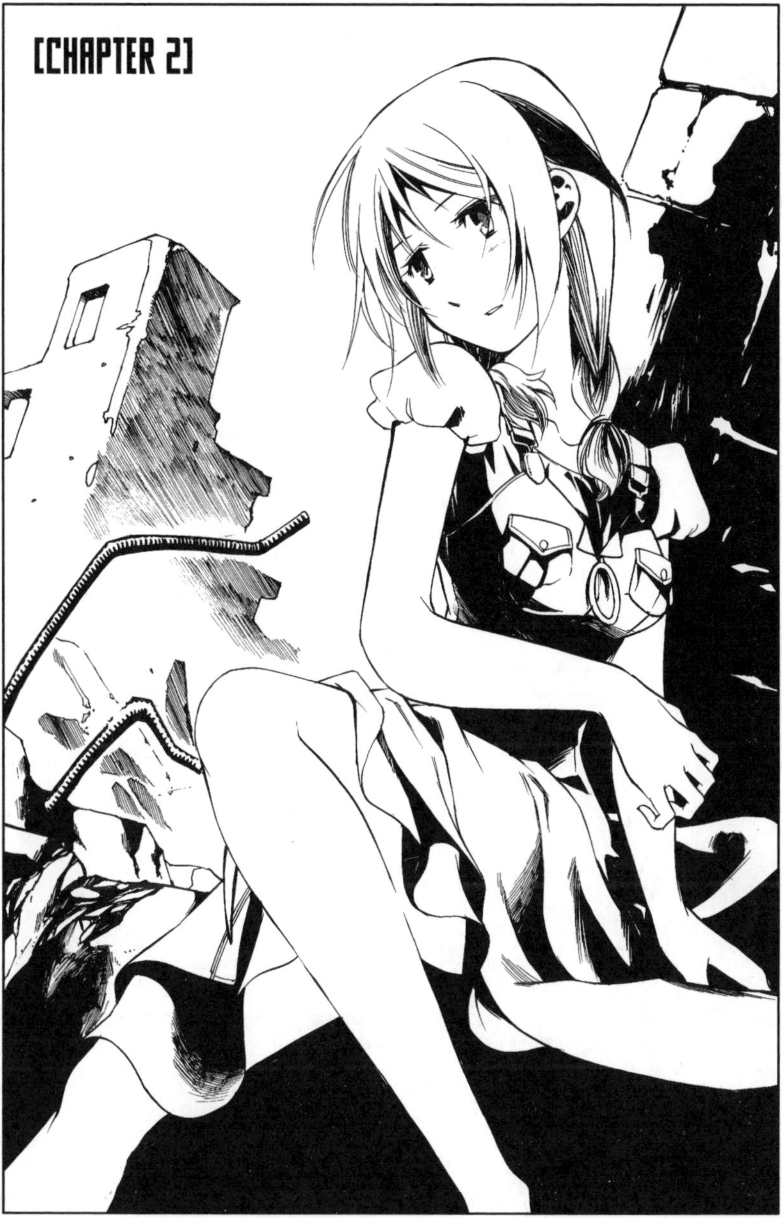
[CHAPTER 2]

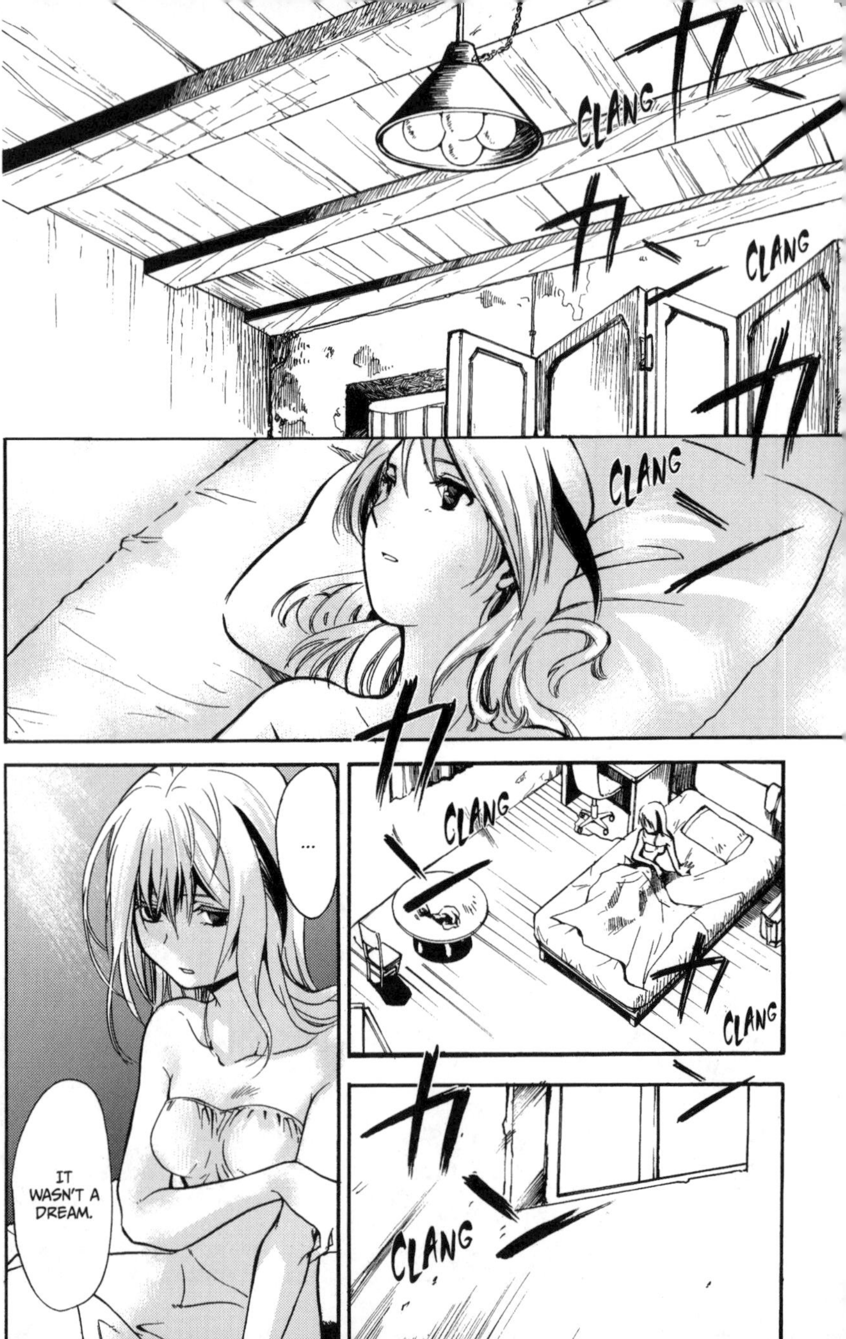
CLANG
CLANG
CLANG
CLANG
CLANG
CLANG
...
IT WASN'T A DREAM.

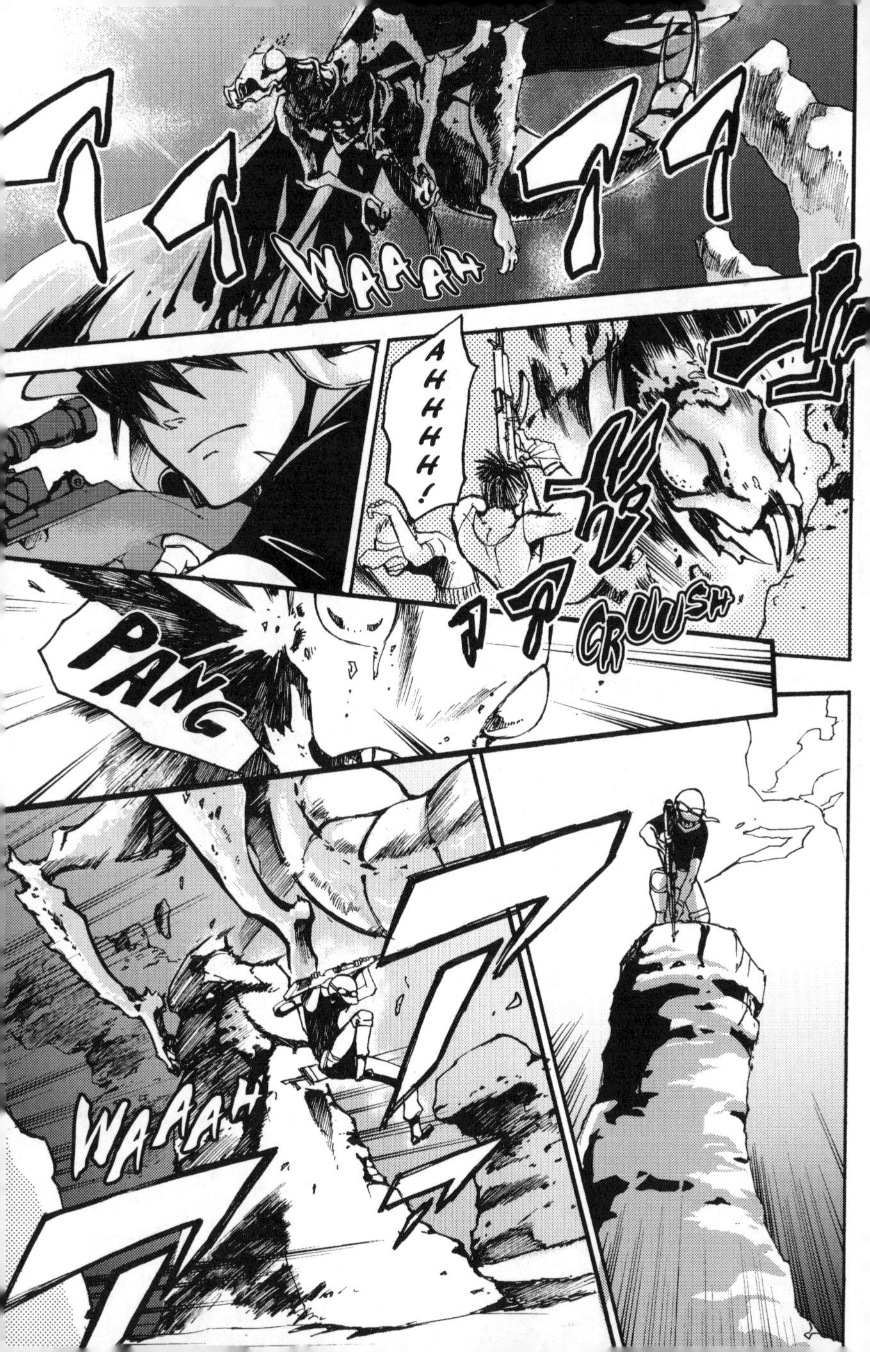
WAAAH
AHHHHH!
CRUUUSH
PANG
WAAAH

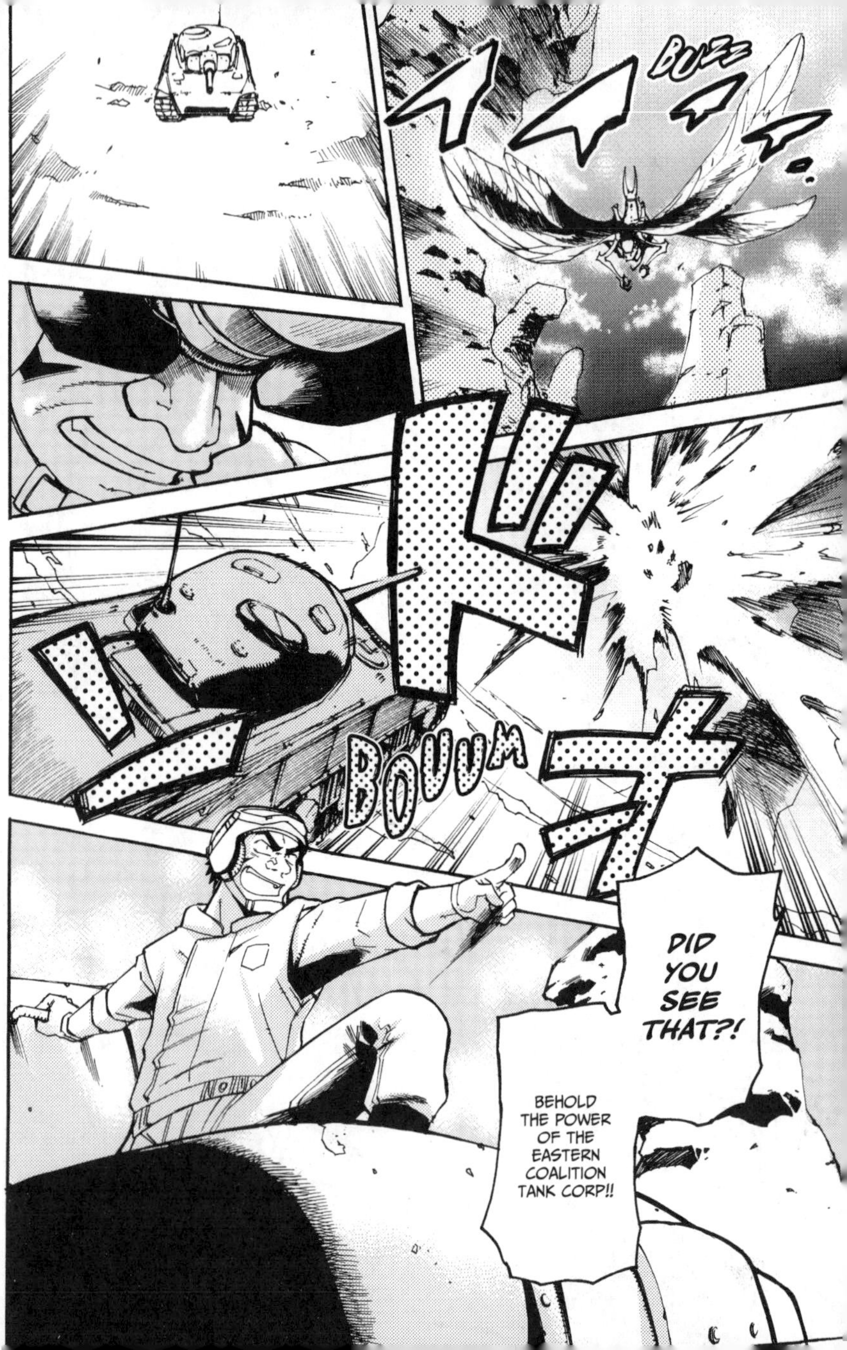

BUZZ
BOUUM
DID YOU SEE THAT?!
BEHOLD THE POWER OF THE EASTERN COALITION TANK CORP!!

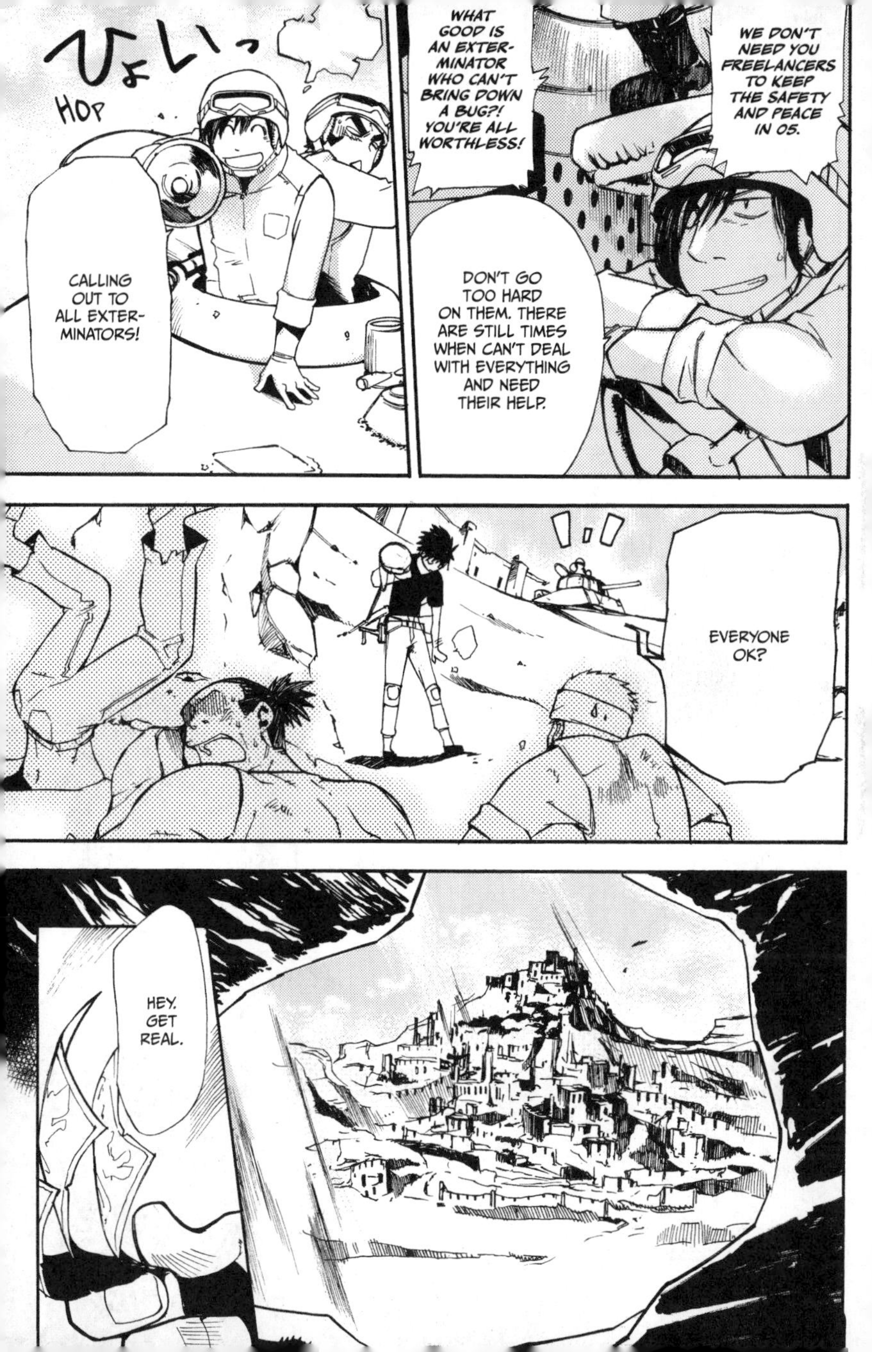
WE DON'T NEED YOU FREELANCERS TO KEEP THE SAFETY AND PEACE IN 05.
WHAT GOOD IS AN EXTERMINATOR WHO CAN'T BRING DOWN A BUG?! YOU'RE ALL WORTHLESS!
DON'T GO TOO HARD ON THEM. THERE ARE STILL TIMES WHEN CAN'T DEAL WITH EVERYTHING AND NEED THEIR HELP.
ひょいっ
HOP
CALLING OUT TO ALL EXTERMINATORS!
EVERYONE OK?
HEY. GET REAL.

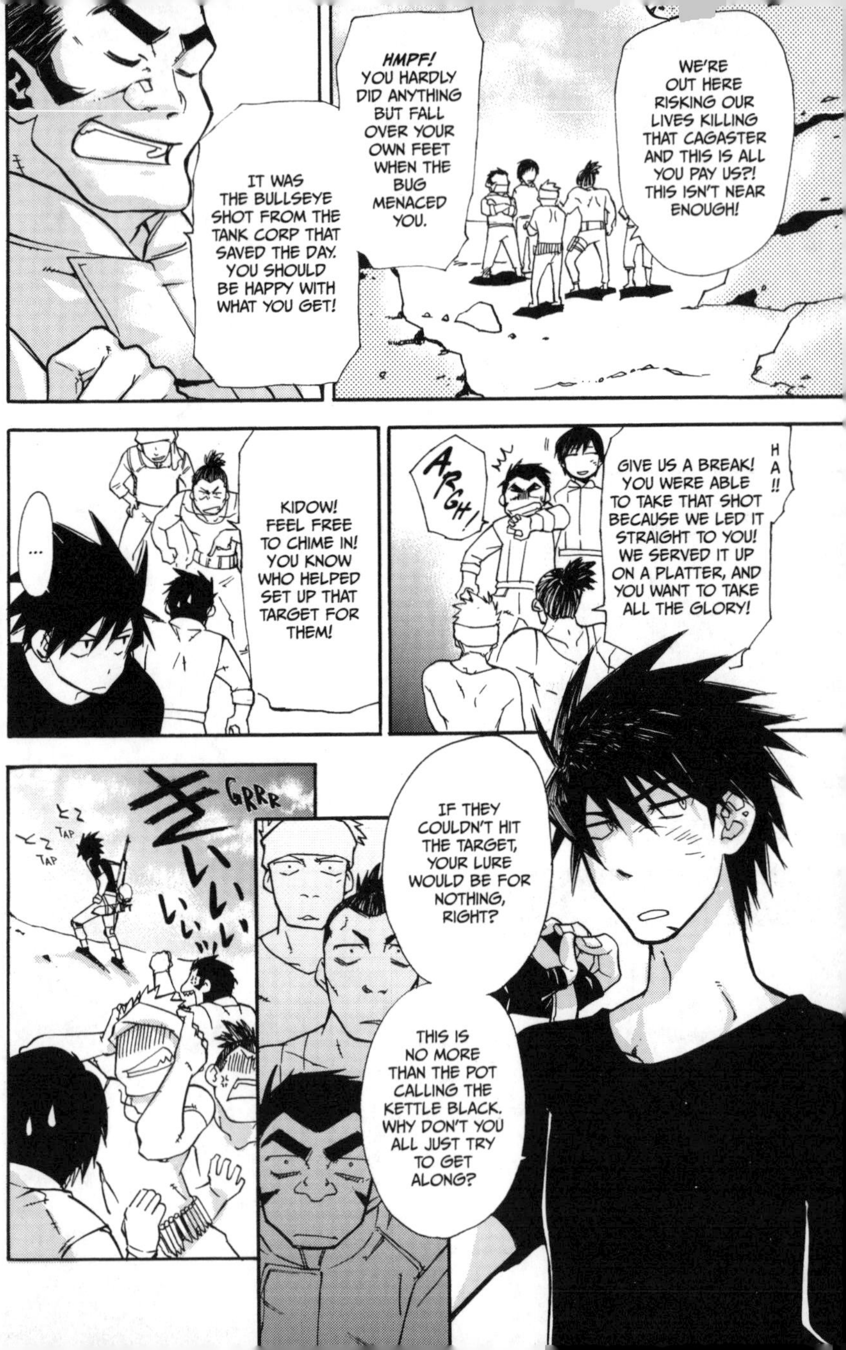
WE'RE OUT HERE RISKING OUR LIVES KILLING THAT CAGASTER AND THIS IS ALL YOU PAY US?! THIS ISN'T NEAR ENOUGH!
HMPF! YOU HARDLY DID ANYTHING BUT FALL OVER YOUR OWN FEET WHEN THE BUG MENACED YOU.
IT WAS THE BULLSEYE SHOT FROM THE TANK CORP THAT SAVED THE DAY. YOU SHOULD BE HAPPY WITH WHAT YOU GET!
HA!!
GIVE US A BREAK! YOU WERE ABLE TO TAKE THAT SHOT BECAUSE WE LED IT STRAIGHT TO YOU! WE SERVED IT UP ON A PLATTER, AND YOU WANT TO TAKE ALL THE GLORY!
ARGH!
KIDOW! FEEL FREE TO CHIME IN! YOU KNOW WHO HELPED SET UP THAT TARGET FOR THEM!
...
IF THEY COULDN'T HIT THE TARGET, YOUR LURE WOULD BE FOR NOTHING, RIGHT?
THIS IS NO MORE THAN THE POT CALLING THE KETTLE BLACK. WHY DON'T YOU ALL JUST TRY TO GET ALONG?
GRRR
TAP
TAP

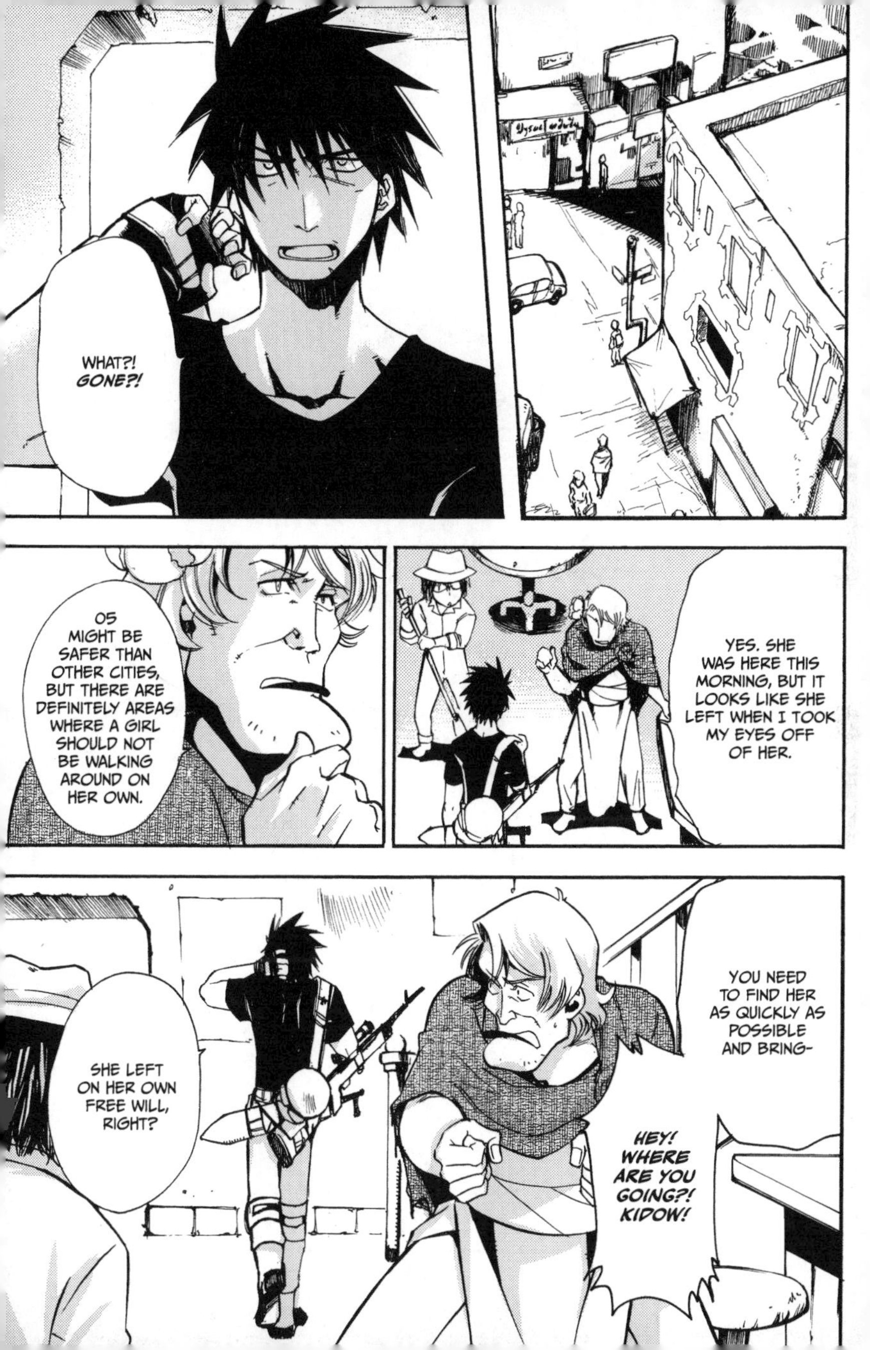
WHAT?! GONE?!
YES. SHE WAS HERE THIS MORNING, BUT IT LOOKS LIKE SHE LEFT WHEN I TOOK MY EYES OFF OF HER.
05 MIGHT BE SAFER THAN OTHER CITIES, BUT THERE ARE DEFINITELY AREAS WHERE A GIRL SHOULD NOT BE WALKING AROUND ON HER OWN.
YOU NEED TO FIND HER AS QUICKLY AS POSSIBLE AND BRING-
SHE LEFT ON HER OWN FREE WILL, RIGHT?
HEY! WHERE ARE YOU GOING?! KIDOW!

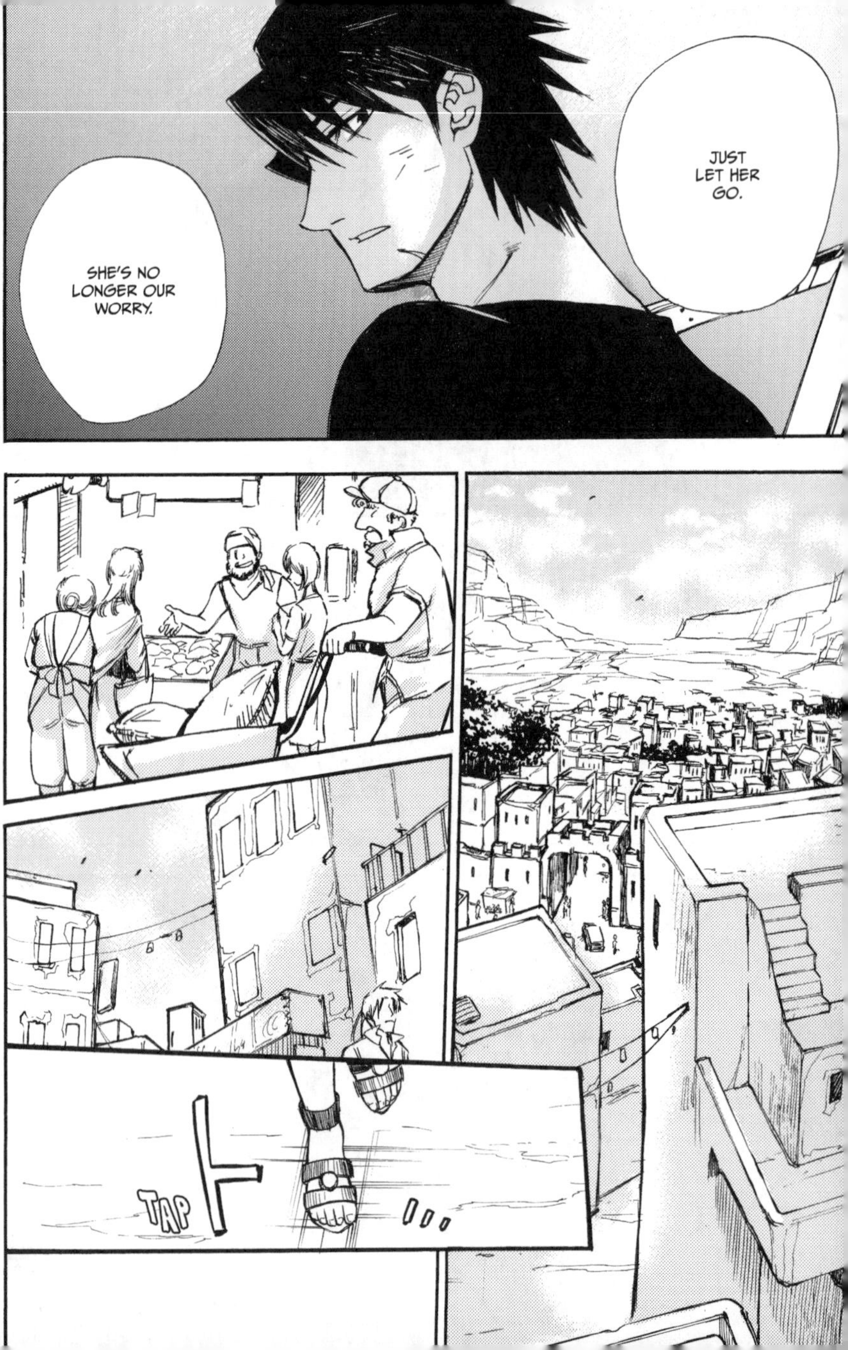
JUST LET HER GO.
SHE'S NO LONGER OUR WORRY.
TAP

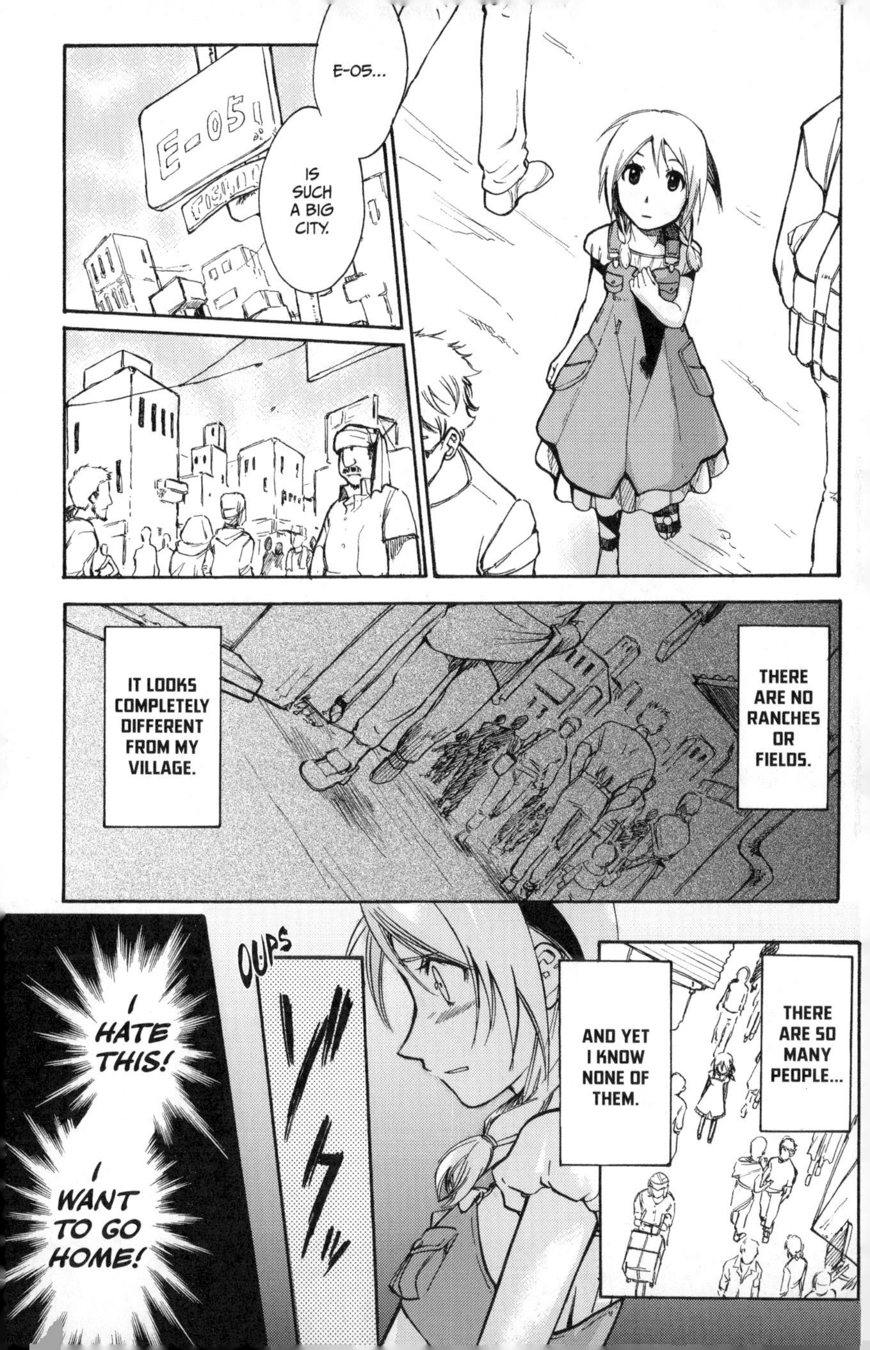
E-05...
IS SUCH A BIG CITY.
E-05
THERE ARE NO RANCHES OR FIELDS.
IT LOOKS COMPLETELY DIFFERENT FROM MY VILLAGE.
THERE ARE SO MANY PEOPLE...
AND YET I KNOW NONE OF THEM.
OUPS
I HATE THIS!
I WANT TO GO HOME!

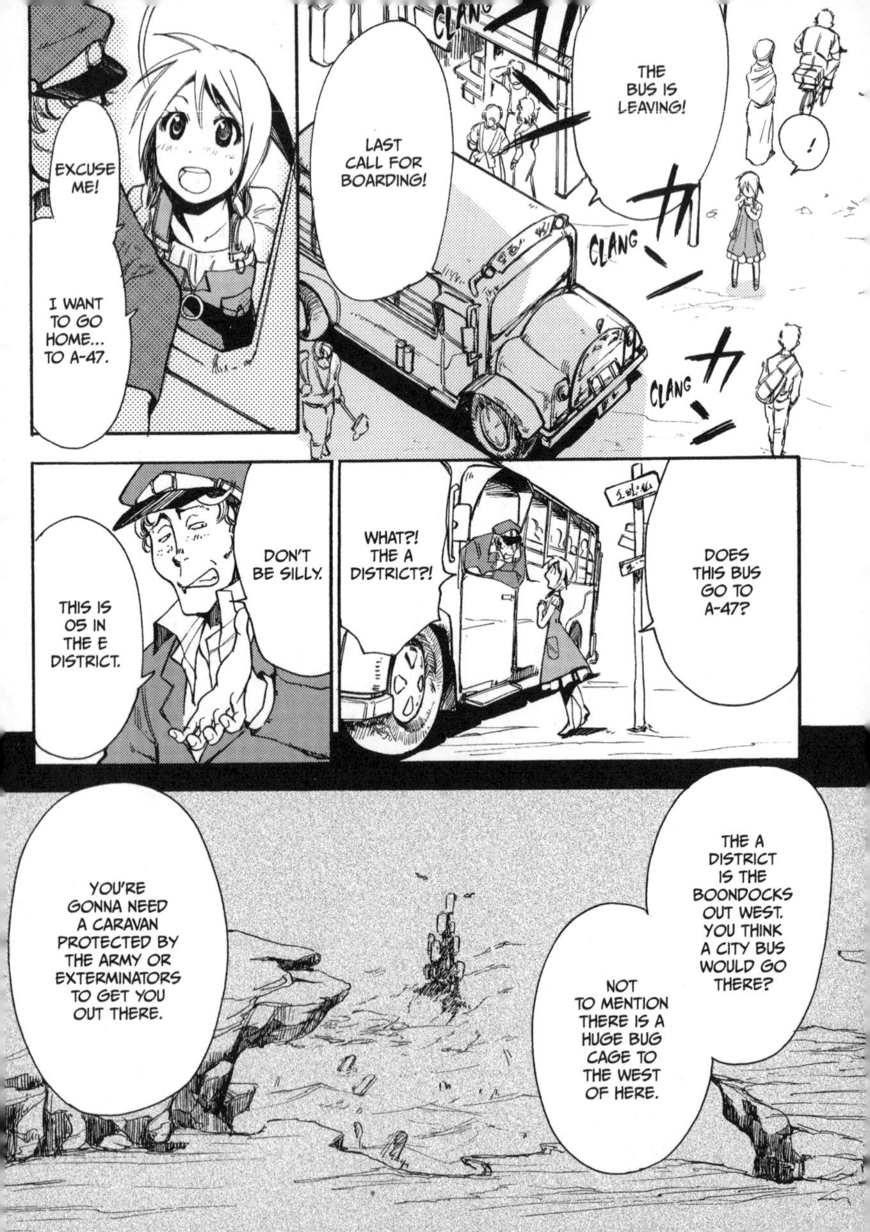
THE BUS IS LEAVING!
!
LAST CALL FOR BOARDING!
CLANG
CLANG
EXCUSE ME!
I WANT TO GO HOME... TO A-47.
DOES THIS BUS GO TO A-47?
WHAT?! THE A DISTRICT?!
DON'T BE SILLY.
THIS IS 05 IN THE E DISTRICT.
THE A DISTRICT IS THE BOONDOCKS OUT WEST. YOU THINK A CITY BUS WOULD GO THERE?
NOT TO MENTION THERE IS A HUGE BUG CAGE TO THE WEST OF HERE.
YOU'RE GONNA NEED A CARAVAN PROTECTED BY THE ARMY OR EXTERMINATORS TO GET YOU OUT THERE.

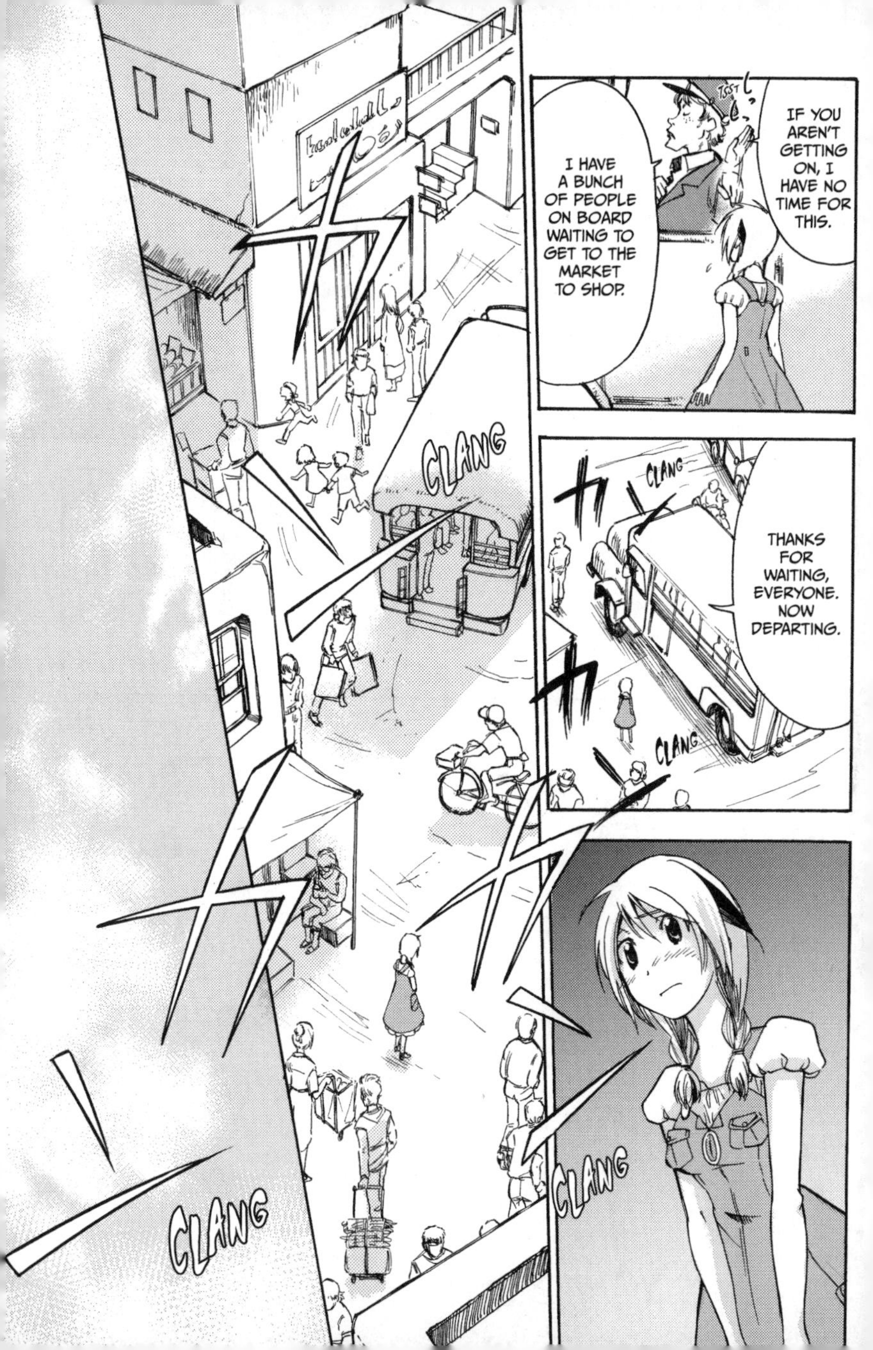
IF YOU AREN'T GETTING ON, I HAVE NO TIME FOR THIS.
I HAVE A BUNCH OF PEOPLE ON BOARD WAITING TO GET TO THE MARKET TO SHOP.
CLANG
THANKS FOR WAITING, EVERYONE. NOW DEPARTING.
CLANG
CLANG
CLANG
CLANG

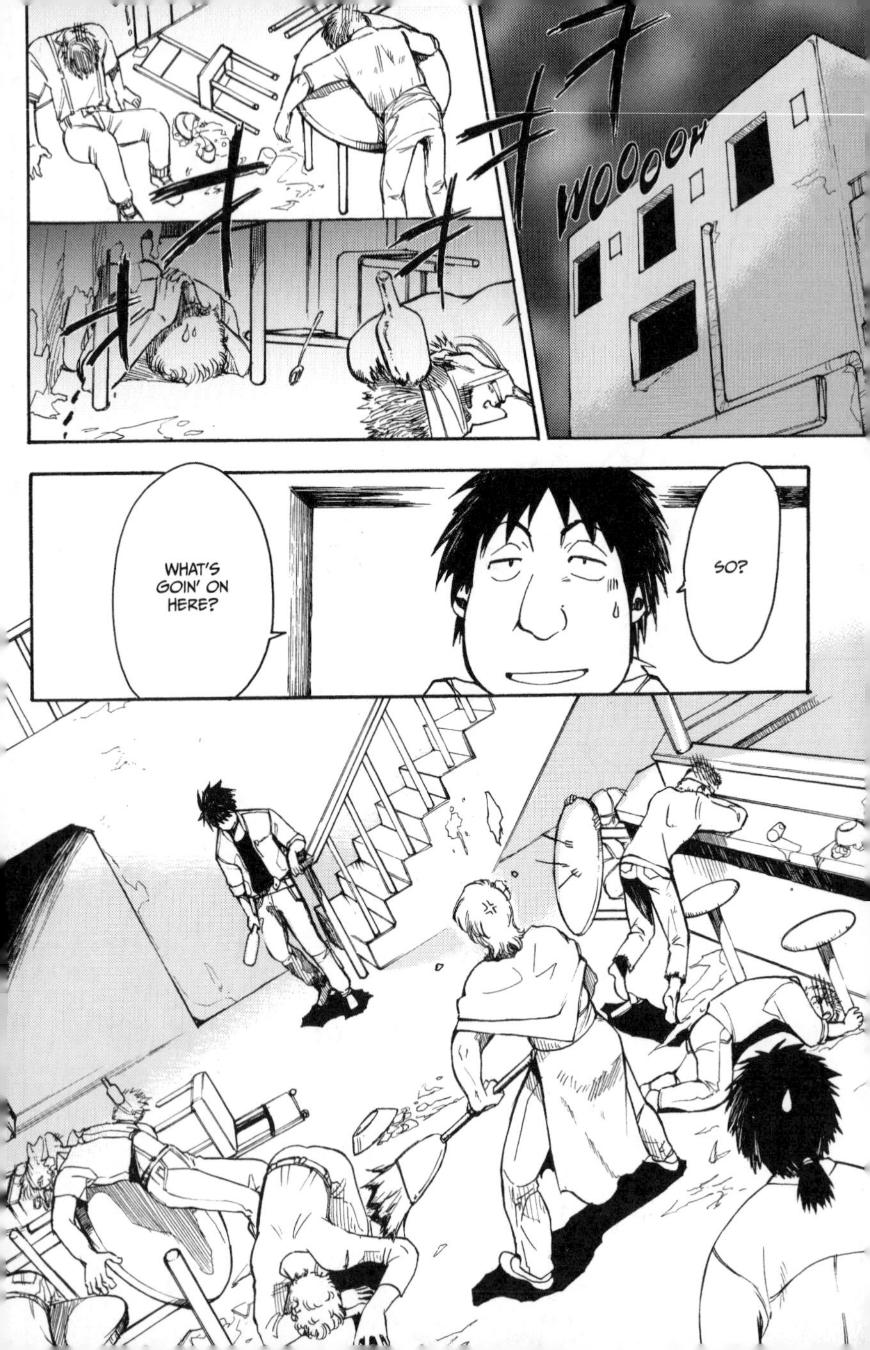
WOOOOOH
SO?
WHAT'S GOIN' ON HERE?

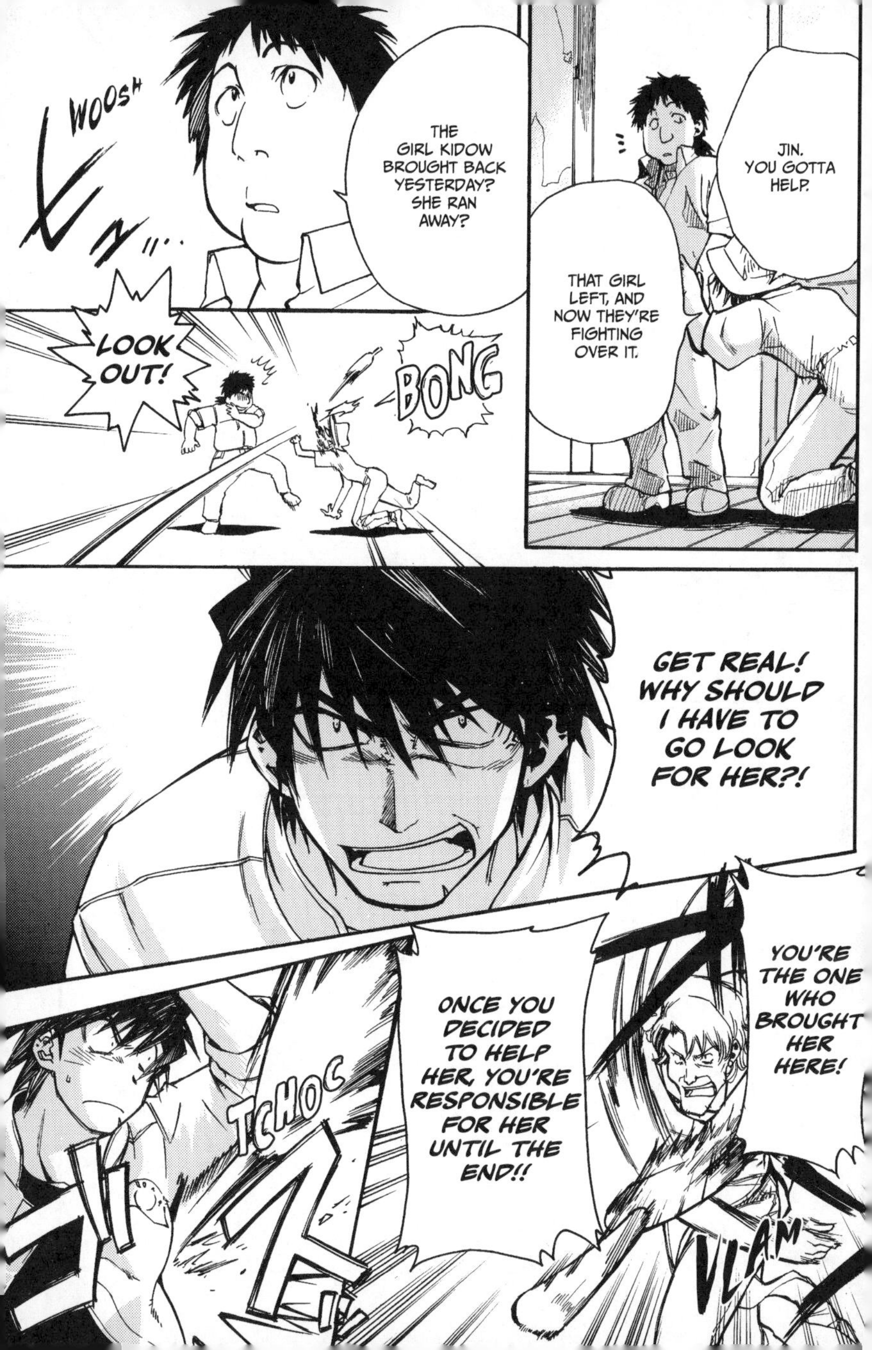
JIN. YOU GOTTA HELP.
THAT GIRL LEFT, AND NOW THEY'RE FIGHTING OVER IT.
WOOSH
THE GIRL KIDOW BROUGHT BACK YESTERDAY? SHE RAN AWAY?
BONG
LOOK OUT!
GET REAL! WHY SHOULD I HAVE TO GO LOOK FOR HER?!
YOU'RE THE ONE WHO BROUGHT HER HERE!
VLAM
ONCE YOU DECIDED TO HELP HER, YOU'RE RESPONSIBLE FOR HER UNTIL THE END!!
TCHOC

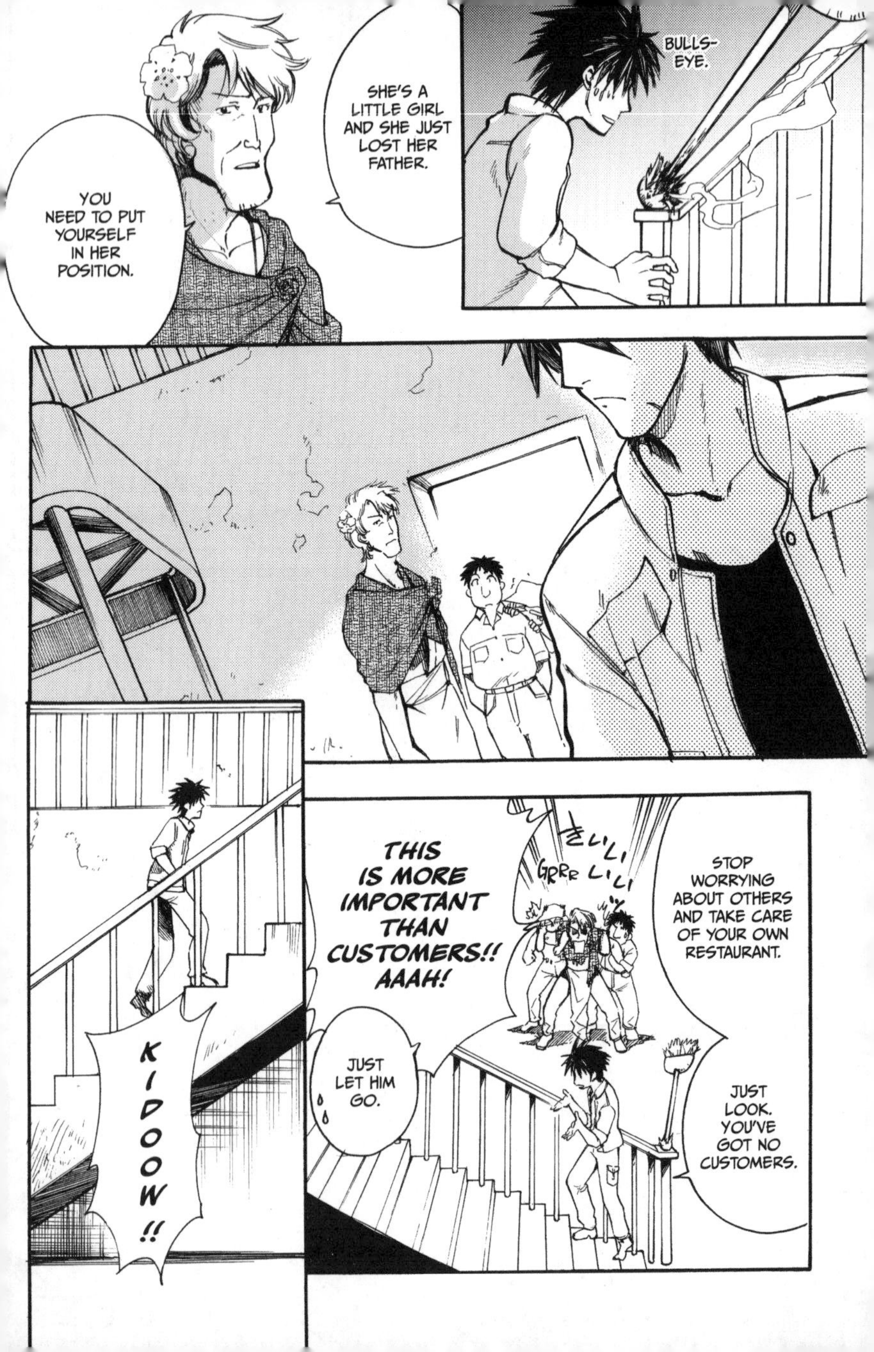
BULLS-EYE.
SHE'S A LITTLE GIRL AND SHE JUST LOST HER FATHER.
YOU NEED TO PUT YOURSELF IN HER POSITION.
STOP WORRYING ABOUT OTHERS AND TAKE CARE OF YOUR OWN RESTAURANT.
THIS IS MORE IMPORTANT THAN CUSTOMERS!! AAAH!
GRRR
JUST LOOK. YOU'VE GOT NO CUSTOMERS.
JUST LET HIM GO.
KIDOOOW!!

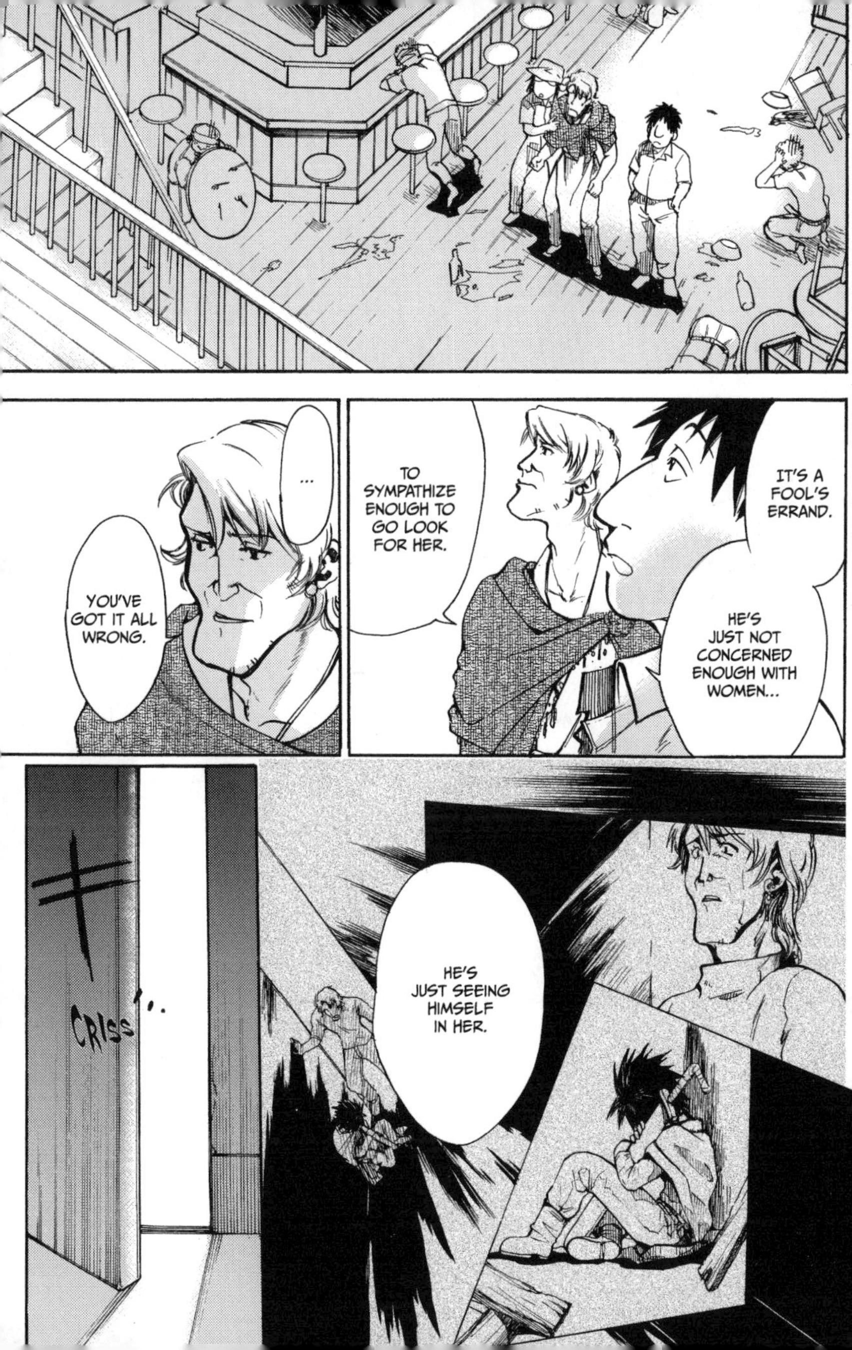
IT'S A FOOL'S ERRAND.
HE'S JUST NOT CONCERNED ENOUGH WITH WOMEN...
TO SYMPATHIZE ENOUGH TO GO LOOK FOR HER.
...
YOU'VE GOT IT ALL WRONG.
HE'S JUST SEEING HIMSELF IN HER.
CRISS...

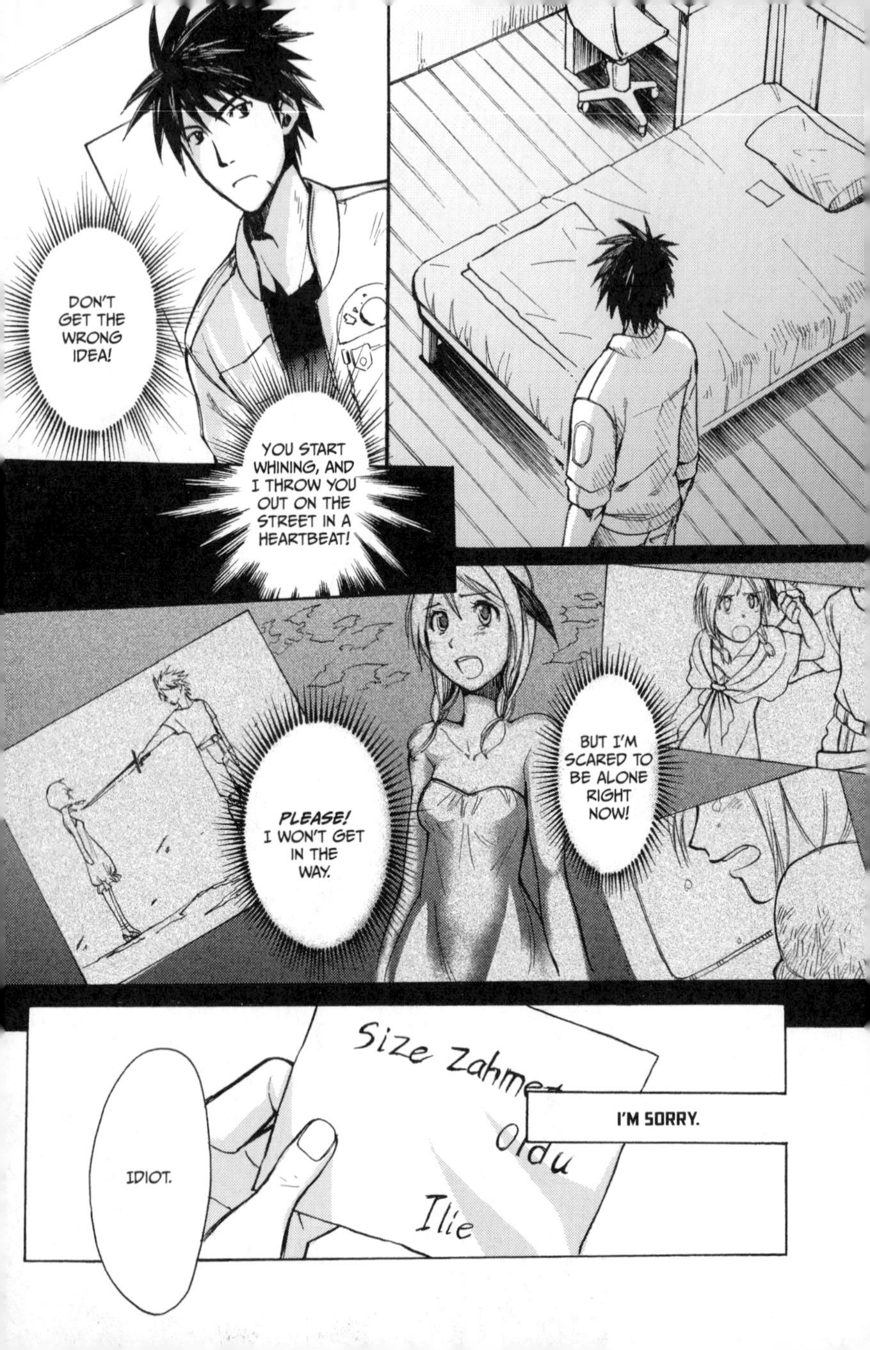
DON'T GET THE WRONG IDEA!
YOU START WHINING, AND I THROW YOU OUT ON THE STREET IN A HEARTBEAT!
PLEASE! I WON'T GET IN THE WAY.
BUT I'M SCARED TO BE ALONE RIGHT NOW!
Size Zahmet Oldu
Ilie
I'M SORRY.
IDIOT.

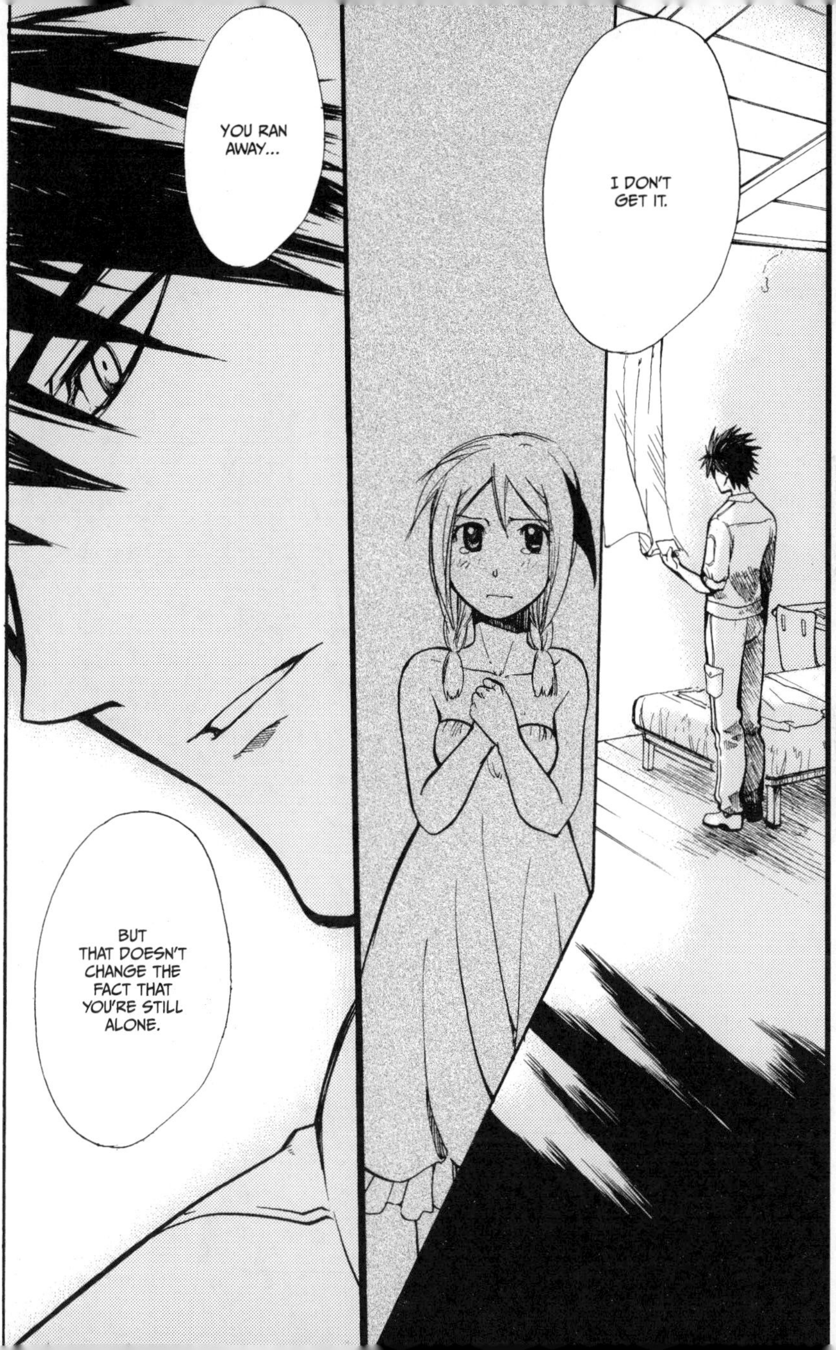
I DON'T GET IT.
YOU RAN AWAY...
BUT THAT DOESN'T CHANGE THE FACT THAT YOU'RE STILL ALONE.

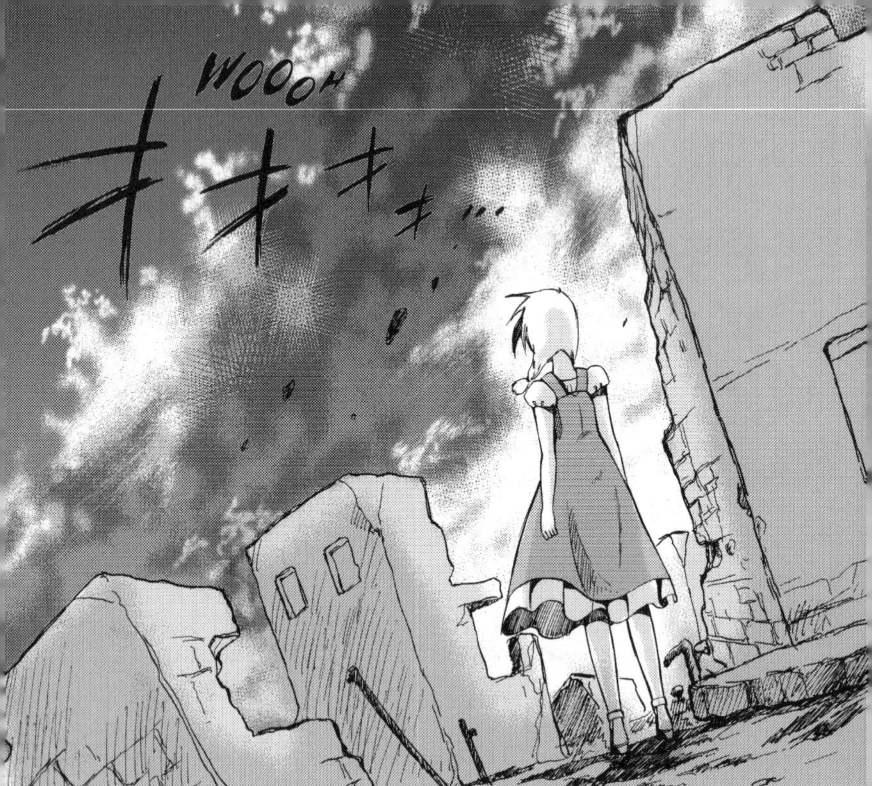
WOOOOH
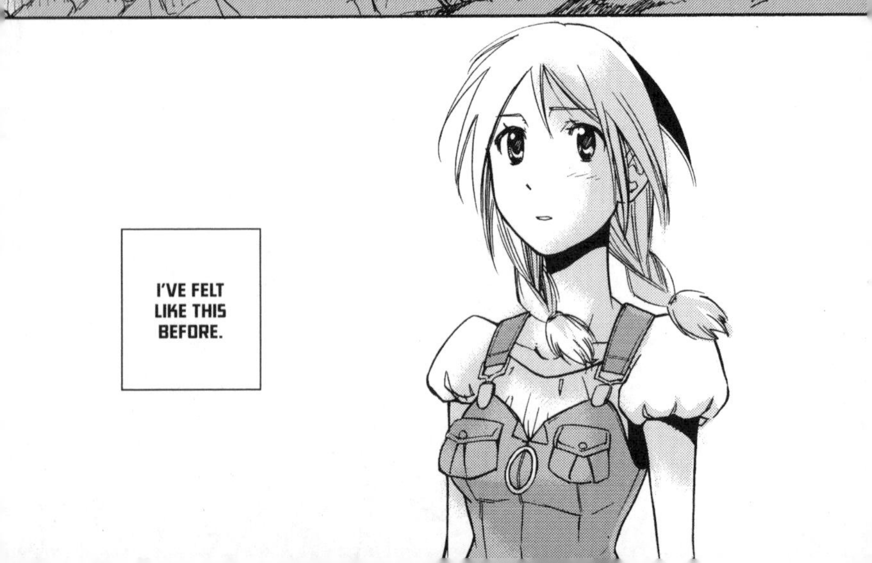
I'VE FELT LIKE THIS BEFORE.

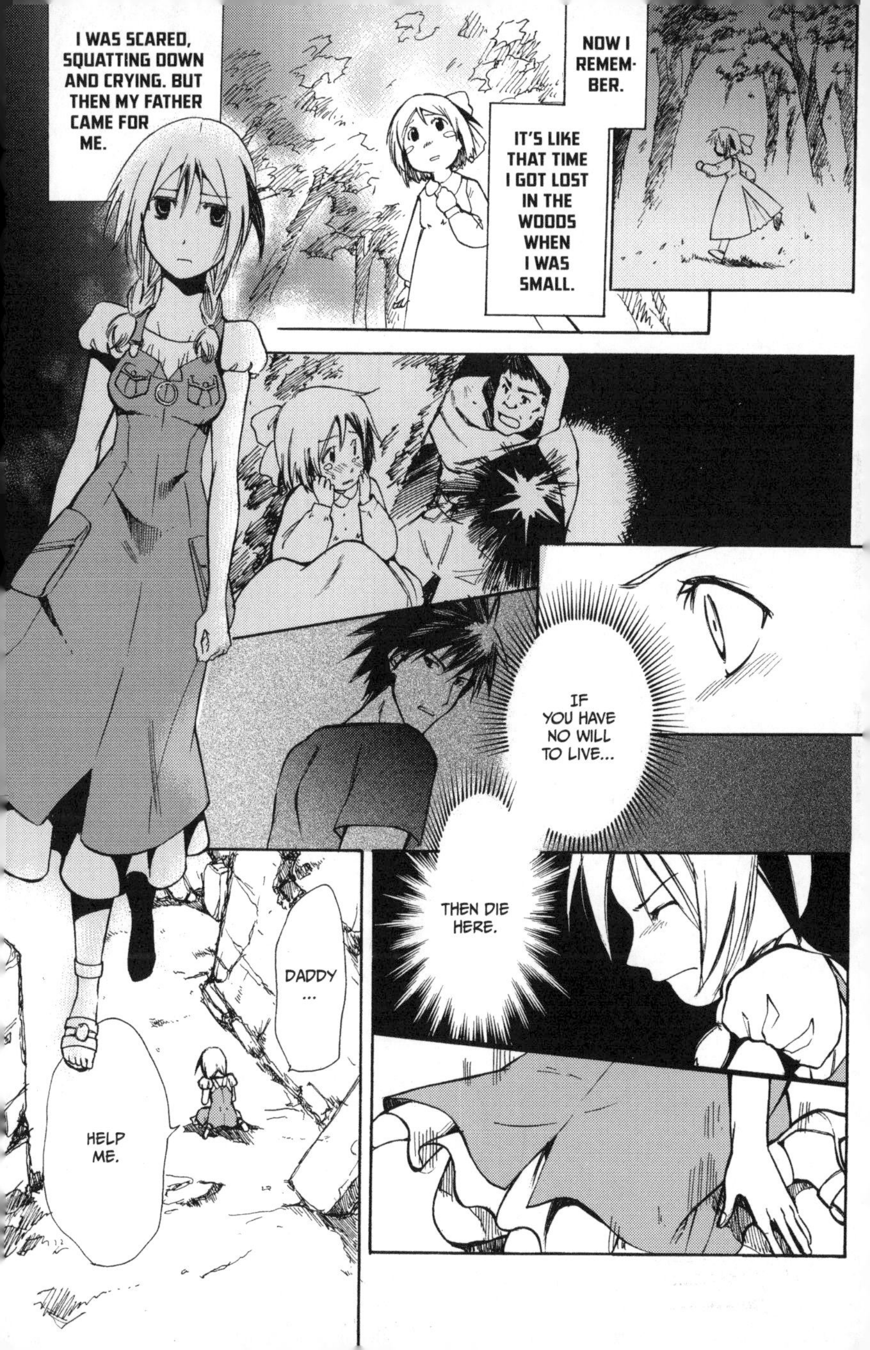
NOW I REMEMBER.
IT'S LIKE THAT TIME I GOT LOST IN THE WOODS WHEN I WAS SMALL.
I WAS SCARED, SQUATTING DOWN AND CRYING. BUT THEN MY FATHER CAME FOR ME.
IF YOU HAVE NO WILL TO LIVE...
THEN DIE HERE.
DADDY ...
HELP ME.

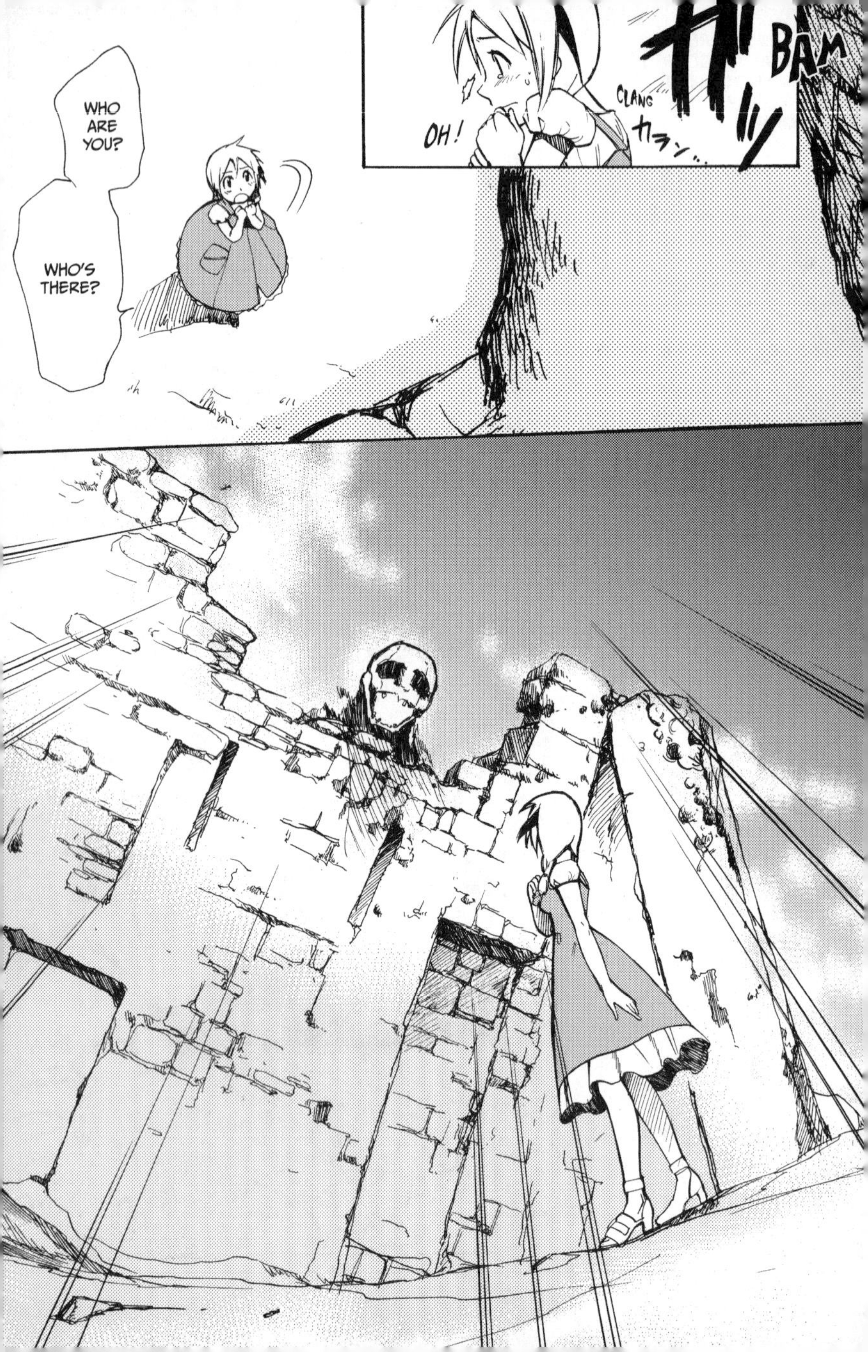
BAM
CLANG
カラン…
OH!
WHO ARE YOU?
WHO'S THERE?

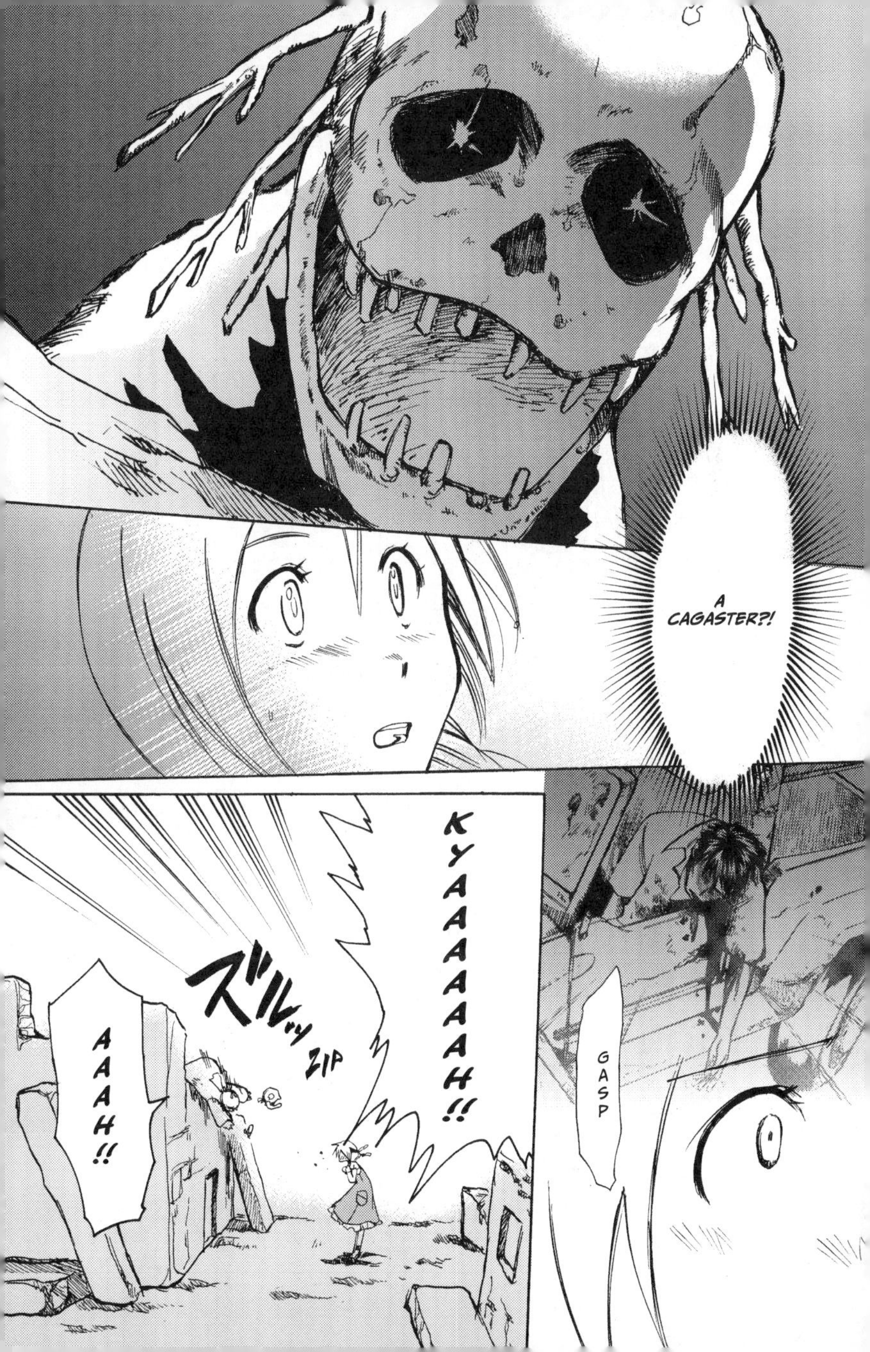
A CAGASTER?!
GASP
KYAAAAAAAAAH!!
ズルッ
ZIP
AAAAH!!

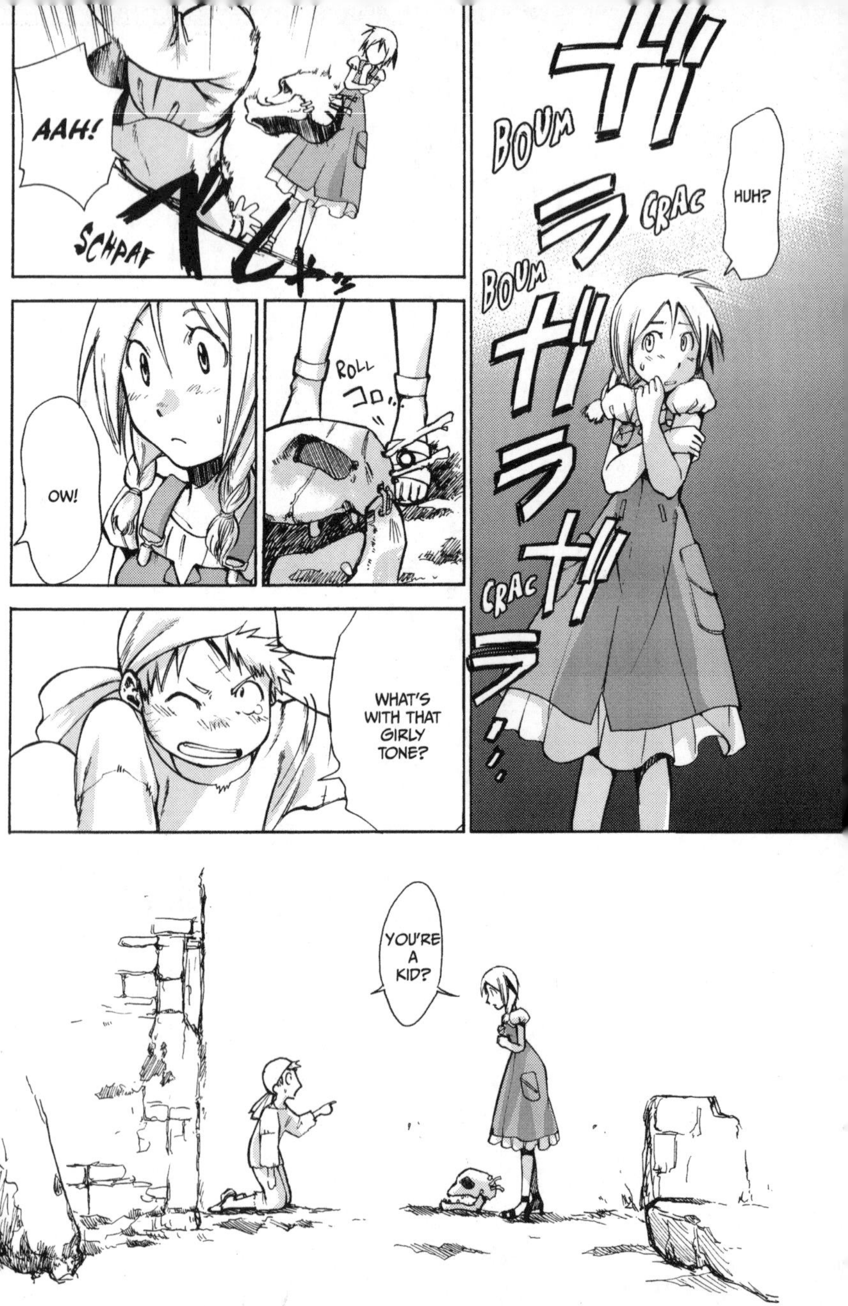
BOUM
CRAC
HUH?
BOUM
CRAC
AAH!
SCHPAF
ROLL
OW!
WHAT'S WITH THAT GIRLY TONE?
YOU'RE A KID?

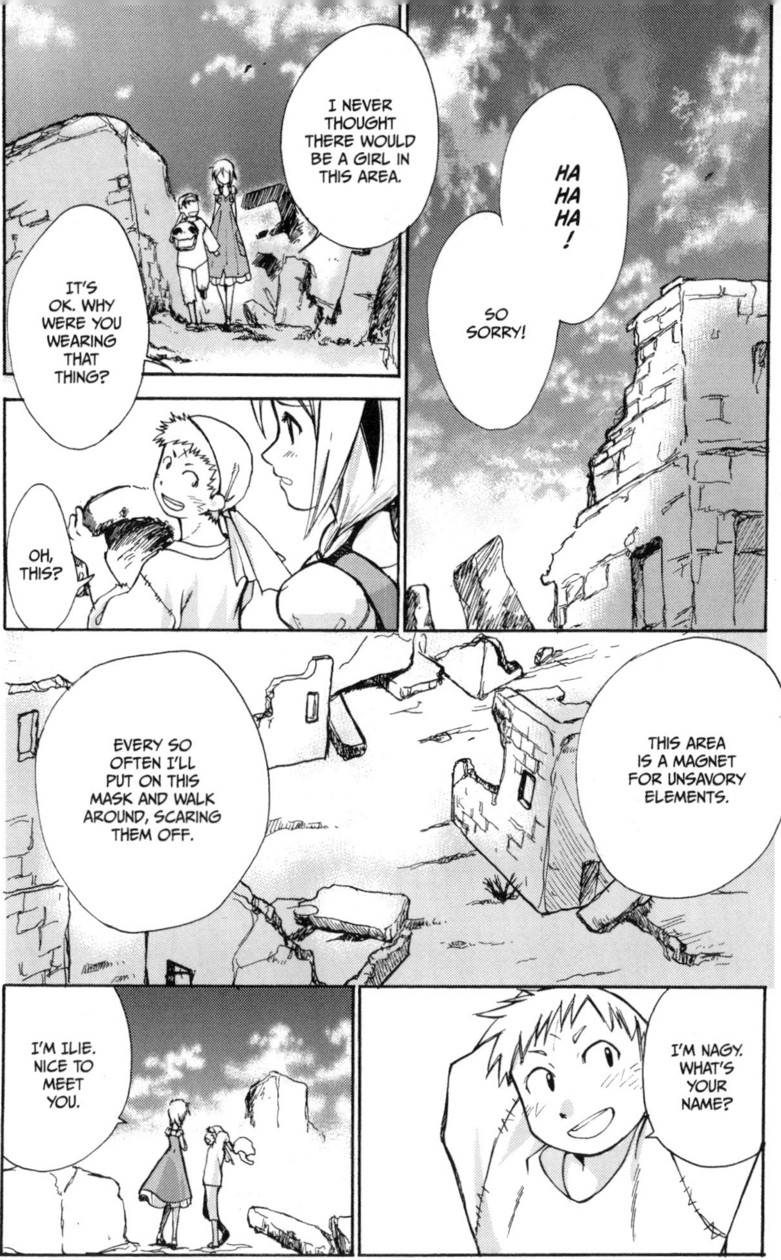
HA HA HA!
SO SORRY!
I NEVER THOUGHT THERE WOULD BE A GIRL IN THIS AREA.
IT'S OK. WHY WERE YOU WEARING THAT THING?
OH, THIS?
THIS AREA IS A MAGNET FOR UNSAVORY ELEMENTS.
EVERY SO OFTEN I'LL PUT ON THIS MASK AND WALK AROUND, SCARING THEM OFF.
I'M NAGY. WHAT'S YOUR NAME?
I'M ILIE. NICE TO MEET YOU.

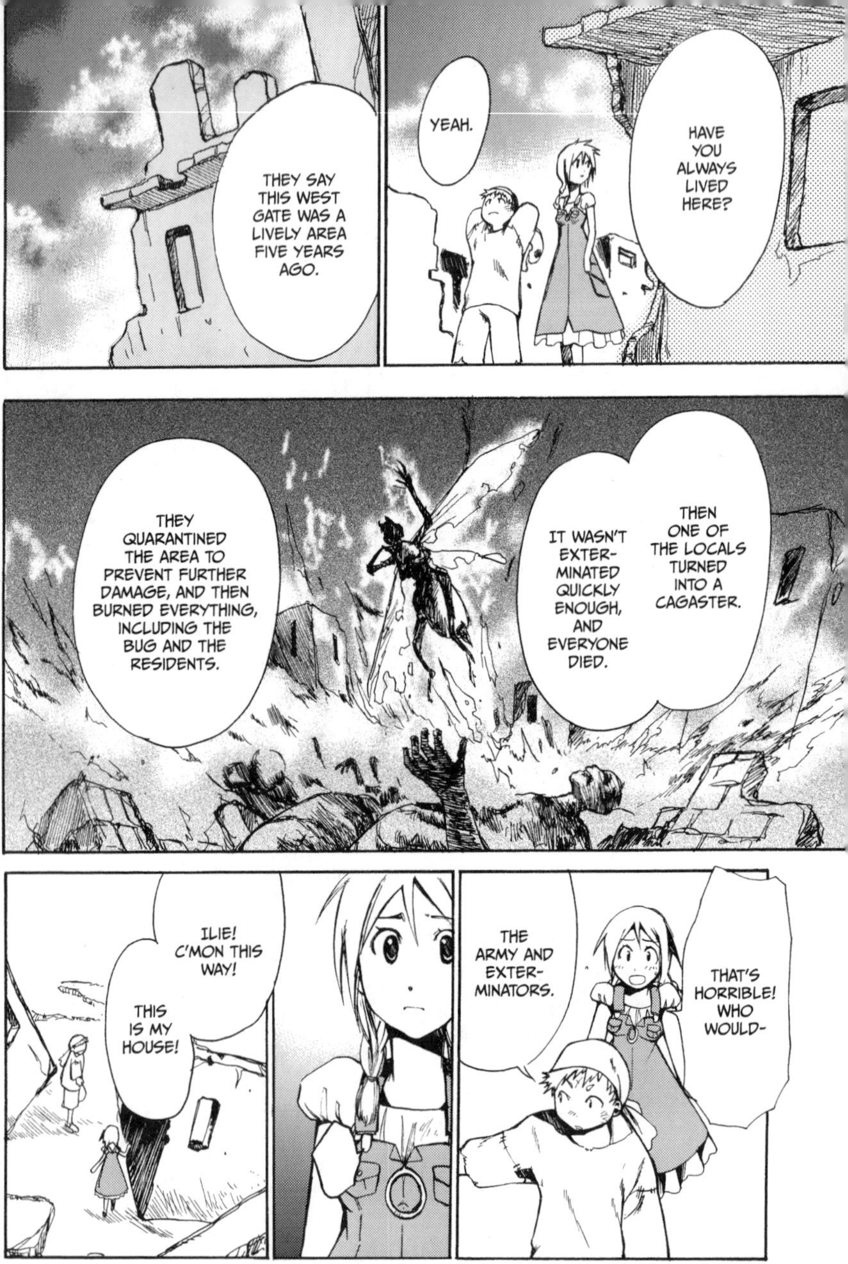
HAVE YOU ALWAYS LIVED HERE?
YEAH.
THEY SAY THIS WEST GATE WAS A LIVELY AREA FIVE YEARS AGO.
THEN ONE OF THE LOCALS TURNED INTO A CAGASTER.
IT WASN'T EXTER-MINATED QUICKLY ENOUGH, AND EVERYONE DIED.
THEY QUARANTINED THE AREA TO PREVENT FURTHER DAMAGE, AND THEN BURNED EVERYTHING, INCLUDING THE BUG AND THE RESIDENTS.
THAT'S HORRIBLE! WHO WOULD-
THE ARMY AND EXTER-MINATORS.
ILIE! C'MON THIS WAY!
THIS IS MY HOUSE!

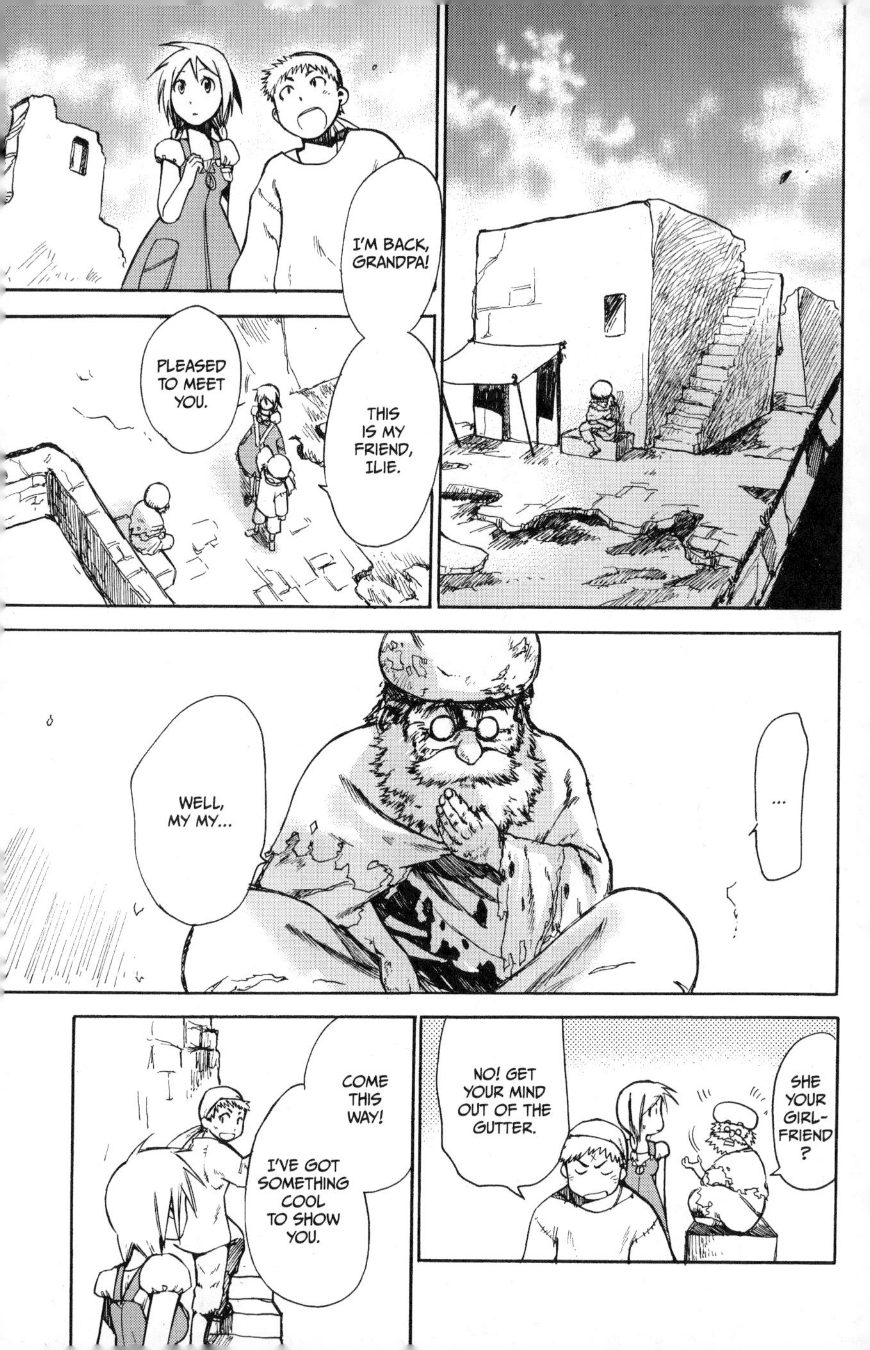
I'M BACK, GRANDPA!
THIS IS MY FRIEND, ILIE.
PLEASED TO MEET YOU.
...
WELL, MY MY...
SHE YOUR GIRL-FRIEND?
NO! GET YOUR MIND OUT OF THE GUTTER.
COME THIS WAY!
I'VE GOT SOMETHING COOL TO SHOW YOU.

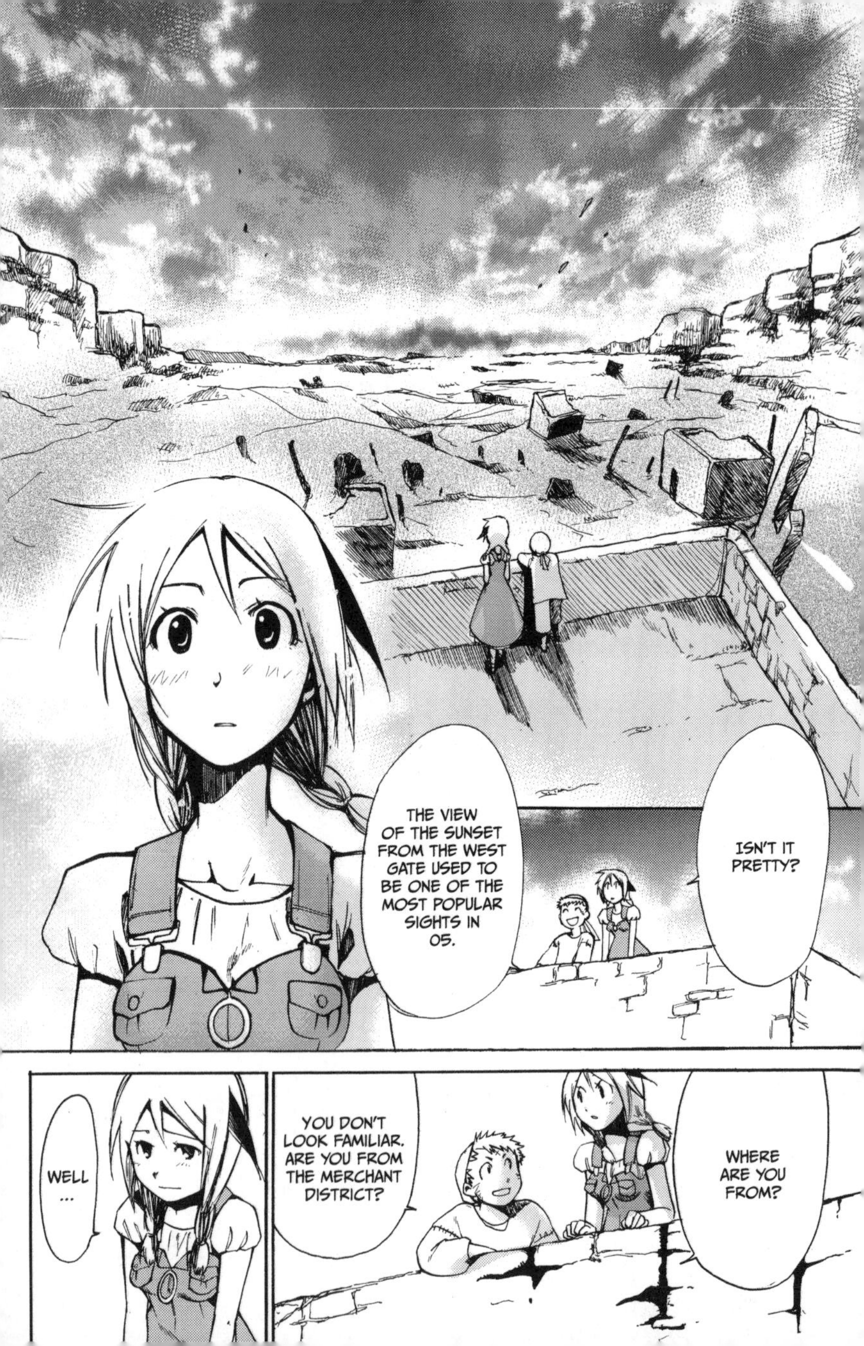
ISN'T IT PRETTY?
THE VIEW OF THE SUNSET FROM THE WEST GATE USED TO BE ONE OF THE MOST POPULAR SIGHTS IN 05.
WHERE ARE YOU FROM?
YOU DON'T LOOK FAMILIAR. ARE YOU FROM THE MERCHANT DISTRICT?
WELL ...

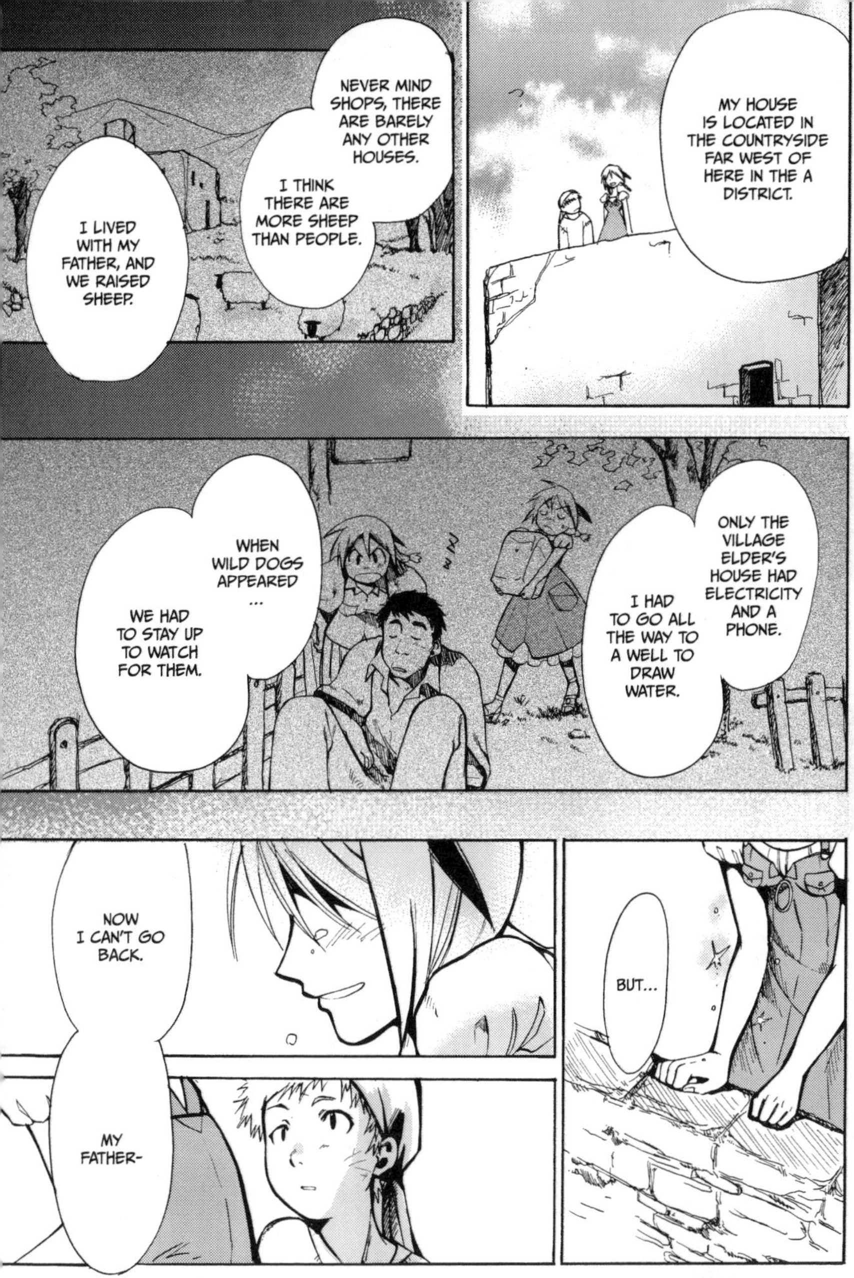
MY HOUSE IS LOCATED IN THE COUNTRYSIDE FAR WEST OF HERE IN THE A DISTRICT.
NEVER MIND SHOPS, THERE ARE BARELY ANY OTHER HOUSES.
I THINK THERE ARE MORE SHEEP THAN PEOPLE.
I LIVED WITH MY FATHER, AND WE RAISED SHEEP.
ONLY THE VILLAGE ELDER'S HOUSE HAD ELECTRICITY AND A PHONE.
I HAD TO GO ALL THE WAY TO A WELL TO DRAW WATER.
WHEN WILD DOGS APPEARED ...
WE HAD TO STAY UP TO WATCH FOR THEM.
BUT...
NOW I CAN'T GO BACK.
MY FATHER-

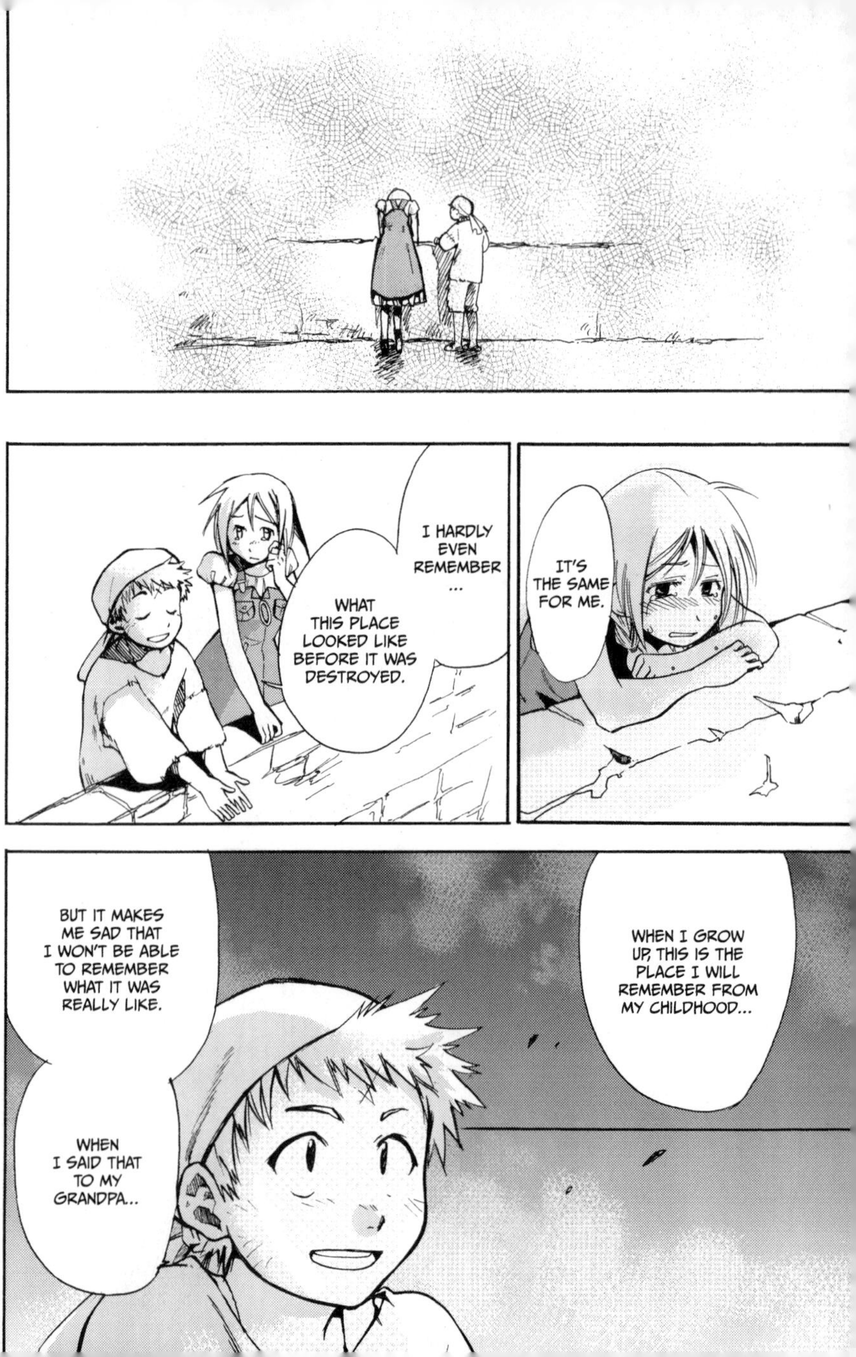
IT'S THE SAME FOR ME.
I HARDLY EVEN REMEMBER...
WHAT THIS PLACE LOOKED LIKE BEFORE IT WAS DESTROYED.
WHEN I GROW UP, THIS IS THE PLACE I WILL REMEMBER FROM MY CHILDHOOD...
BUT IT MAKES ME SAD THAT I WON'T BE ABLE TO REMEMBER WHAT IT WAS REALLY LIKE.
WHEN I SAID THAT TO MY GRANDPA...

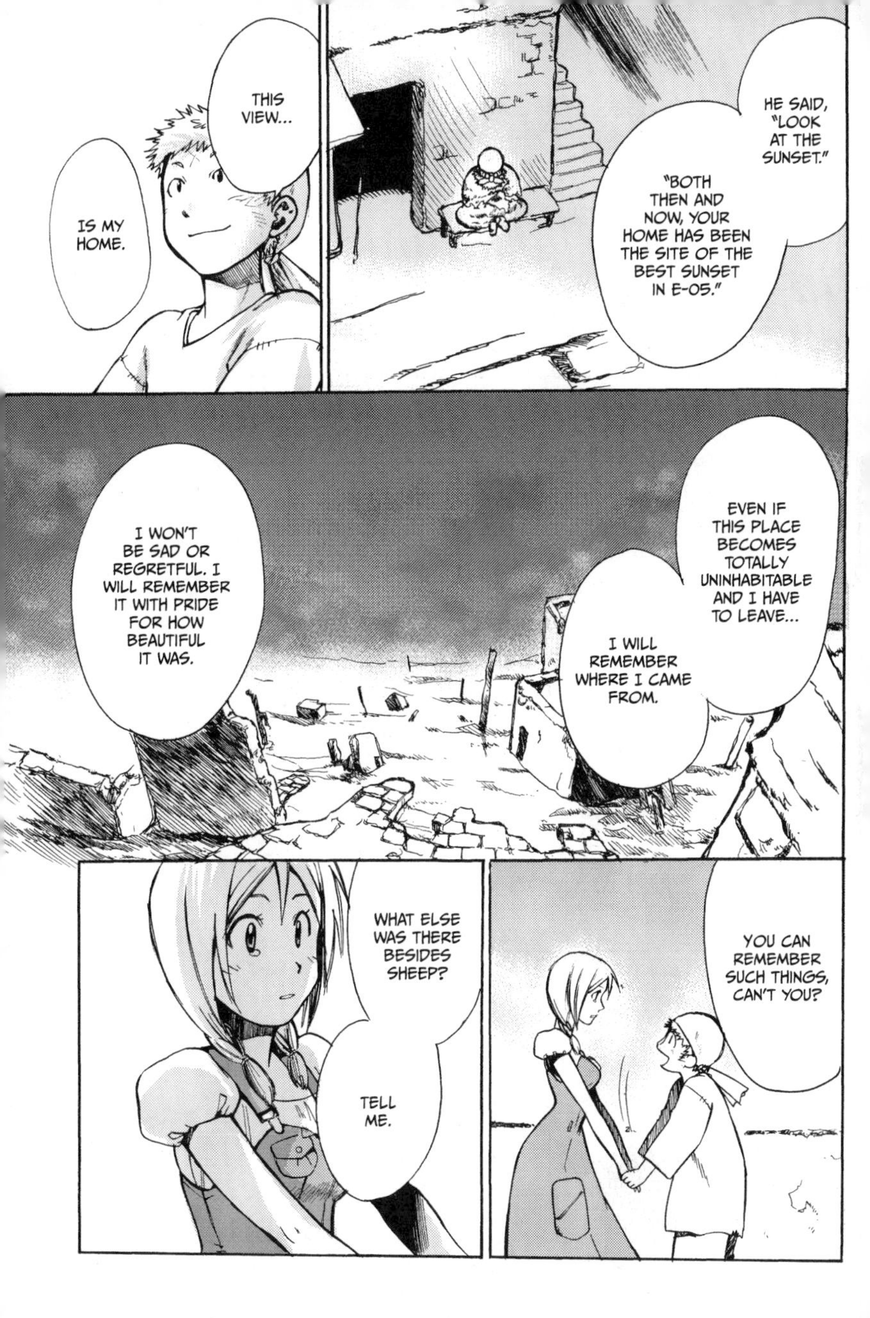
HE SAID, "LOOK AT THE SUNSET."
"BOTH THEN AND NOW, YOUR HOME HAS BEEN THE SITE OF THE BEST SUNSET IN E-05."
THIS VIEW...
IS MY HOME.
EVEN IF THIS PLACE BECOMES TOTALLY UNINHABITABLE AND I HAVE TO LEAVE...
I WILL REMEMBER WHERE I CAME FROM.
I WON'T BE SAD OR REGRETFUL. I WILL REMEMBER IT WITH PRIDE FOR HOW BEAUTIFUL IT WAS.
YOU CAN REMEMBER SUCH THINGS, CAN'T YOU?
WHAT ELSE WAS THERE BESIDES SHEEP?
TELL ME.

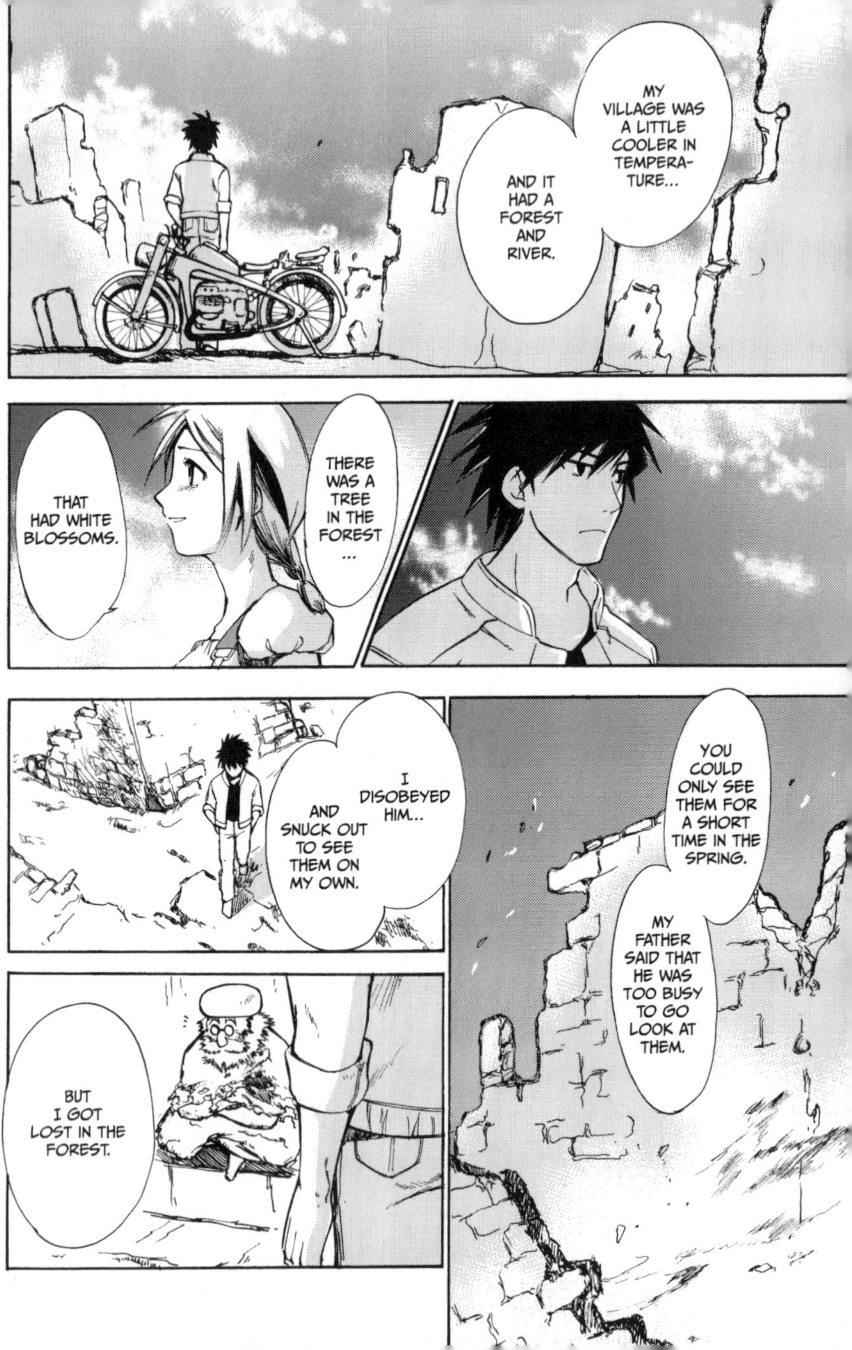
MY VILLAGE WAS A LITTLE COOLER IN TEMPERATURE...
AND IT HAD A FOREST AND RIVER.
THERE WAS A TREE IN THE FOREST...
THAT HAD WHITE BLOSSOMS.
YOU COULD ONLY SEE THEM FOR A SHORT TIME IN THE SPRING.
MY FATHER SAID THAT HE WAS TOO BUSY TO GO LOOK AT THEM.
I DISOBEYED HIM...
AND SNUCK OUT TO SEE THEM ON MY OWN.
BUT I GOT LOST IN THE FOREST.

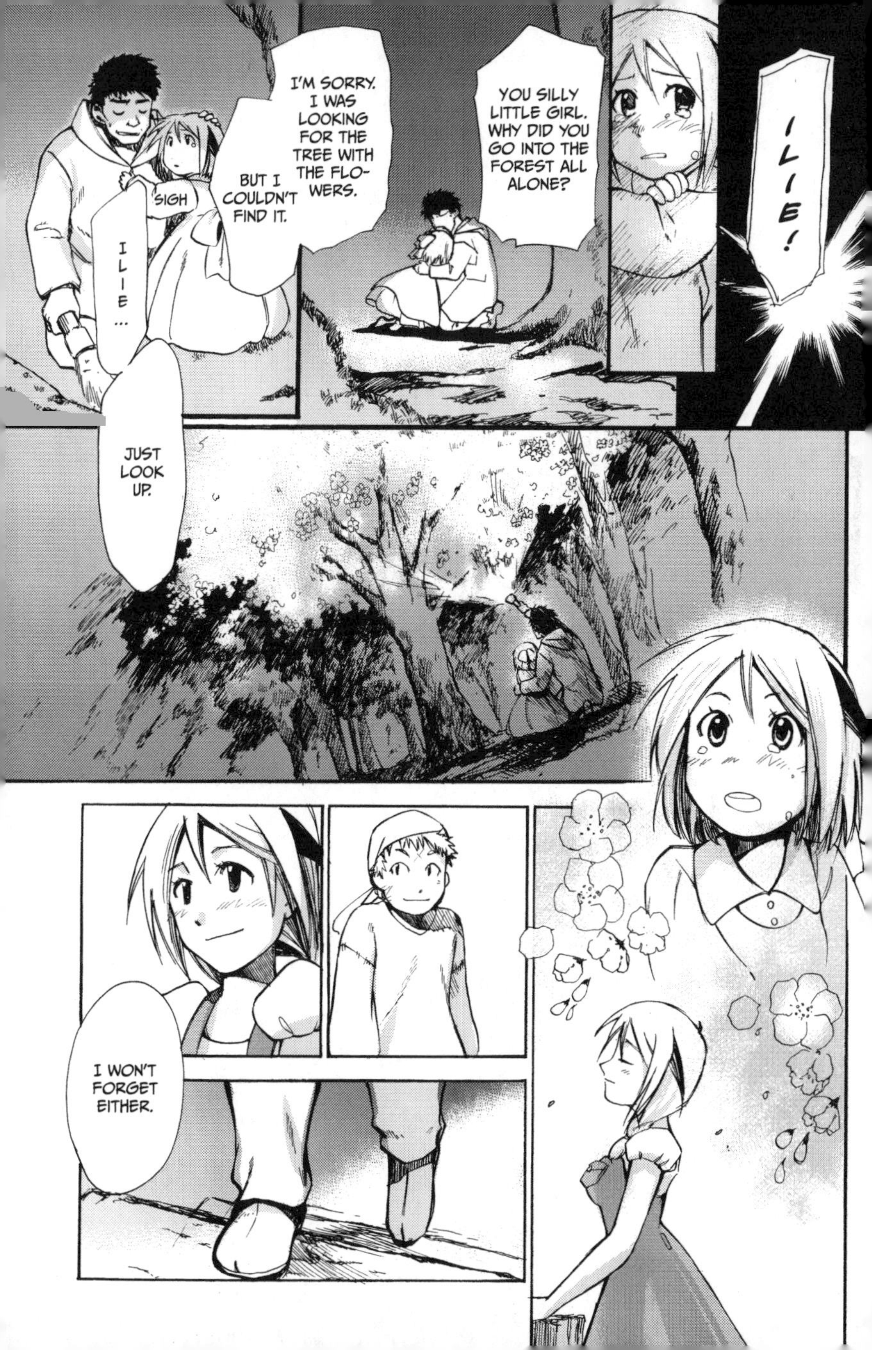
ILIE!
YOU SILLY LITTLE GIRL. WHY DID YOU GO INTO THE FOREST ALL ALONE?
I'M SORRY. I WAS LOOKING FOR THE TREE WITH THE FLO- WERS.
BUT I COULDN'T FIND IT.
SIGH
ILIE...
JUST LOOK UP.
I WON'T FORGET EITHER.

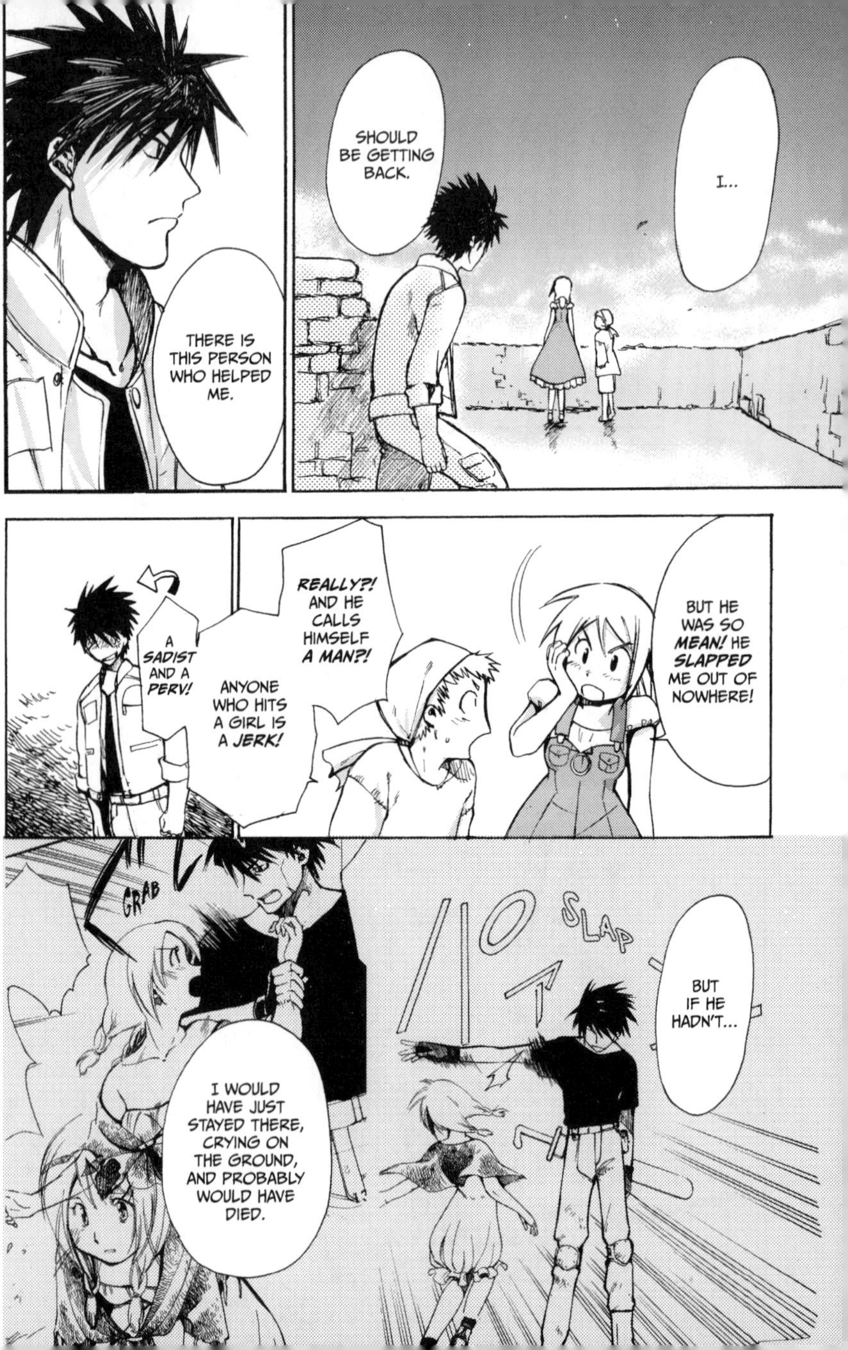
I...
SHOULD BE GETTING BACK.
THERE IS THIS PERSON WHO HELPED ME.
BUT HE WAS SO *MEAN!* HE *SLAPPED* ME OUT OF NOWHERE!
*REALLY?!* AND HE CALLS HIMSELF *A MAN?!*
ANYONE WHO HITS A GIRL IS A *JERK!*
A *SADIST* AND A *PERV!*
BUT IF HE HADN'T...
SLAP
GRAB
I WOULD HAVE JUST STAYED THERE, CRYING ON THE GROUND, AND PROBABLY WOULD HAVE DIED.

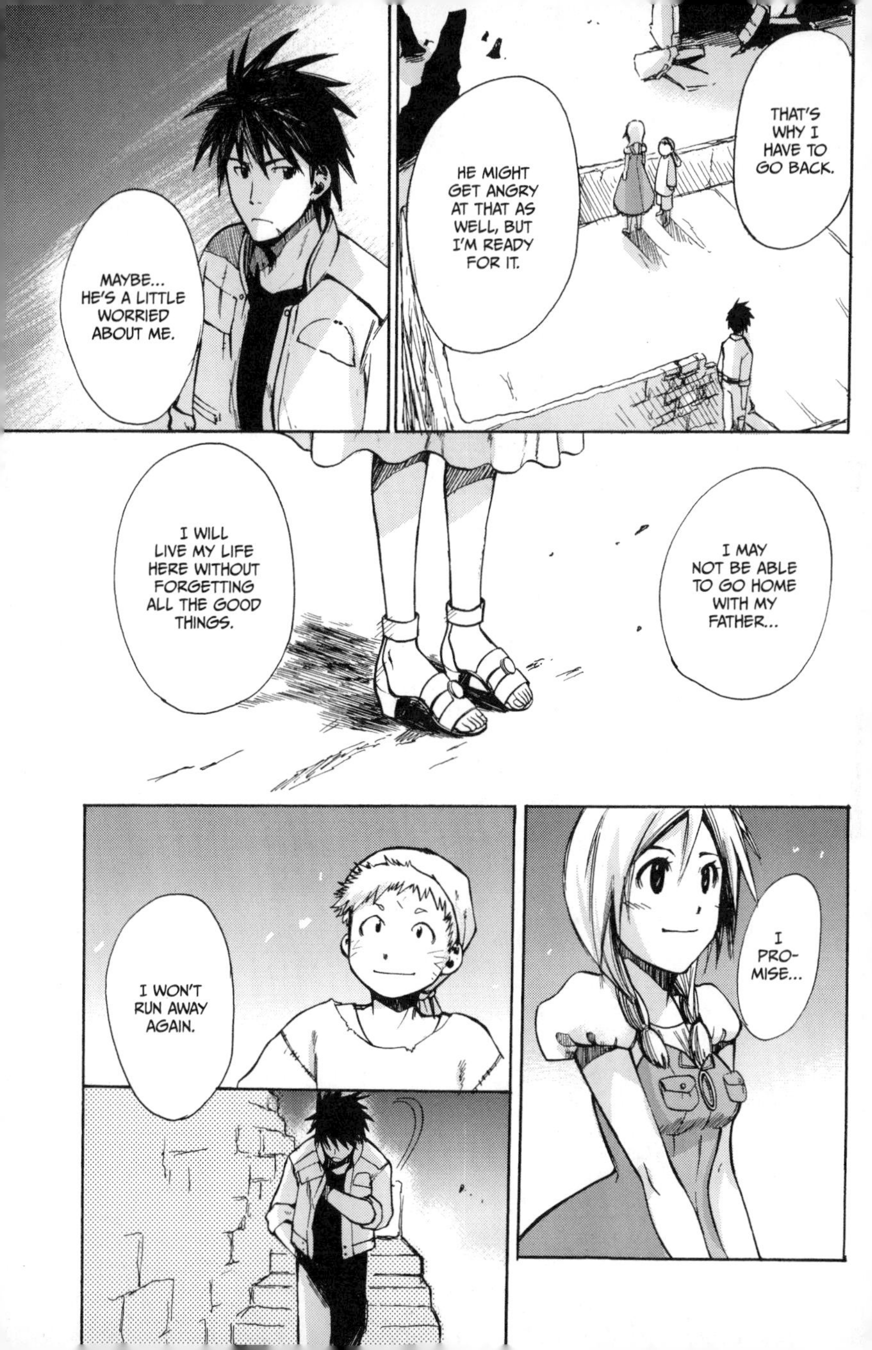
THAT'S WHY I HAVE TO GO BACK.
HE MIGHT GET ANGRY AT THAT AS WELL, BUT I'M READY FOR IT.
MAYBE... HE'S A LITTLE WORRIED ABOUT ME.
I MAY NOT BE ABLE TO GO HOME WITH MY FATHER...
I WILL LIVE MY LIFE HERE WITHOUT FORGETTING ALL THE GOOD THINGS.
I PRO-MISE...
I WON'T RUN AWAY AGAIN.

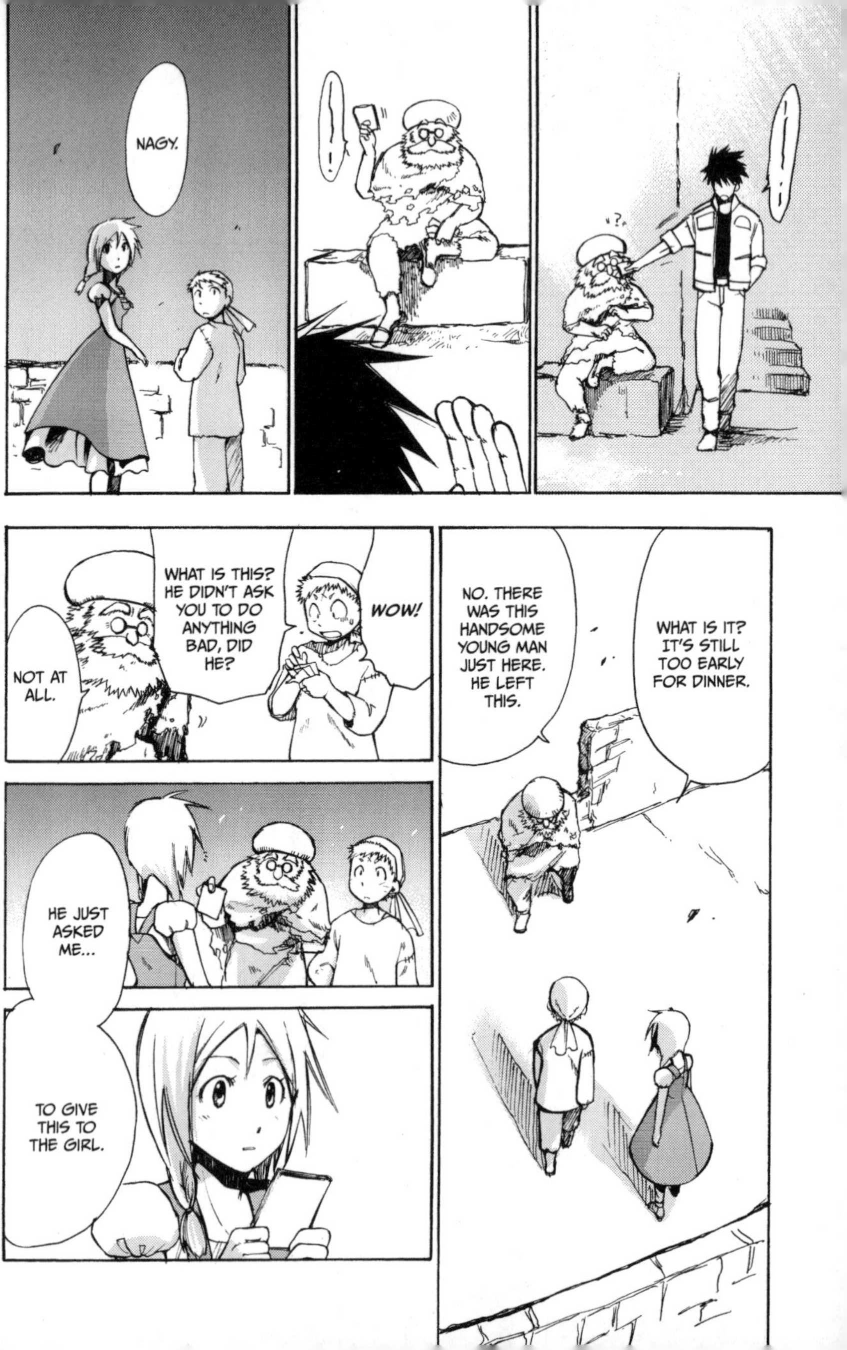

!
?
!
NAGY.
WHAT IS IT? IT'S STILL TOO EARLY FOR DINNER.
NO. THERE WAS THIS HANDSOME YOUNG MAN JUST HERE. HE LEFT THIS.
WOW!
WHAT IS THIS? HE DIDN'T ASK YOU TO DO ANYTHING BAD, DID HE?
NOT AT ALL.
HE JUST ASKED ME...
TO GIVE THIS TO THE GIRL.

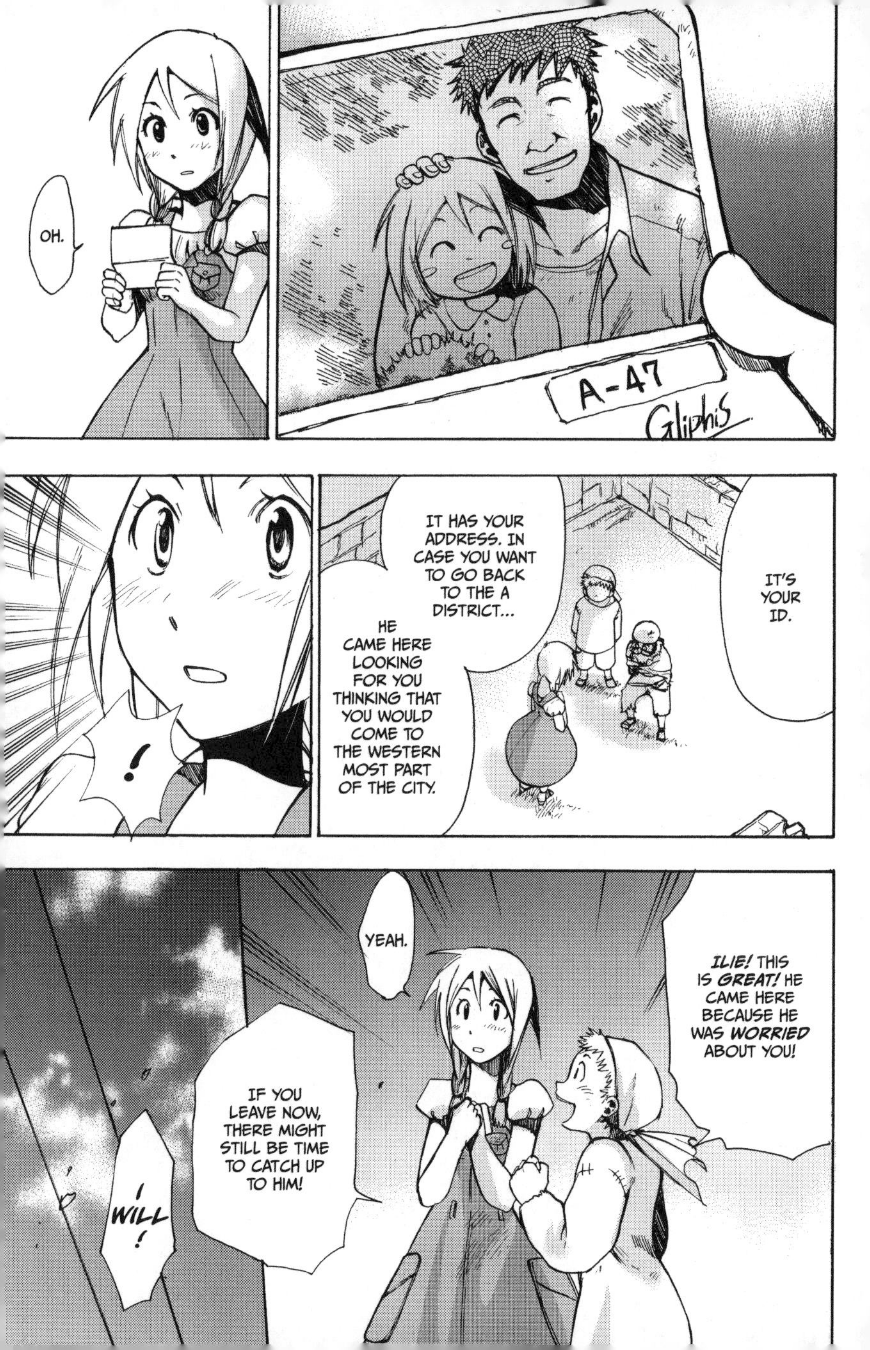

A-47
Gliphis
OH.
IT'S YOUR ID.
IT HAS YOUR ADDRESS. IN CASE YOU WANT TO GO BACK TO THE A DISTRICT...
HE CAME HERE LOOKING FOR YOU THINKING THAT YOU WOULD COME TO THE WESTERN MOST PART OF THE CITY.
!
*ILIE!* THIS IS *GREAT!* HE CAME HERE BECAUSE HE WAS *WORRIED* ABOUT YOU!
YEAH.
IF YOU LEAVE NOW, THERE MIGHT STILL BE TIME TO CATCH UP TO HIM!
I *WILL*!

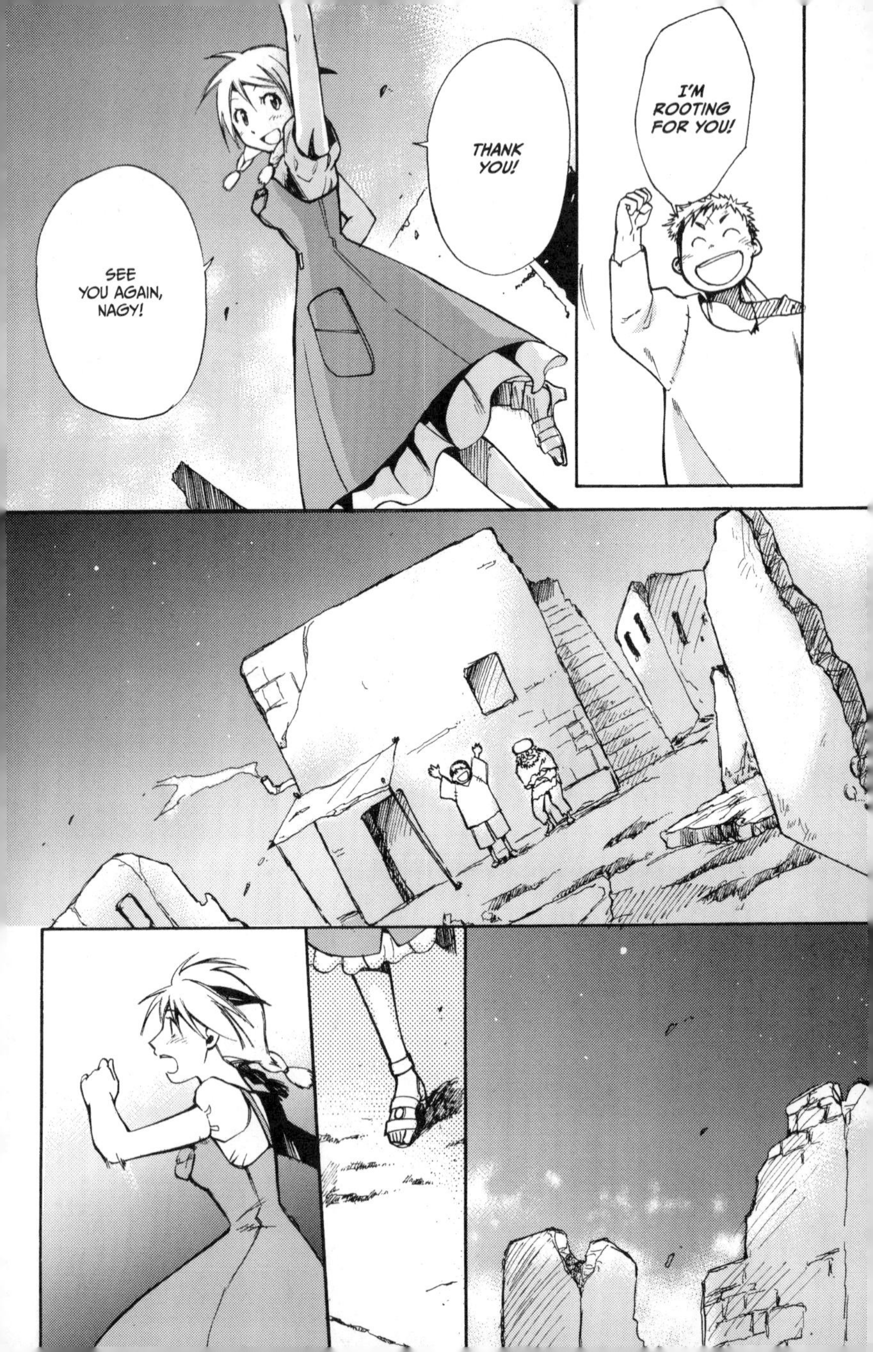
I'M ROOTING FOR YOU!
THANK YOU!
SEE YOU AGAIN, NAGY!

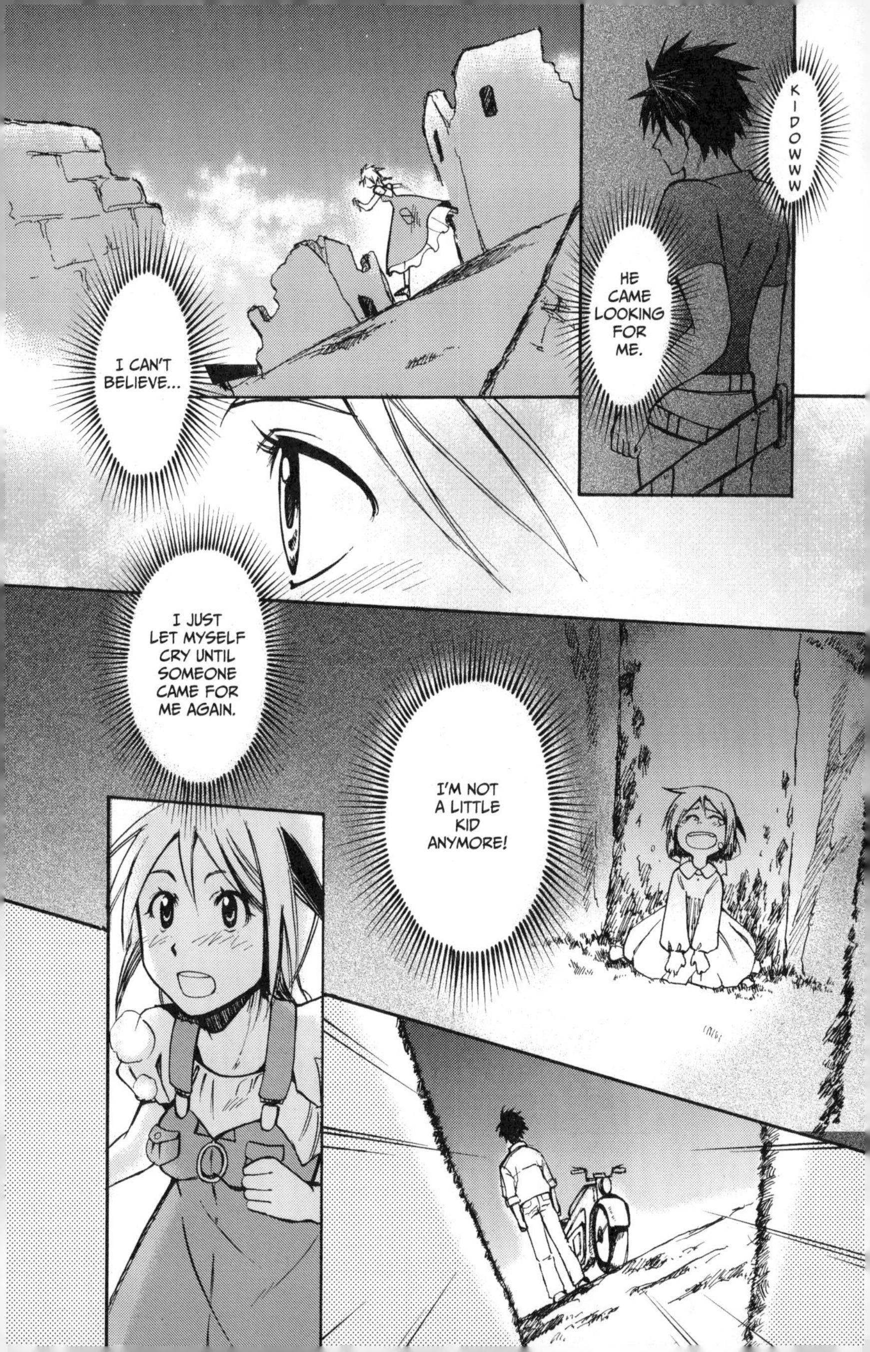
KIDOWWW
HE CAME LOOKING FOR ME.
I CAN'T BELIEVE...
I JUST LET MYSELF CRY UNTIL SOMEONE CAME FOR ME AGAIN.
I'M NOT A LITTLE KID ANYMORE!

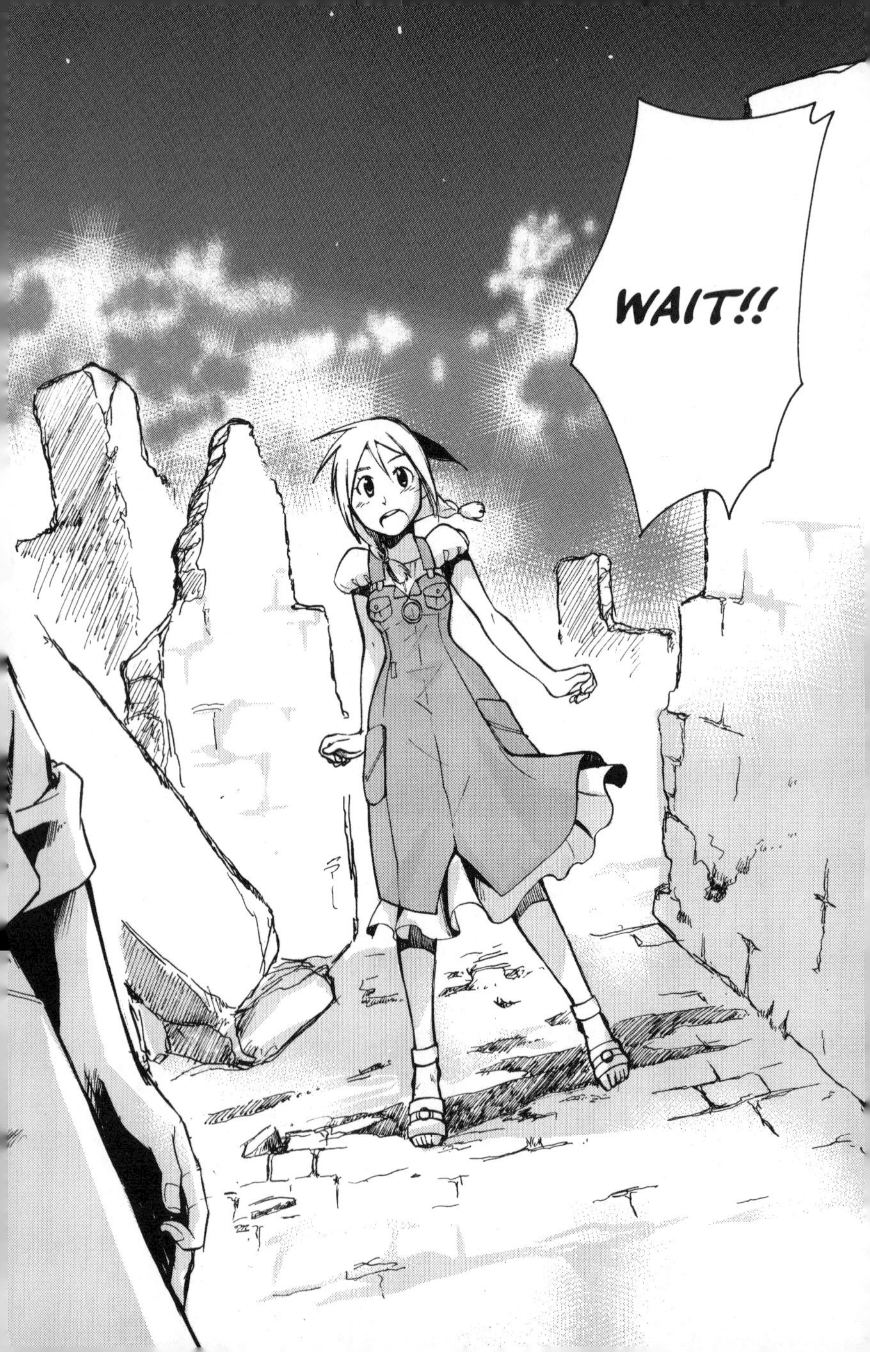
WAIT!!

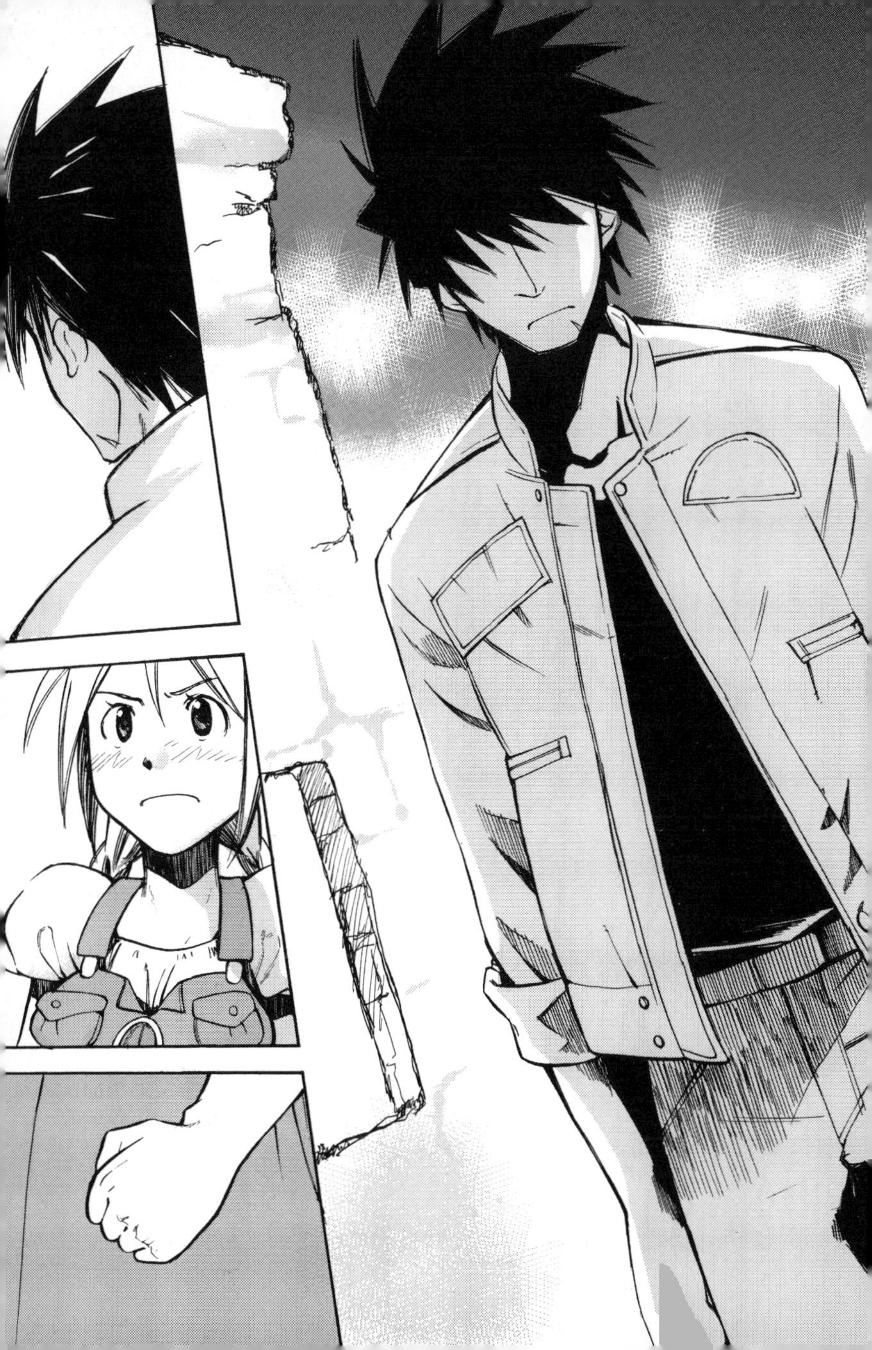

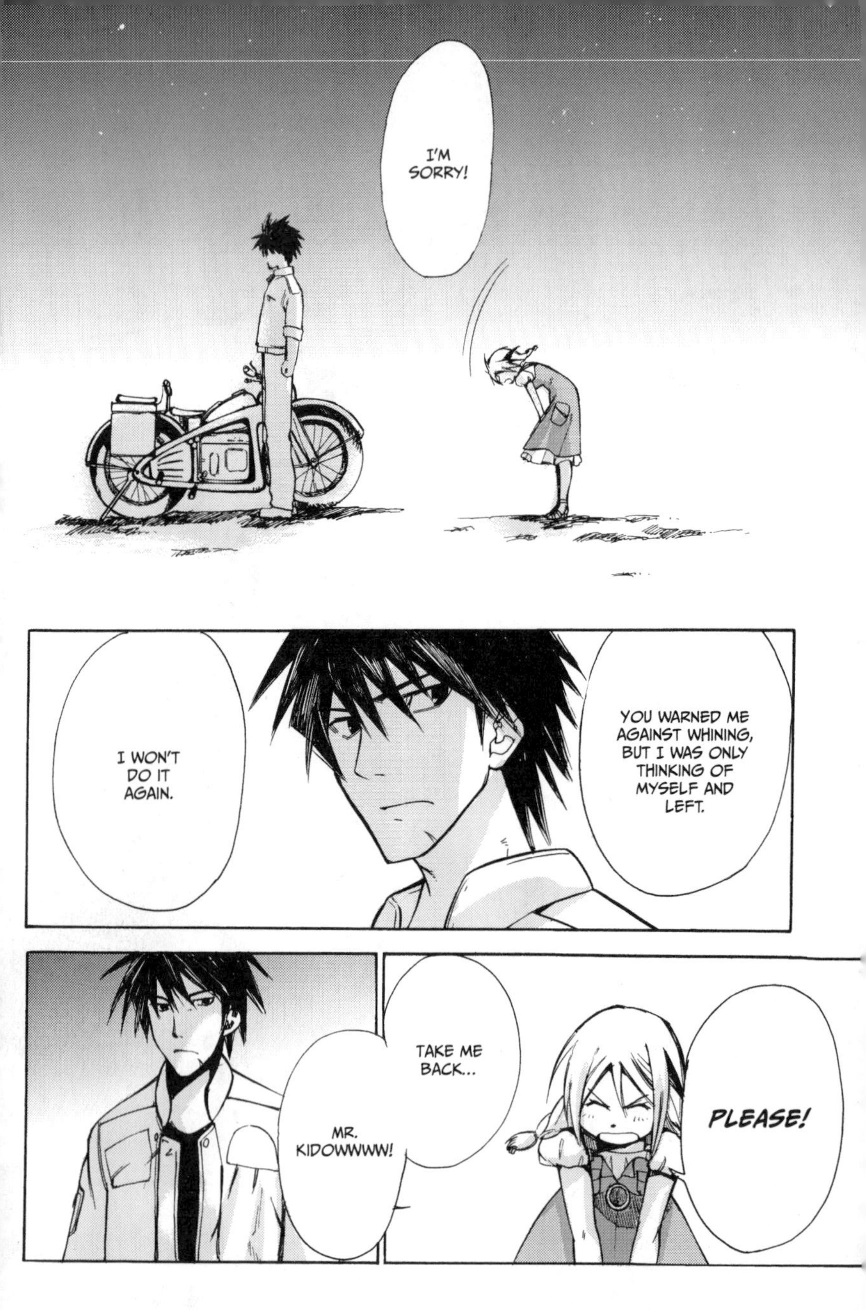
I'M SORRY!
YOU WARNED ME AGAINST WHINING, BUT I WAS ONLY THINKING OF MYSELF AND LEFT.
I WON'T DO IT AGAIN.
PLEASE!
TAKE ME BACK...
MR. KIDOWWWW!

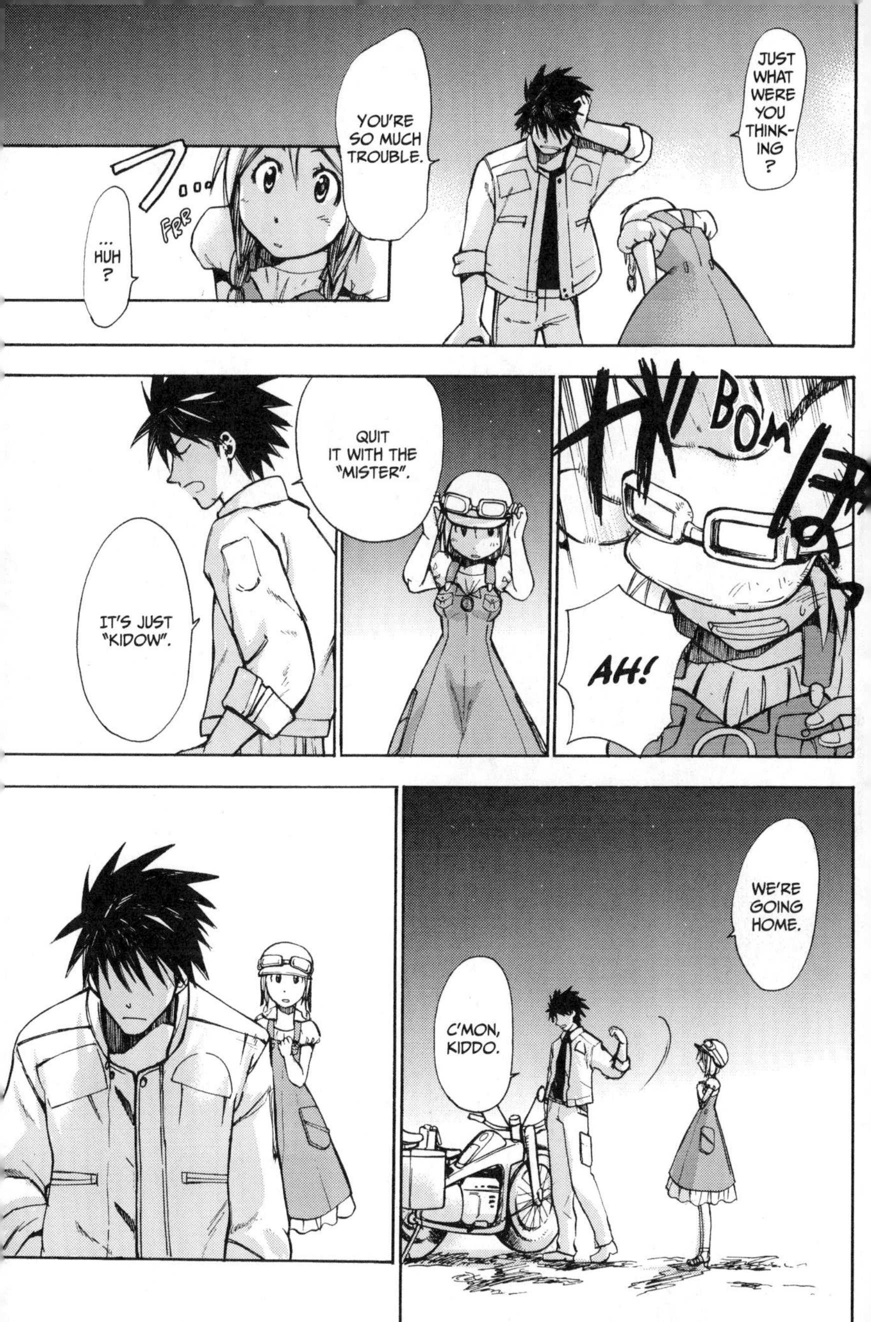
JUST WHAT WERE YOU THINKING-ING?
YOU'RE SO MUCH TROUBLE.
...HUH?
BOM
AH!
QUIT IT WITH THE "MISTER".
IT'S JUST "KIDOW".
WE'RE GOING HOME.
C'MON, KIDDO.

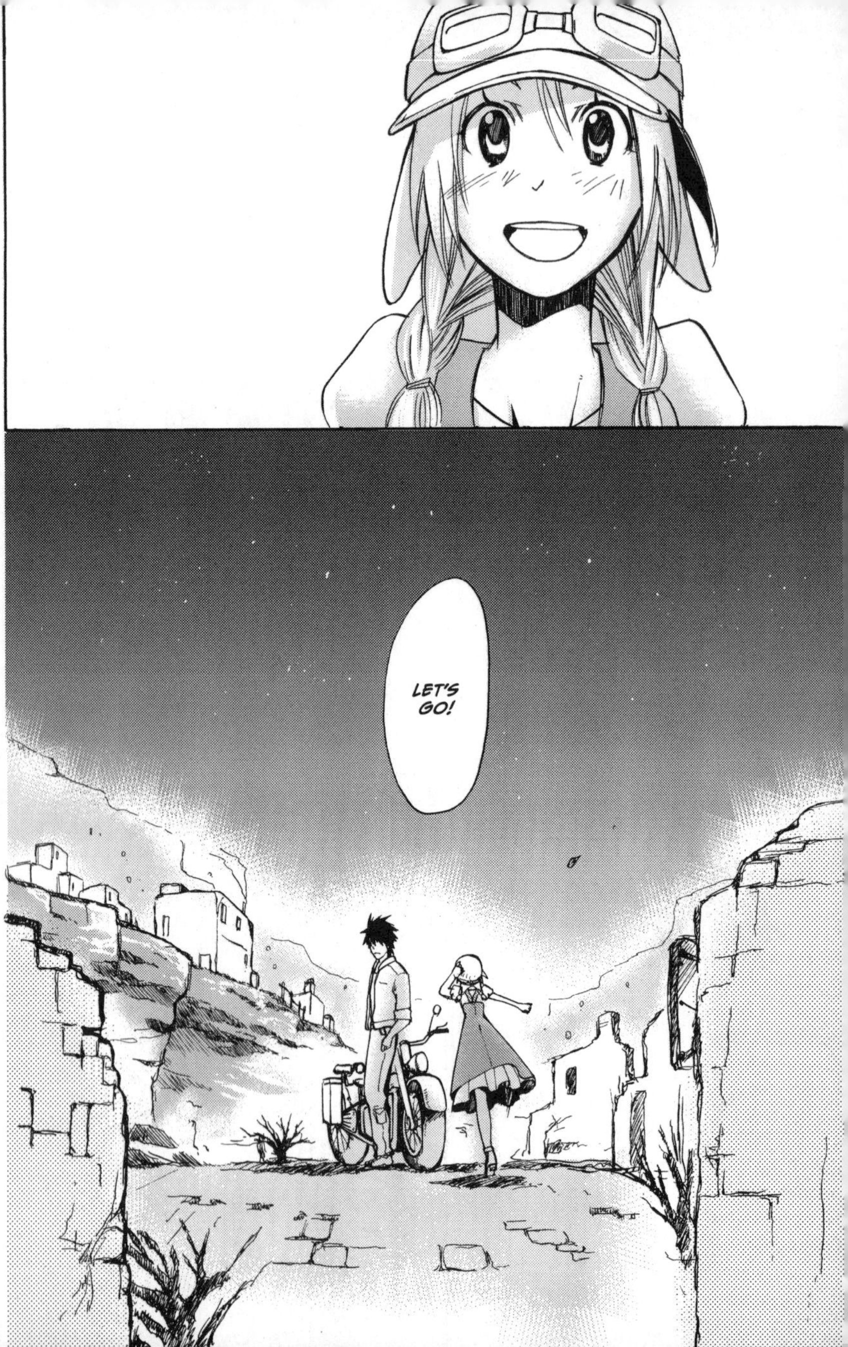
LET'S GO!

# [CHAPTER 3]

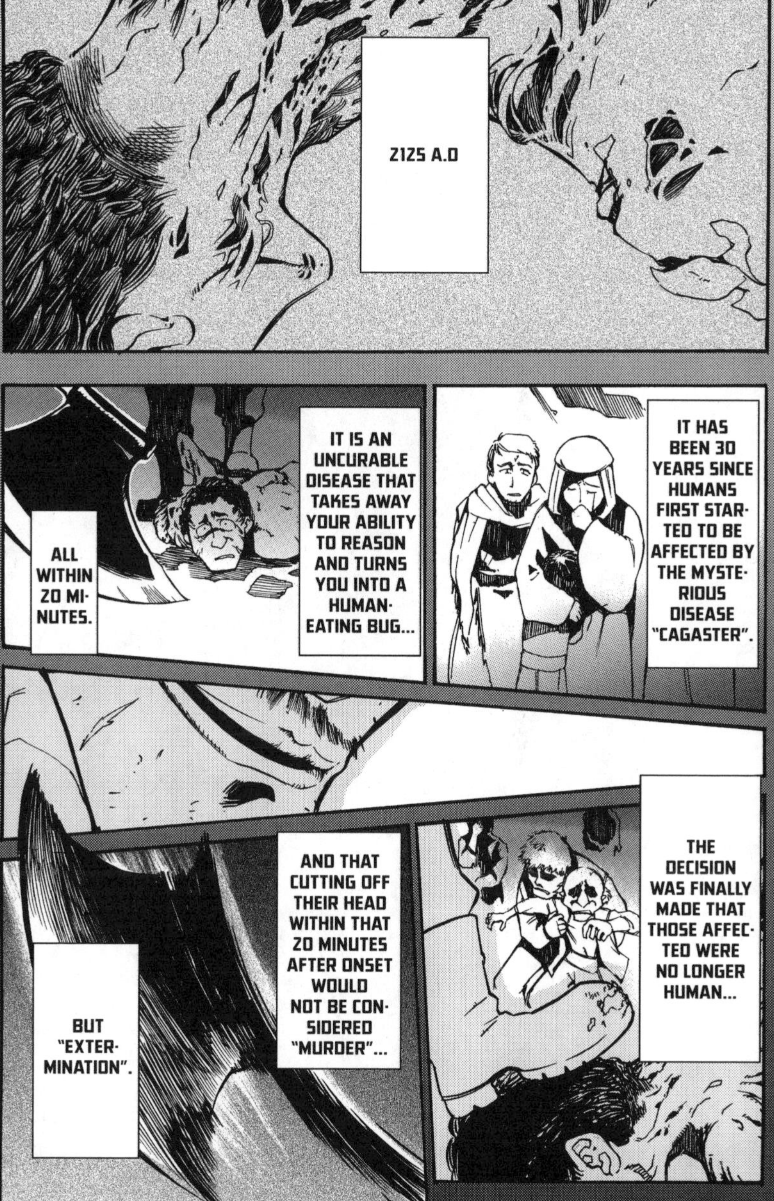
2125 A.D
IT HAS BEEN 30 YEARS SINCE HUMANS FIRST STAR-TED TO BE AFFECTED BY THE MYSTE-RIOUS DISEASE "CAGASTER".
IT IS AN UNCURABLE DISEASE THAT TAKES AWAY YOUR ABILITY TO REASON AND TURNS YOU INTO A HUMAN-EATING BUG...
ALL WITHIN 20 MI-NUTES.
THE DECISION WAS FINALLY MADE THAT THOSE AFFEC-TED WERE NO LONGER HUMAN...
AND THAT CUTTING OFF THEIR HEAD WITHIN THAT 20 MINUTES AFTER ONSET WOULD NOT BE CON-SIDERED "MURDER"...
BUT "EXTER-MINATION".

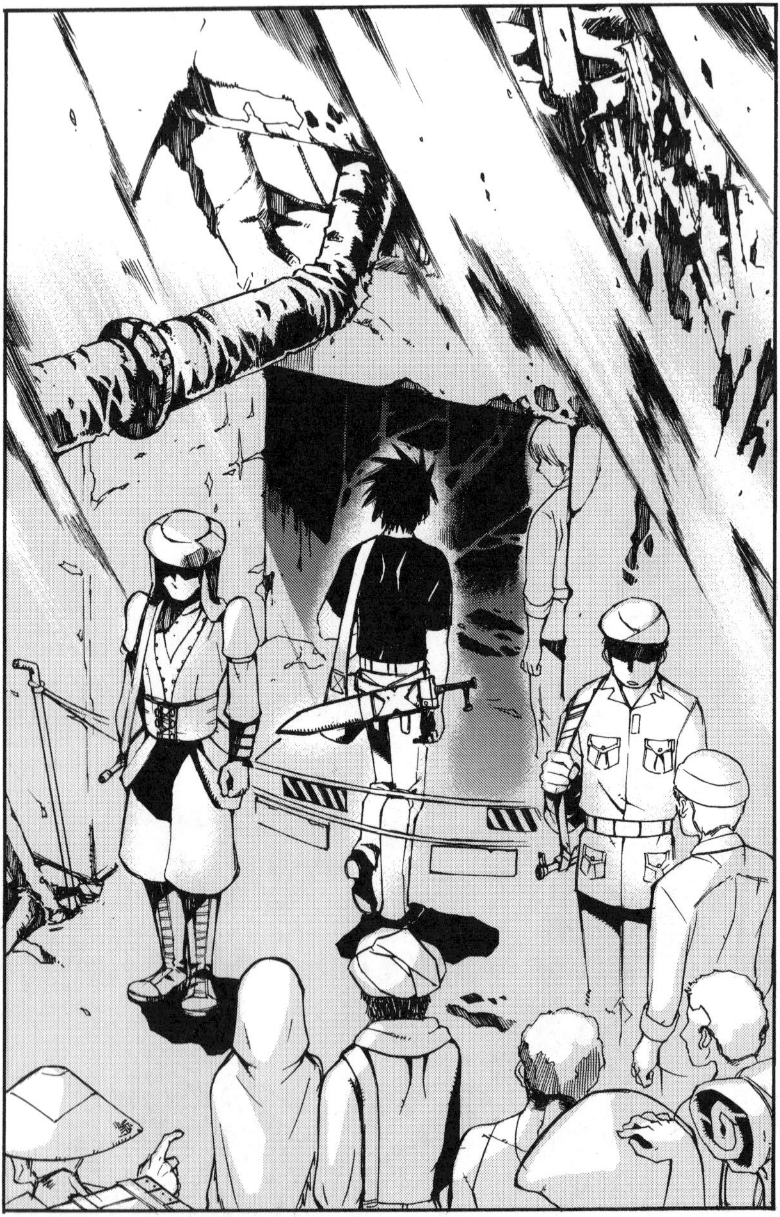

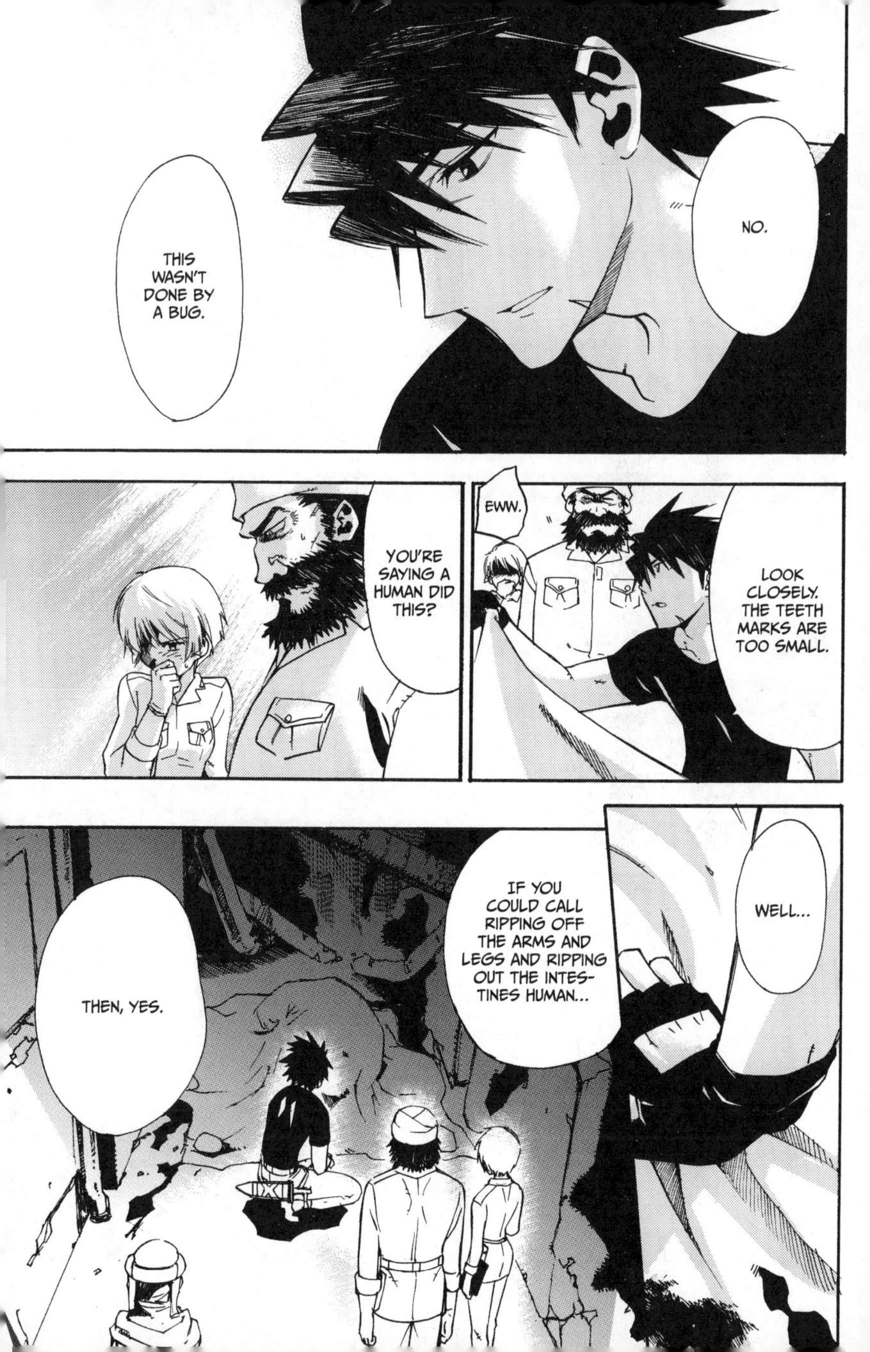
NO.
THIS WASN'T DONE BY A BUG.
LOOK CLOSELY. THE TEETH MARKS ARE TOO SMALL.
EWW.
YOU'RE SAYING A HUMAN DID THIS?
WELL...
IF YOU COULD CALL RIPPING OFF THE ARMS AND LEGS AND RIPPING OUT THE INTES-TINES HUMAN...
THEN, YES.

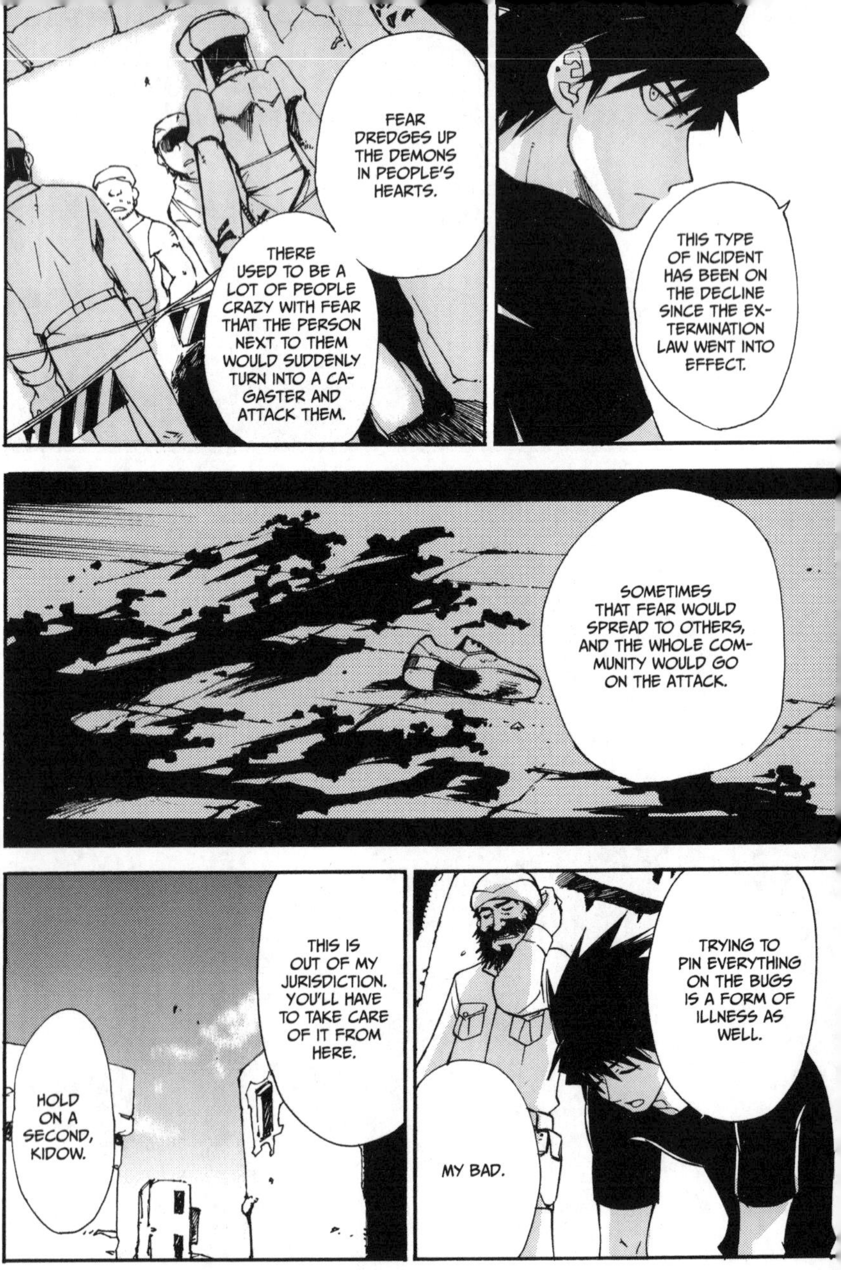
THIS TYPE OF INCIDENT HAS BEEN ON THE DECLINE SINCE THE EXTERMINATION LAW WENT INTO EFFECT.
FEAR DREDGES UP THE DEMONS IN PEOPLE'S HEARTS.
THERE USED TO BE A LOT OF PEOPLE CRAZY WITH FEAR THAT THE PERSON NEXT TO THEM WOULD SUDDENLY TURN INTO A CAGASTER AND ATTACK THEM.
SOMETIMES THAT FEAR WOULD SPREAD TO OTHERS, AND THE WHOLE COMMUNITY WOULD GO ON THE ATTACK.
TRYING TO PIN EVERYTHING ON THE BUGS IS A FORM OF ILLNESS AS WELL.
MY BAD.
THIS IS OUT OF MY JURISDICTION. YOU'LL HAVE TO TAKE CARE OF IT FROM HERE.
HOLD ON A SECOND, KIDOW.

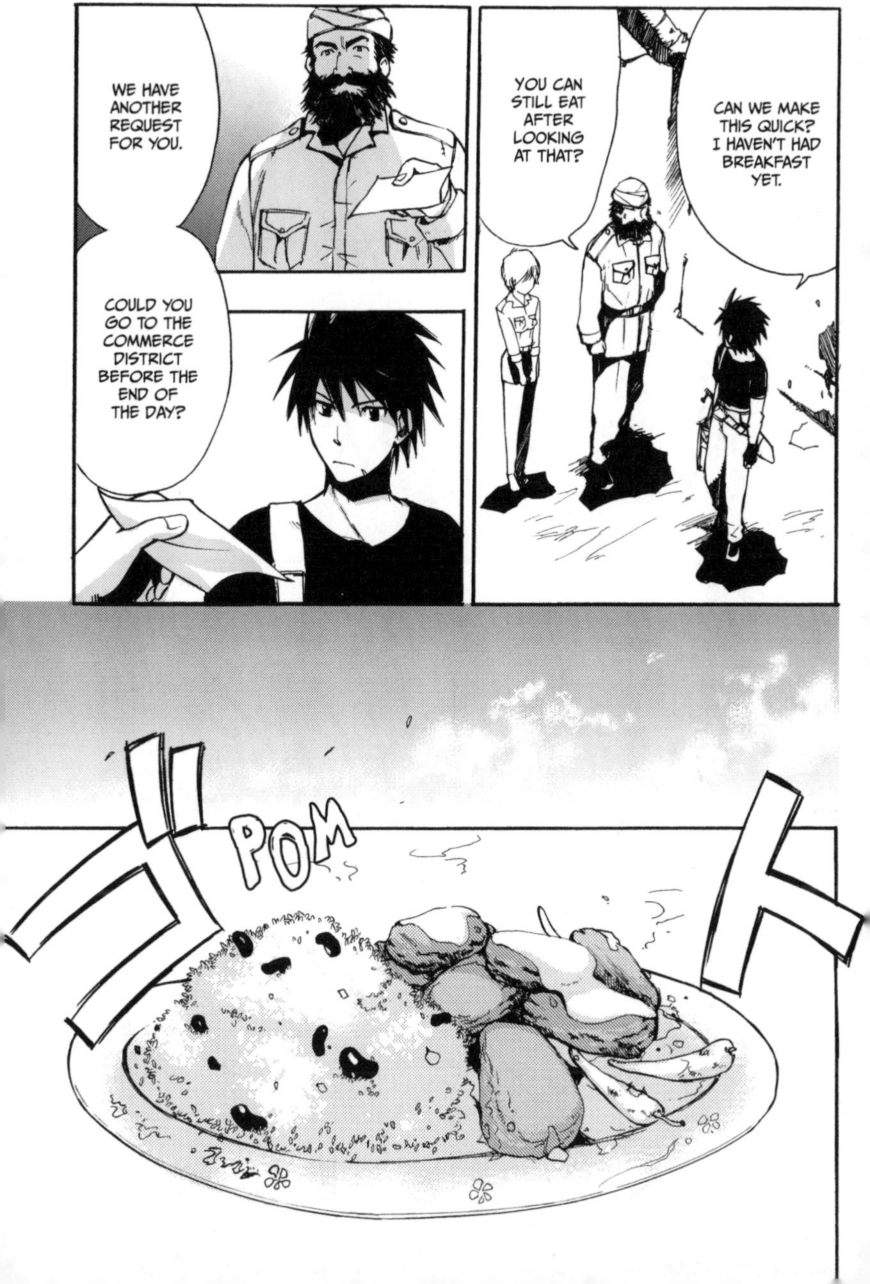
CAN WE MAKE THIS QUICK? I HAVEN'T HAD BREAKFAST YET.
YOU CAN STILL EAT AFTER LOOKING AT THAT?
WE HAVE ANOTHER REQUEST FOR YOU.
COULD YOU GO TO THE COMMERCE DISTRICT BEFORE THE END OF THE DAY?
POM

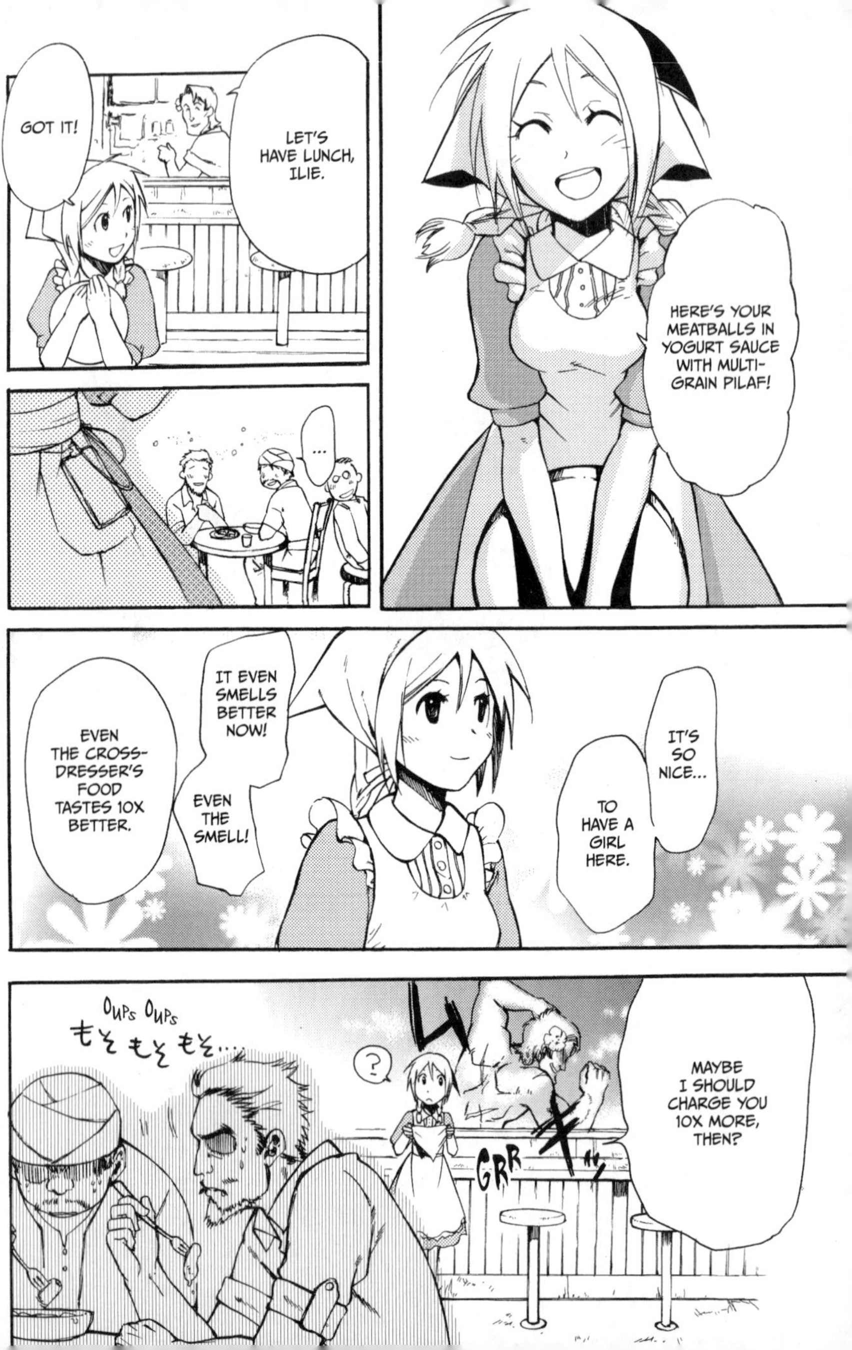
HERE'S YOUR MEATBALLS IN YOGURT SAUCE WITH MULTI-GRAIN PILAF!
LET'S HAVE LUNCH, ILIE.
GOT IT!
...
IT'S SO NICE...
TO HAVE A GIRL HERE.
IT EVEN SMELLS BETTER NOW!
EVEN THE SMELL!
EVEN THE CROSS-DRESSER'S FOOD TASTES 10X BETTER.
MAYBE I SHOULD CHARGE YOU 10X MORE, THEN?
GRR
?
もそもそもそ...
OUPS OUPS

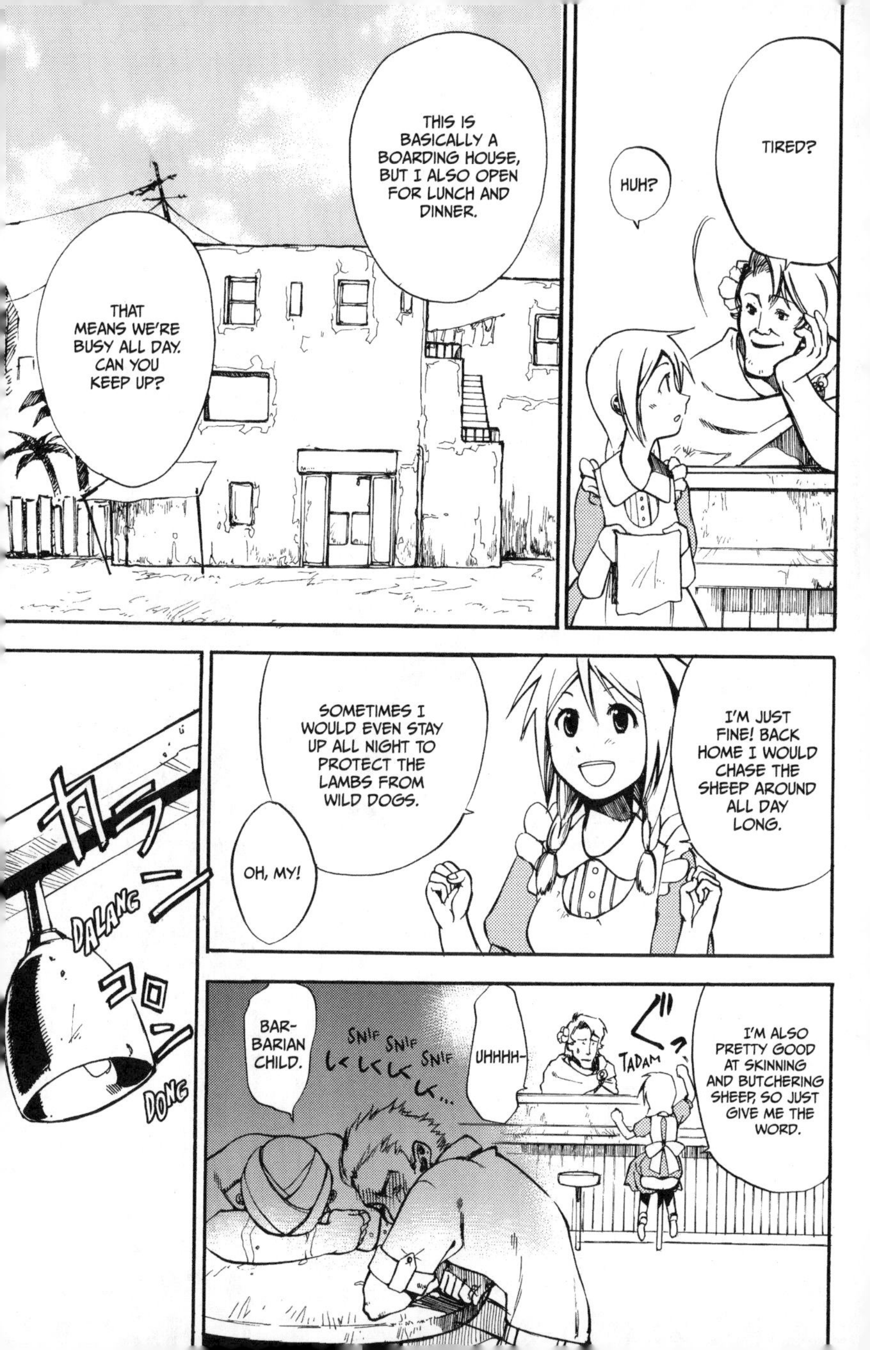
TIRED?
HUH?
THIS IS BASICALLY A BOARDING HOUSE, BUT I ALSO OPEN FOR LUNCH AND DINNER.
THAT MEANS WE'RE BUSY ALL DAY. CAN YOU KEEP UP?
I'M JUST FINE! BACK HOME I WOULD CHASE THE SHEEP AROUND ALL DAY LONG.
SOMETIMES I WOULD EVEN STAY UP ALL NIGHT TO PROTECT THE LAMBS FROM WILD DOGS.
OH, MY!
I'M ALSO PRETTY GOOD AT SKINNING AND BUTCHERING SHEEP, SO JUST GIVE ME THE WORD.
TADAM
UHHHH-
SNIF SNIF SNIF
BAR-BARIAN CHILD.
DALANG
DONG

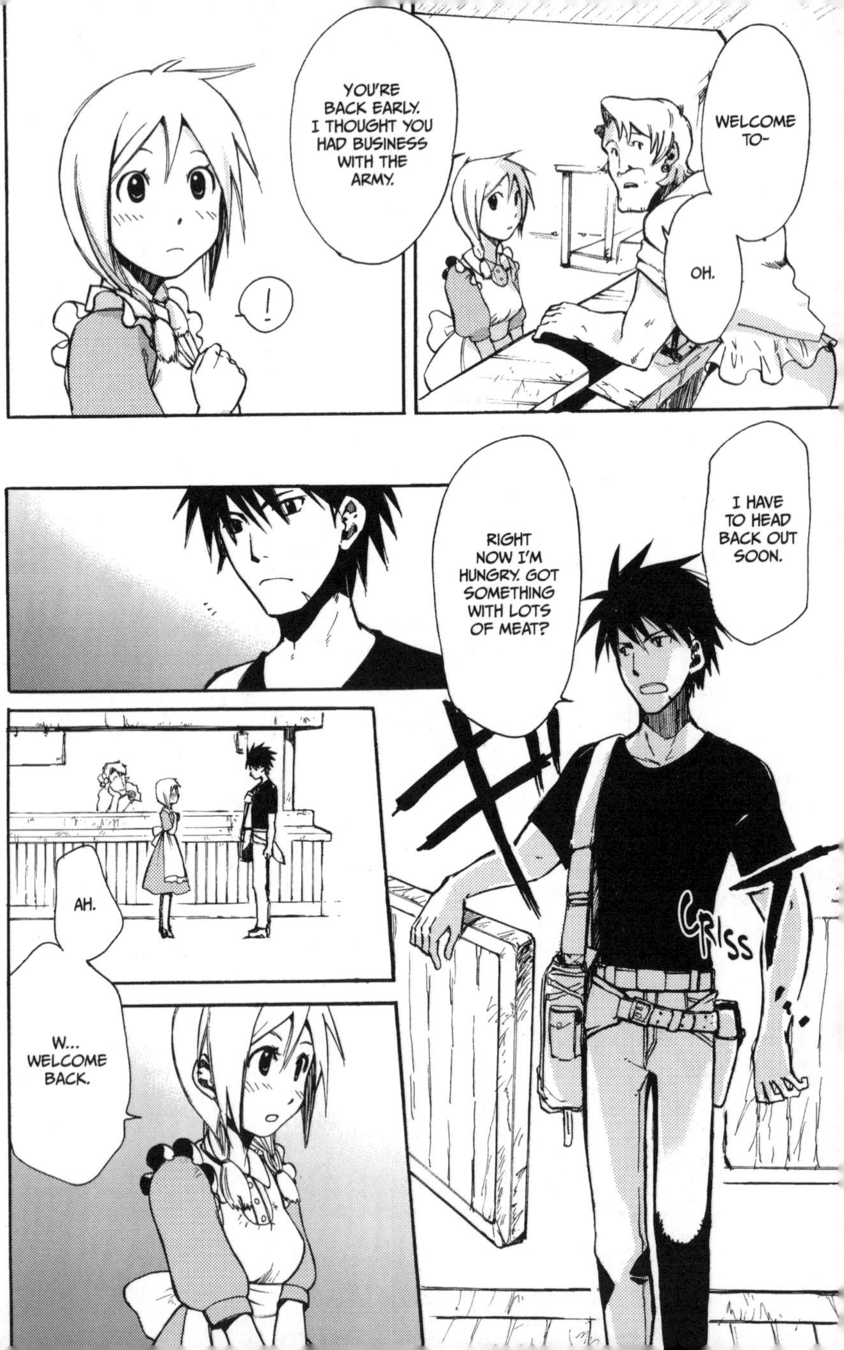
WELCOME TO-
OH.
YOU'RE BACK EARLY. I THOUGHT YOU HAD BUSINESS WITH THE ARMY.
!
I HAVE TO HEAD BACK OUT SOON.
RIGHT NOW I'M HUNGRY. GOT SOMETHING WITH LOTS OF MEAT?
CRISS
AH.
W... WELCOME BACK.

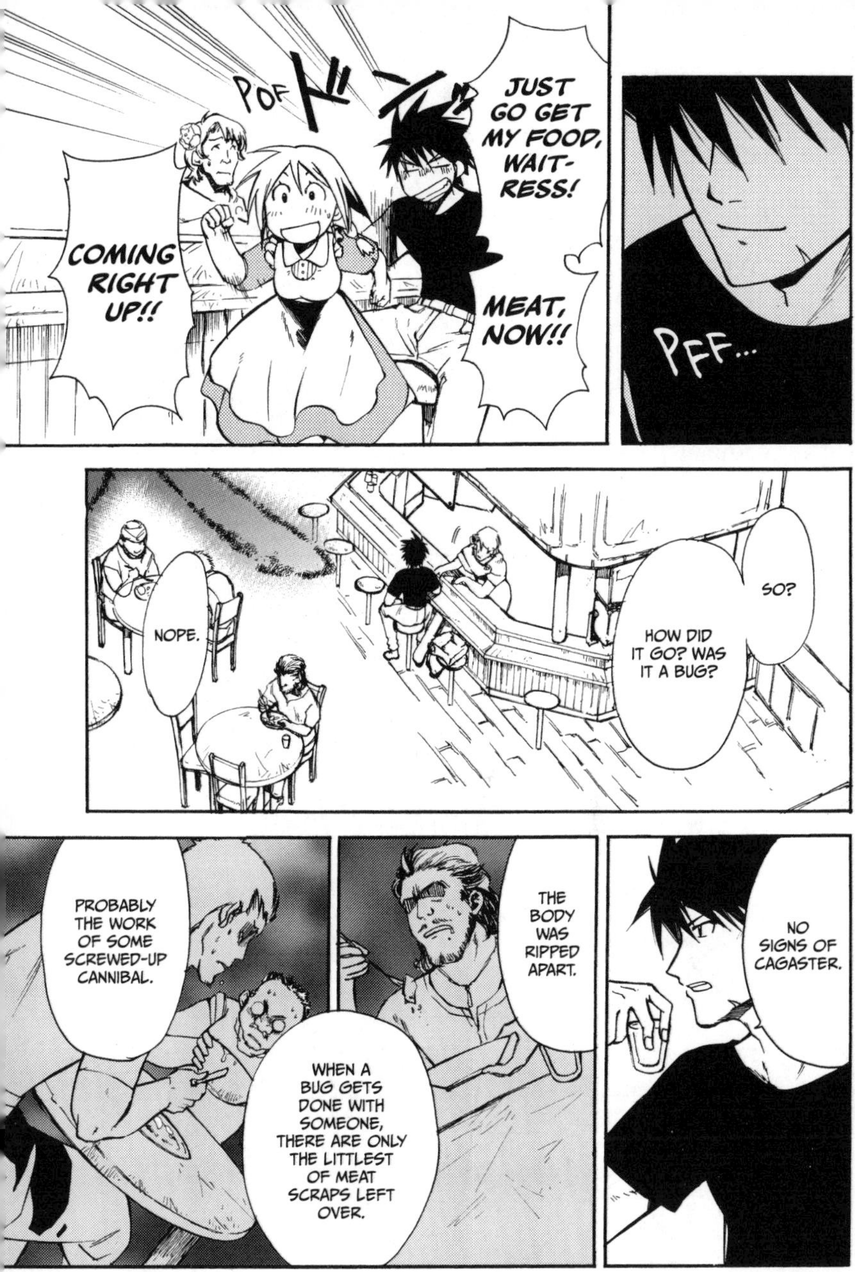
PFF...
JUST GO GET MY FOOD, WAIT-RESS!
POF
MEAT, NOW!!
COMING RIGHT UP!!
SO?
HOW DID IT GO? WAS IT A BUG?
NOPE.
NO SIGNS OF CAGASTER.
THE BODY WAS RIPPED APART.
WHEN A BUG GETS DONE WITH SOMEONE, THERE ARE ONLY THE LITTLEST OF MEAT SCRAPS LEFT OVER.
PROBABLY THE WORK OF SOME SCREWED-UP CANNIBAL.

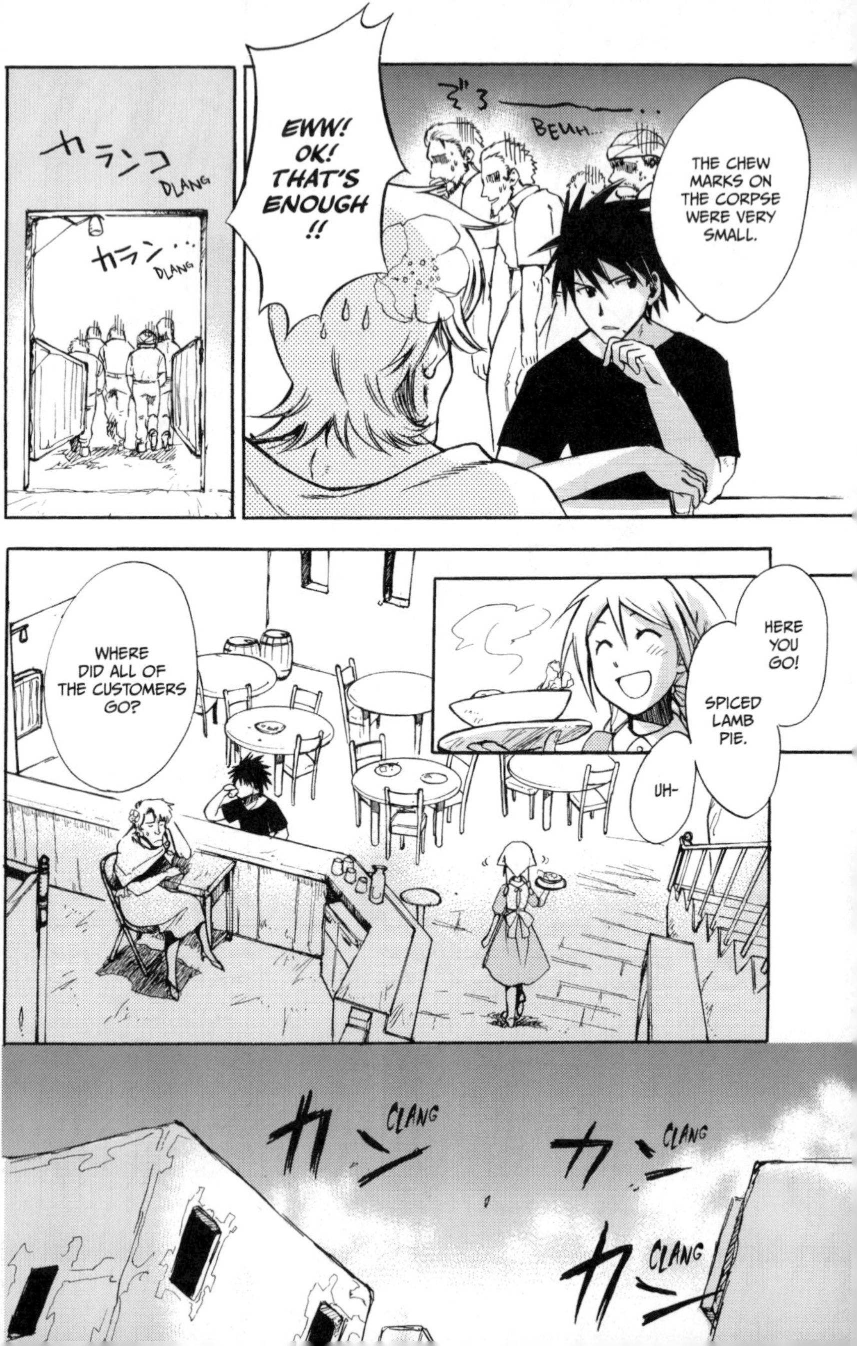
THE CHEW MARKS ON THE CORPSE WERE VERY SMALL.
BEUH...
EWW! OK! THAT'S ENOUGH !!
カランコ
DLANG
カラン…
DLANG
HERE YOU GO!
SPICED LAMB PIE.
UH-
WHERE DID ALL OF THE CUSTOMERS GO?
カン
CLANG
カン
CLANG
カン
CLANG

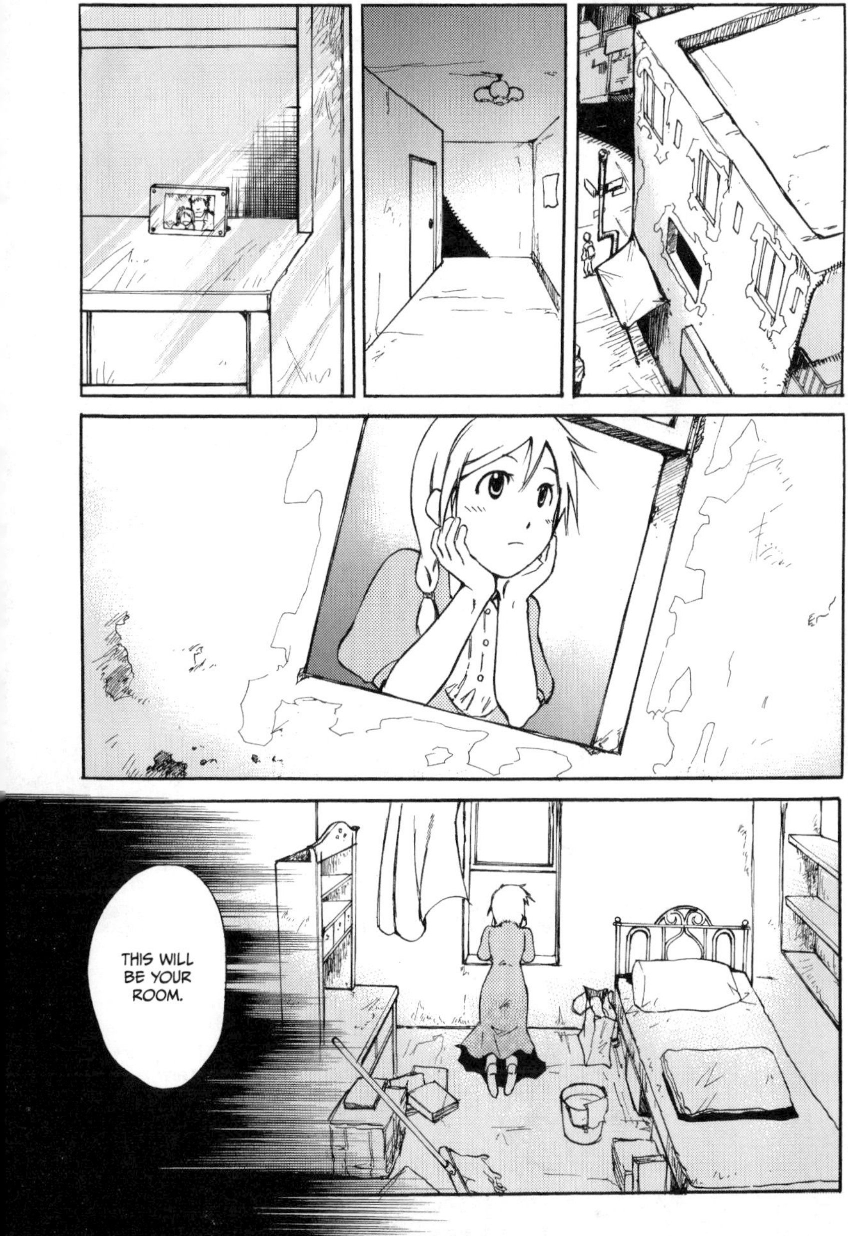
THIS WILL BE YOUR ROOM.

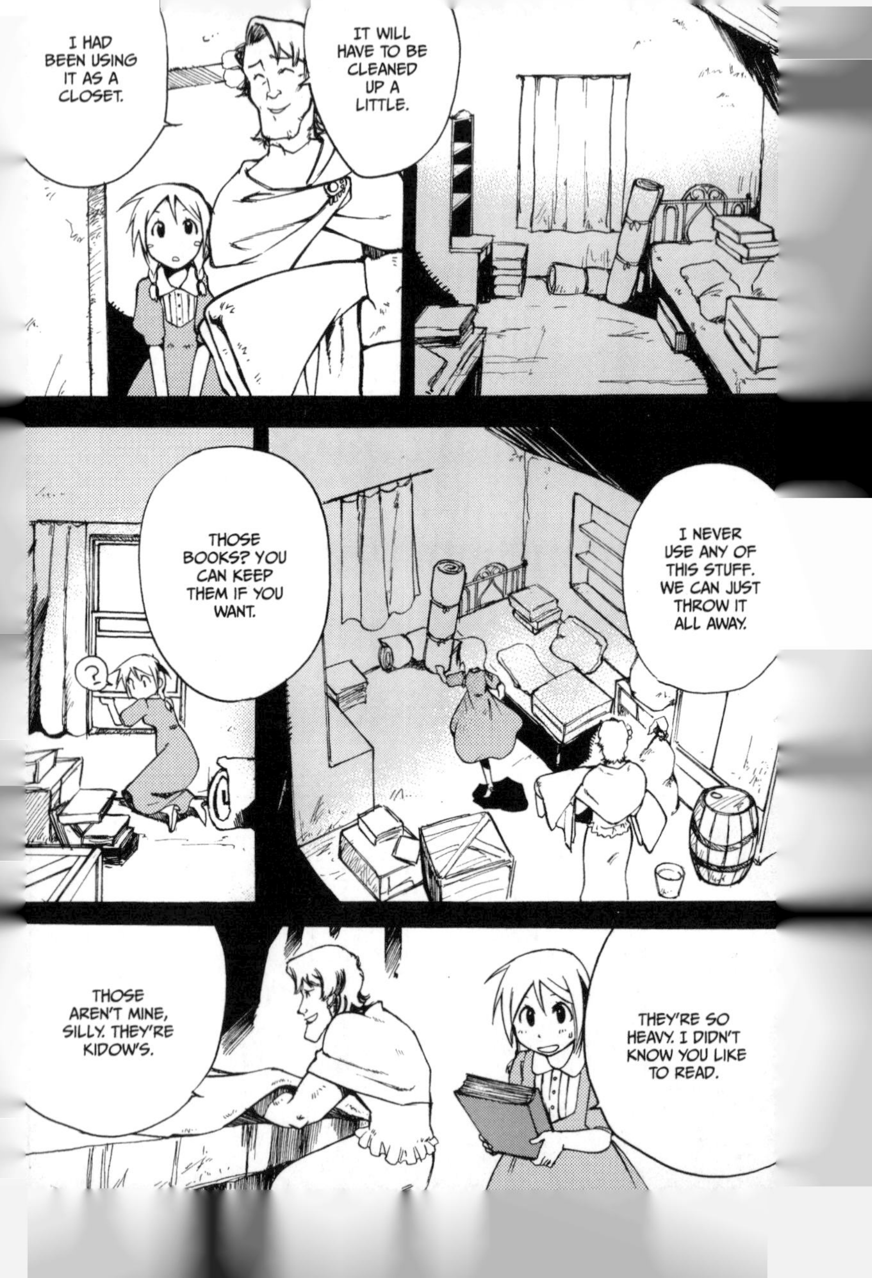
IT WILL HAVE TO BE CLEANED UP A LITTLE.
I HAD BEEN USING IT AS A CLOSET.
I NEVER USE ANY OF THIS STUFF. WE CAN JUST THROW IT ALL AWAY.
THOSE BOOKS? YOU CAN KEEP THEM IF YOU WANT.
?
THEY'RE SO HEAVY. I DIDN'T KNOW YOU LIKE TO READ.
THOSE AREN'T MINE, SILLY. THEY'RE KIDOW'S.

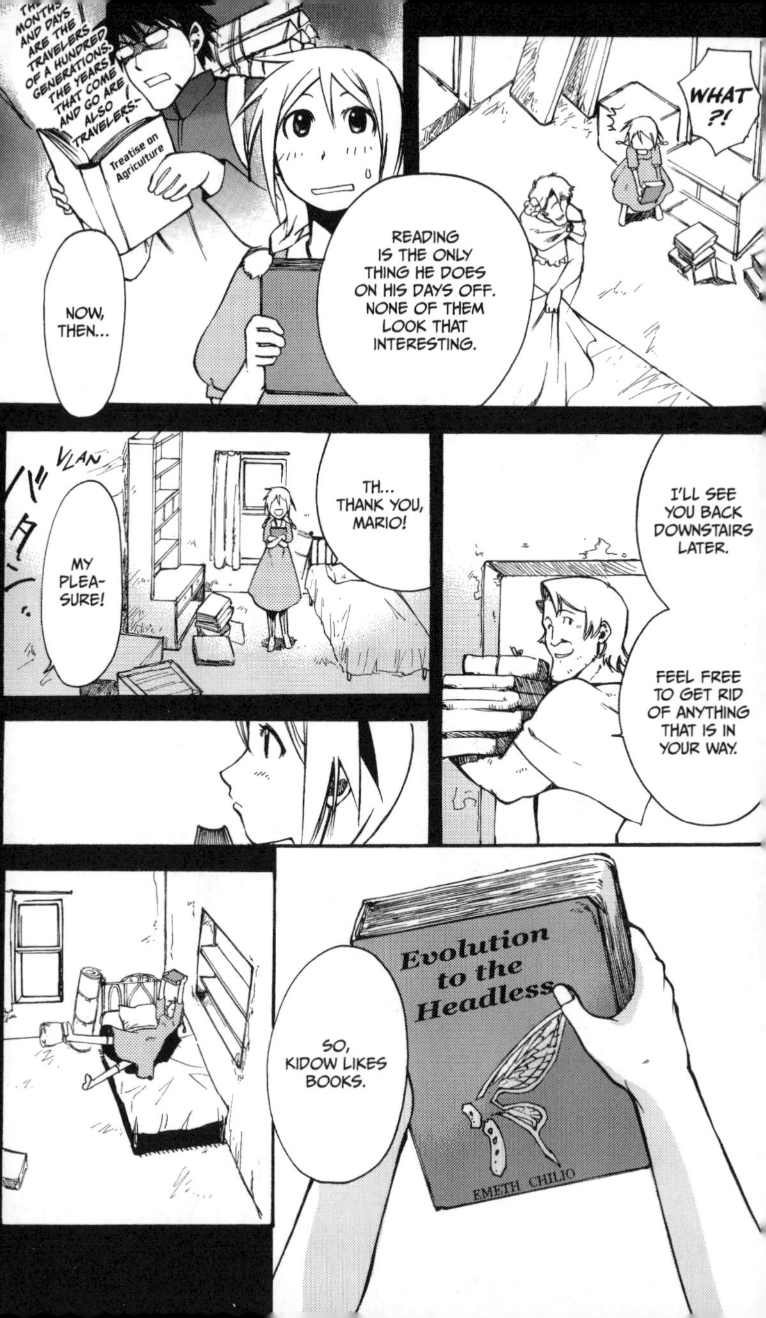

WHAT?!
MONTHS AND DAYS ARE THE TRAVELERS OF A HUNDRED GENERATIONS. THE YEARS THAT COME AND GO ARE ALSO TRAVELERS.
Treatise on Agriculture
READING IS THE ONLY THING HE DOES ON HIS DAYS OFF. NONE OF THEM LOOK THAT INTERESTING.
NOW, THEN...
I'LL SEE YOU BACK DOWNSTAIRS LATER.
FEEL FREE TO GET RID OF ANYTHING THAT IS IN YOUR WAY.
TH... THANK YOU, MARIO!
VLAN
MY PLEASURE!
Evolution to the Headless
EMETH CHILIO
SO, KIDOW LIKES BOOKS.

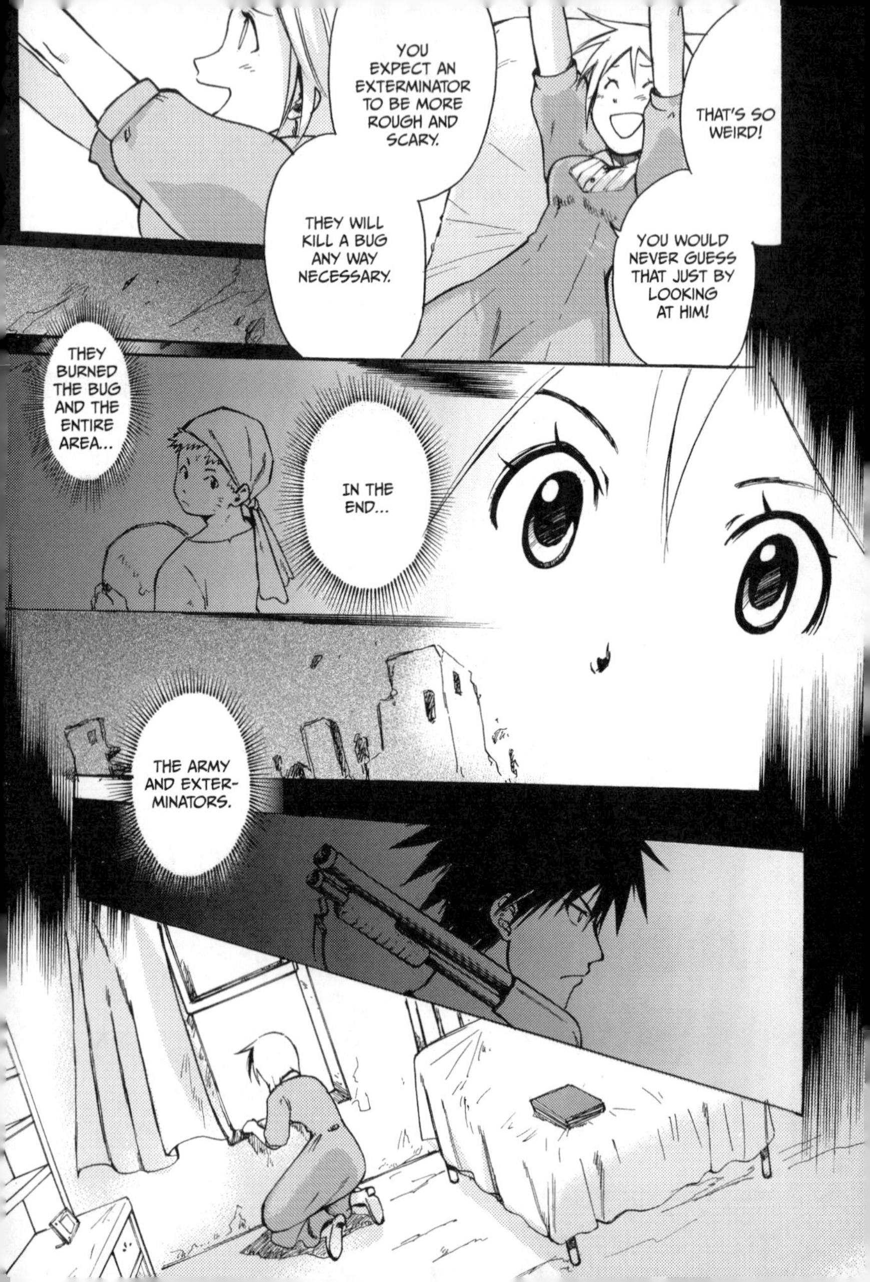
THAT'S SO WEIRD!
YOU WOULD NEVER GUESS THAT JUST BY LOOKING AT HIM!
YOU EXPECT AN EXTERMINATOR TO BE MORE ROUGH AND SCARY.
THEY WILL KILL A BUG ANY WAY NECESSARY.
IN THE END...
THEY BURNED THE BUG AND THE ENTIRE AREA...
THE ARMY AND EXTER- MINATORS.

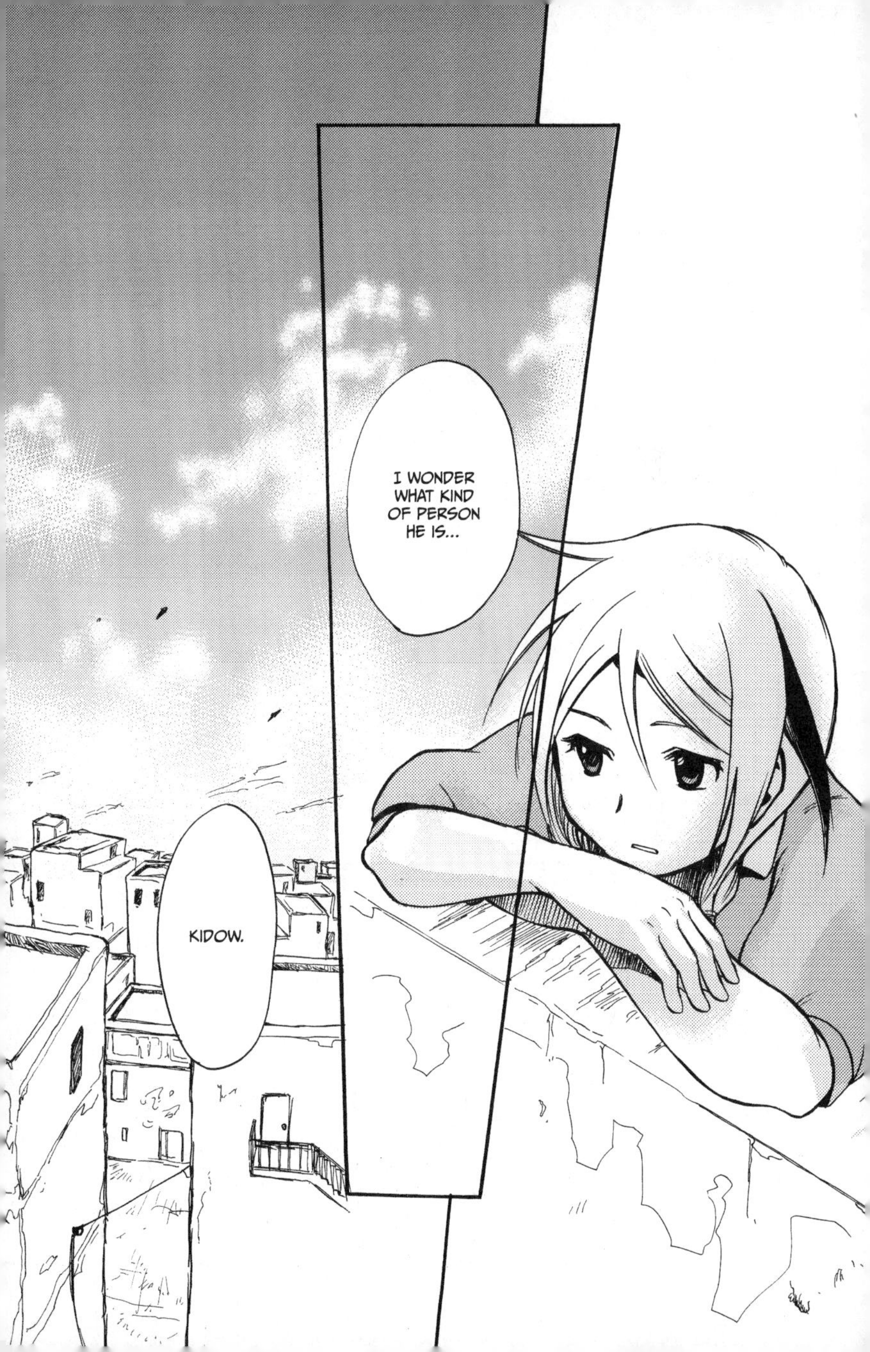
I WONDER WHAT KIND OF PERSON HE IS...
KIDOW.

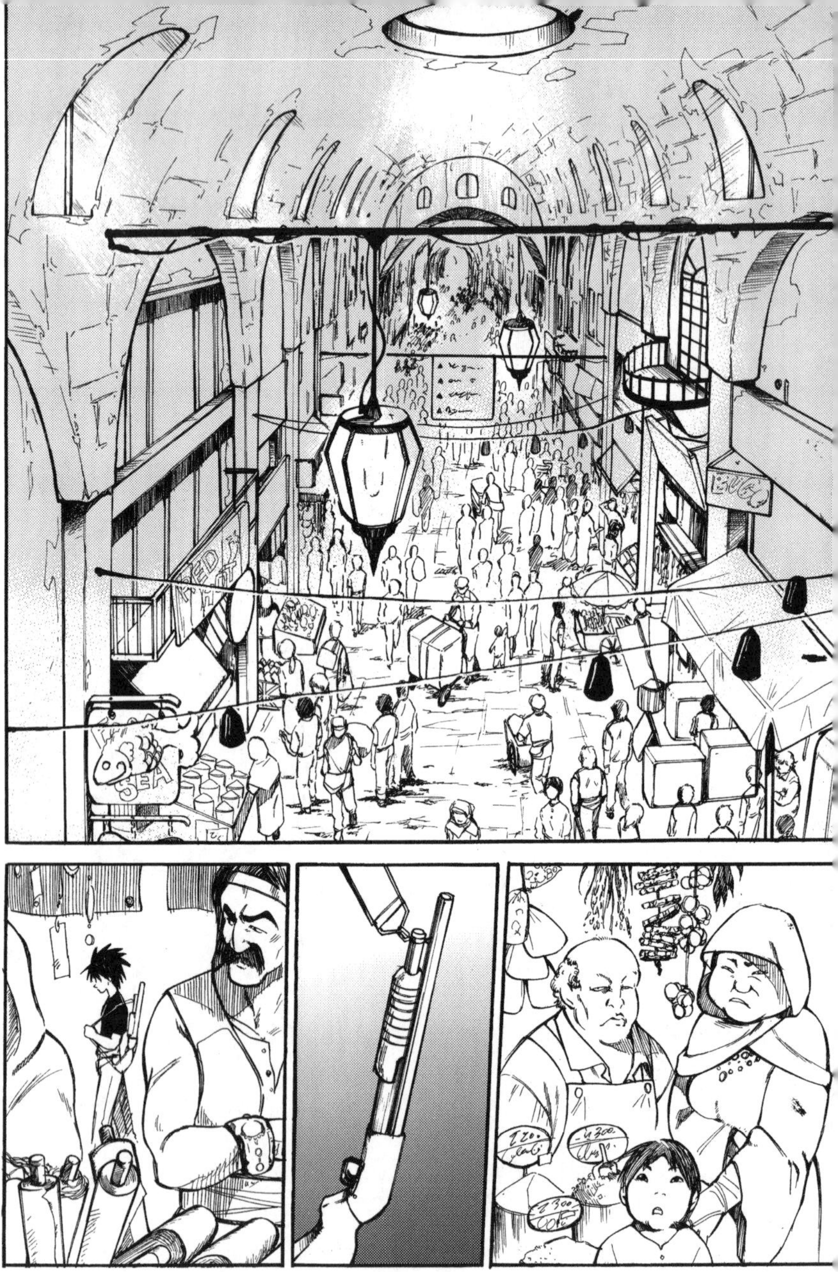
SEA

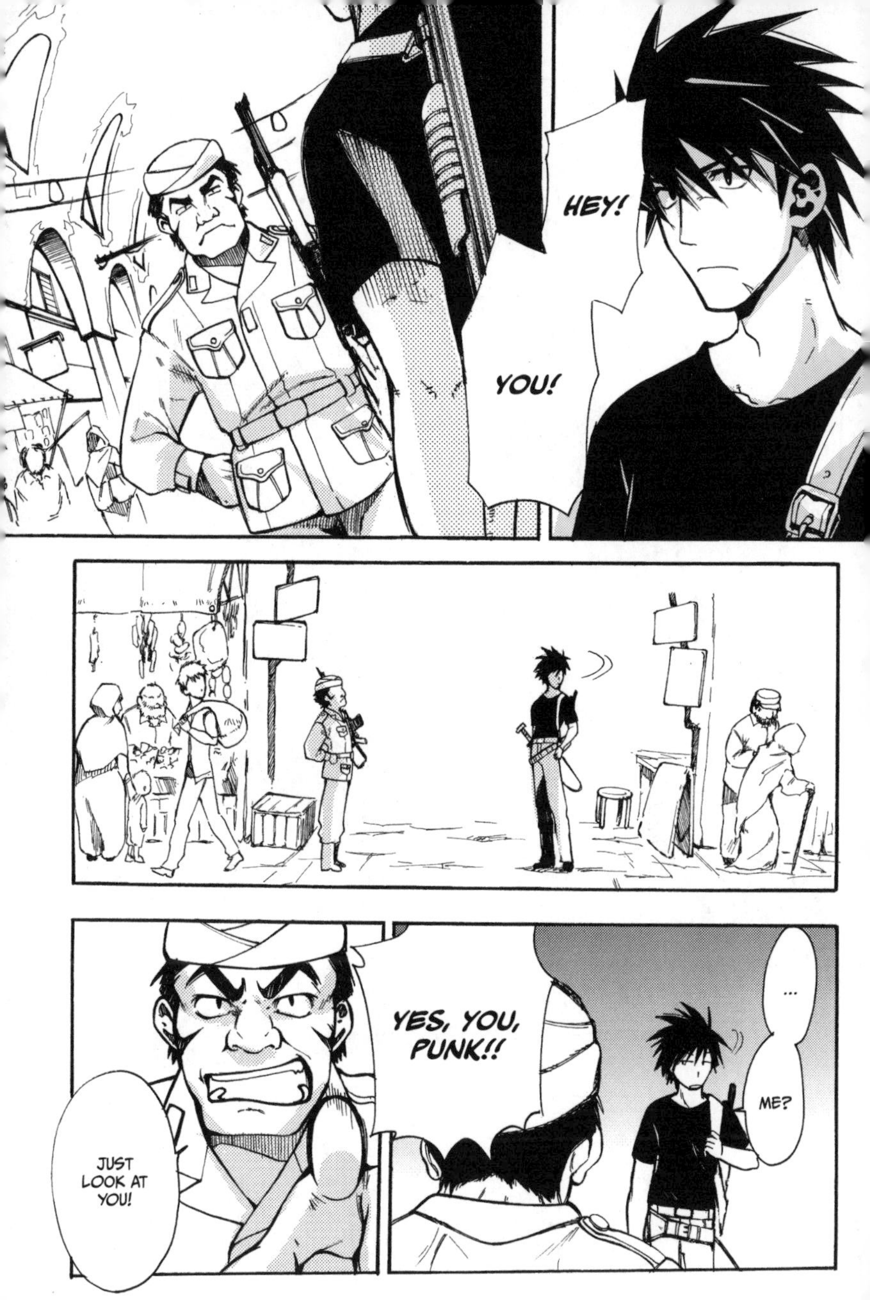
HEY!
YOU!
...
ME?
YES, YOU, PUNK!!
JUST LOOK AT YOU!

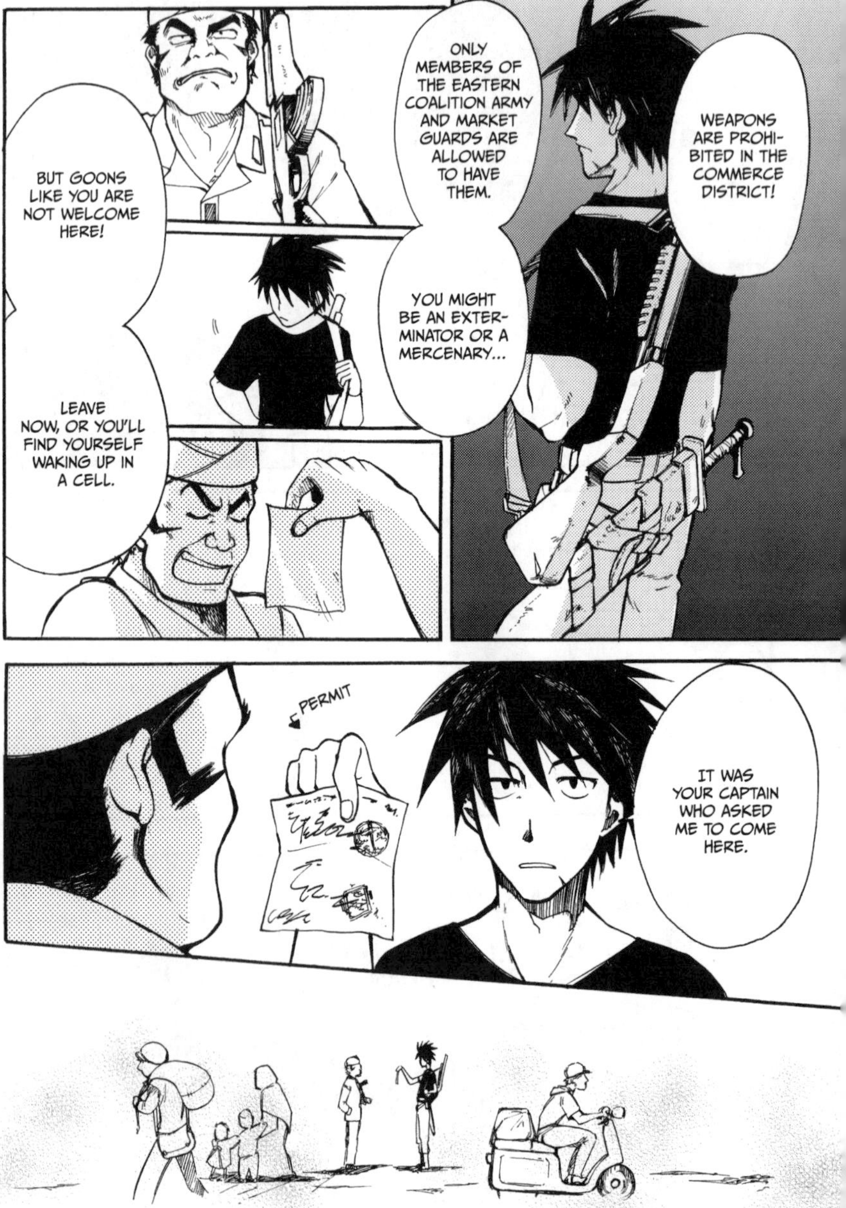
WEAPONS ARE PROHIBITED IN THE COMMERCE DISTRICT!
ONLY MEMBERS OF THE EASTERN COALITION ARMY AND MARKET GUARDS ARE ALLOWED TO HAVE THEM.
YOU MIGHT BE AN EXTERMINATOR OR A MERCENARY...
BUT GOONS LIKE YOU ARE NOT WELCOME HERE!
LEAVE NOW, OR YOU'LL FIND YOURSELF WAKING UP IN A CELL.
IT WAS YOUR CAPTAIN WHO ASKED ME TO COME HERE.
PERMIT

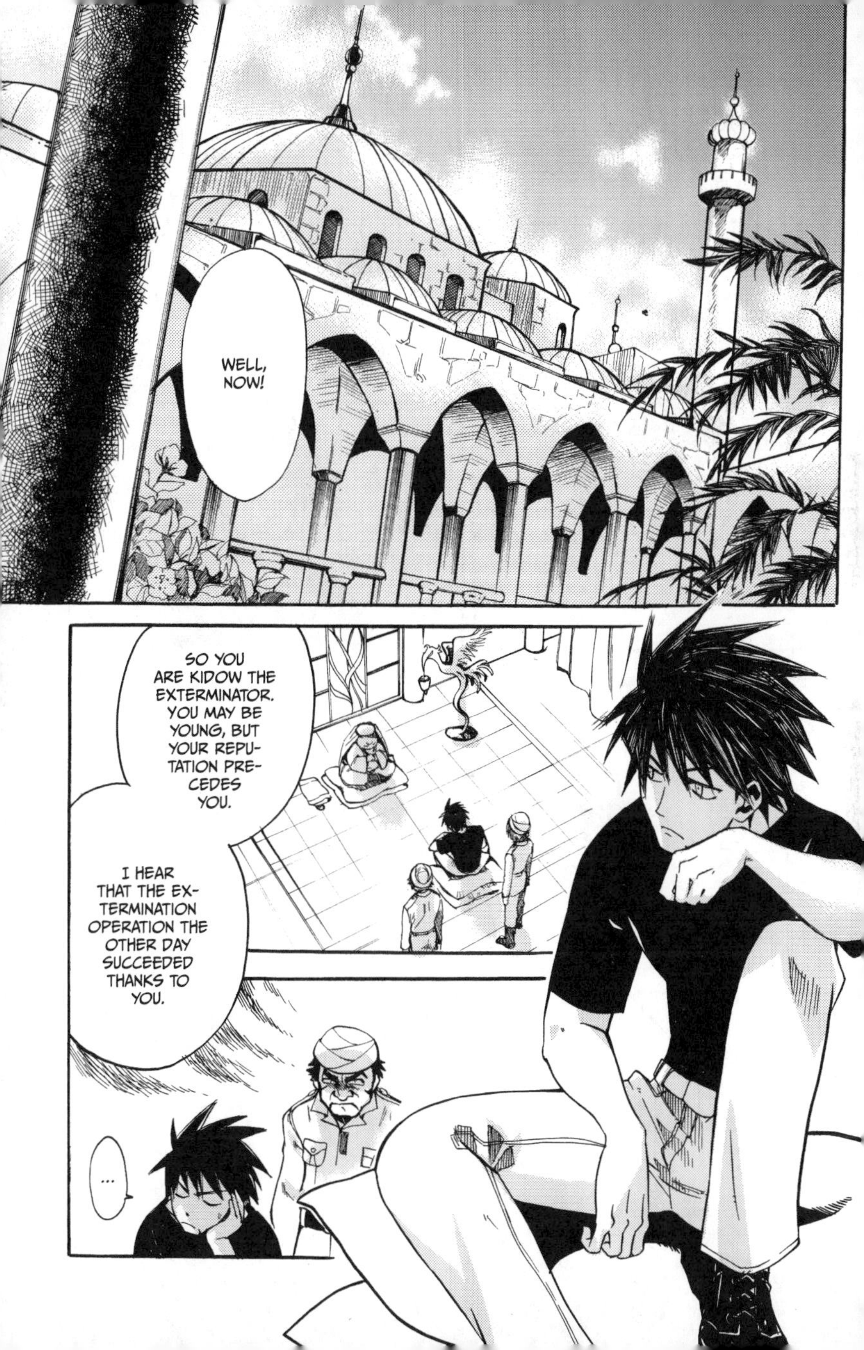
WELL, NOW!
SO YOU ARE KIDOW THE EXTERMINATOR. YOU MAY BE YOUNG, BUT YOUR REPUTATION PRECEDES YOU.
I HEAR THAT THE EXTERMINATION OPERATION THE OTHER DAY SUCCEEDED THANKS TO YOU.
...

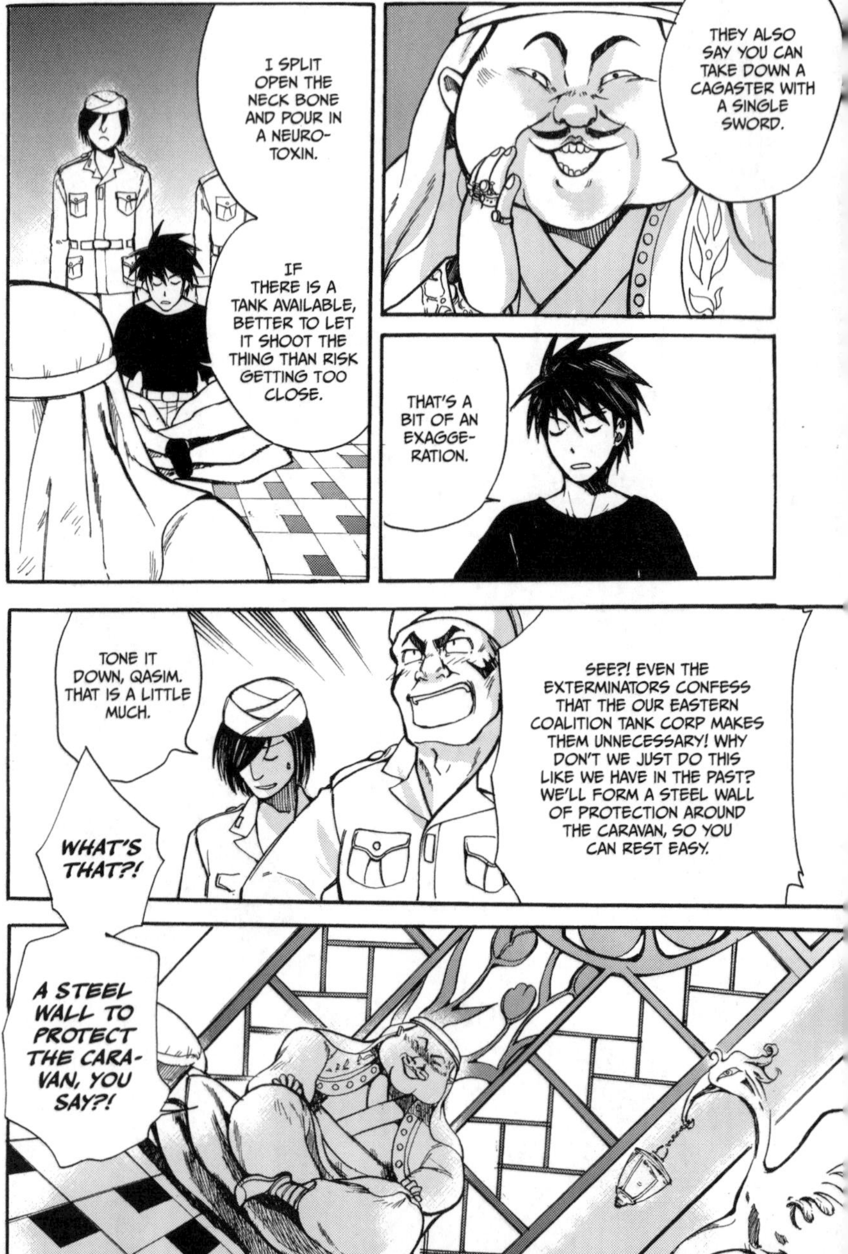
THEY ALSO SAY YOU CAN TAKE DOWN A CAGASTER WITH A SINGLE SWORD.
THAT'S A BIT OF AN EXAGGE-RATION.
I SPLIT OPEN THE NECK BONE AND POUR IN A NEURO-TOXIN.
IF THERE IS A TANK AVAILABLE, BETTER TO LET IT SHOOT THE THING THAN RISK GETTING TOO CLOSE.
SEE?! EVEN THE EXTERMINATORS CONFESS THAT THE OUR EASTERN COALITION TANK CORP MAKES THEM UNNECESSARY! WHY DON'T WE JUST DO THIS LIKE WE HAVE IN THE PAST? WE'LL FORM A STEEL WALL OF PROTECTION AROUND THE CARAVAN, SO YOU CAN REST EASY.
TONE IT DOWN, QASIM. THAT IS A LITTLE MUCH.
WHAT'S THAT?!
A STEEL WALL TO PROTECT THE CARA-VAN, YOU SAY?!

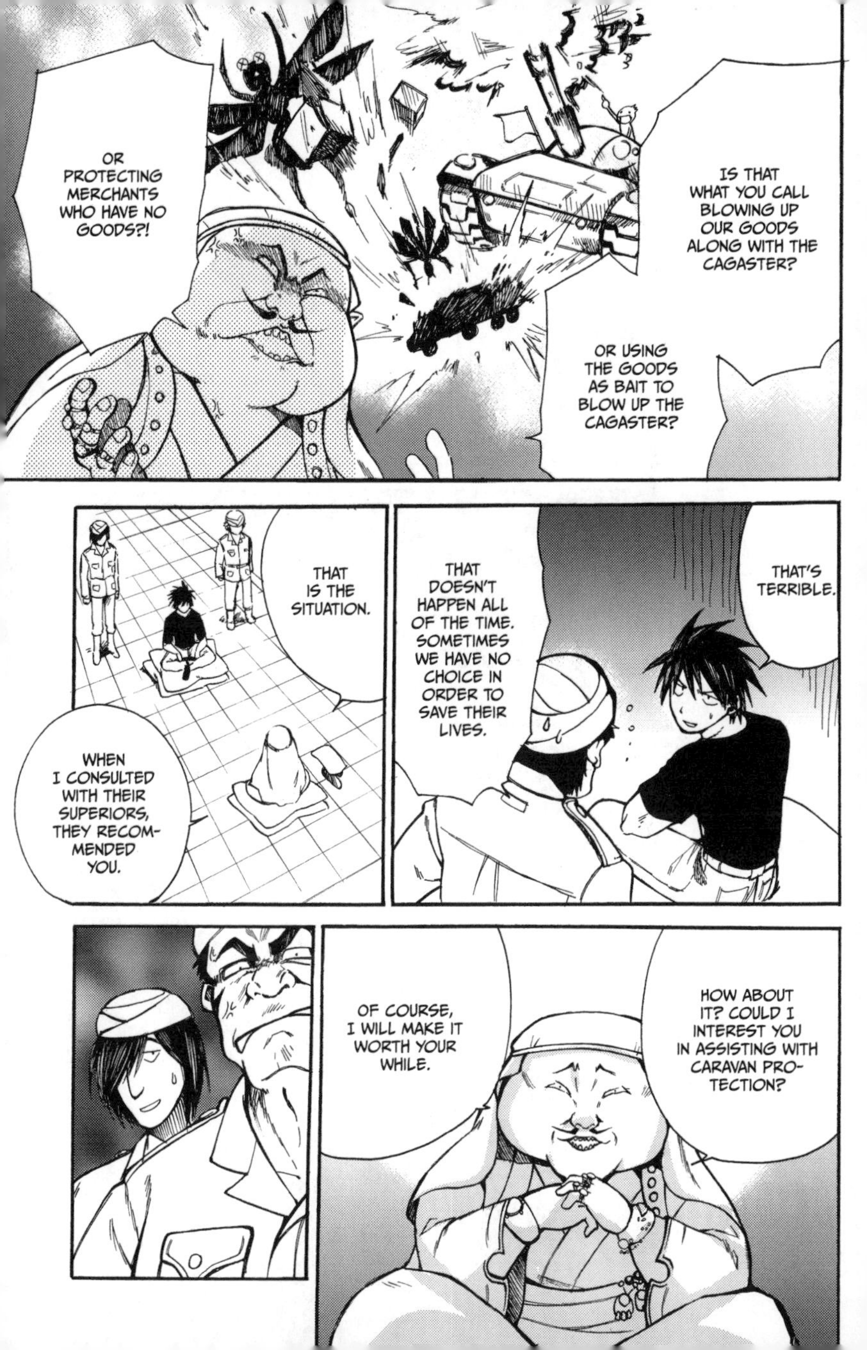
IS THAT WHAT YOU CALL BLOWING UP OUR GOODS ALONG WITH THE CAGASTER?
OR USING THE GOODS AS BAIT TO BLOW UP THE CAGASTER?
OR PROTECTING MERCHANTS WHO HAVE NO GOODS?!
THAT'S TERRIBLE.
THAT DOESN'T HAPPEN ALL OF THE TIME. SOMETIMES WE HAVE NO CHOICE IN ORDER TO SAVE THEIR LIVES.
THAT IS THE SITUATION.
WHEN I CONSULTED WITH THEIR SUPERIORS, THEY RECOMMENDED YOU.
HOW ABOUT IT? COULD I INTEREST YOU IN ASSISTING WITH CARAVAN PROTECTION?
OF COURSE, I WILL MAKE IT WORTH YOUR WHILE.

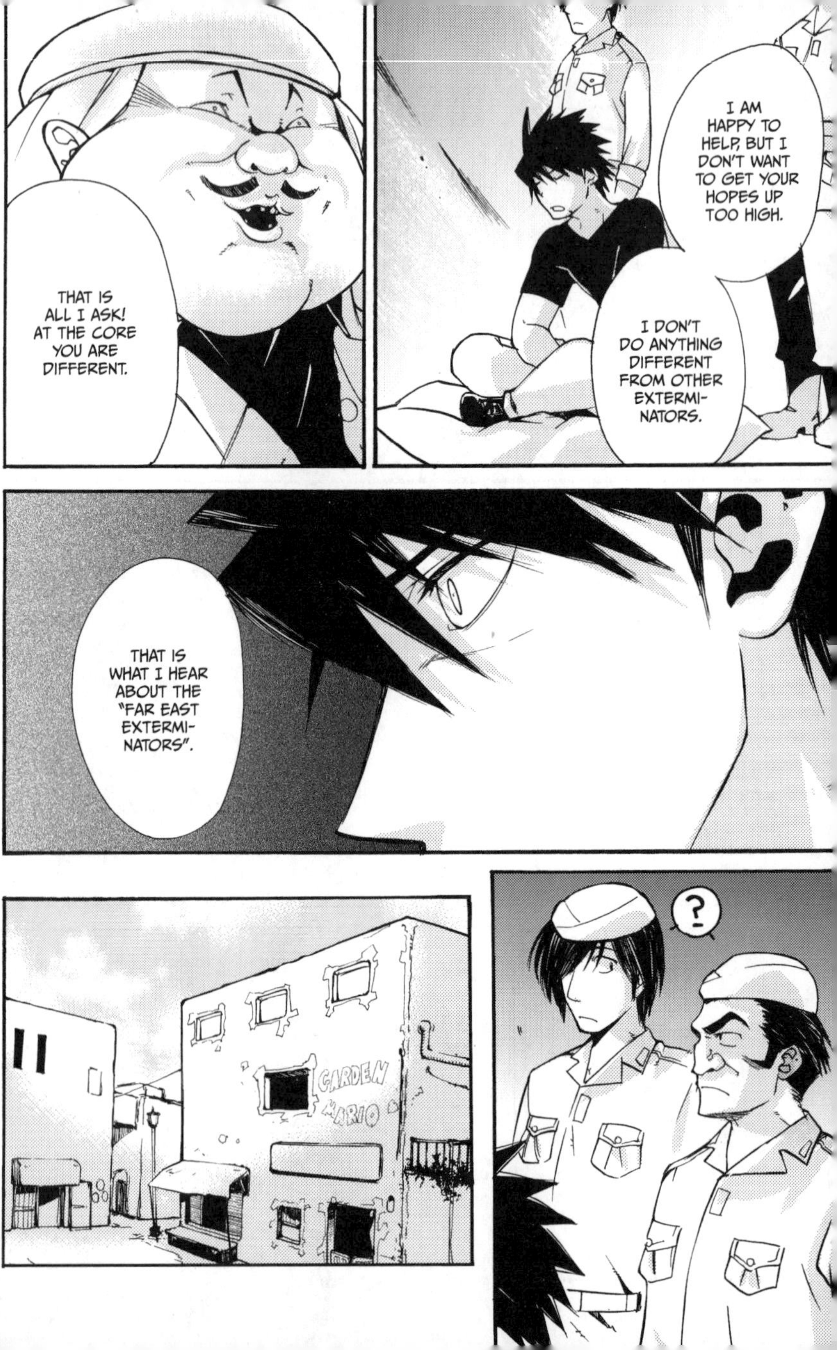
I AM HAPPY TO HELP, BUT I DON'T WANT TO GET YOUR HOPES UP TOO HIGH.
I DON'T DO ANYTHING DIFFERENT FROM OTHER EXTERMI-NATORS.
THAT IS ALL I ASK! AT THE CORE YOU ARE DIFFERENT.
THAT IS WHAT I HEAR ABOUT THE "FAR EAST EXTERMI-NATORS".
?
GARDEN MARIO

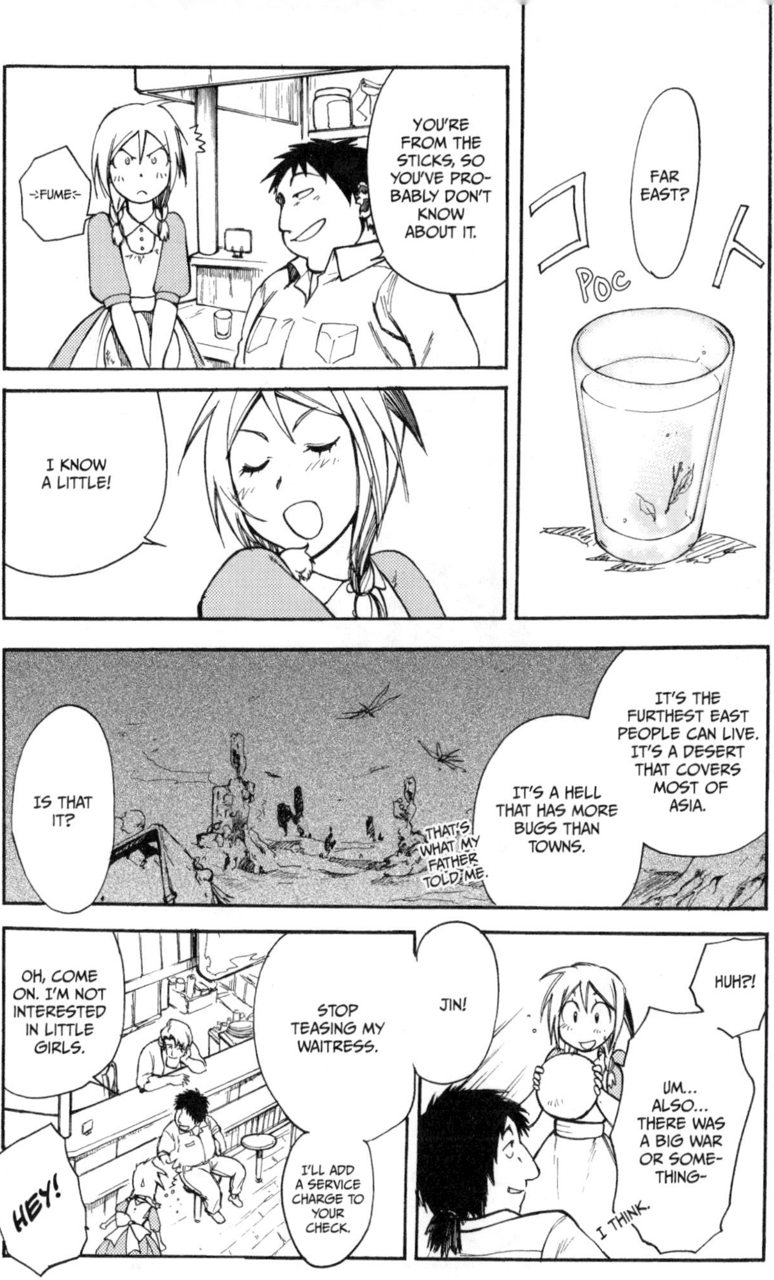
FAR EAST?
コト
POC
YOU'RE FROM THE STICKS, SO YOU'VE PRO-BABLY DON'T KNOW ABOUT IT.
FUME
I KNOW A LITTLE!
IT'S THE FURTHEST EAST PEOPLE CAN LIVE. IT'S A DESERT THAT COVERS MOST OF ASIA.
IT'S A HELL THAT HAS MORE BUGS THAN TOWNS.
THAT'S WHAT MY FATHER TOLD ME.
IS THAT IT?
HUH?!
UM... ALSO... THERE WAS A BIG WAR OR SOME-THING-
I THINK.
JIN!
STOP TEASING MY WAITRESS.
I'LL ADD A SERVICE CHARGE TO YOUR CHECK.
OH, COME ON. I'M NOT INTERESTED IN LITTLE GIRLS.
HEY!

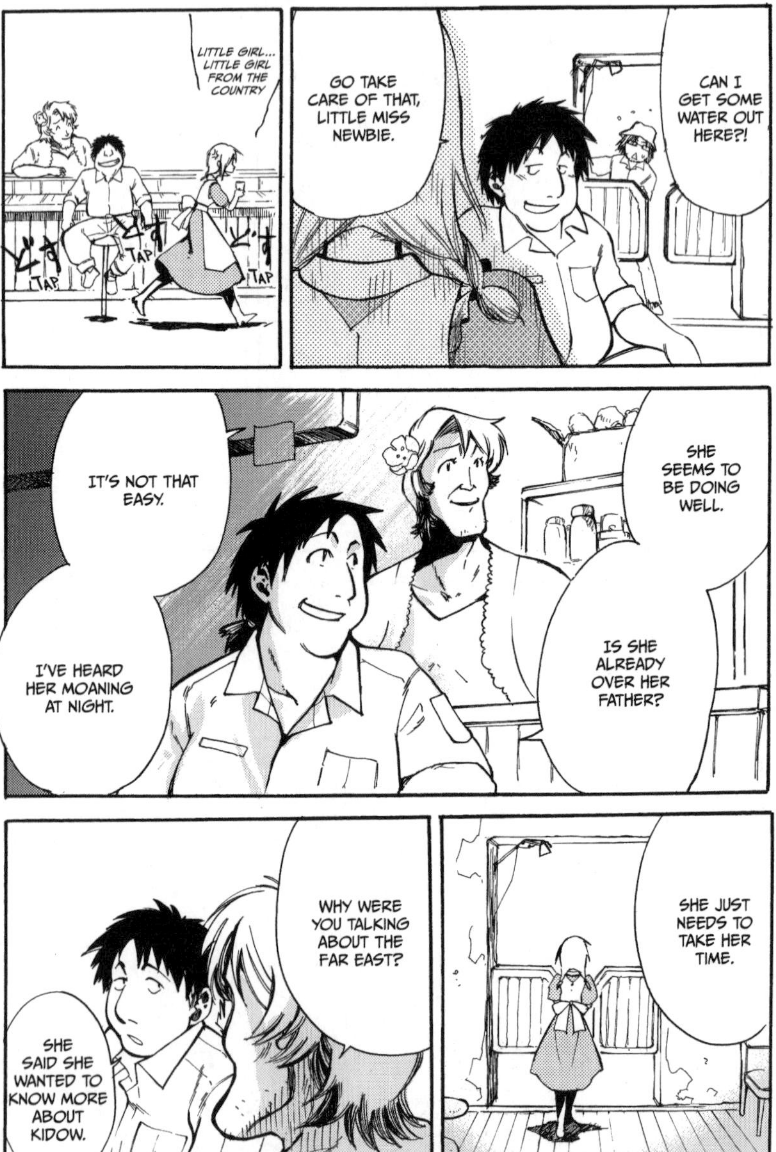
CAN I GET SOME WATER OUT HERE?!
GO TAKE CARE OF THAT, LITTLE MISS NEWBIE.
LITTLE GIRL... LITTLE GIRL FROM THE COUNTRY
TAP
TAP
TAP
SHE SEEMS TO BE DOING WELL.
IS SHE ALREADY OVER HER FATHER?
IT'S NOT THAT EASY.
I'VE HEARD HER MOANING AT NIGHT.
SHE JUST NEEDS TO TAKE HER TIME.
WHY WERE YOU TALKING ABOUT THE FAR EAST?
SHE SAID SHE WANTED TO KNOW MORE ABOUT KIDOW.

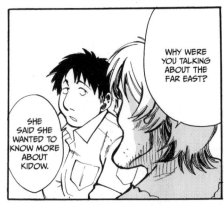

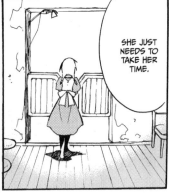

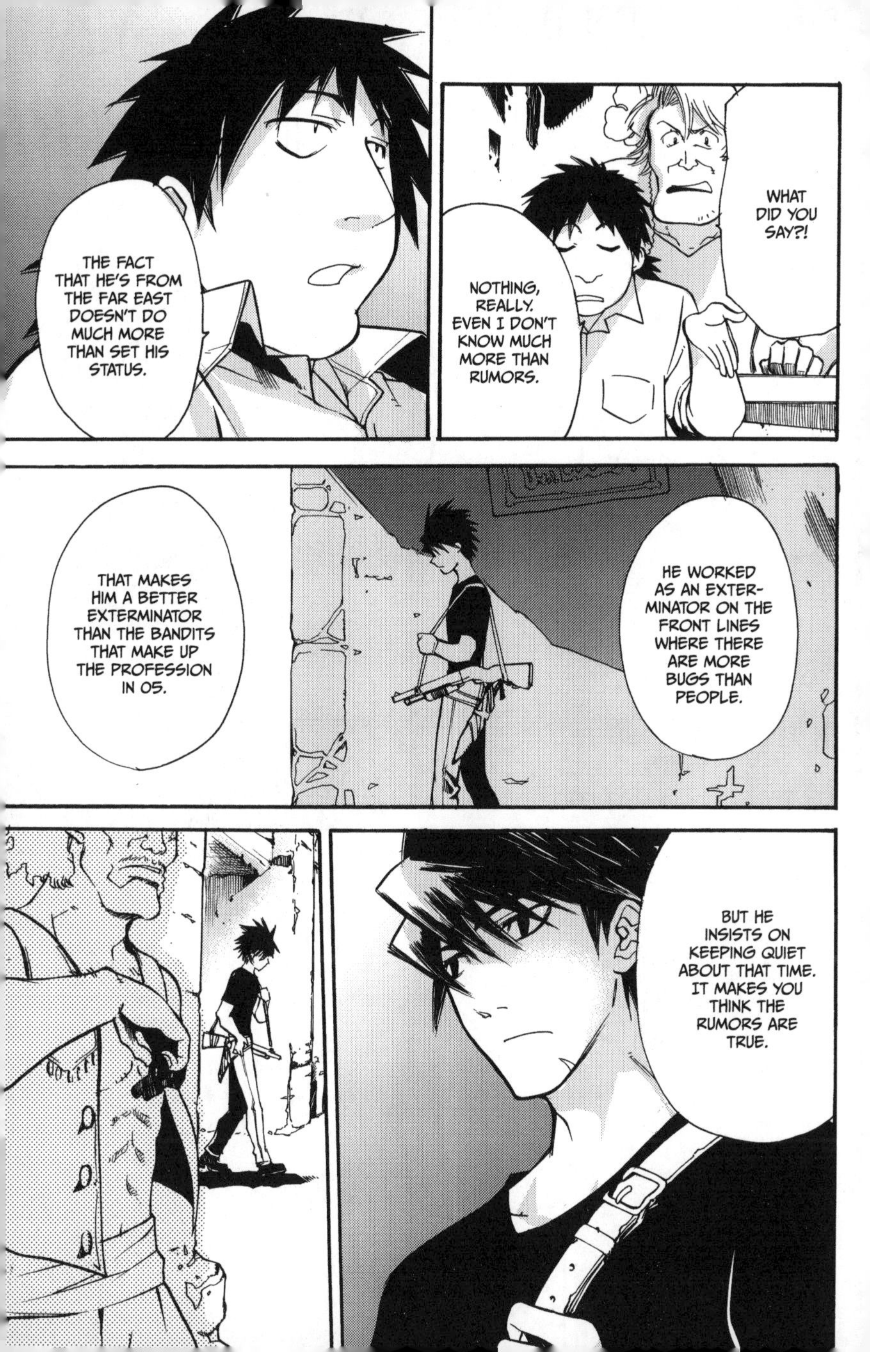
WHAT DID YOU SAY?!
NOTHING, REALLY. EVEN I DON'T KNOW MUCH MORE THAN RUMORS.
THE FACT THAT HE'S FROM THE FAR EAST DOESN'T DO MUCH MORE THAN SET HIS STATUS.
HE WORKED AS AN EXTER-MINATOR ON THE FRONT LINES WHERE THERE ARE MORE BUGS THAN PEOPLE.
THAT MAKES HIM A BETTER EXTERMINATOR THAN THE BANDITS THAT MAKE UP THE PROFESSION IN 05.
BUT HE INSISTS ON KEEPING QUIET ABOUT THAT TIME. IT MAKES YOU THINK THE RUMORS ARE TRUE.

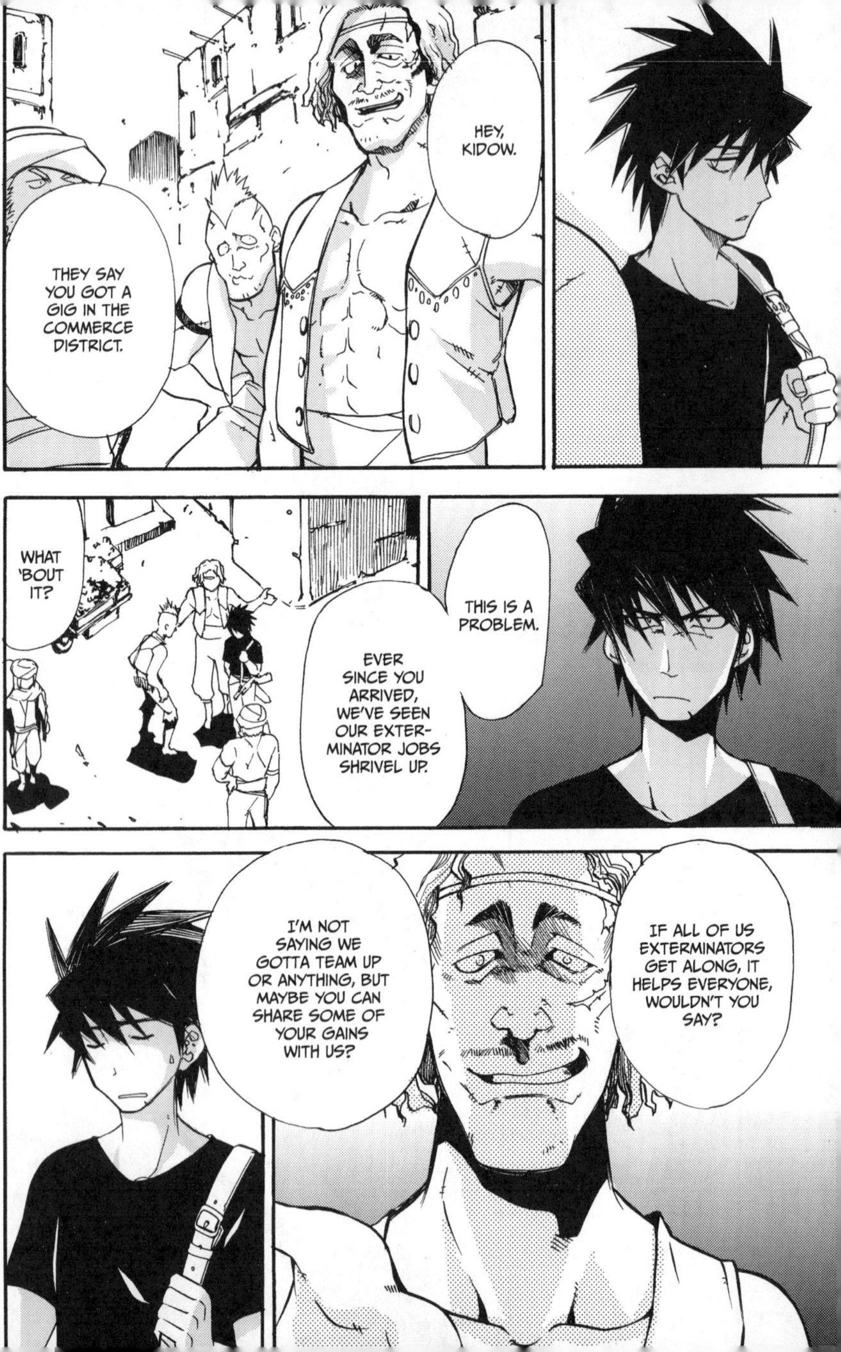
HEY, KIDOW.
THEY SAY YOU GOT A GIG IN THE COMMERCE DISTRICT.
WHAT 'BOUT IT?
THIS IS A PROBLEM.
EVER SINCE YOU ARRIVED, WE'VE SEEN OUR EXTER-MINATOR JOBS SHRIVEL UP.
I'M NOT SAYING WE GOTTA TEAM UP OR ANYTHING, BUT MAYBE YOU CAN SHARE SOME OF YOUR GAINS WITH US?
IF ALL OF US EXTERMINATORS GET ALONG, IT HELPS EVERYONE, WOULDN'T YOU SAY?

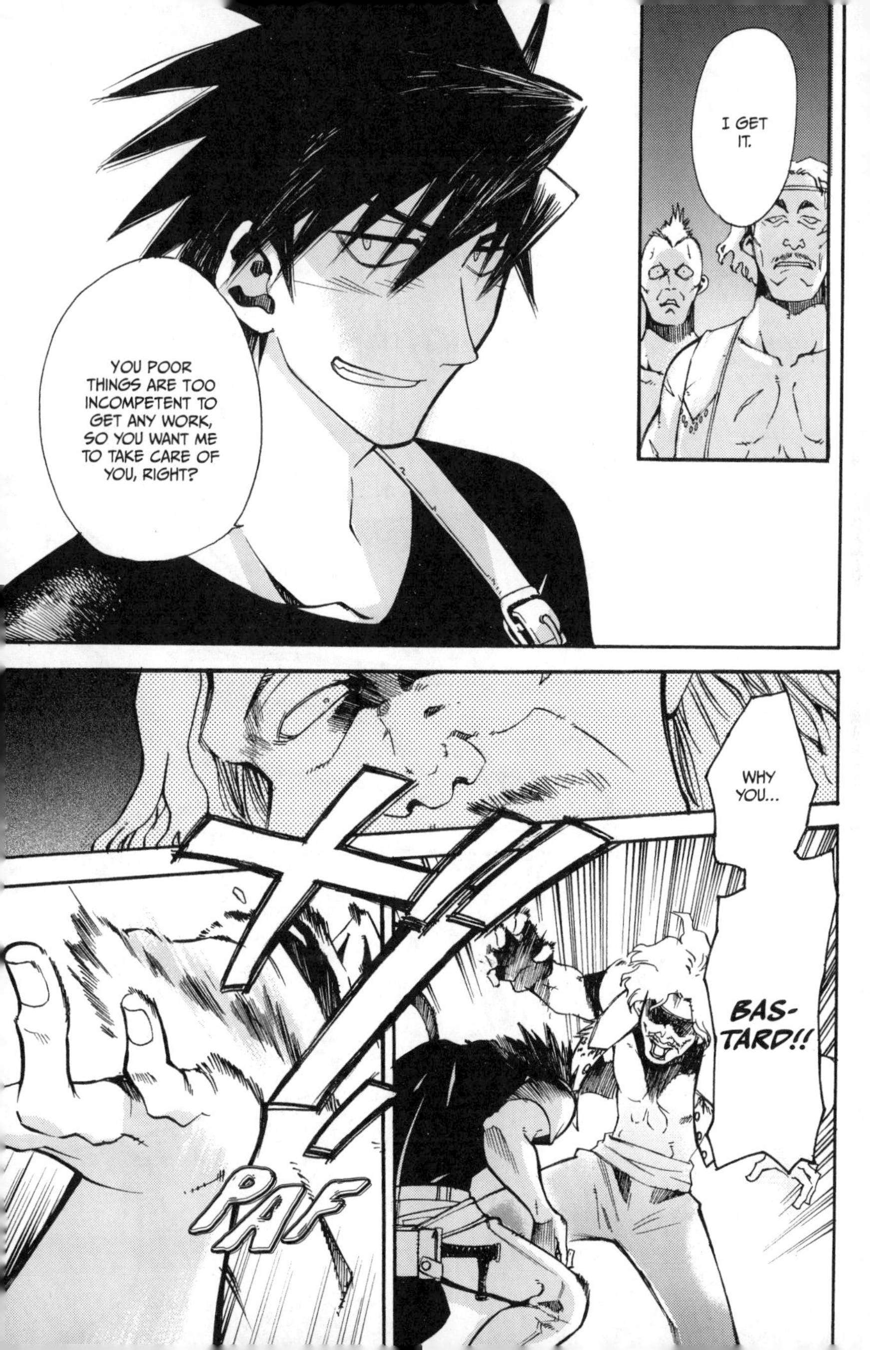
I GET IT.
YOU POOR THINGS ARE TOO INCOMPETENT TO GET ANY WORK, SO YOU WANT ME TO TAKE CARE OF YOU, RIGHT?
WHY YOU...
BAS-TARD!!
RAF

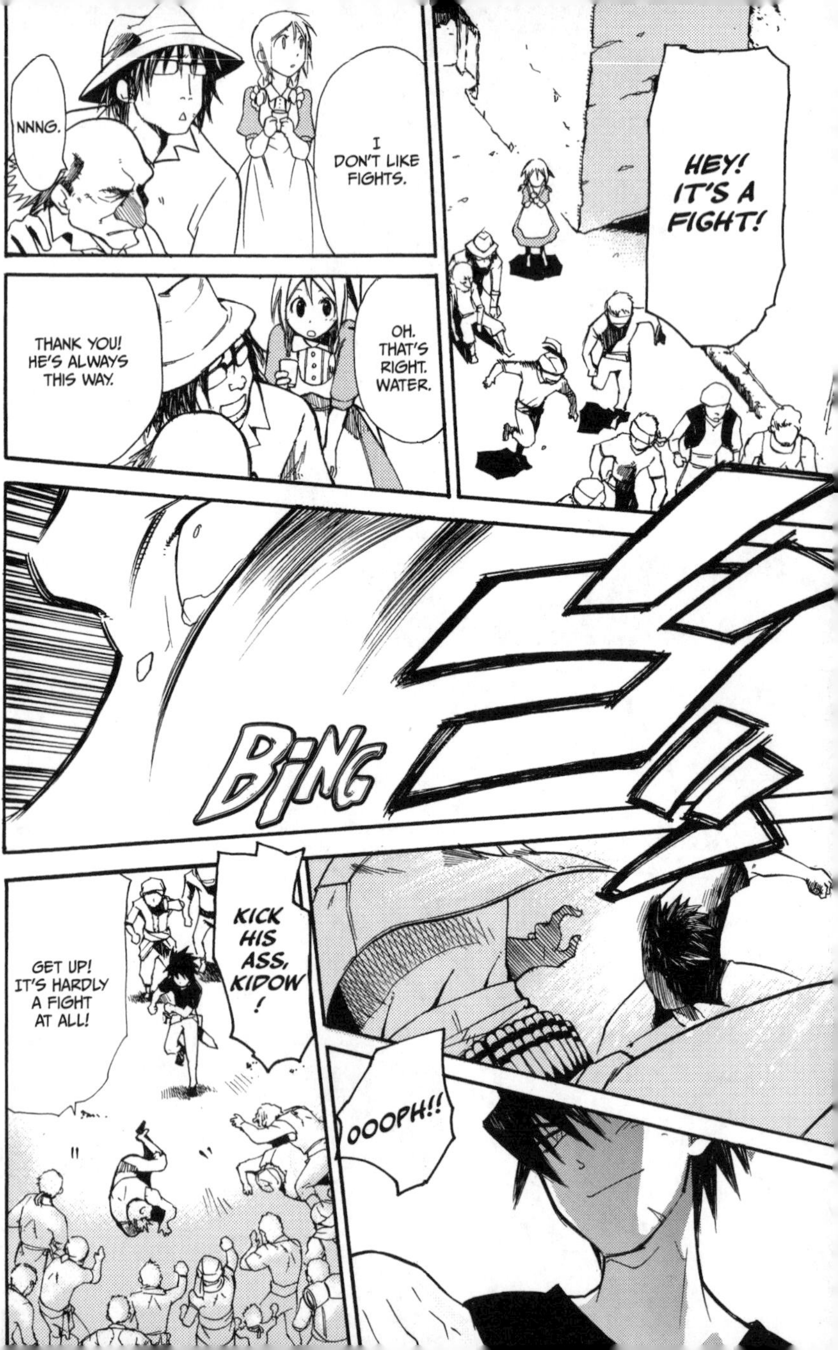
HEY! IT'S A FIGHT!
I DON'T LIKE FIGHTS.
NNNG.
OH. THAT'S RIGHT. WATER.
THANK YOU! HE'S ALWAYS THIS WAY.
BING
OOOPH!!
KICK HIS ASS, KIDOW!
GET UP! IT'S HARDLY A FIGHT AT ALL!

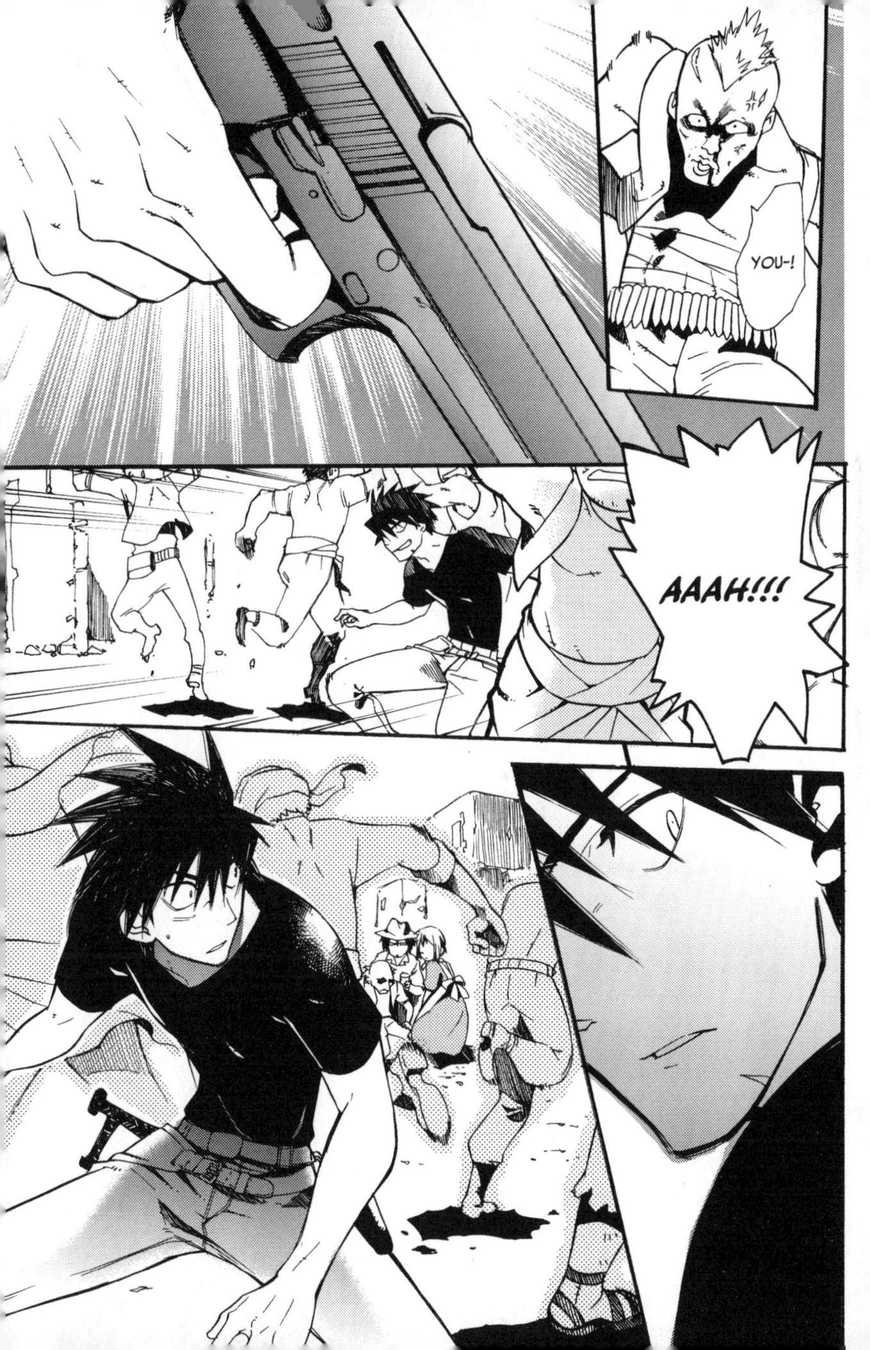
YOU-!
AAAH!!!

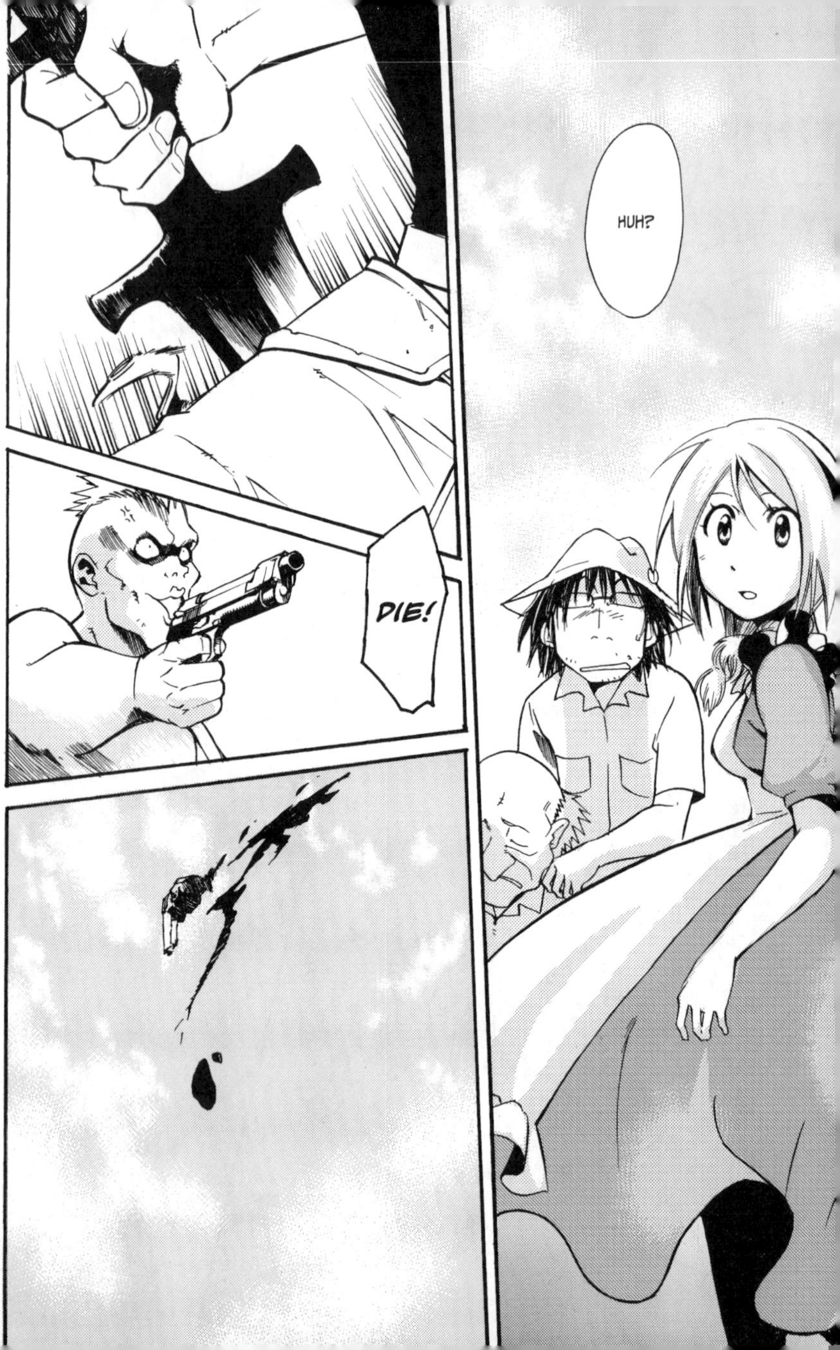
HUH?
DIE!

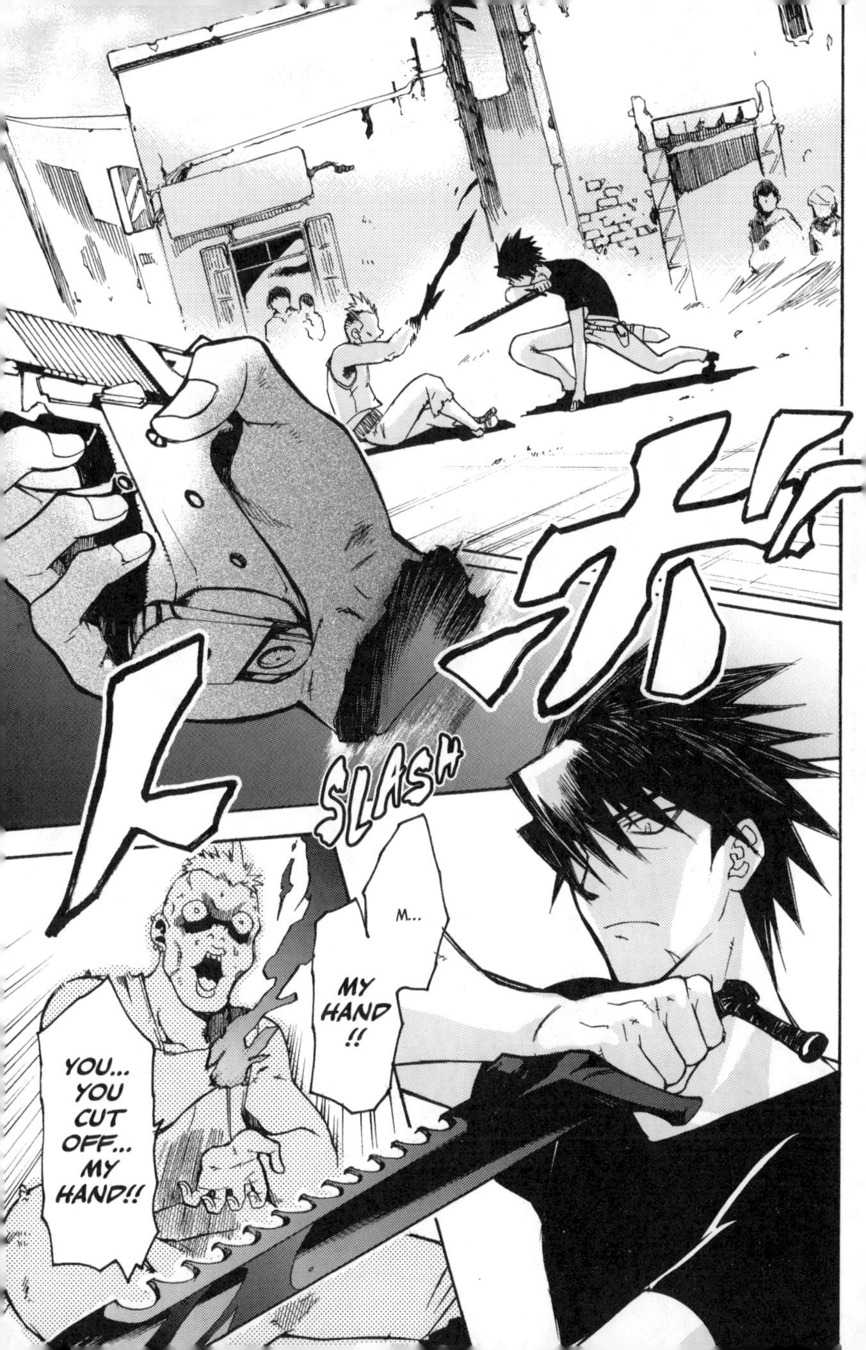
SLASH
M...
MY HAND!!
YOU... YOU CUT OFF... MY HAND!!

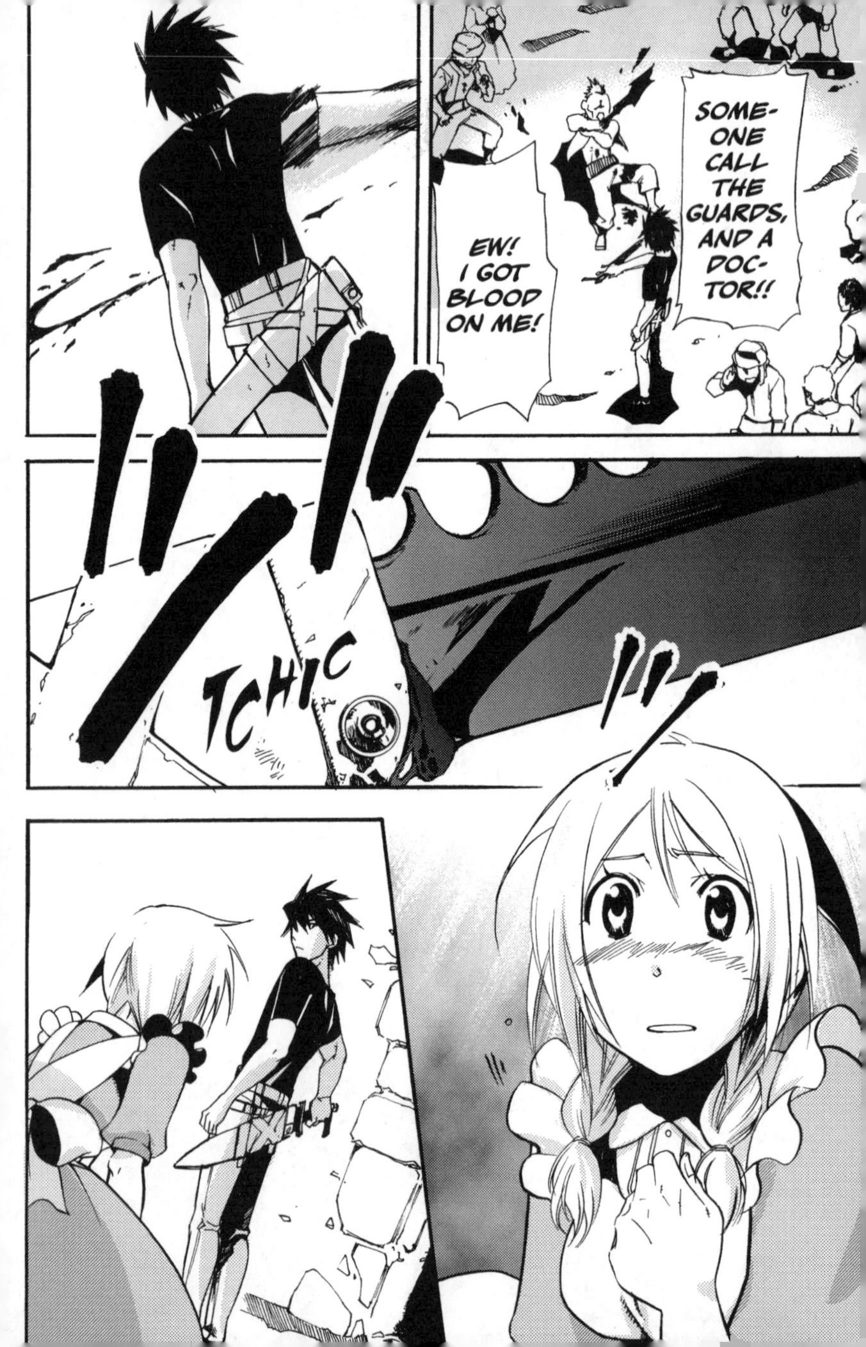
SOME-ONE CALL THE GUARDS, AND A DOC-TOR!!
EW! I GOT BLOOD ON ME!
TCHIC

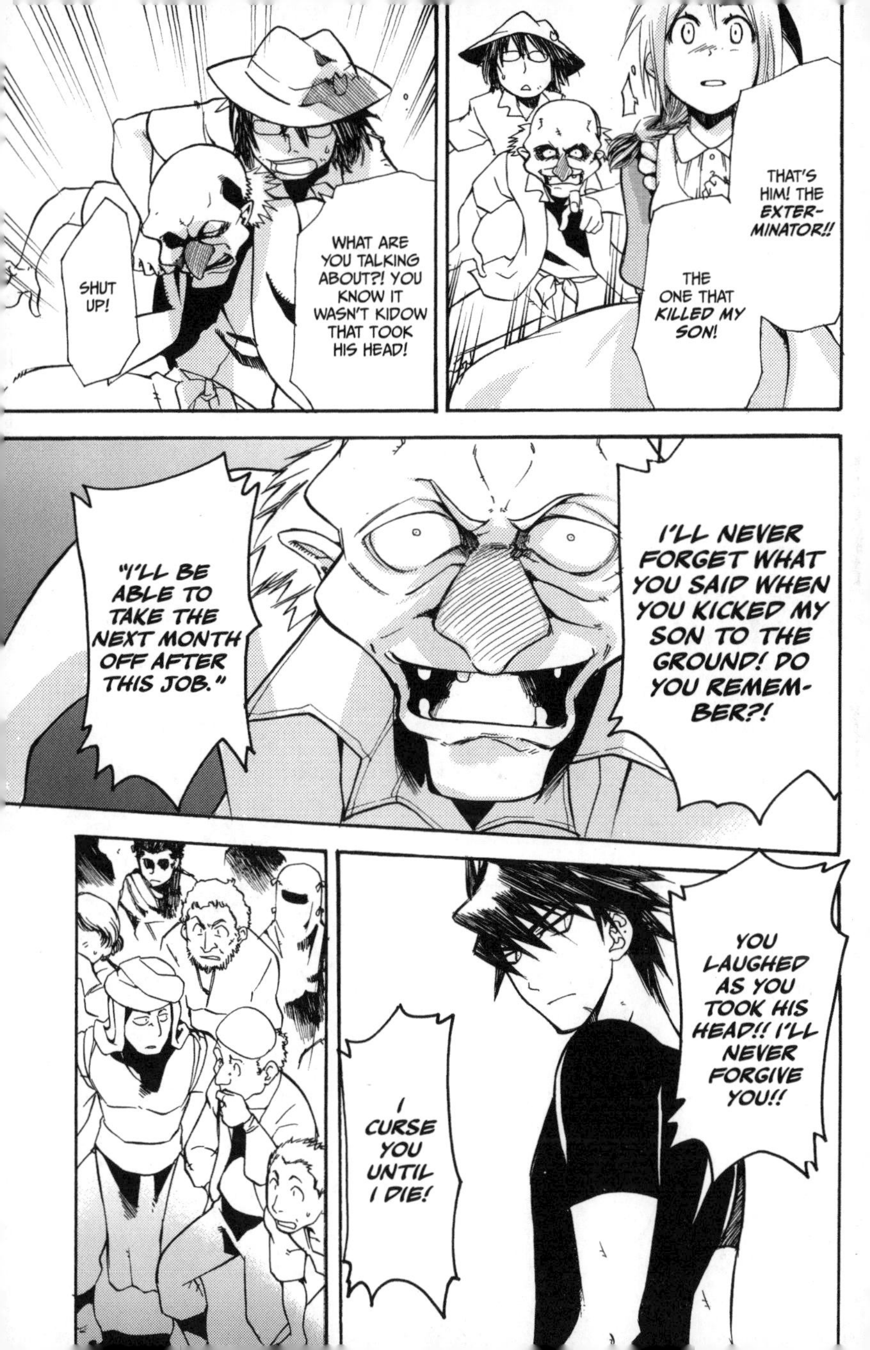
THAT'S HIM! THE EXTER-MINATOR!!
THE ONE THAT KILLED MY SON!
WHAT ARE YOU TALKING ABOUT?! YOU KNOW IT WASN'T KIDOW THAT TOOK HIS HEAD!
SHUT UP!
I'LL NEVER FORGET WHAT YOU SAID WHEN YOU KICKED MY SON TO THE GROUND! DO YOU REMEM-BER?!
"I'LL BE ABLE TO TAKE THE NEXT MONTH OFF AFTER THIS JOB."
YOU LAUGHED AS YOU TOOK HIS HEAD!! I'LL NEVER FORGIVE YOU!!
I CURSE YOU UNTIL I DIE!

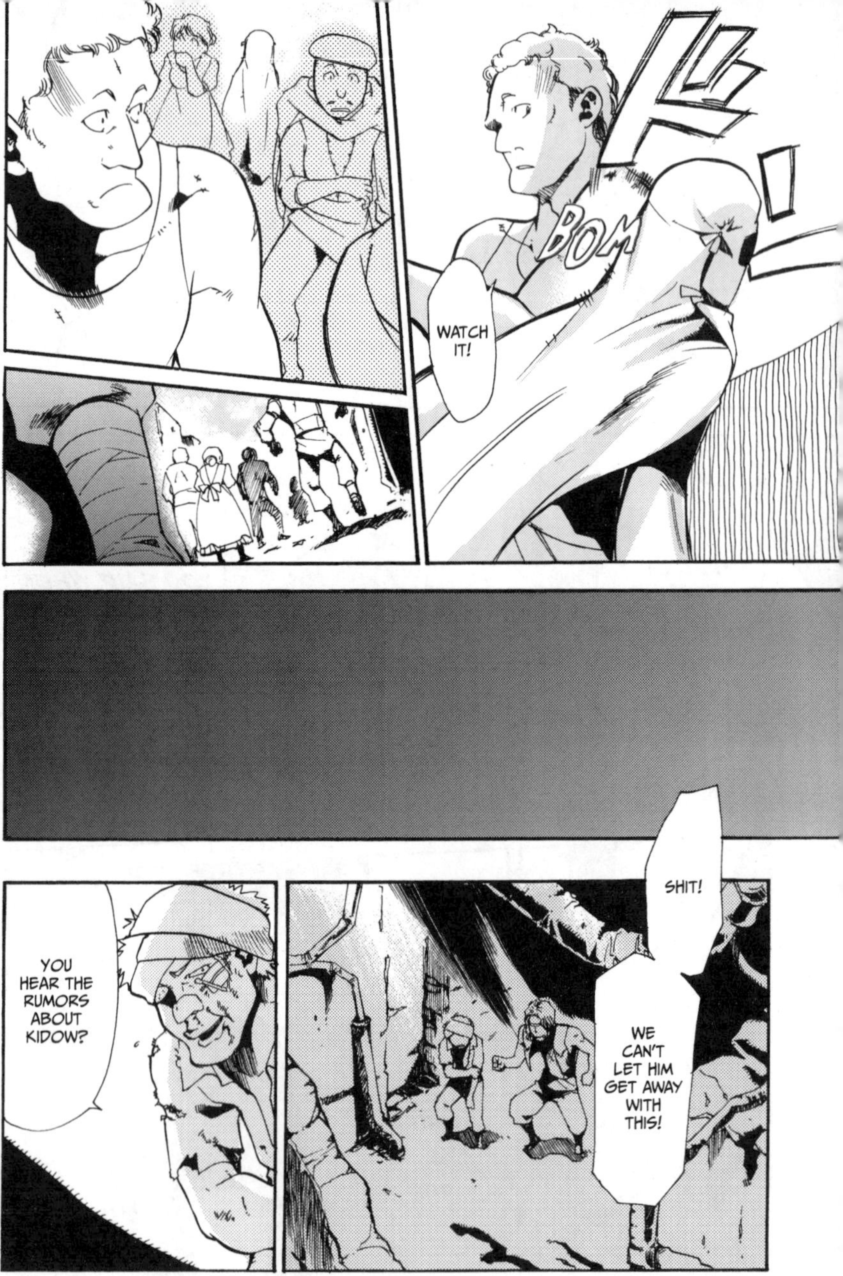
BOM
WATCH IT!
SHIT!
WE CAN'T LET HIM GET AWAY WITH THIS!
YOU HEAR THE RUMORS ABOUT KIDOW?

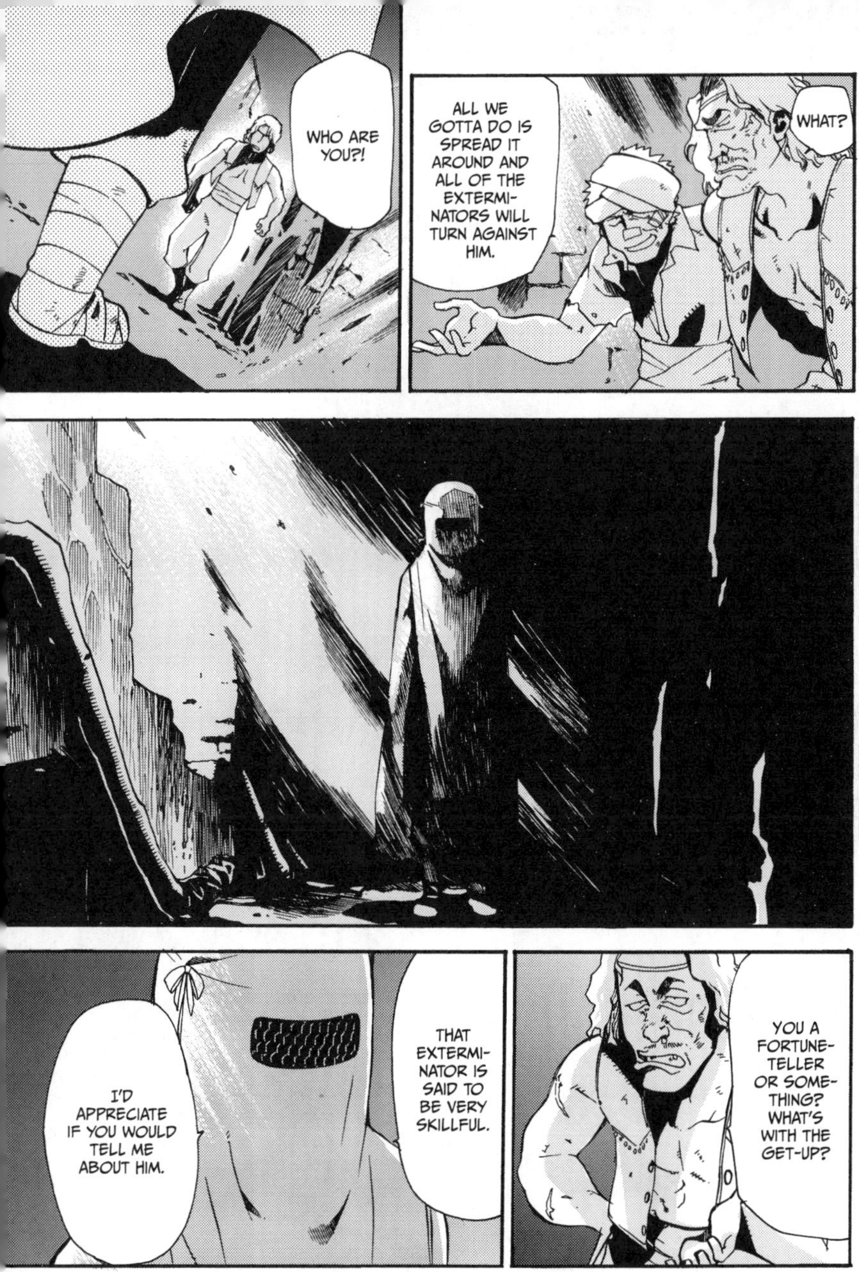
WHAT?
ALL WE GOTTA DO IS SPREAD IT AROUND AND ALL OF THE EXTERMINATORS WILL TURN AGAINST HIM.
WHO ARE YOU?!
YOU A FORTUNE-TELLER OR SOMETHING? WHAT'S WITH THE GET-UP?
THAT EXTERMINATOR IS SAID TO BE VERY SKILLFUL.
I'D APPRECIATE IF YOU WOULD TELL ME ABOUT HIM.

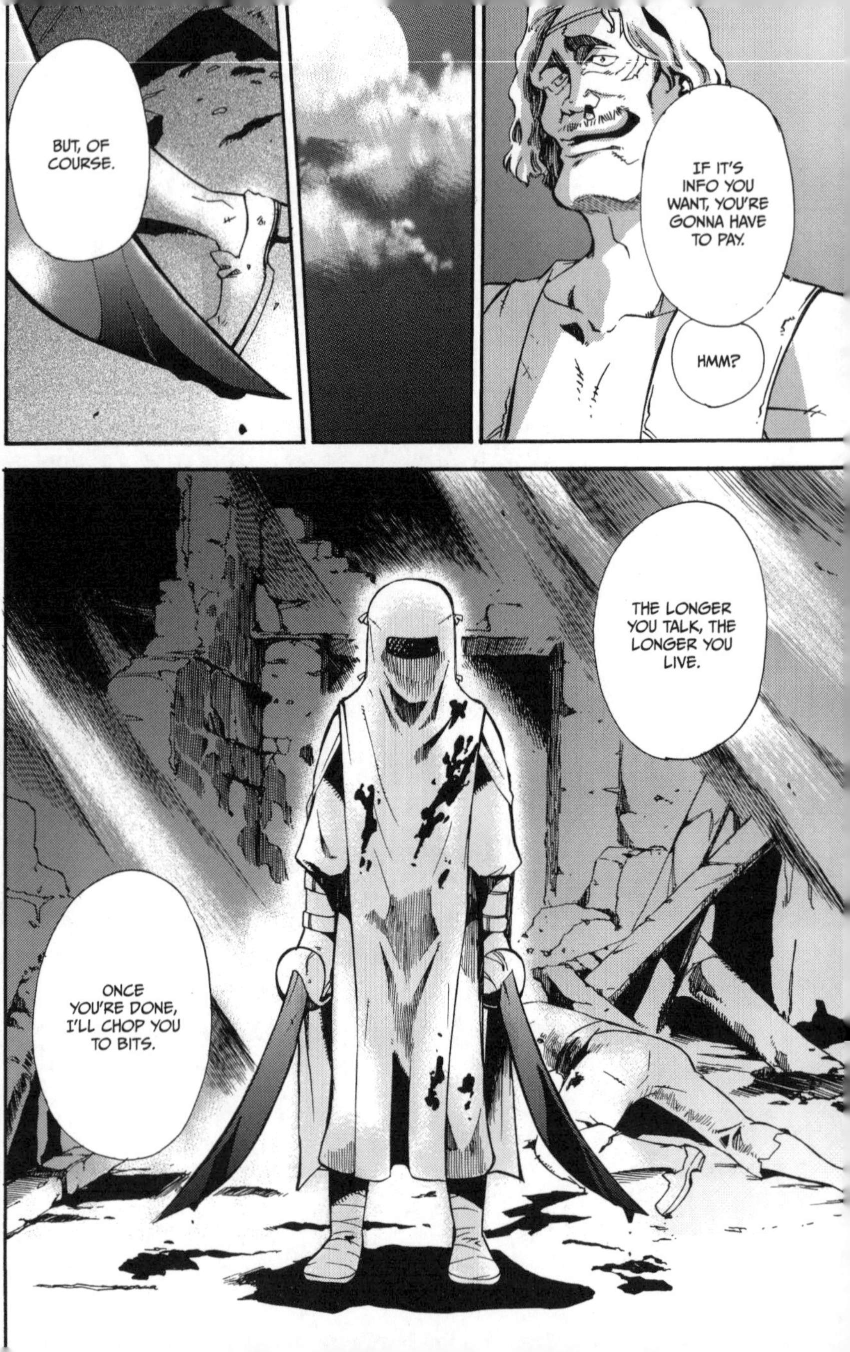
IF IT'S INFO YOU WANT, YOU'RE GONNA HAVE TO PAY.
HMM?
BUT, OF COURSE.
THE LONGER YOU TALK, THE LONGER YOU LIVE.
ONCE YOU'RE DONE, I'LL CHOP YOU TO BITS.

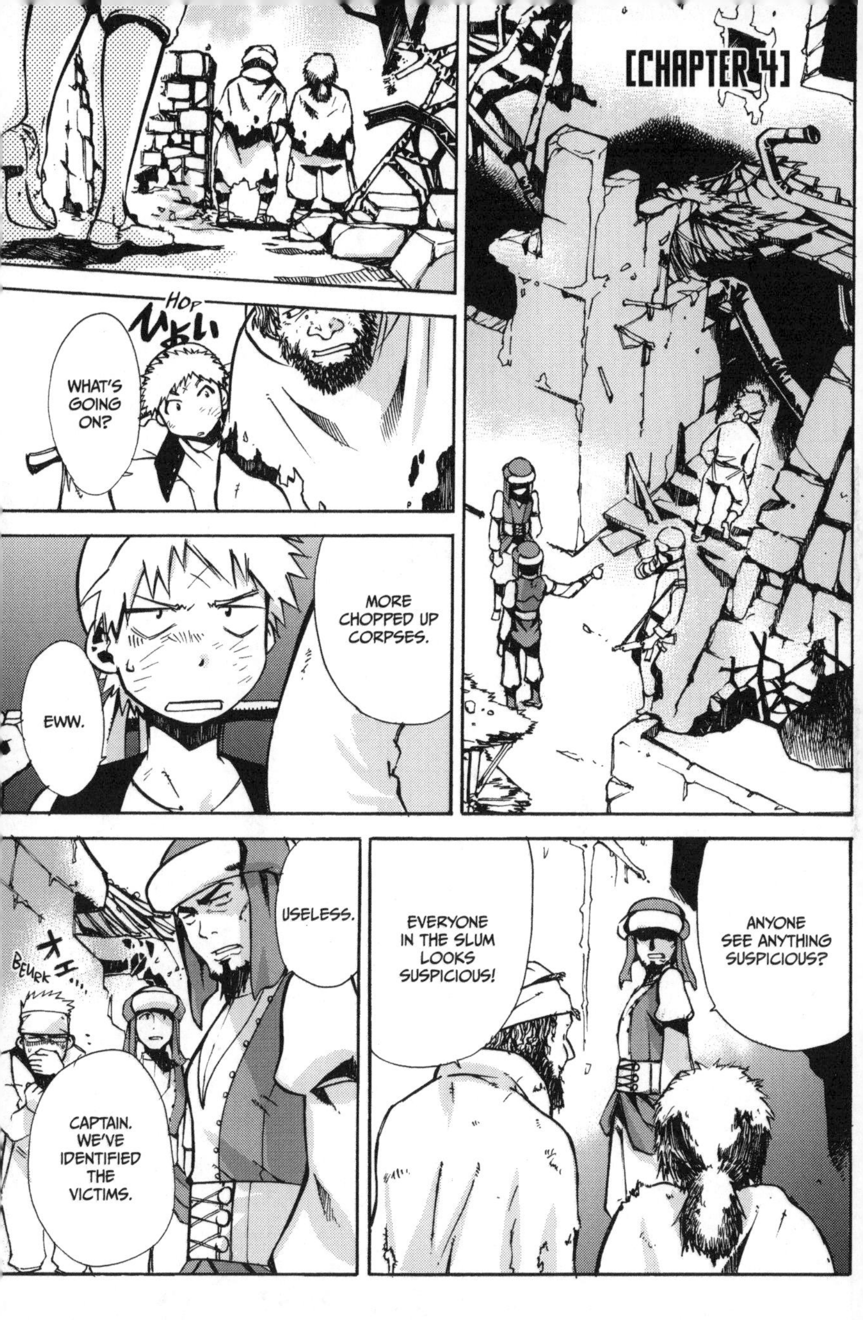
[CHAPTER 4]
HOP
ひょい
WHAT'S GOING ON?
MORE CHOPPED UP CORPSES.
EWW.
ANYONE SEE ANYTHING SUSPICIOUS?
EVERYONE IN THE SLUM LOOKS SUSPICIOUS!
USELESS.
オエ...
BEURK
CAPTAIN. WE'VE IDENTIFIED THE VICTIMS.

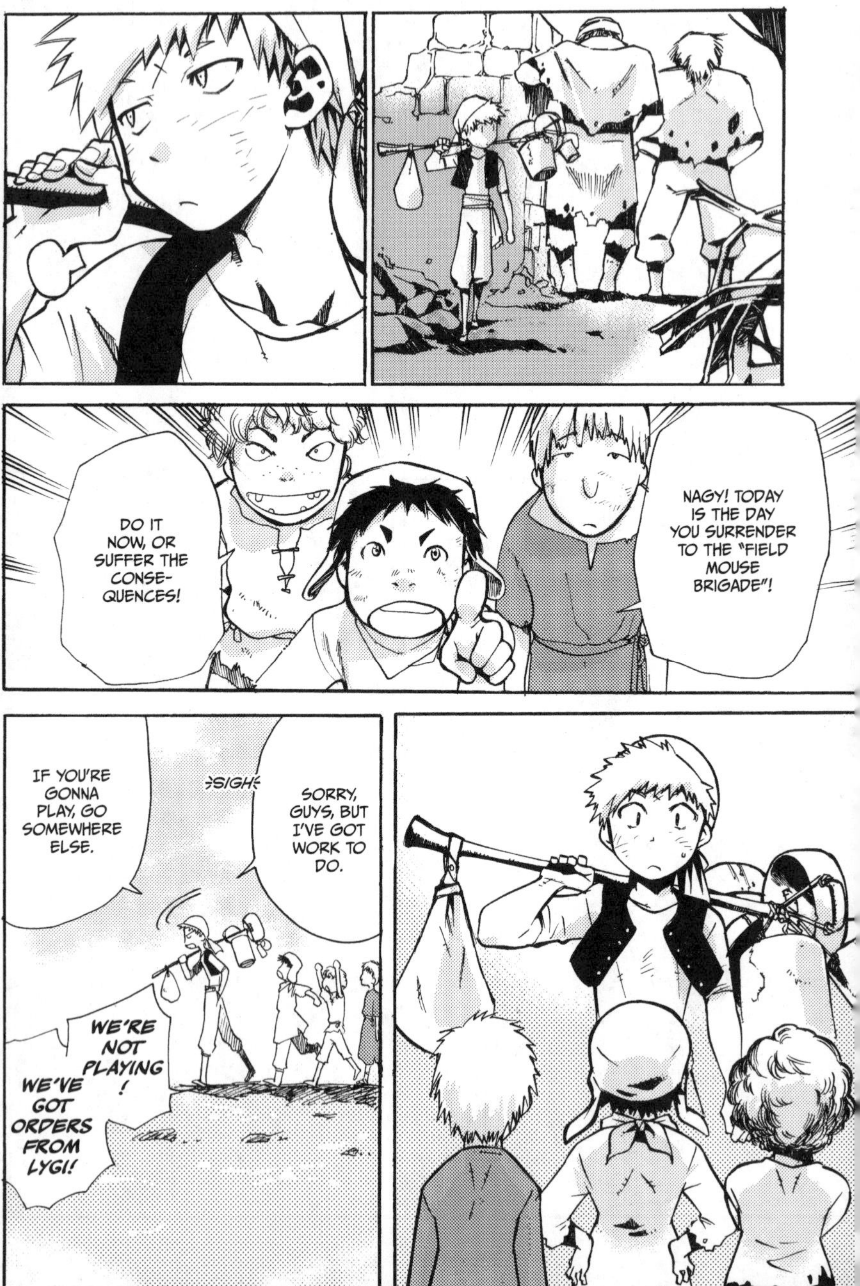
NAGY! TODAY IS THE DAY YOU SURRENDER TO THE "FIELD MOUSE BRIGADE"!
DO IT NOW, OR SUFFER THE CONSE-QUENCES!
SORRY, GUYS, BUT I'VE GOT WORK TO DO.
SIGH
IF YOU'RE GONNA PLAY, GO SOMEWHERE ELSE.
WE'RE NOT PLAYING!
WE'VE GOT ORDERS FROM LYGI!

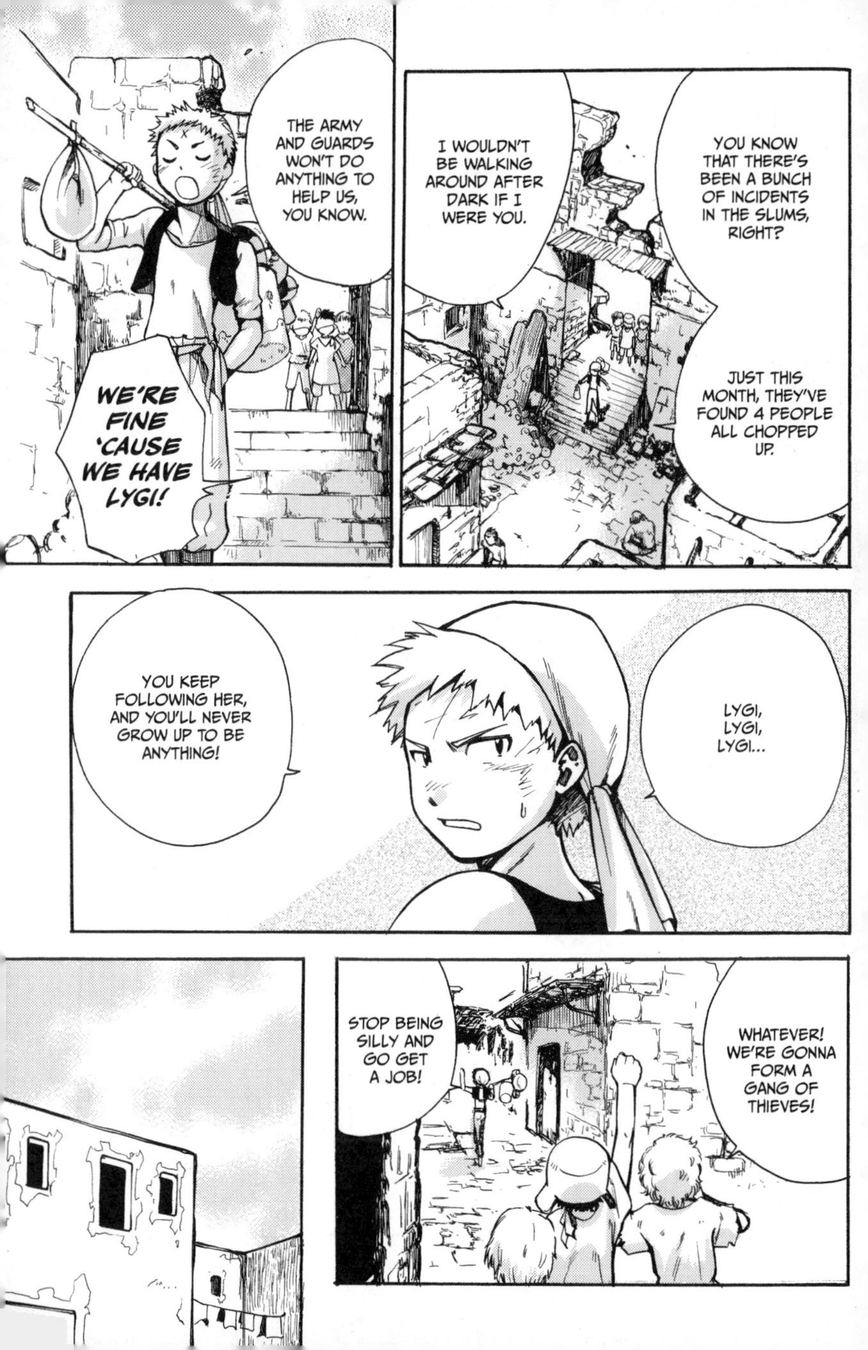
YOU KNOW THAT THERE'S BEEN A BUNCH OF INCIDENTS IN THE SLUMS, RIGHT?
I WOULDN'T BE WALKING AROUND AFTER DARK IF I WERE YOU.
JUST THIS MONTH, THEY'VE FOUND 4 PEOPLE ALL CHOPPED UP.
THE ARMY AND GUARDS WON'T DO ANYTHING TO HELP US, YOU KNOW.
WE'RE FINE 'CAUSE WE HAVE LYGI!
LYGI, LYGI, LYGI...
YOU KEEP FOLLOWING HER, AND YOU'LL NEVER GROW UP TO BE ANYTHING!
WHATEVER! WE'RE GONNA FORM A GANG OF THIEVES!
STOP BEING SILLY AND GO GET A JOB!

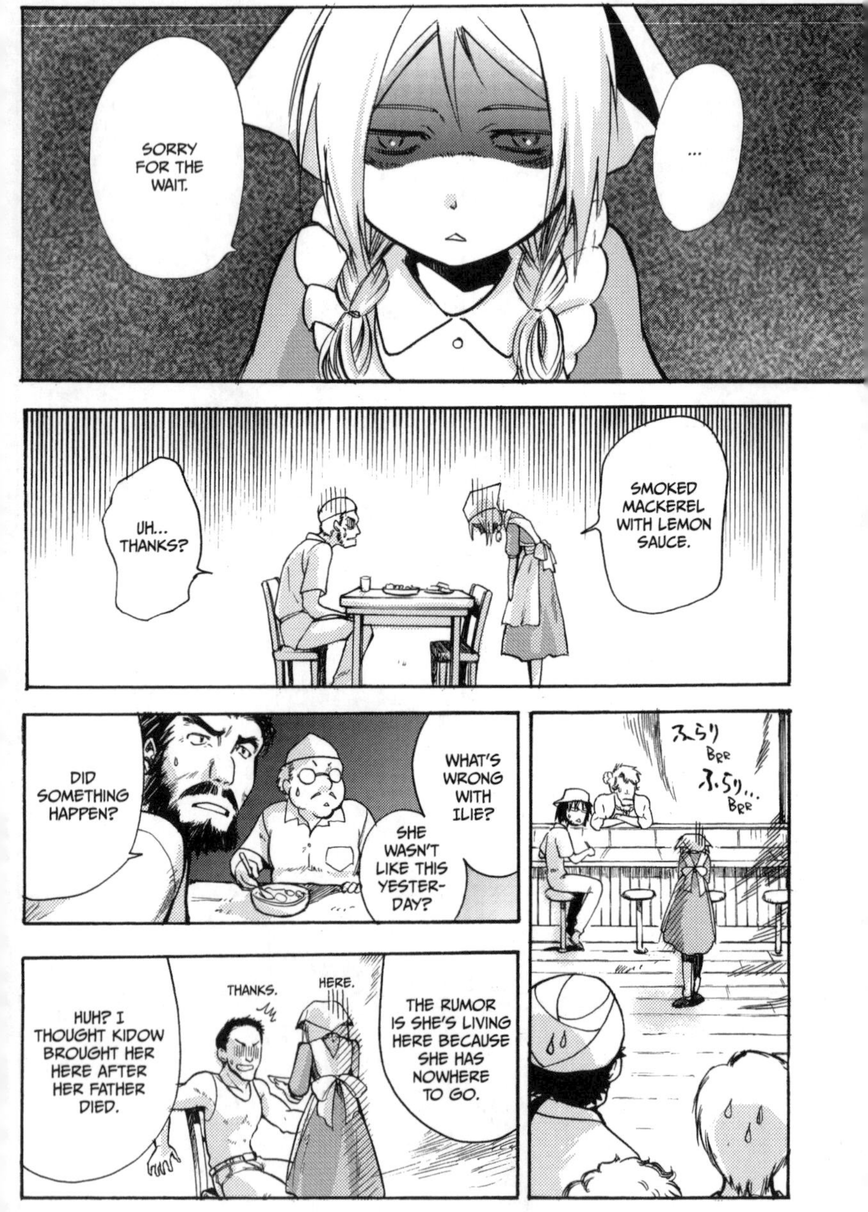
...
SORRY FOR THE WAIT.
SMOKED MACKEREL WITH LEMON SAUCE.
UH... THANKS?
ふらり
Brr
ふらり...
Brr
WHAT'S WRONG WITH ILIE?
SHE WASN'T LIKE THIS YESTER-DAY?
DID SOMETHING HAPPEN?
THE RUMOR IS SHE'S LIVING HERE BECAUSE SHE HAS NOWHERE TO GO.
HERE.
THANKS.
HUH? I THOUGHT KIDOW BROUGHT HER HERE AFTER HER FATHER DIED.

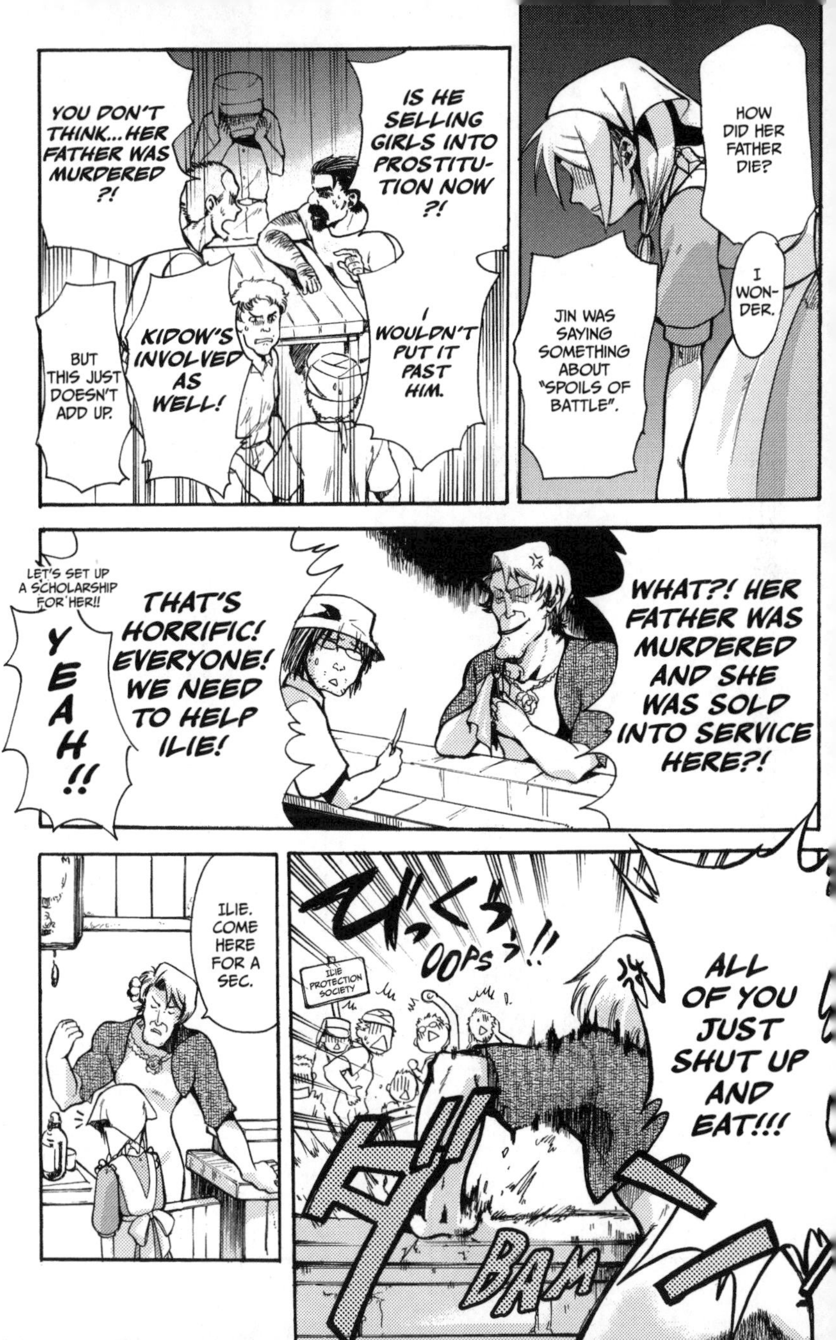
HOW DID HER FATHER DIE?
I WONDER.
JIN WAS SAYING SOMETHING ABOUT "SPOILS OF BATTLE".
IS HE SELLING GIRLS INTO PROSTITUTION NOW ?!
YOU DON'T THINK...HER FATHER WAS MURDERED ?!
I WOULDN'T PUT IT PAST HIM.
KIDOW'S INVOLVED AS WELL!
BUT THIS JUST DOESN'T ADD UP.
WHAT?! HER FATHER WAS MURDERED AND SHE WAS SOLD INTO SERVICE HERE?!
THAT'S HORRIFIC! EVERYONE! WE NEED TO HELP ILIE!
YEAH!!
LET'S SET UP A SCHOLARSHIP FOR HER!!
OOPS
ILIE PROTECTION SOCIETY
ALL OF YOU JUST SHUT UP AND EAT!!!
BAM
ILIE. COME HERE FOR A SEC.

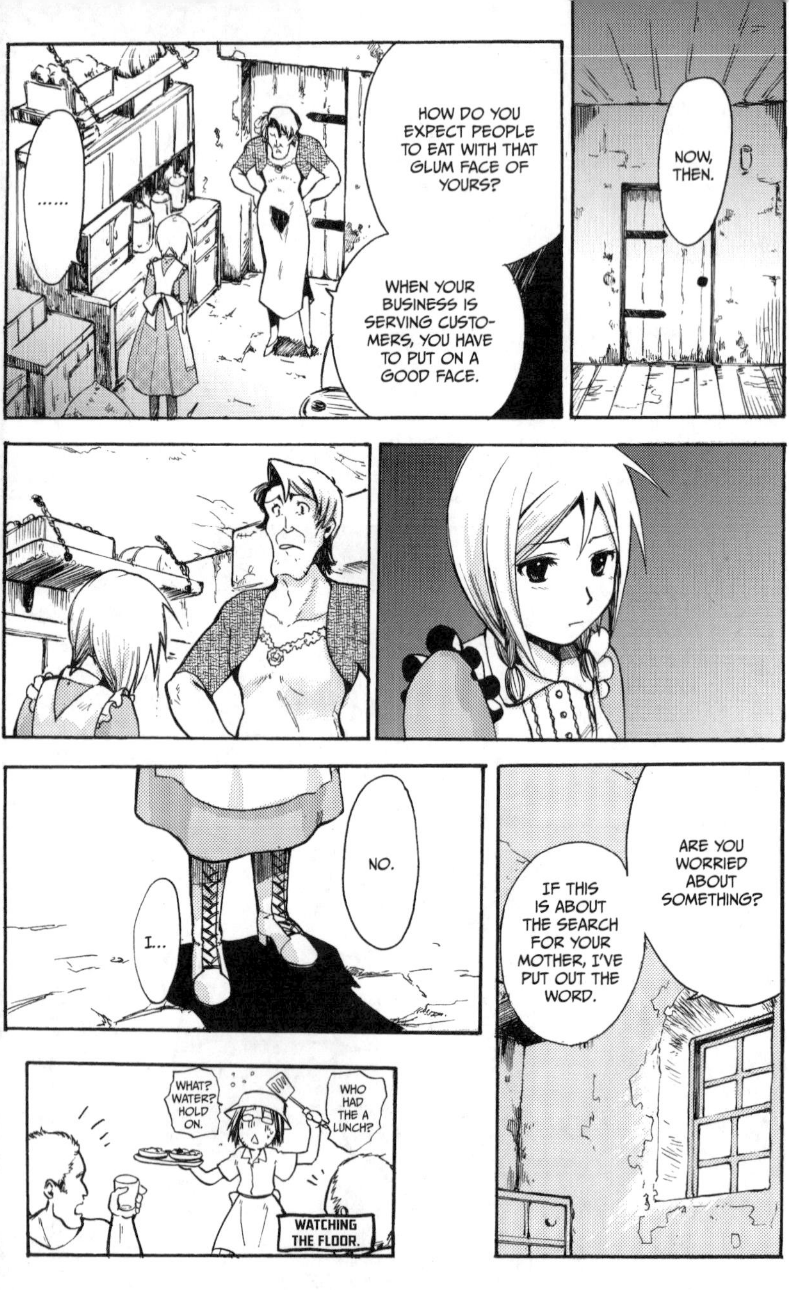
NOW, THEN.
HOW DO YOU EXPECT PEOPLE TO EAT WITH THAT GLUM FACE OF YOURS?
WHEN YOUR BUSINESS IS SERVING CUSTOMERS, YOU HAVE TO PUT ON A GOOD FACE.
......
ARE YOU WORRIED ABOUT SOMETHING?
IF THIS IS ABOUT THE SEARCH FOR YOUR MOTHER, I'VE PUT OUT THE WORD.
NO.
I...
WHO HAD THE A LUNCH?
WHAT? WATER? HOLD ON.
WATCHING THE FLOOR.

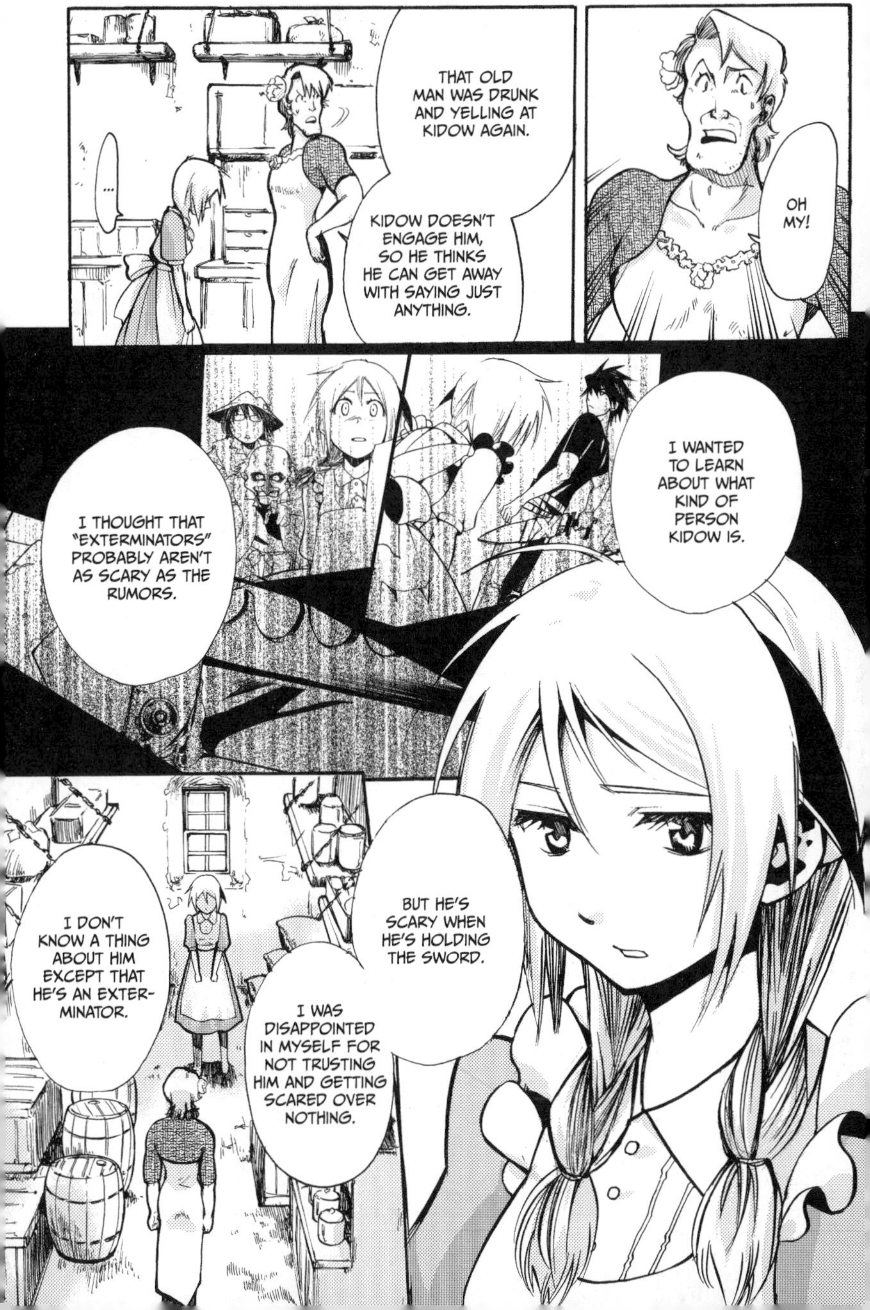
OH MY!
THAT OLD MAN WAS DRUNK AND YELLING AT KIDOW AGAIN.
...
KIDOW DOESN'T ENGAGE HIM, SO HE THINKS HE CAN GET AWAY WITH SAYING JUST ANYTHING.
I WANTED TO LEARN ABOUT WHAT KIND OF PERSON KIDOW IS.
I THOUGHT THAT "EXTERMINATORS" PROBABLY AREN'T AS SCARY AS THE RUMORS.
BUT HE'S SCARY WHEN HE'S HOLDING THE SWORD.
I WAS DISAPPOINTED IN MYSELF FOR NOT TRUSTING HIM AND GETTING SCARED OVER NOTHING.
I DON'T KNOW A THING ABOUT HIM EXCEPT THAT HE'S AN EXTER-MINATOR.

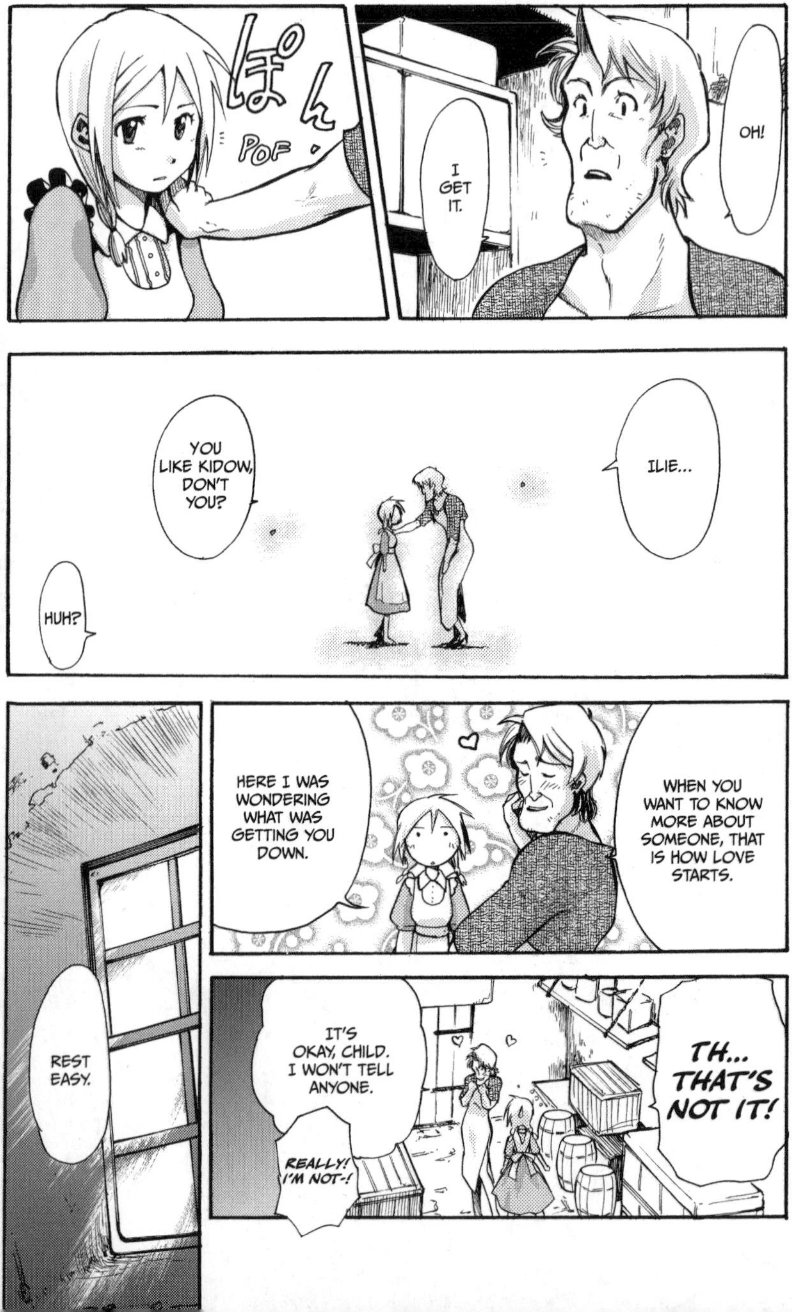
OH!
I GET IT.
ぽん
POF
ILIE...
YOU LIKE KIDOW, DON'T YOU?
HUH?
WHEN YOU WANT TO KNOW MORE ABOUT SOMEONE, THAT IS HOW LOVE STARTS.
HERE I WAS WONDERING WHAT WAS GETTING YOU DOWN.
TH... THAT'S NOT IT!
IT'S OKAY, CHILD. I WON'T TELL ANYONE.
REALLY! I'M NOT-!
REST EASY.

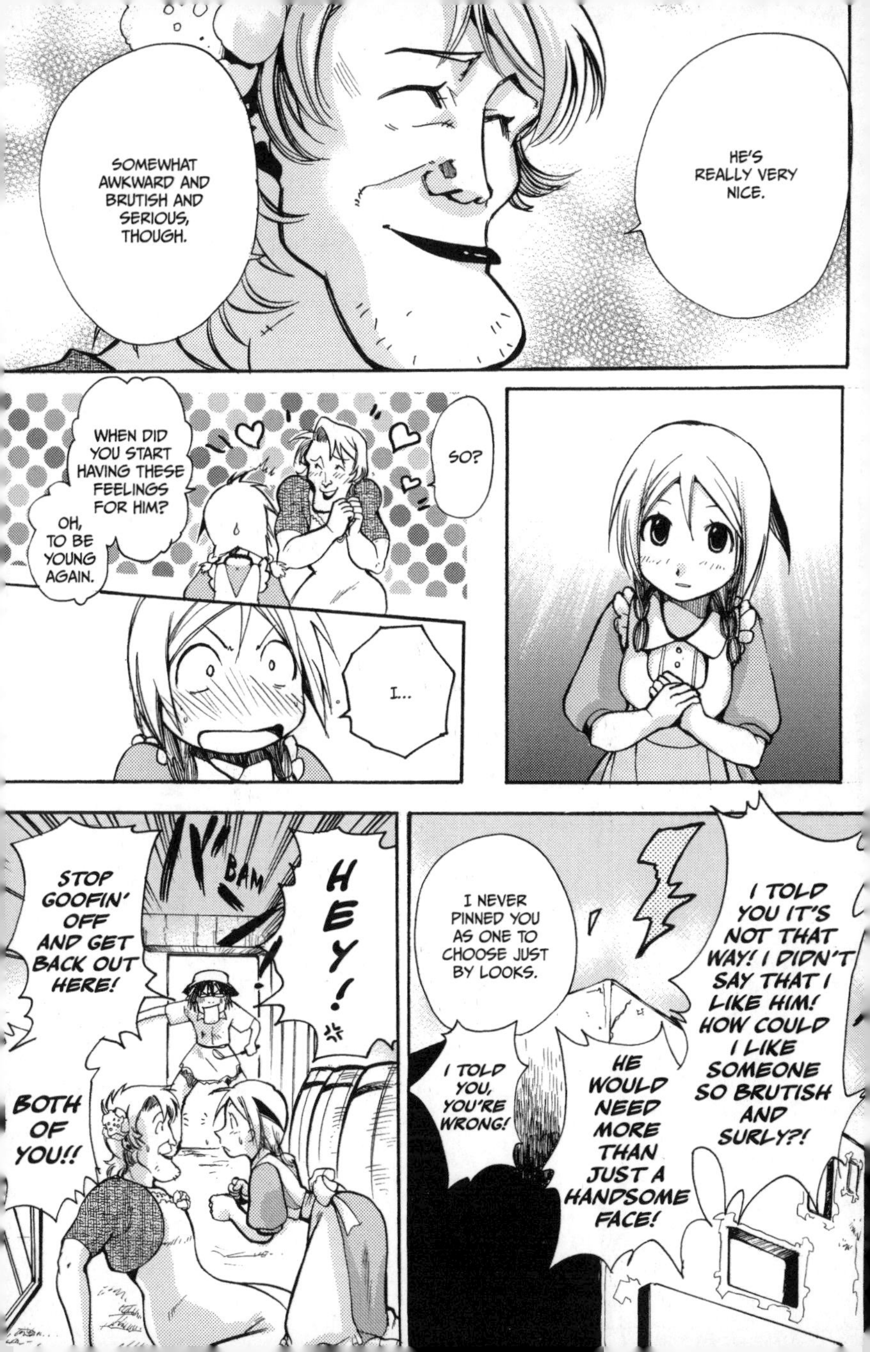
HE'S REALLY VERY NICE.
SOMEWHAT AWKWARD AND BRUTISH AND SERIOUS, THOUGH.
SO?
WHEN DID YOU START HAVING THESE FEELINGS FOR HIM?
OH, TO BE YOUNG AGAIN.
I...
I TOLD YOU IT'S NOT THAT WAY! I DIDN'T SAY THAT I LIKE HIM! HOW COULD I LIKE SOMEONE SO BRUTISH AND SURLY?!
I NEVER PINNED YOU AS ONE TO CHOOSE JUST BY LOOKS.
HE WOULD NEED MORE THAN JUST A HANDSOME FACE!
I TOLD YOU, YOU'RE WRONG!
HEY!
BAM
STOP GOOFIN' OFF AND GET BACK OUT HERE!
BOTH OF YOU!!

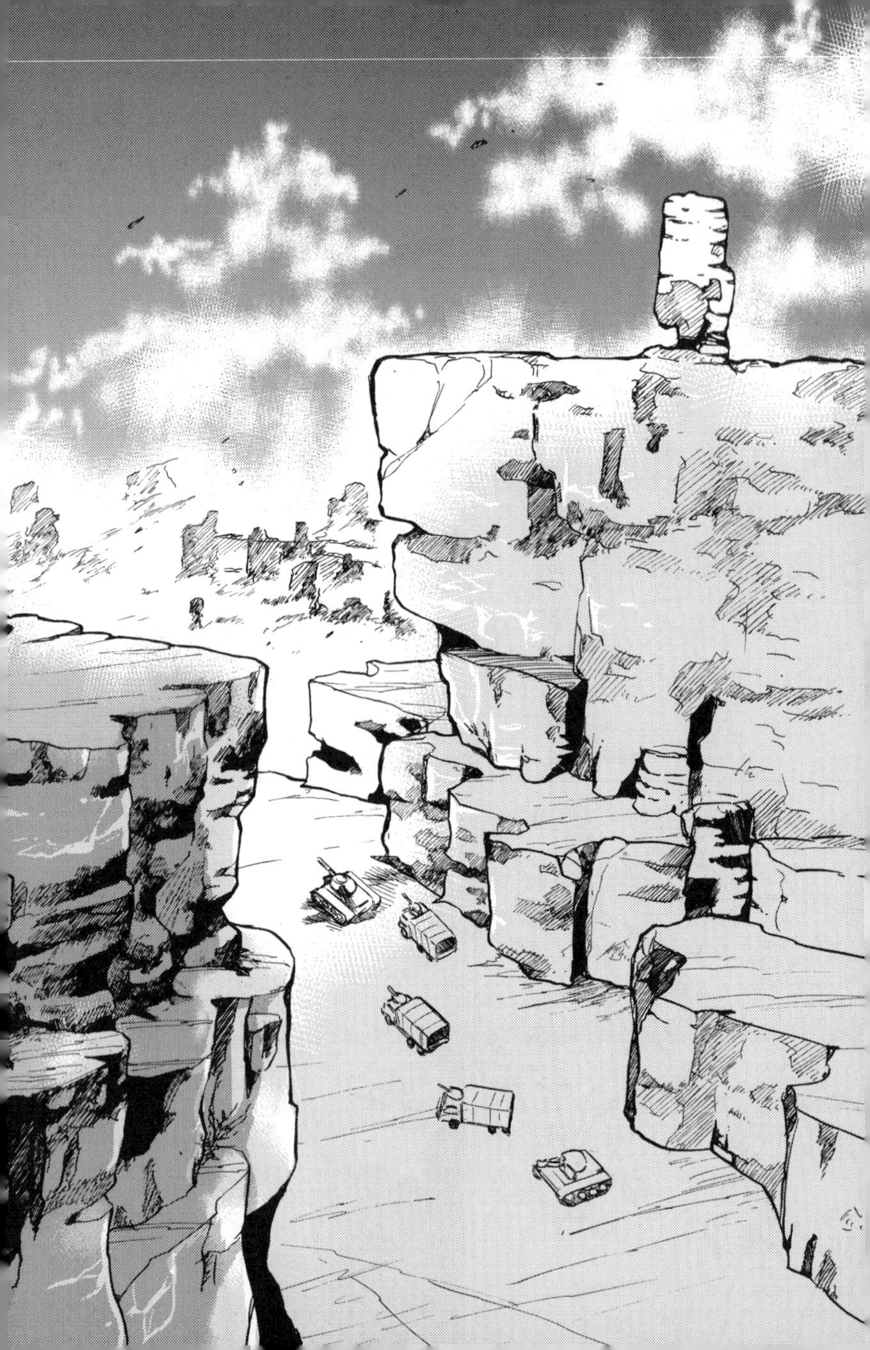

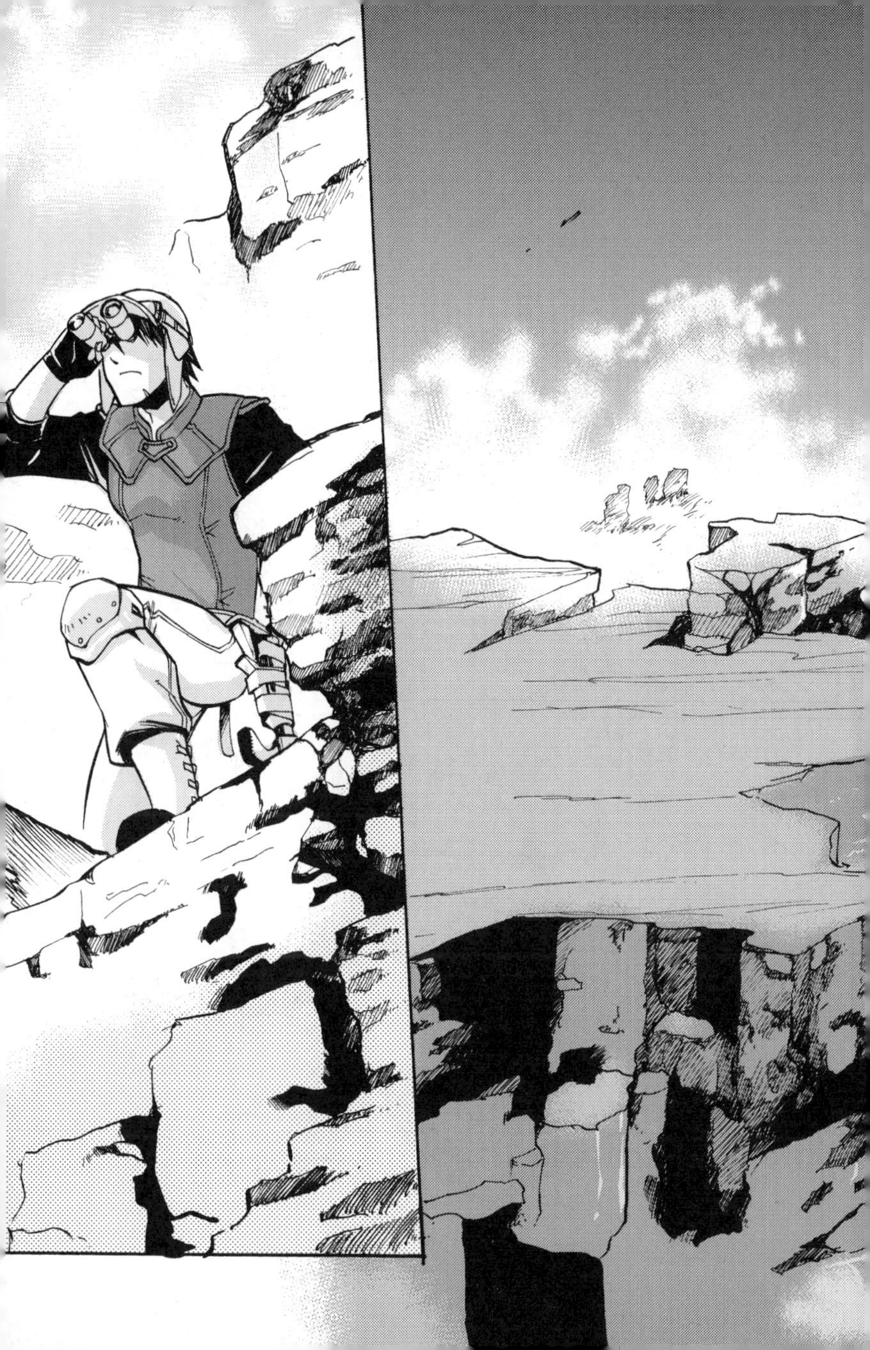

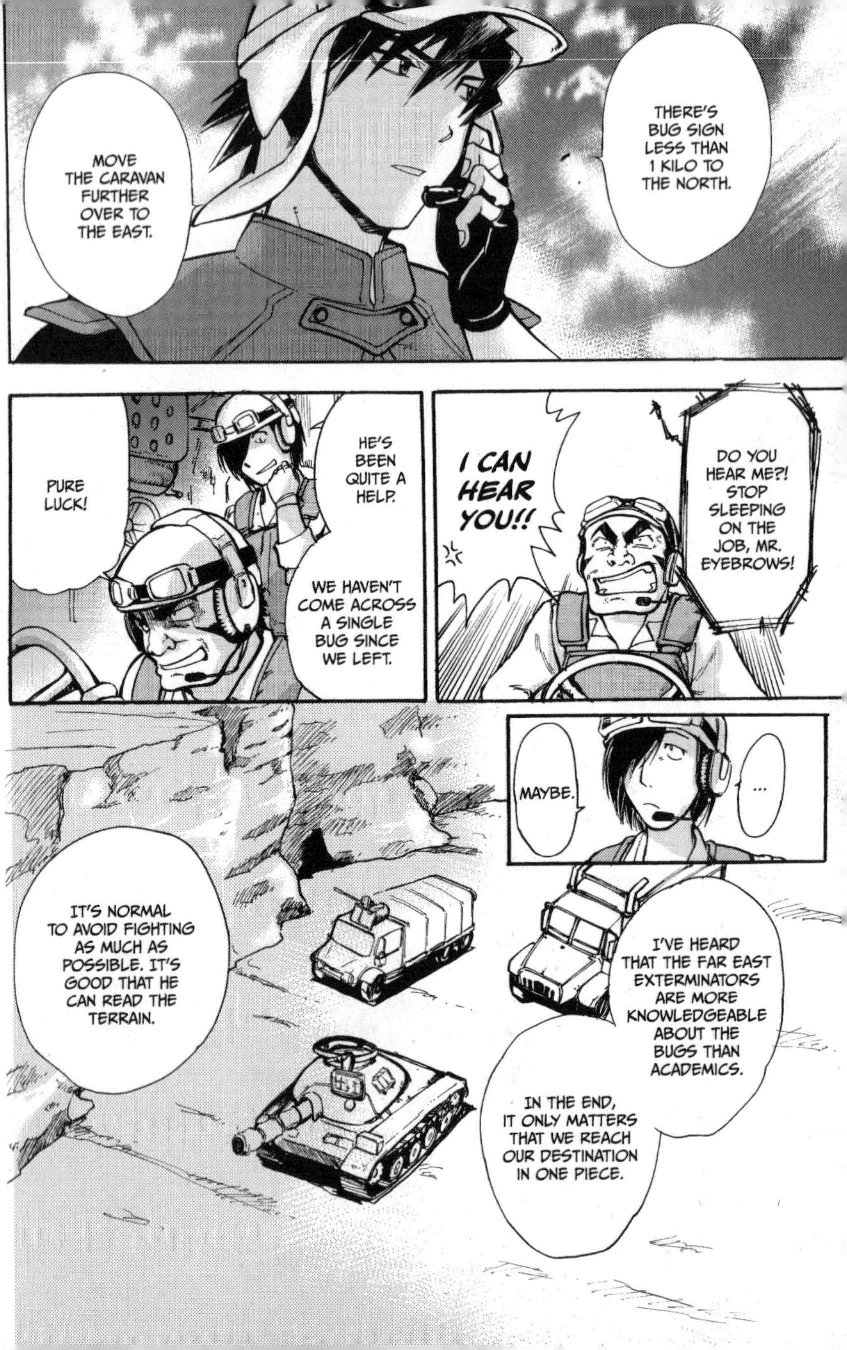
THERE'S BUG SIGN LESS THAN 1 KILO TO THE NORTH.
MOVE THE CARAVAN FURTHER OVER TO THE EAST.
DO YOU HEAR ME?! STOP SLEEPING ON THE JOB, MR. EYEBROWS!
I CAN HEAR YOU!!
HE'S BEEN QUITE A HELP.
WE HAVEN'T COME ACROSS A SINGLE BUG SINCE WE LEFT.
PURE LUCK!
...
MAYBE.
I'VE HEARD THAT THE FAR EAST EXTERMINATORS ARE MORE KNOWLEDGEABLE ABOUT THE BUGS THAN ACADEMICS.
IN THE END, IT ONLY MATTERS THAT WE REACH OUR DESTINATION IN ONE PIECE.
IT'S NORMAL TO AVOID FIGHTING AS MUCH AS POSSIBLE. IT'S GOOD THAT HE CAN READ THE TERRAIN.

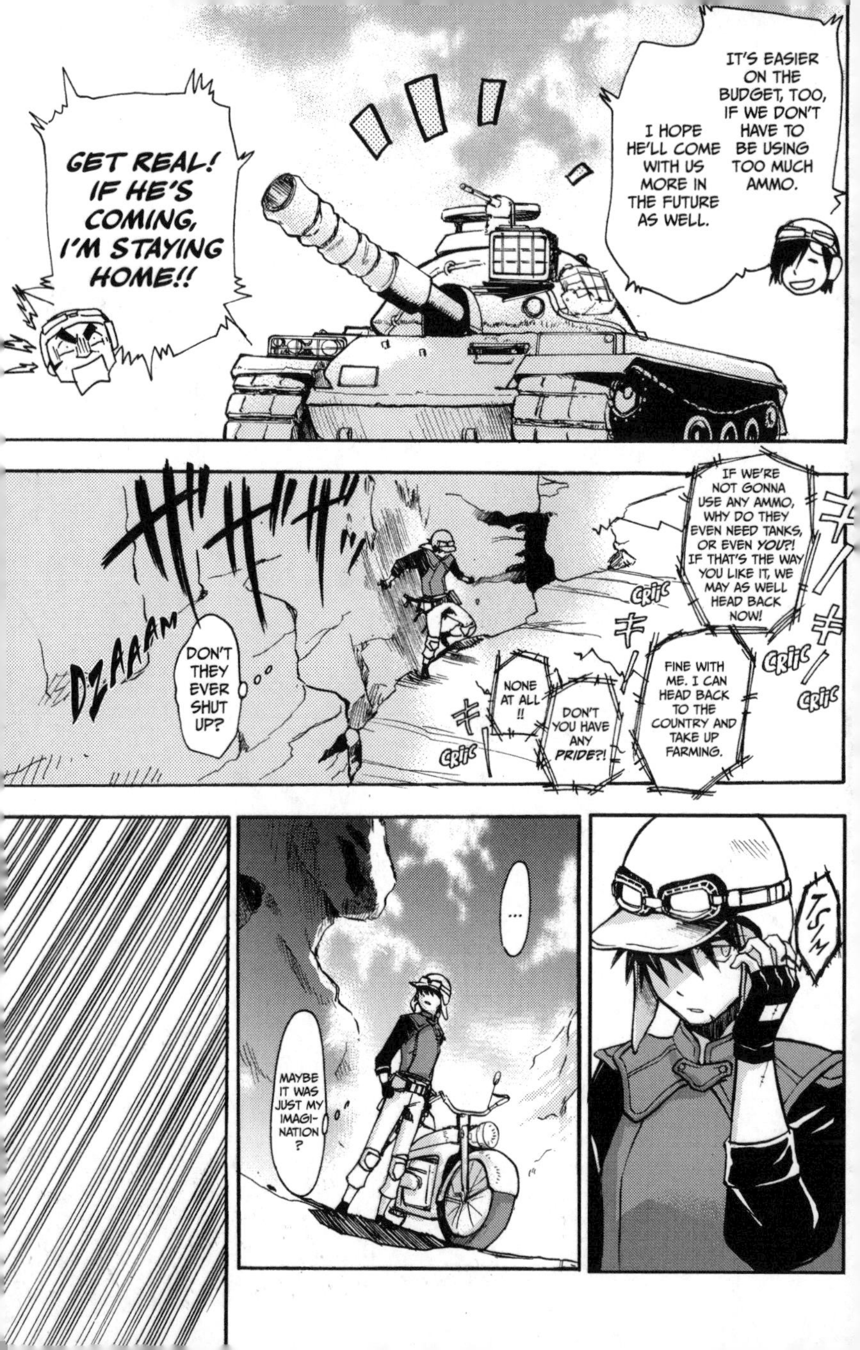
I HOPE HE'LL COME WITH US MORE IN THE FUTURE AS WELL.
IT'S EASIER ON THE BUDGET, TOO, IF WE DON'T HAVE TO BE USING TOO MUCH AMMO.
GET REAL! IF HE'S COMING, I'M STAYING HOME!!
IF WE'RE NOT GONNA USE ANY AMMO, WHY DO THEY EVEN NEED TANKS, OR EVEN YOU?! IF THAT'S THE WAY YOU LIKE IT, WE MAY AS WELL HEAD BACK NOW!
CRIIC
CRIIC
CRIIC
FINE WITH ME. I CAN HEAD BACK TO THE COUNTRY AND TAKE UP FARMING.
DON'T YOU HAVE ANY PRIDE?!
NONE AT ALL !!
CRIIC
DON'T THEY EVER SHUT UP?
DZAAAAM
TSIM
...
MAYBE IT WAS JUST MY IMAGI-NATION?

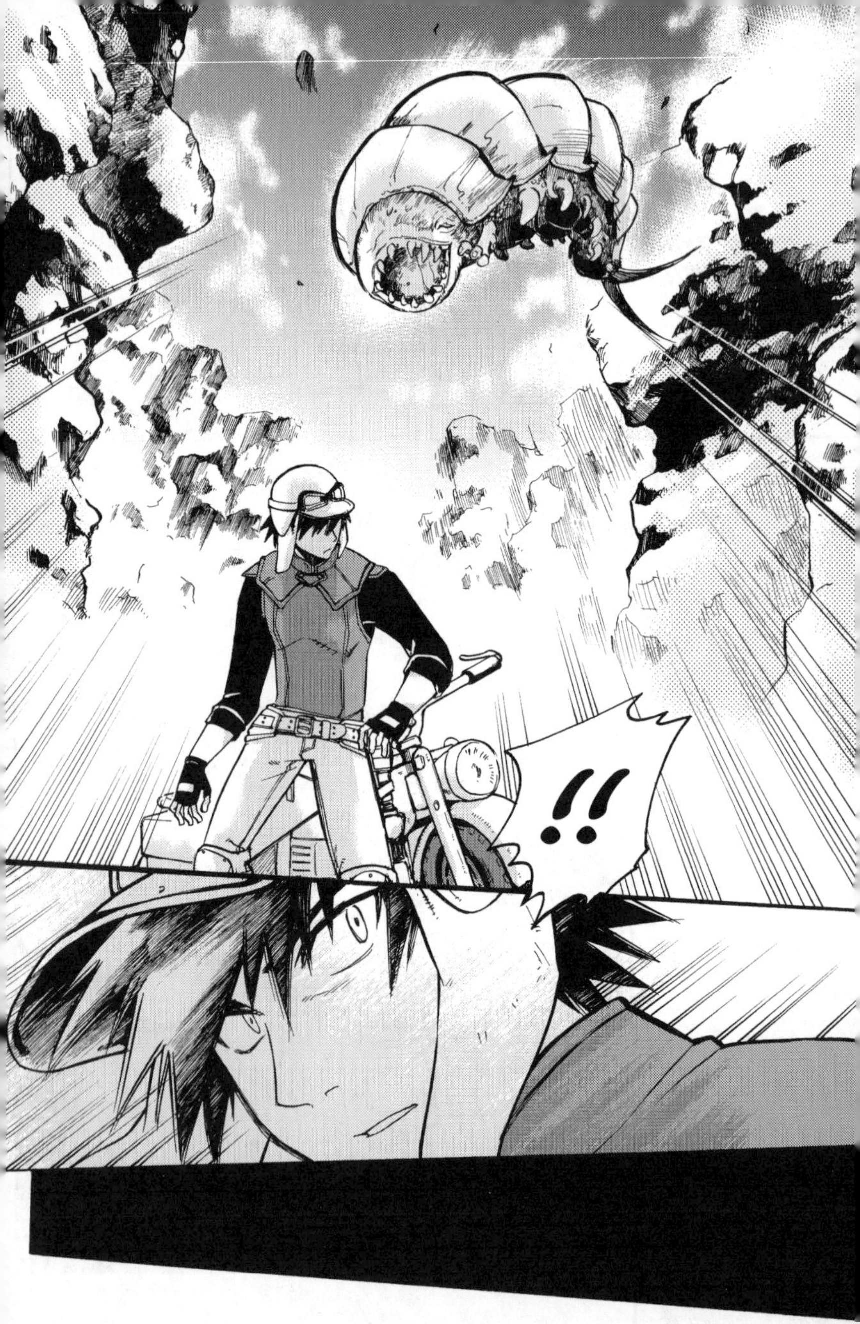
!!

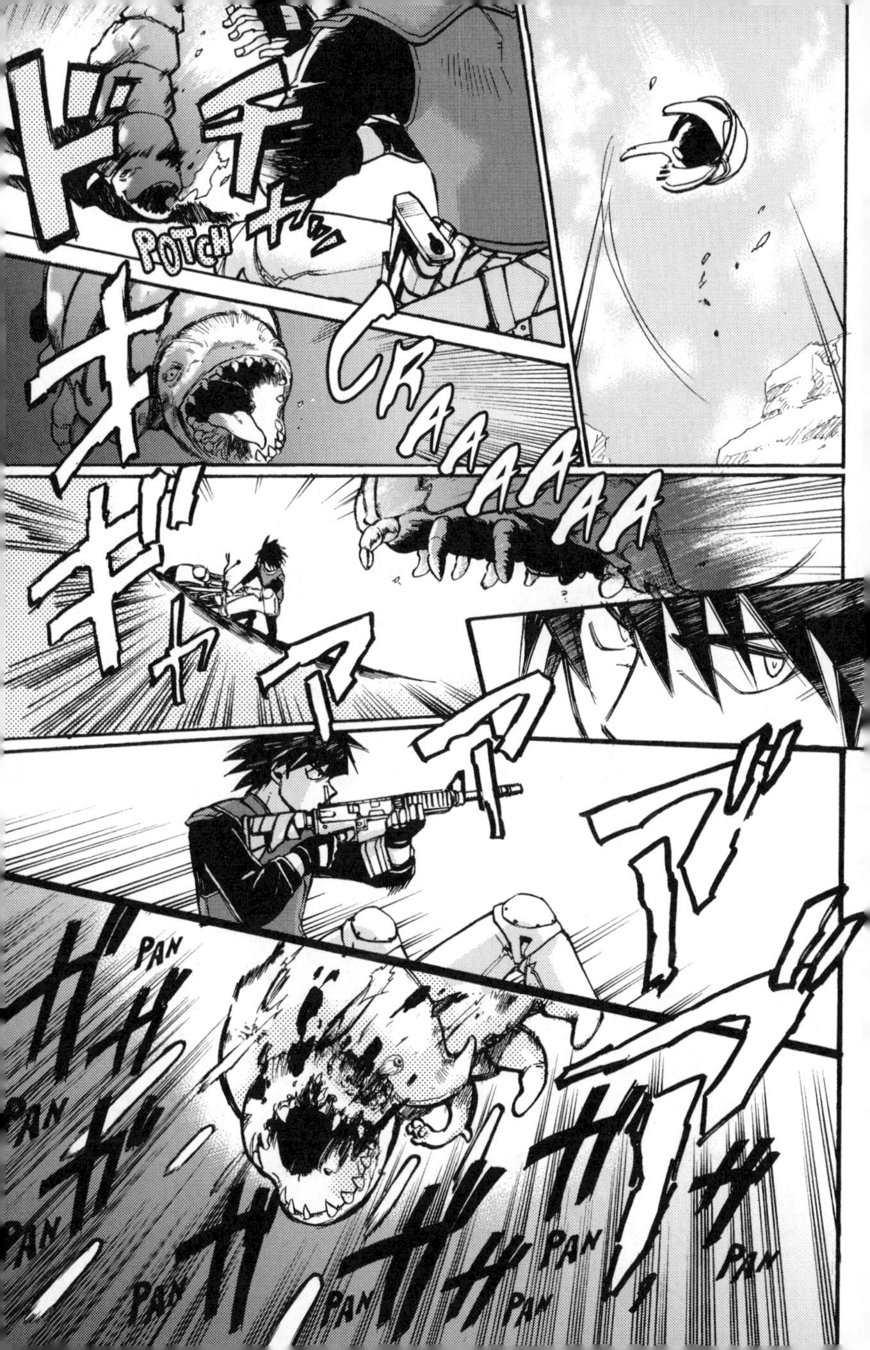
POTCH
CRAAAAAAAA
PAN
PAN
PAN
PAN
PAN
PAN
PAN
PAN

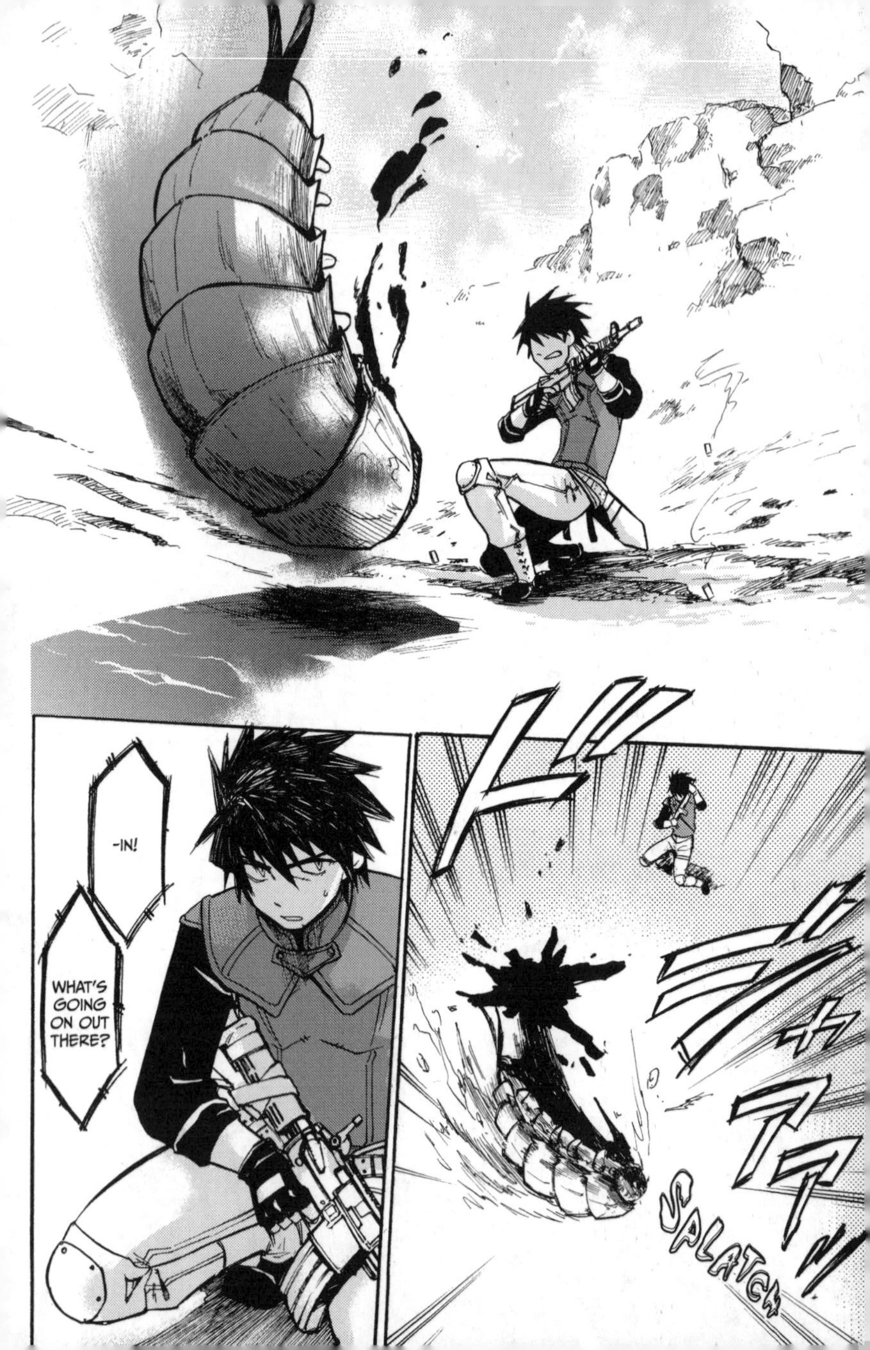
SPLATCH
-IN!
WHAT'S GOING ON OUT THERE?

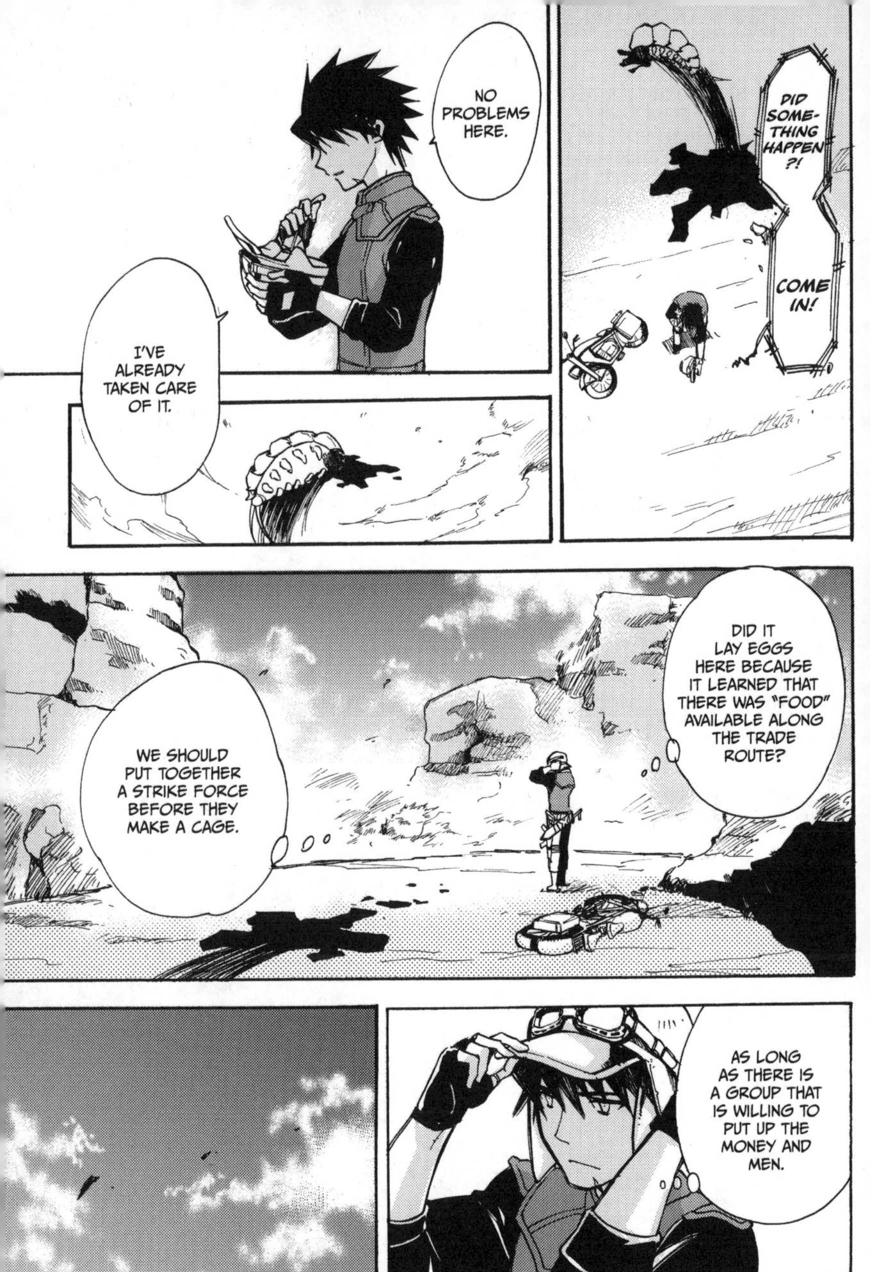
DID SOMETHING HAPPEN?!
COME IN!
NO PROBLEMS HERE.
I'VE ALREADY TAKEN CARE OF IT.
DID IT LAY EGGS HERE BECAUSE IT LEARNED THAT THERE WAS "FOOD" AVAILABLE ALONG THE TRADE ROUTE?
WE SHOULD PUT TOGETHER A STRIKE FORCE BEFORE THEY MAKE A CAGE.
AS LONG AS THERE IS A GROUP THAT IS WILLING TO PUT UP THE MONEY AND MEN.

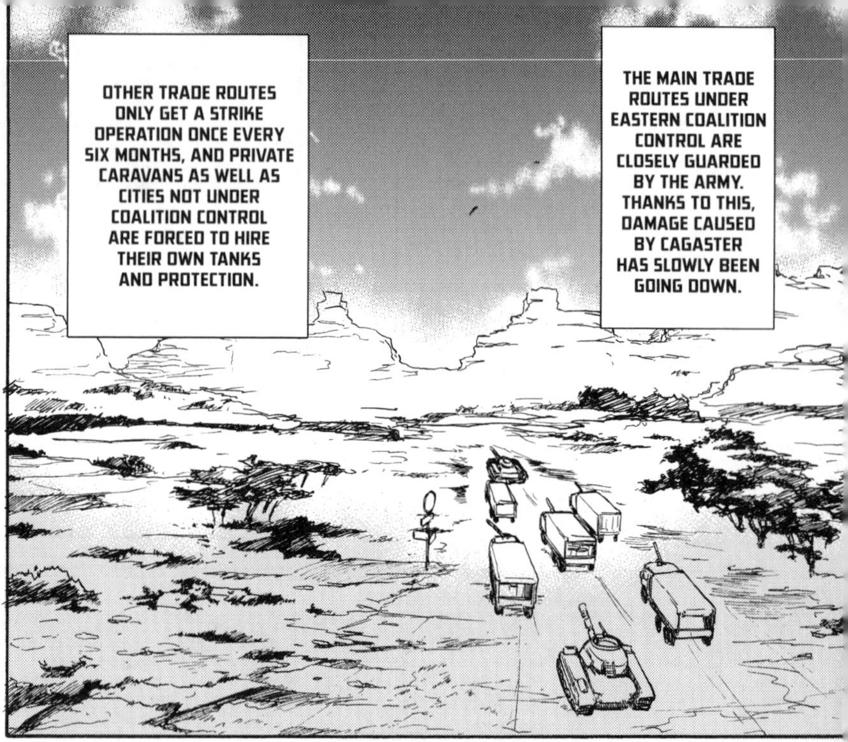
THE MAIN TRADE ROUTES UNDER EASTERN COALITION CONTROL ARE CLOSELY GUARDED BY THE ARMY. THANKS TO THIS, DAMAGE CAUSED BY CAGASTER HAS SLOWLY BEEN GOING DOWN.
OTHER TRADE ROUTES ONLY GET A STRIKE OPERATION ONCE EVERY SIX MONTHS, AND PRIVATE CARAVANS AS WELL AS CITIES NOT UNDER COALITION CONTROL ARE FORCED TO HIRE THEIR OWN TANKS AND PROTECTION.
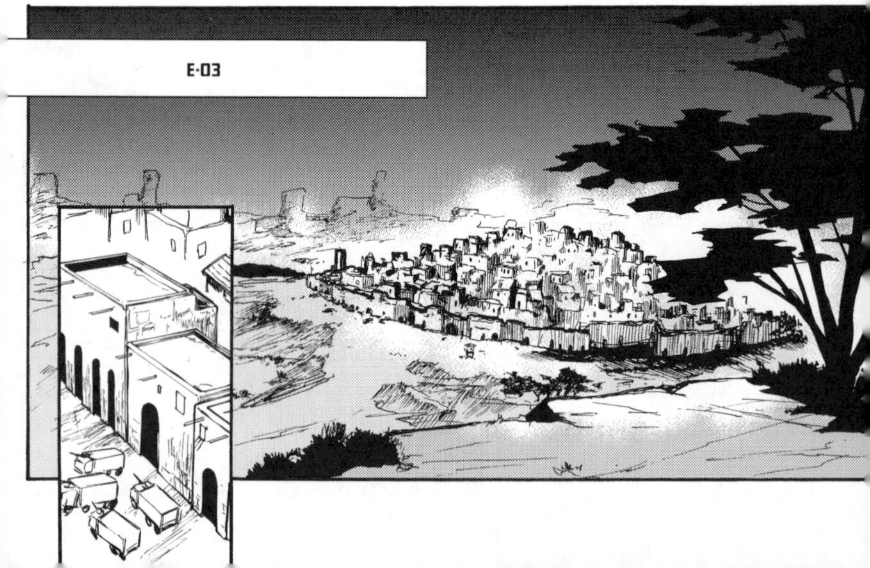
E-03

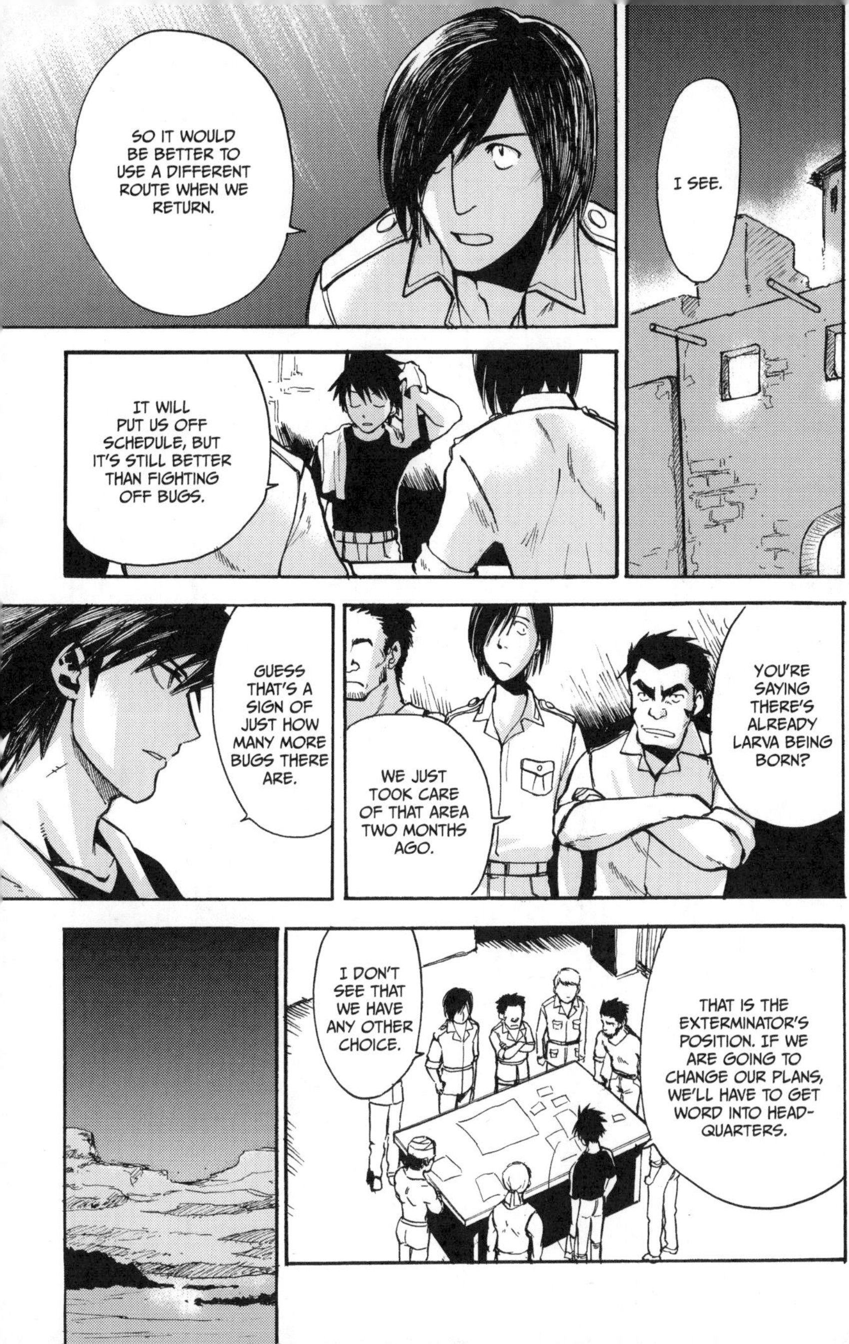
I SEE.
SO IT WOULD BE BETTER TO USE A DIFFERENT ROUTE WHEN WE RETURN.
IT WILL PUT US OFF SCHEDULE, BUT IT'S STILL BETTER THAN FIGHTING OFF BUGS.
YOU'RE SAYING THERE'S ALREADY LARVA BEING BORN?
WE JUST TOOK CARE OF THAT AREA TWO MONTHS AGO.
GUESS THAT'S A SIGN OF JUST HOW MANY MORE BUGS THERE ARE.
THAT IS THE EXTERMINATOR'S POSITION. IF WE ARE GOING TO CHANGE OUR PLANS, WE'LL HAVE TO GET WORD INTO HEAD-QUARTERS.
I DON'T SEE THAT WE HAVE ANY OTHER CHOICE.

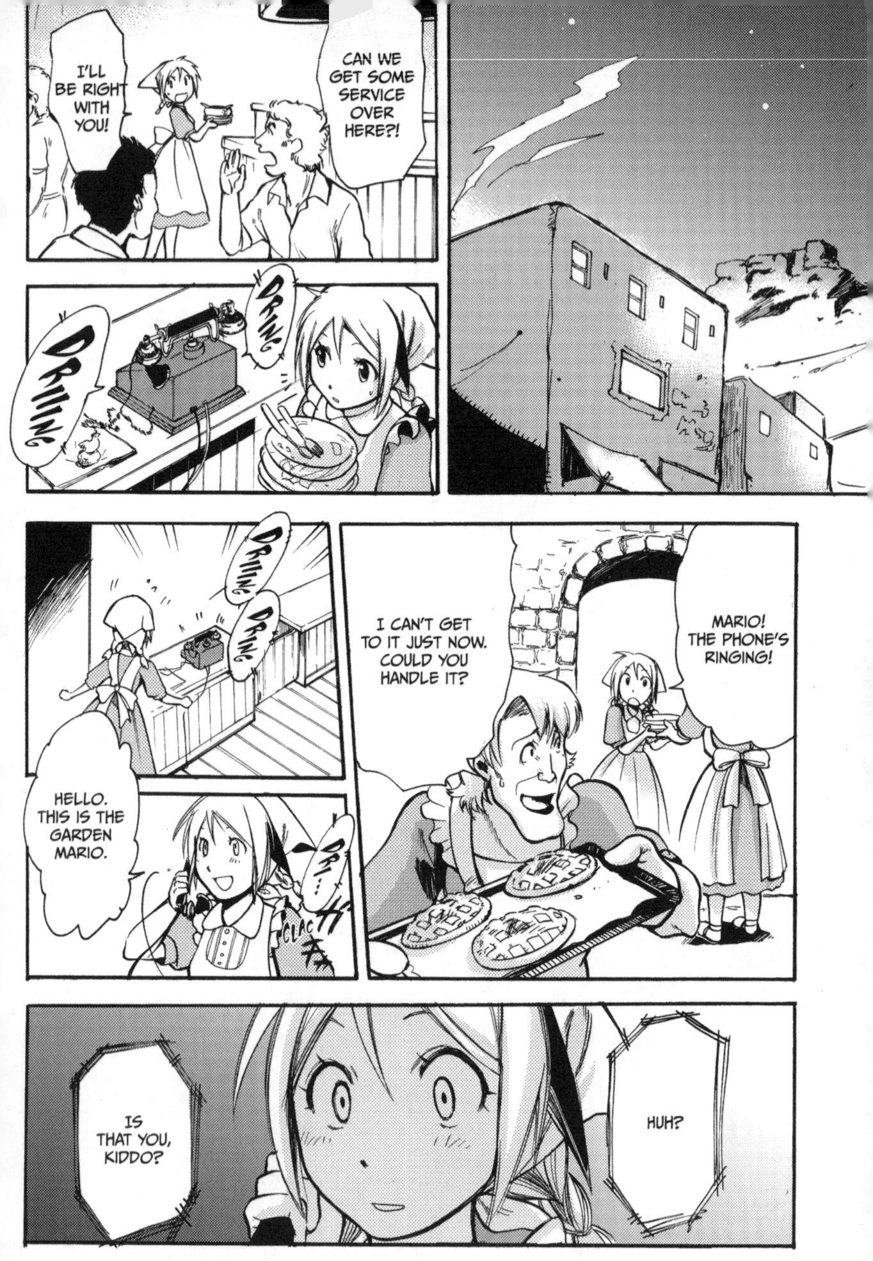
CAN WE GET SOME SERVICE OVER HERE?!
I'LL BE RIGHT WITH YOU!
DRING
DRIIIING
MARIO! THE PHONE'S RINGING!
I CAN'T GET TO IT JUST NOW. COULD YOU HANDLE IT?
DRIIIING
DRING
DRI...
CLAC
HELLO. THIS IS THE GARDEN MARIO.
HUH?
IS THAT YOU, KIDDO?

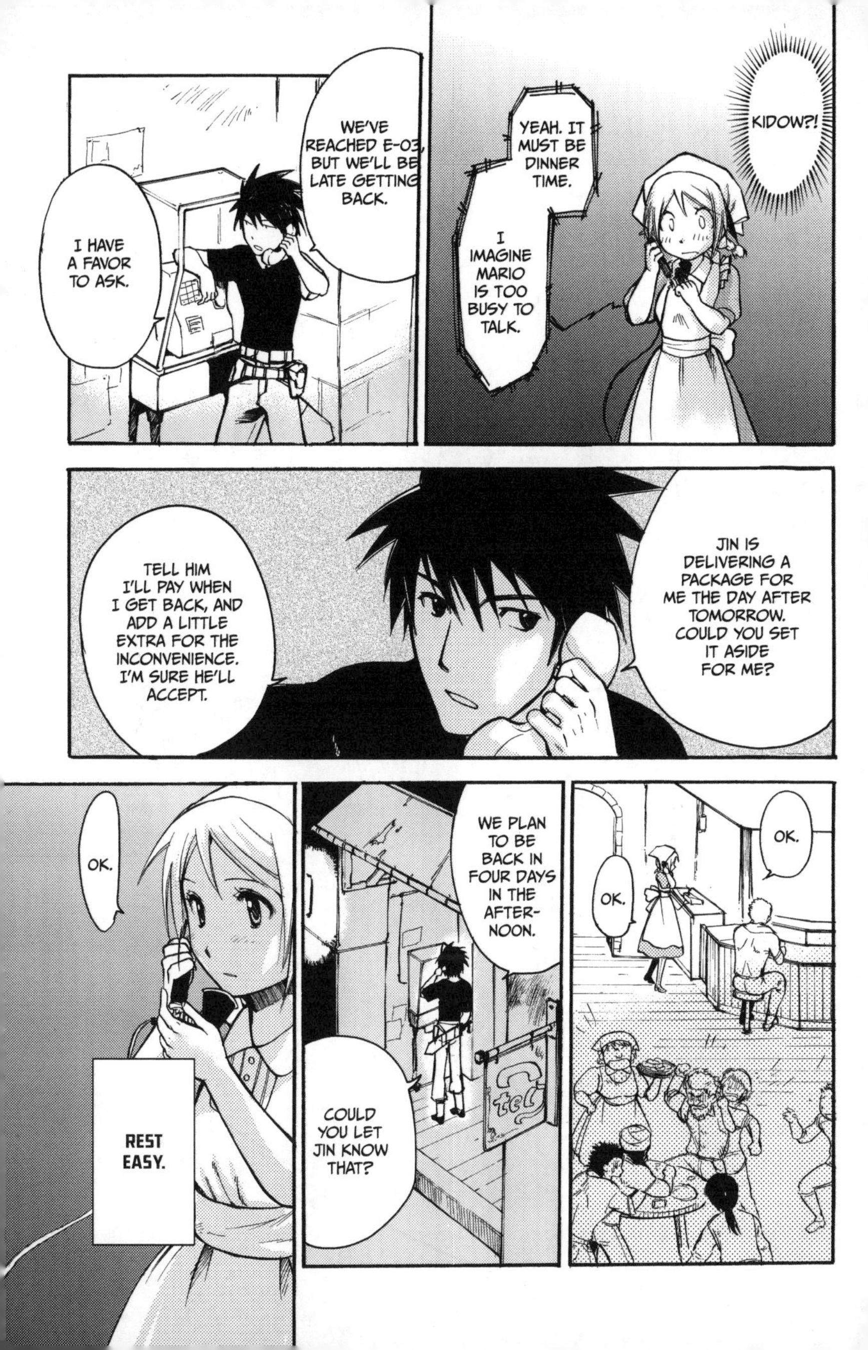
KIDOW?!
YEAH. IT MUST BE DINNER TIME.
I IMAGINE MARIO IS TOO BUSY TO TALK.
WE'VE REACHED E-03, BUT WE'LL BE LATE GETTING BACK.
I HAVE A FAVOR TO ASK.
JIN IS DELIVERING A PACKAGE FOR ME THE DAY AFTER TOMORROW. COULD YOU SET IT ASIDE FOR ME?
TELL HIM I'LL PAY WHEN I GET BACK, AND ADD A LITTLE EXTRA FOR THE INCONVENIENCE. I'M SURE HE'LL ACCEPT.
OK.
OK.
WE PLAN TO BE BACK IN FOUR DAYS IN THE AFTER-NOON.
COULD YOU LET JIN KNOW THAT?
OK.
REST EASY.

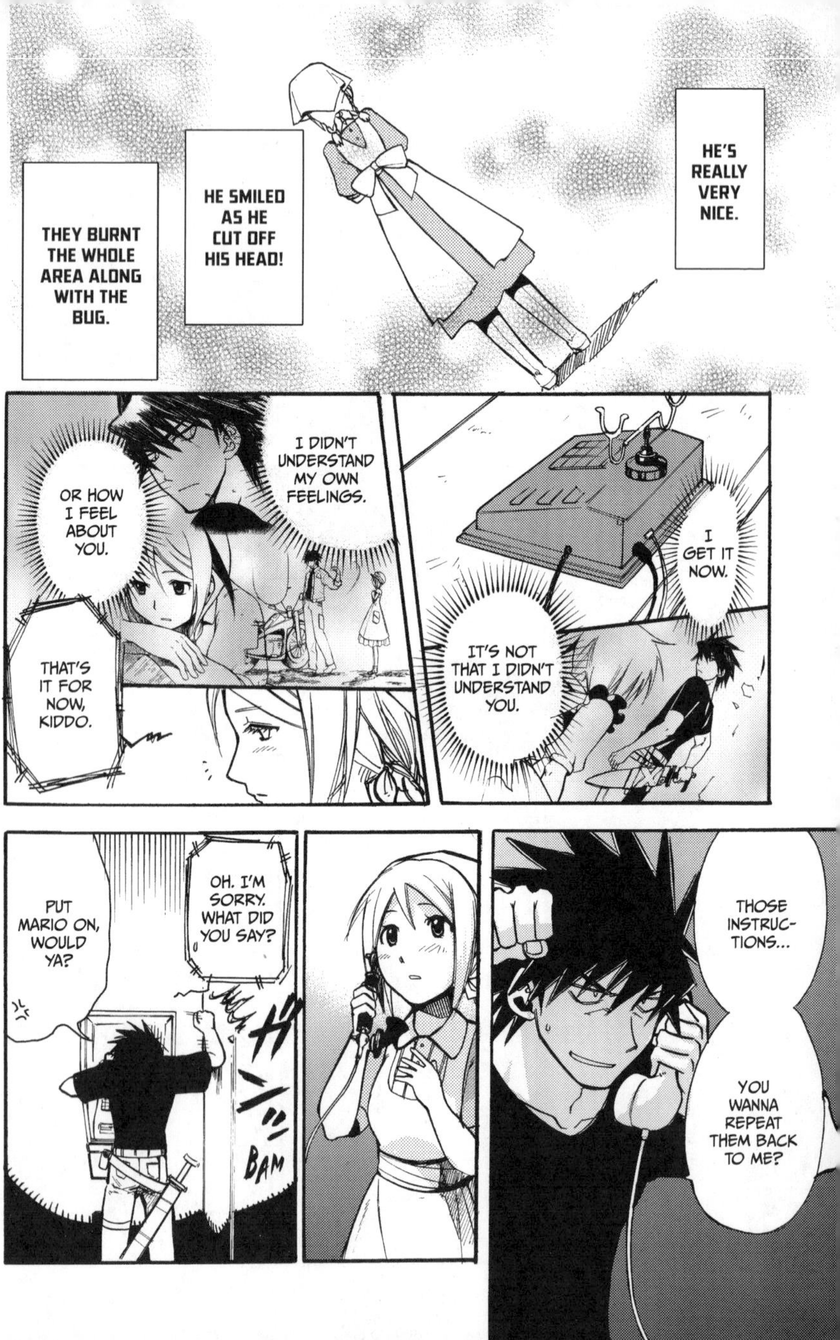

HE'S REALLY VERY NICE.
HE SMILED AS HE CUT OFF HIS HEAD!
THEY BURNT THE WHOLE AREA ALONG WITH THE BUG.
I GET IT NOW.
IT'S NOT THAT I DIDN'T UNDERSTAND YOU.
I DIDN'T UNDERSTAND MY OWN FEELINGS.
OR HOW I FEEL ABOUT YOU.
THAT'S IT FOR NOW, KIDDO.
THOSE INSTRUC-TIONS...
YOU WANNA REPEAT THEM BACK TO ME?
OH. I'M SORRY. WHAT DID YOU SAY?
PUT MARIO ON, WOULD YA?
BAM

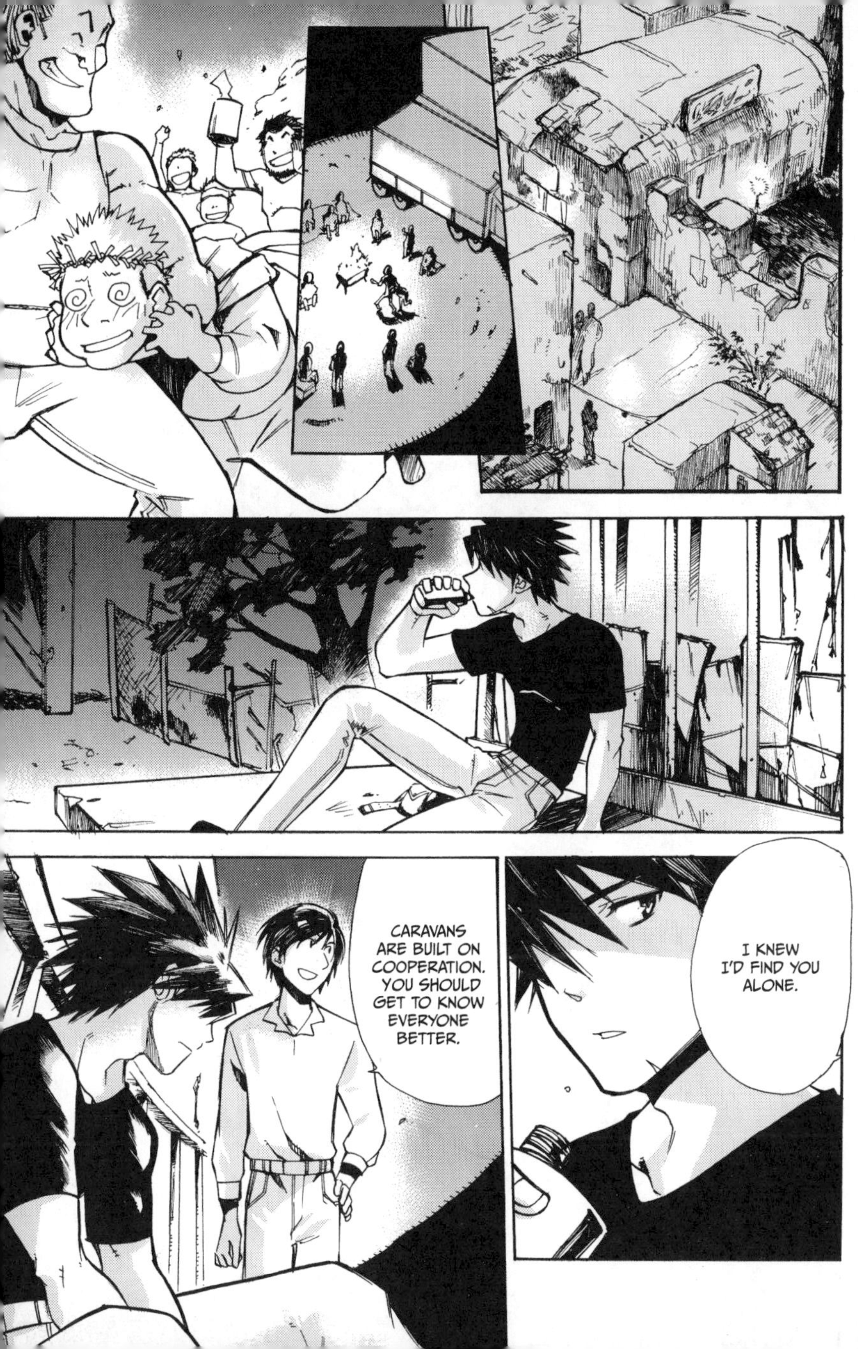
I KNEW I'D FIND YOU ALONE.
CARAVANS ARE BUILT ON COOPERATION. YOU SHOULD GET TO KNOW EVERYONE BETTER.

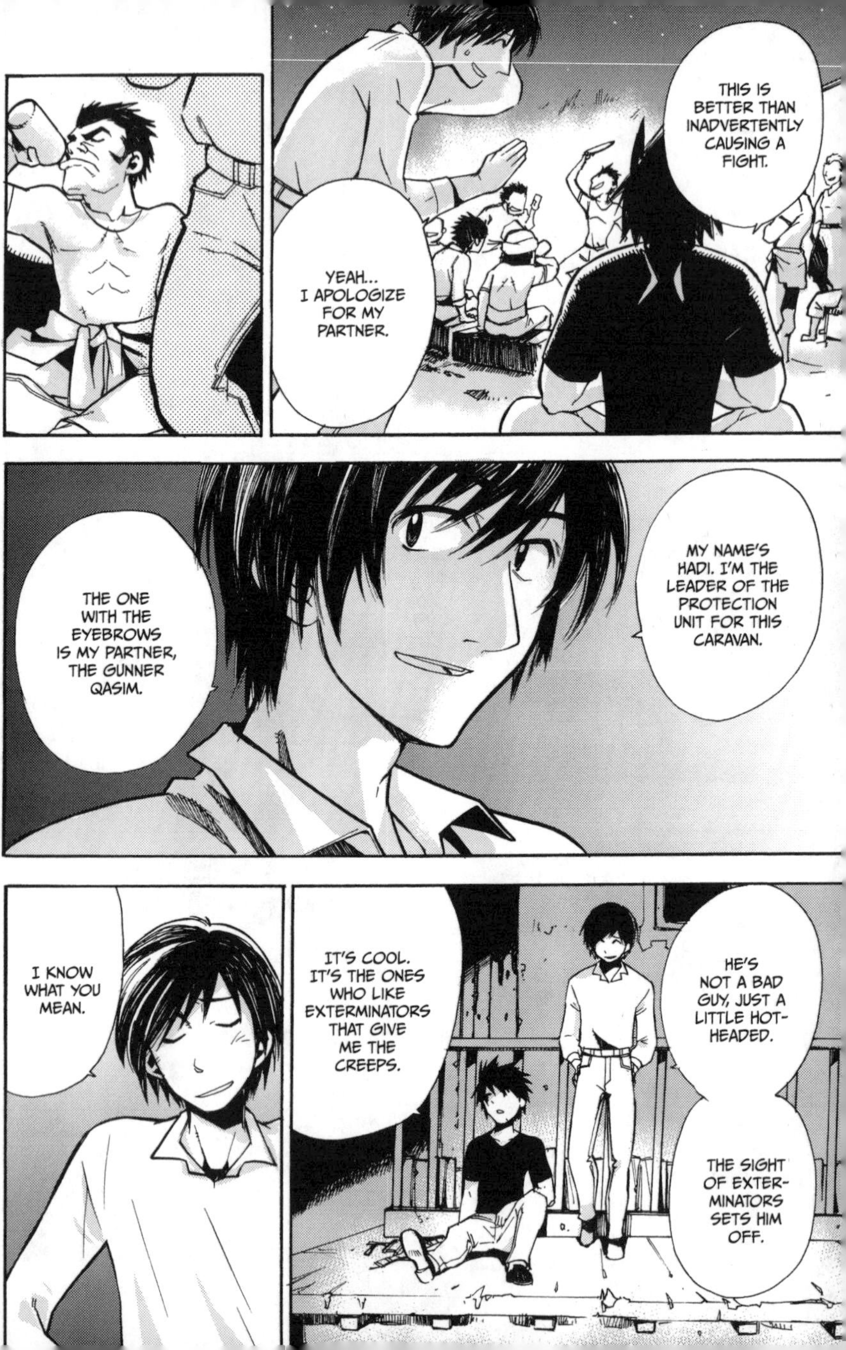

THIS IS BETTER THAN INADVERTENTLY CAUSING A FIGHT.
YEAH... I APOLOGIZE FOR MY PARTNER.
MY NAME'S HADI. I'M THE LEADER OF THE PROTECTION UNIT FOR THIS CARAVAN.
THE ONE WITH THE EYEBROWS IS MY PARTNER, THE GUNNER QASIM.
HE'S NOT A BAD GUY, JUST A LITTLE HOT-HEADED.
THE SIGHT OF EXTER-MINATORS SETS HIM OFF.
IT'S COOL. IT'S THE ONES WHO LIKE EXTERMINATORS THAT GIVE ME THE CREEPS.
I KNOW WHAT YOU MEAN.

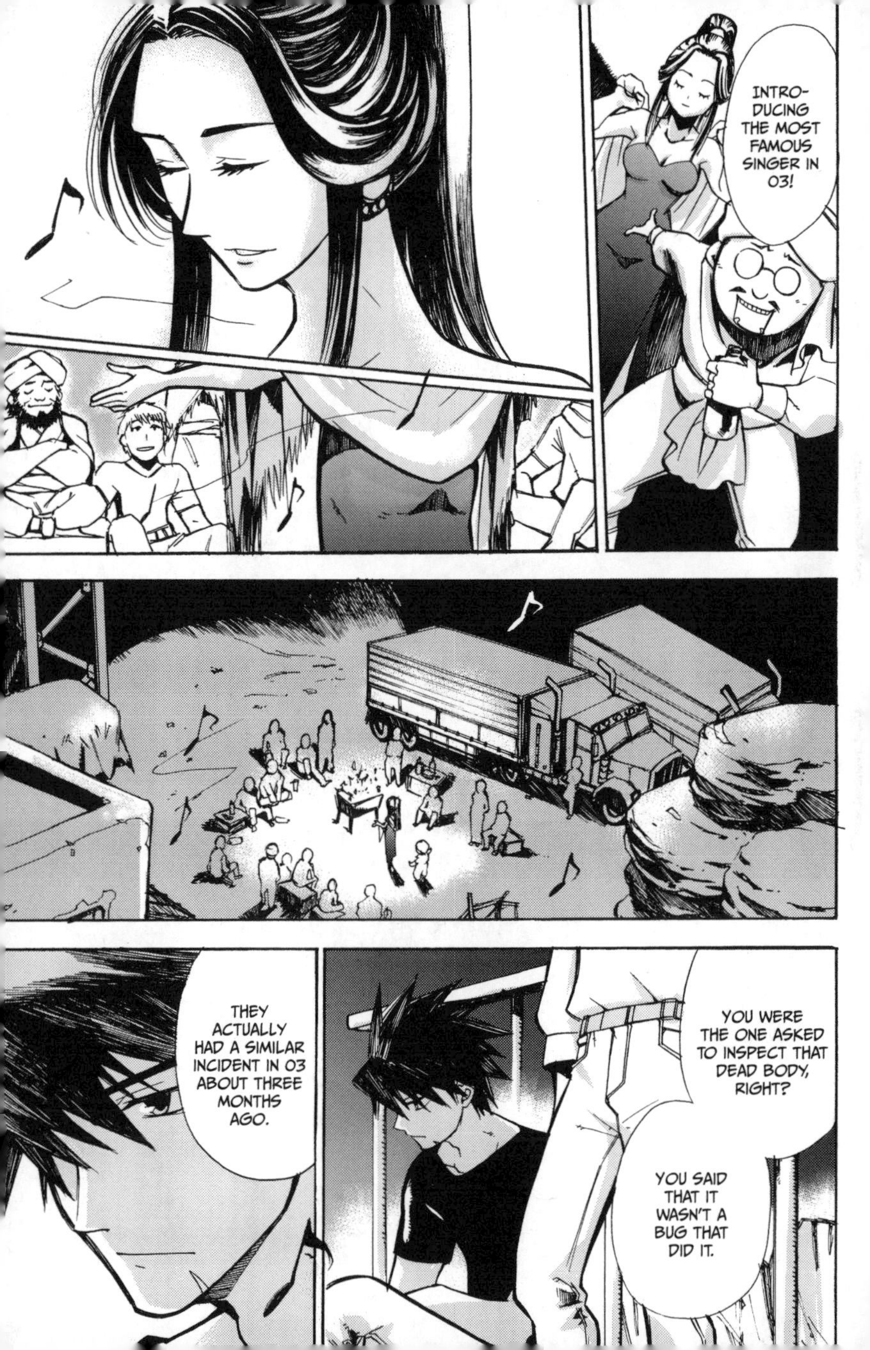
INTRO-DUCING THE MOST FAMOUS SINGER IN 03!
YOU WERE THE ONE ASKED TO INSPECT THAT DEAD BODY, RIGHT?
YOU SAID THAT IT WASN'T A BUG THAT DID IT.
THEY ACTUALLY HAD A SIMILAR INCIDENT IN 03 ABOUT THREE MONTHS AGO.

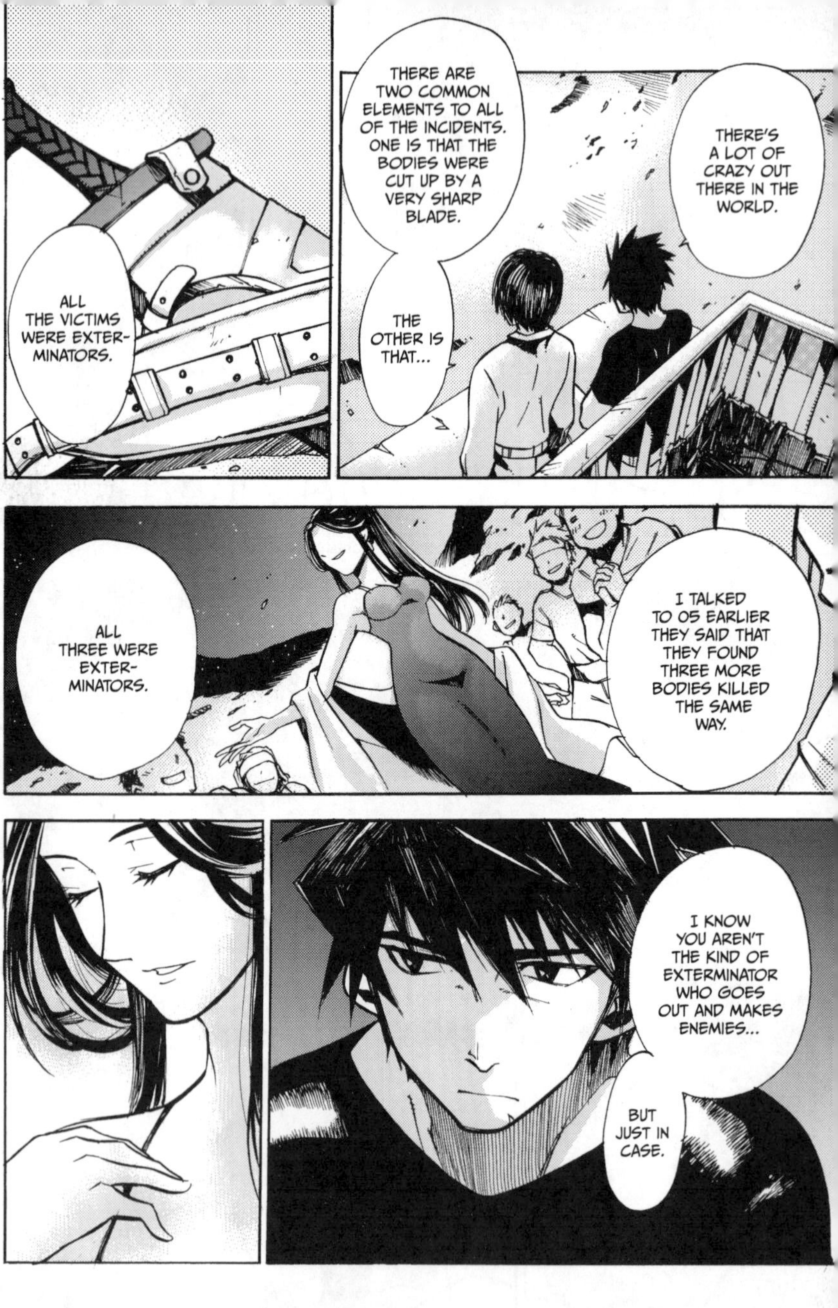
THERE'S A LOT OF CRAZY OUT THERE IN THE WORLD.
THERE ARE TWO COMMON ELEMENTS TO ALL OF THE INCIDENTS. ONE IS THAT THE BODIES WERE CUT UP BY A VERY SHARP BLADE.
THE OTHER IS THAT...
ALL THE VICTIMS WERE EXTER- MINATORS.
I TALKED TO 05 EARLIER THEY SAID THAT THEY FOUND THREE MORE BODIES KILLED THE SAME WAY.
ALL THREE WERE EXTER- MINATORS.
I KNOW YOU AREN'T THE KIND OF EXTERMINATOR WHO GOES OUT AND MAKES ENEMIES...
BUT JUST IN CASE.

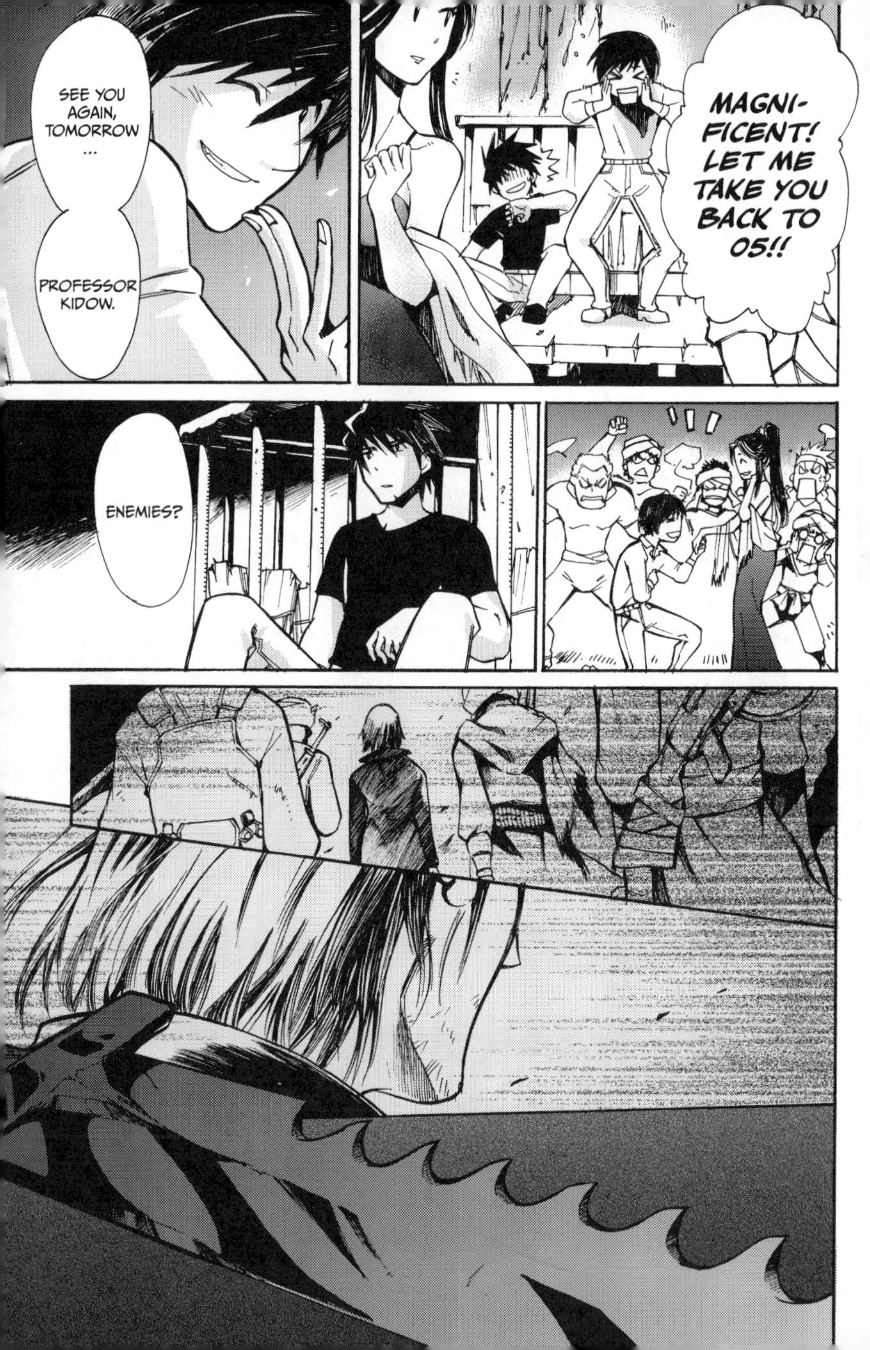
MAGNI-FICENT! LET ME TAKE YOU BACK TO 05!!
SEE YOU AGAIN, TOMORROW ...
PROFESSOR KIDOW.
ENEMIES?

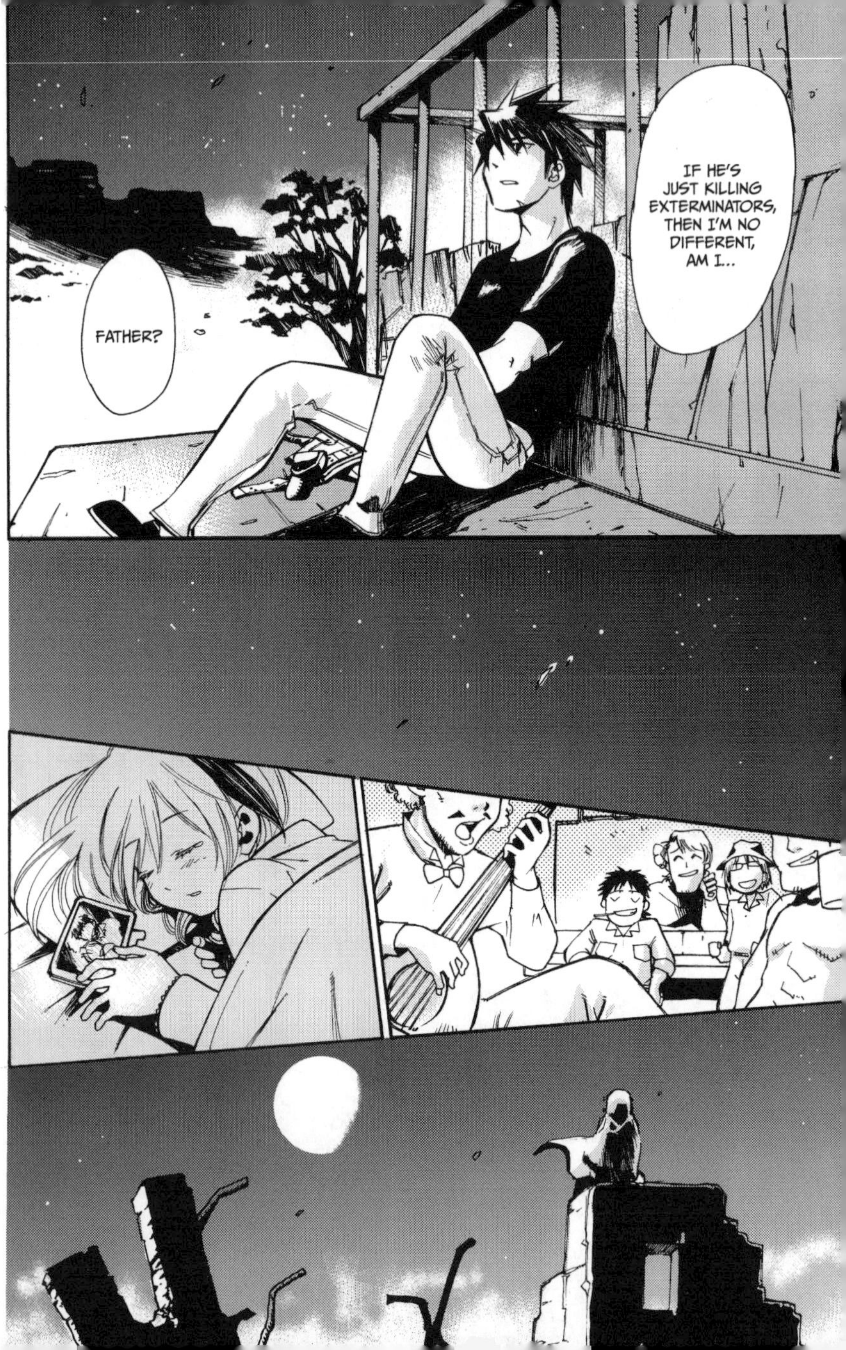
IF HE'S JUST KILLING EXTERMINATORS, THEN I'M NO DIFFERENT, AM I...
FATHER?

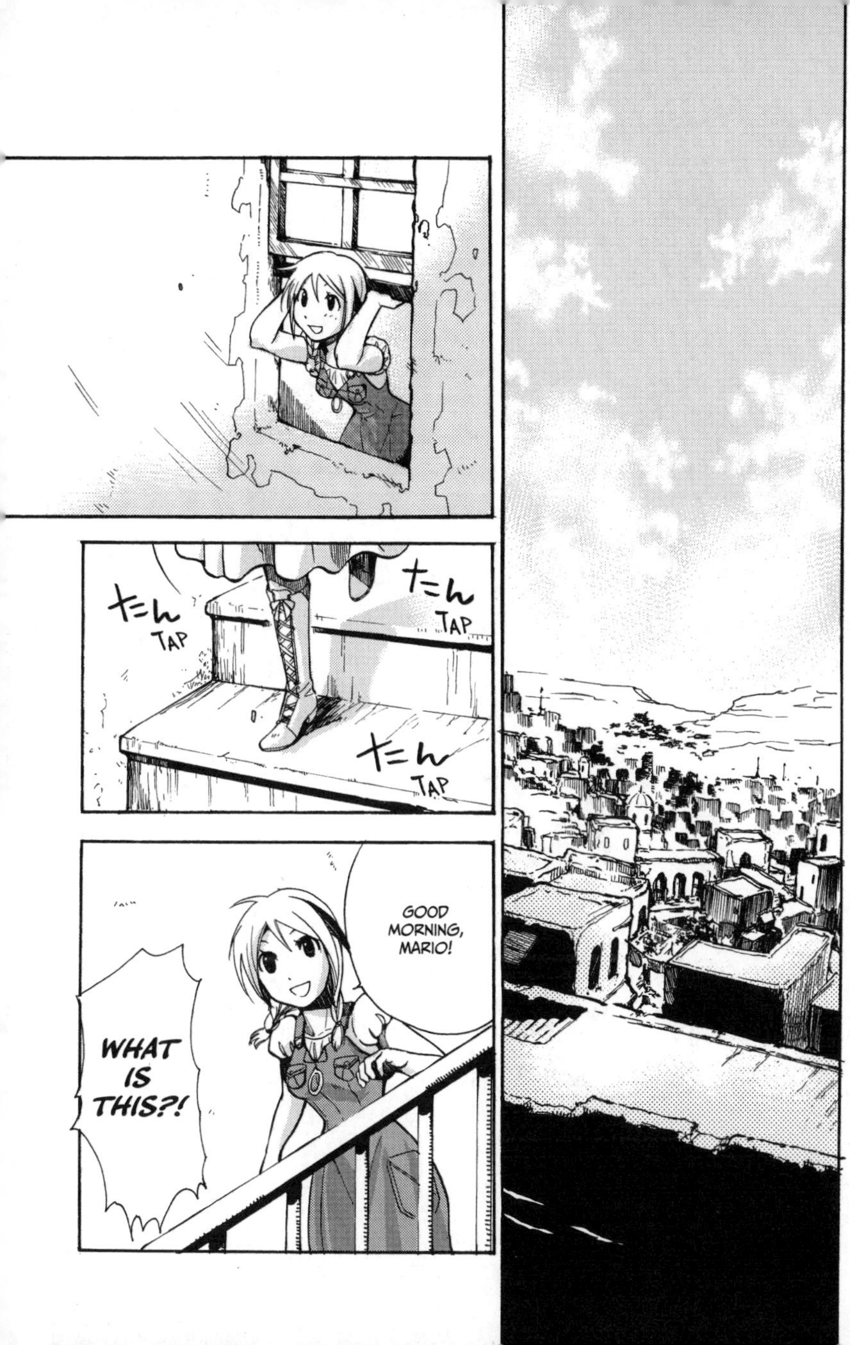
たん TAP
たん TAP
たん TAP
GOOD MORNING, MARIO!
WHAT IS THIS?!

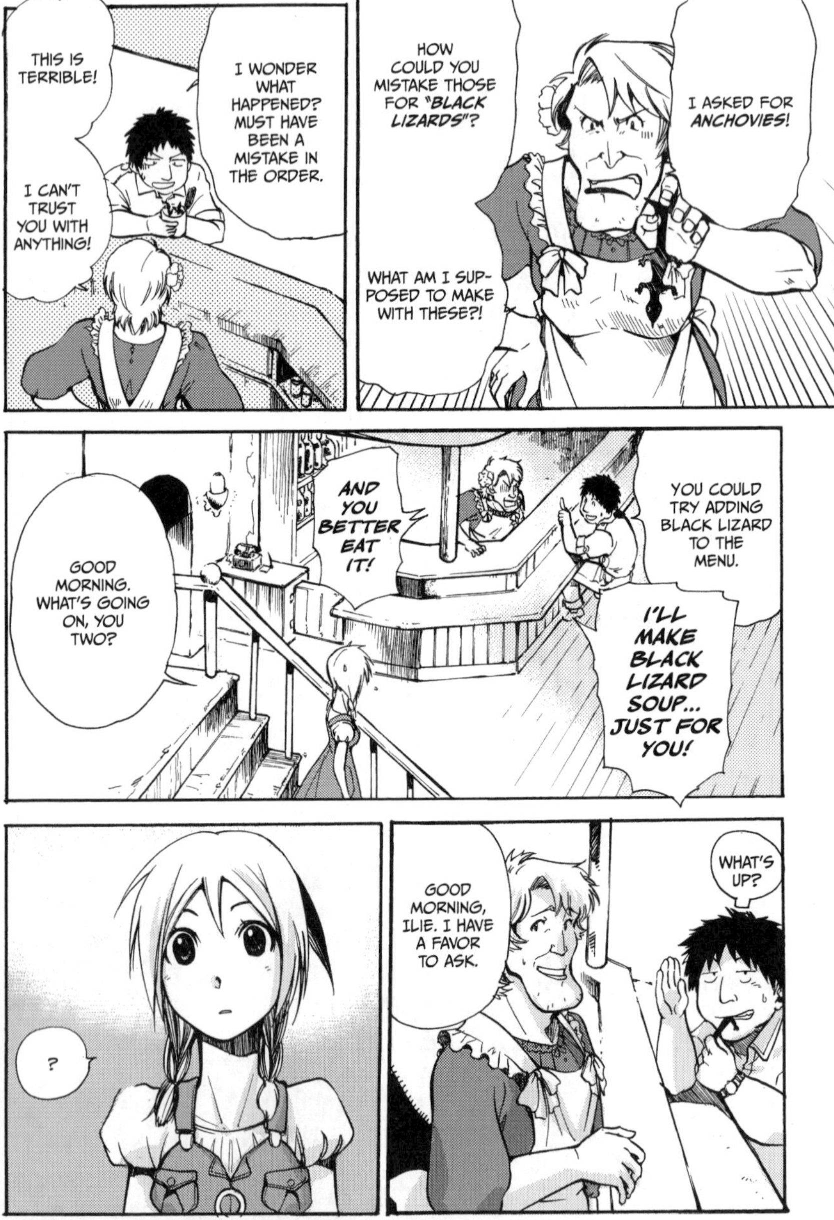
I ASKED FOR ANCHOVIES!
HOW COULD YOU MISTAKE THOSE FOR "BLACK LIZARDS"?
WHAT AM I SUP-POSED TO MAKE WITH THESE?!
I WONDER WHAT HAPPENED? MUST HAVE BEEN A MISTAKE IN THE ORDER.
THIS IS TERRIBLE!
I CAN'T TRUST YOU WITH ANYTHING!
YOU COULD TRY ADDING BLACK LIZARD TO THE MENU.
I'LL MAKE BLACK LIZARD SOUP... JUST FOR YOU!
AND YOU BETTER EAT IT!
GOOD MORNING. WHAT'S GOING ON, YOU TWO?
WHAT'S UP?
GOOD MORNING, ILIE. I HAVE A FAVOR TO ASK.
?

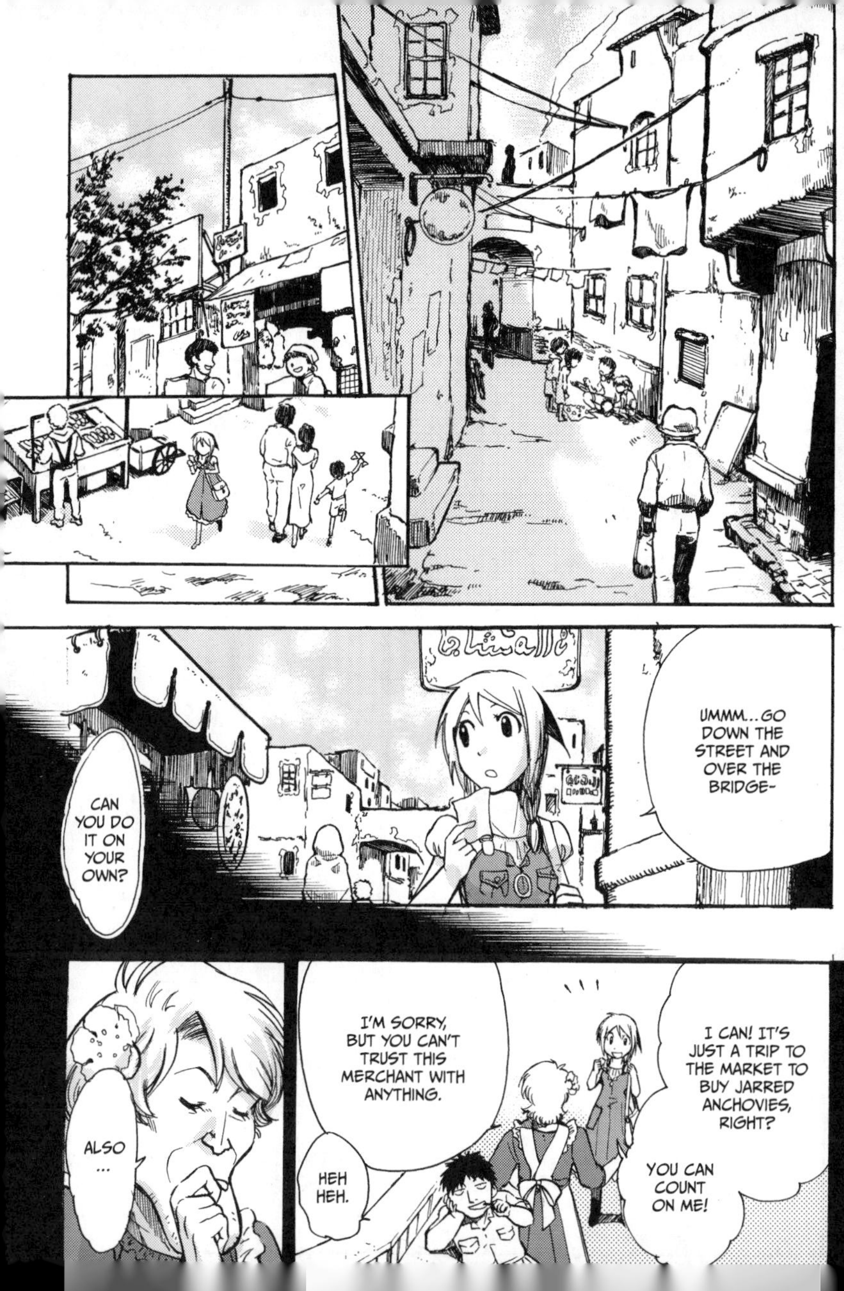
UMMM...GO DOWN THE STREET AND OVER THE BRIDGE-
CAN YOU DO IT ON YOUR OWN?
I CAN! IT'S JUST A TRIP TO THE MARKET TO BUY JARRED ANCHOVIES, RIGHT?
I'M SORRY, BUT YOU CAN'T TRUST THIS MERCHANT WITH ANYTHING.
YOU CAN COUNT ON ME!
HEH HEH.
ALSO ...

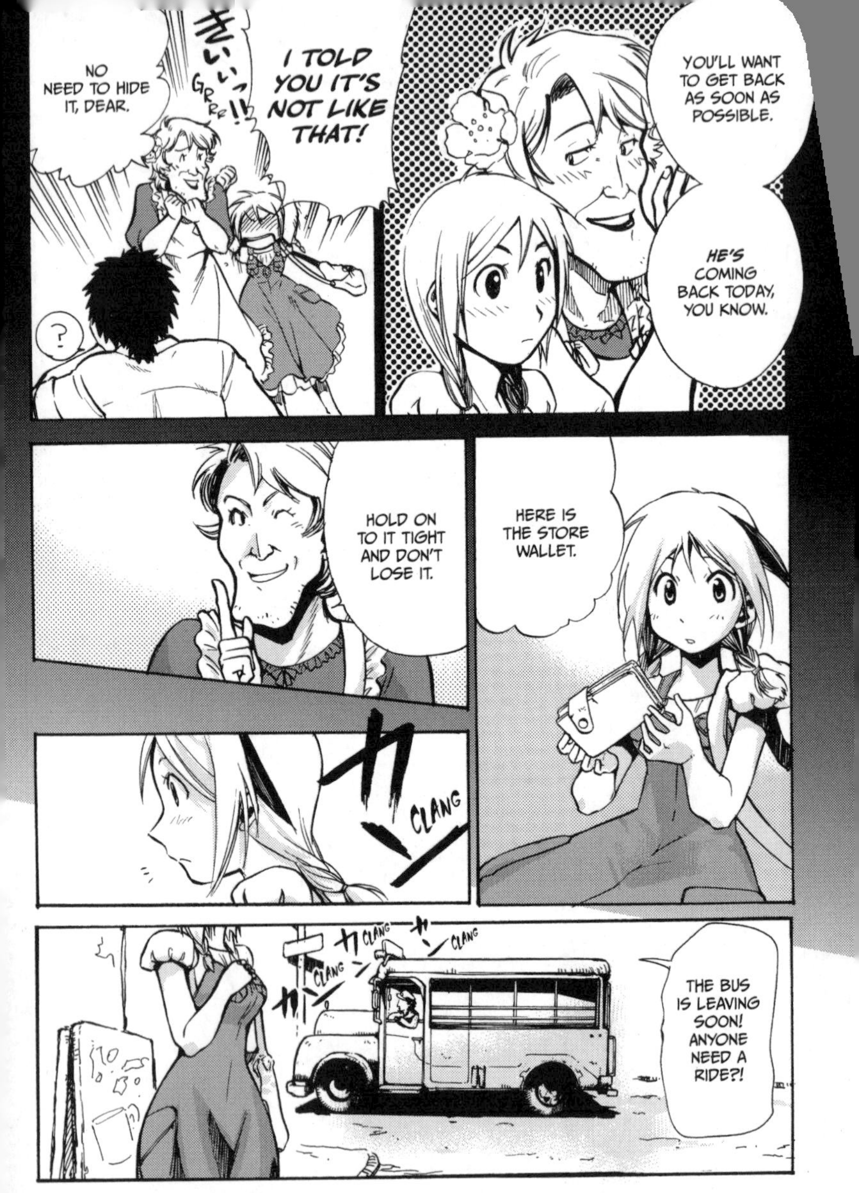
YOU'LL WANT TO GET BACK AS SOON AS POSSIBLE.
HE'S COMING BACK TODAY, YOU KNOW.
I TOLD YOU IT'S NOT LIKE THAT!
きぃぃっ
GRrr!!
NO NEED TO HIDE IT, DEAR.
?
HERE IS THE STORE WALLET.
HOLD ON TO IT TIGHT AND DON'T LOSE IT.
CLANG
THE BUS IS LEAVING SOON! ANYONE NEED A RIDE?!
CLANG
CLANG
CLANG

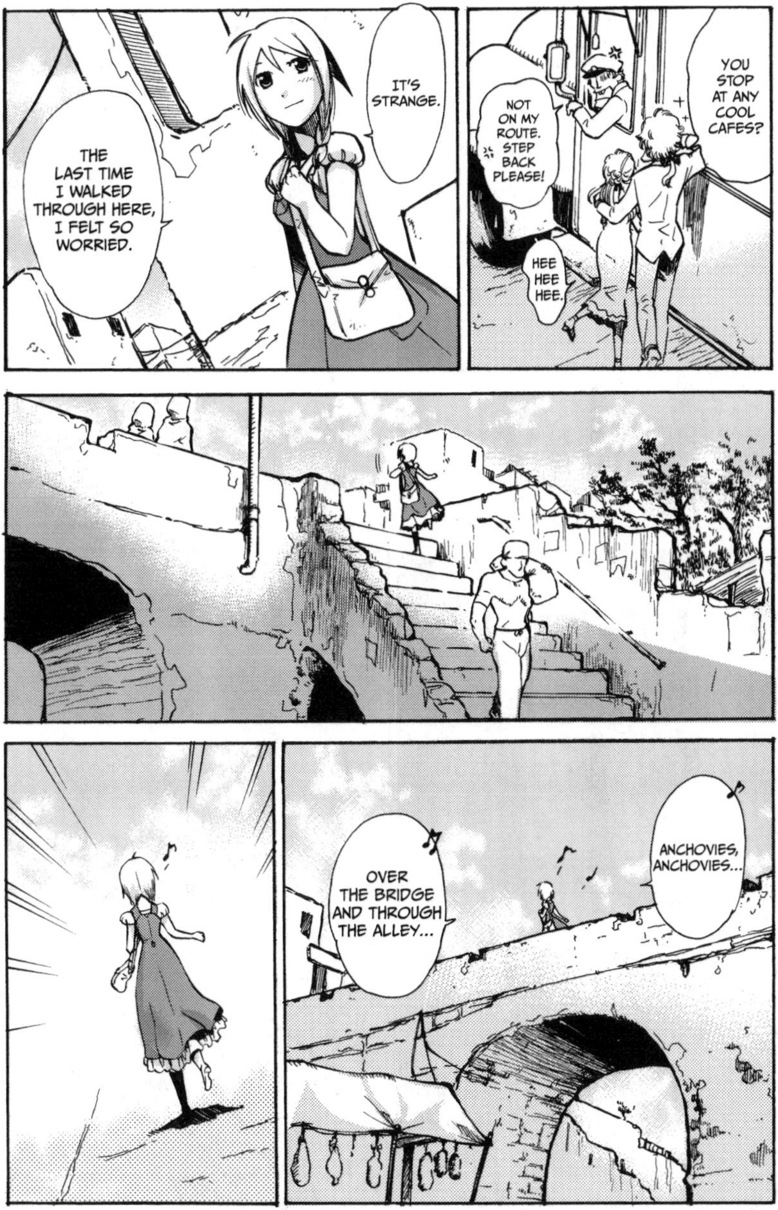
YOU STOP AT ANY COOL CAFES?
NOT ON MY ROUTE. STEP BACK PLEASE!
HEE HEE HEE.
IT'S STRANGE.
THE LAST TIME I WALKED THROUGH HERE, I FELT SO WORRIED.
ANCHOVIES, ANCHOVIES...
OVER THE BRIDGE AND THROUGH THE ALLEY...

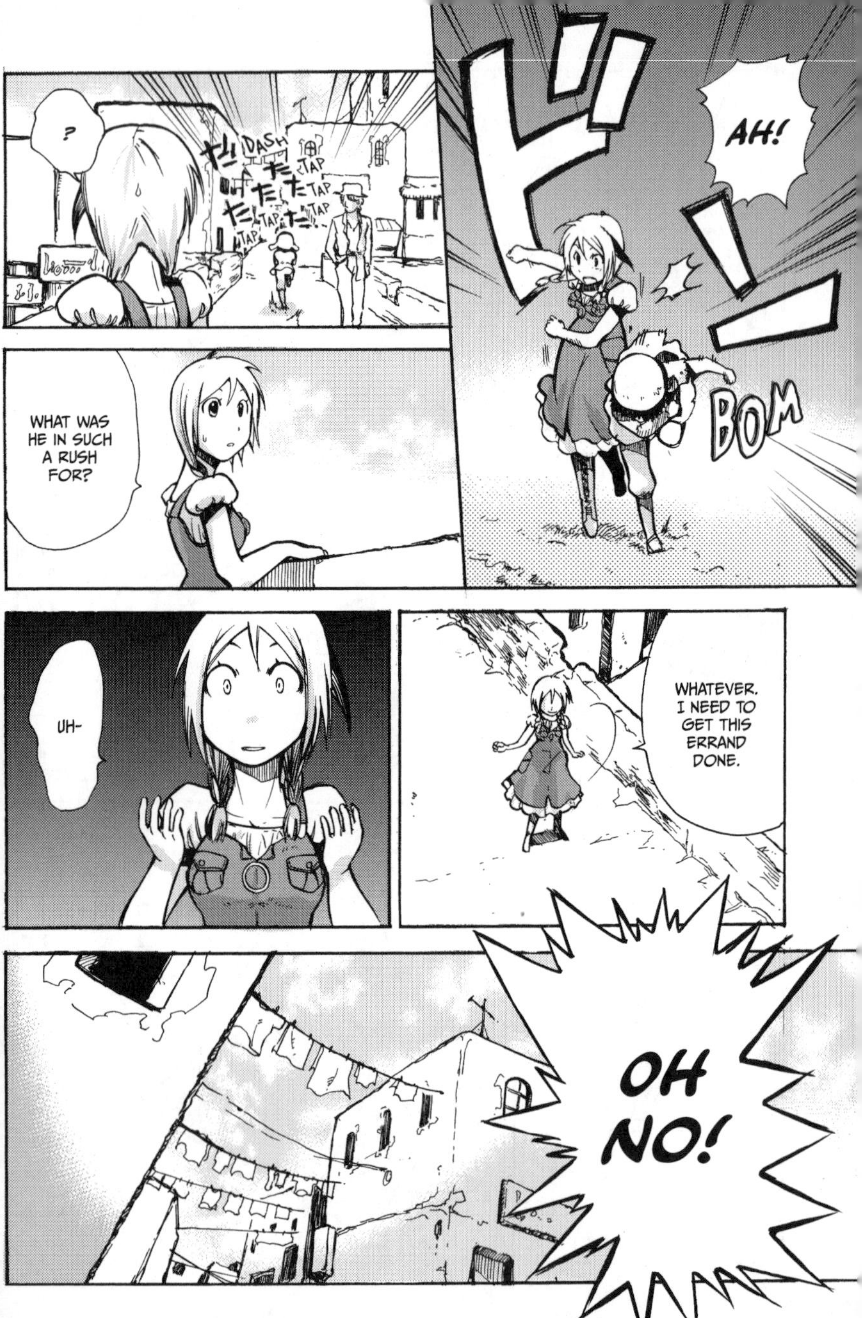
AH!
BOM
?
DASH
TAP
TAP
TAP
TAP
TAP
WHAT WAS HE IN SUCH A RUSH FOR?
WHATEVER. I NEED TO GET THIS ERRAND DONE.
UH-
OH NO!

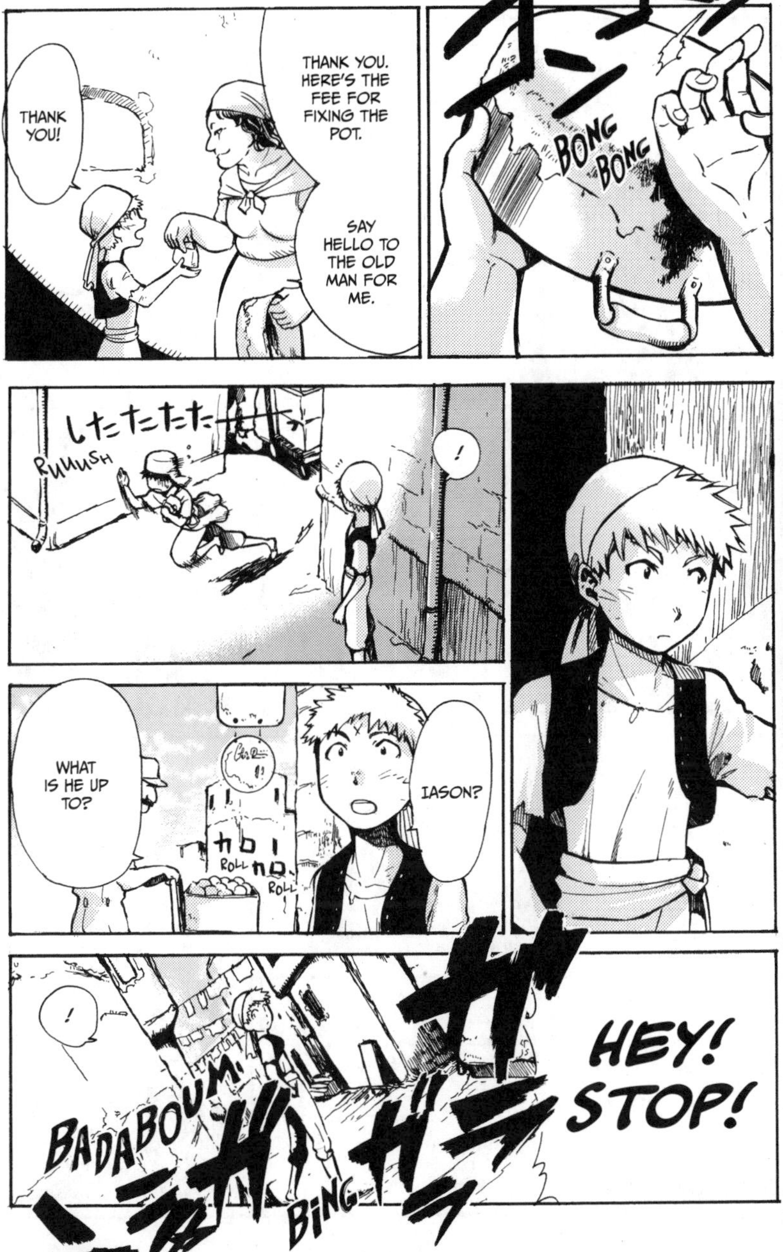
コーンコーン
BONG
BONG
THANK YOU. HERE'S THE FEE FOR FIXING THE POT.
SAY HELLO TO THE OLD MAN FOR ME.
THANK YOU!
したたたたた
RUUUSH
!
IASON?
カロ
ROLL
カロ
ROLL
WHAT IS HE UP TO?
HEY! STOP!
!
BADABOUM
BING

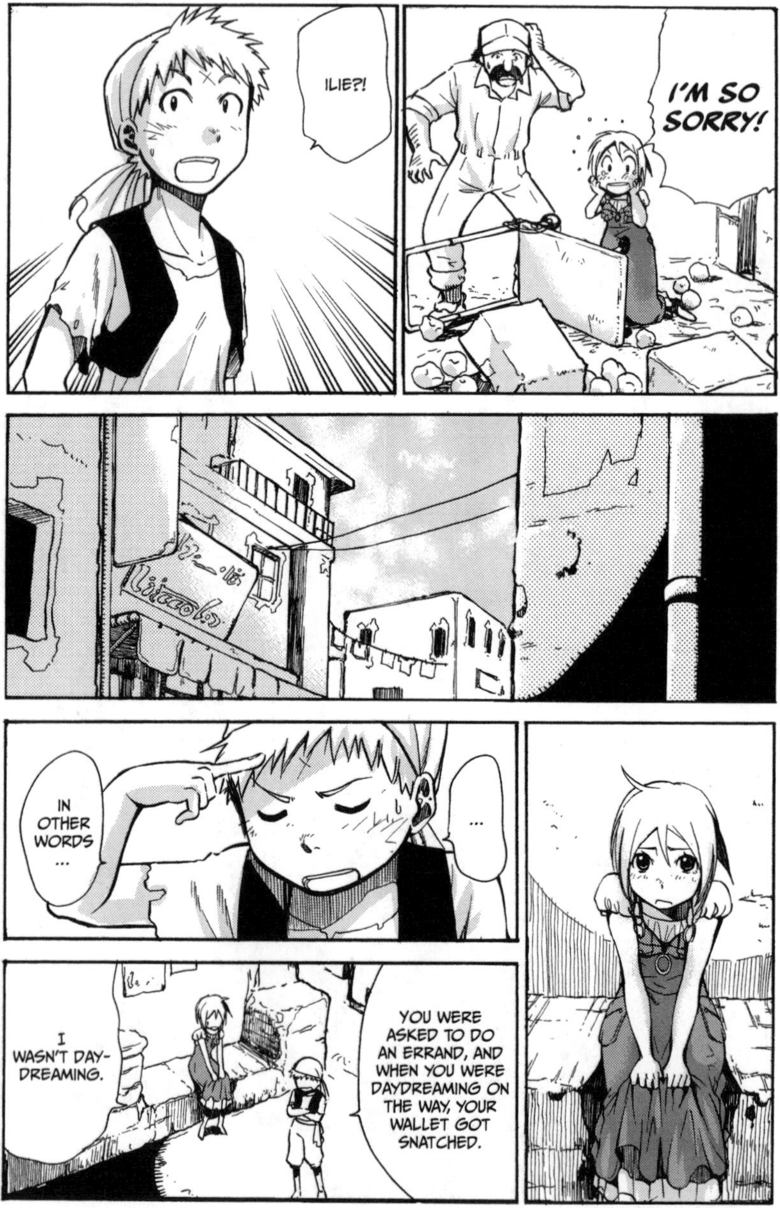
I'M SO SORRY!
!LIE?!
...
IN OTHER WORDS ...
YOU WERE ASKED TO DO AN ERRAND, AND WHEN YOU WERE DAYDREAMING ON THE WAY, YOUR WALLET GOT SNATCHED.
I WASN'T DAY-DREAMING.

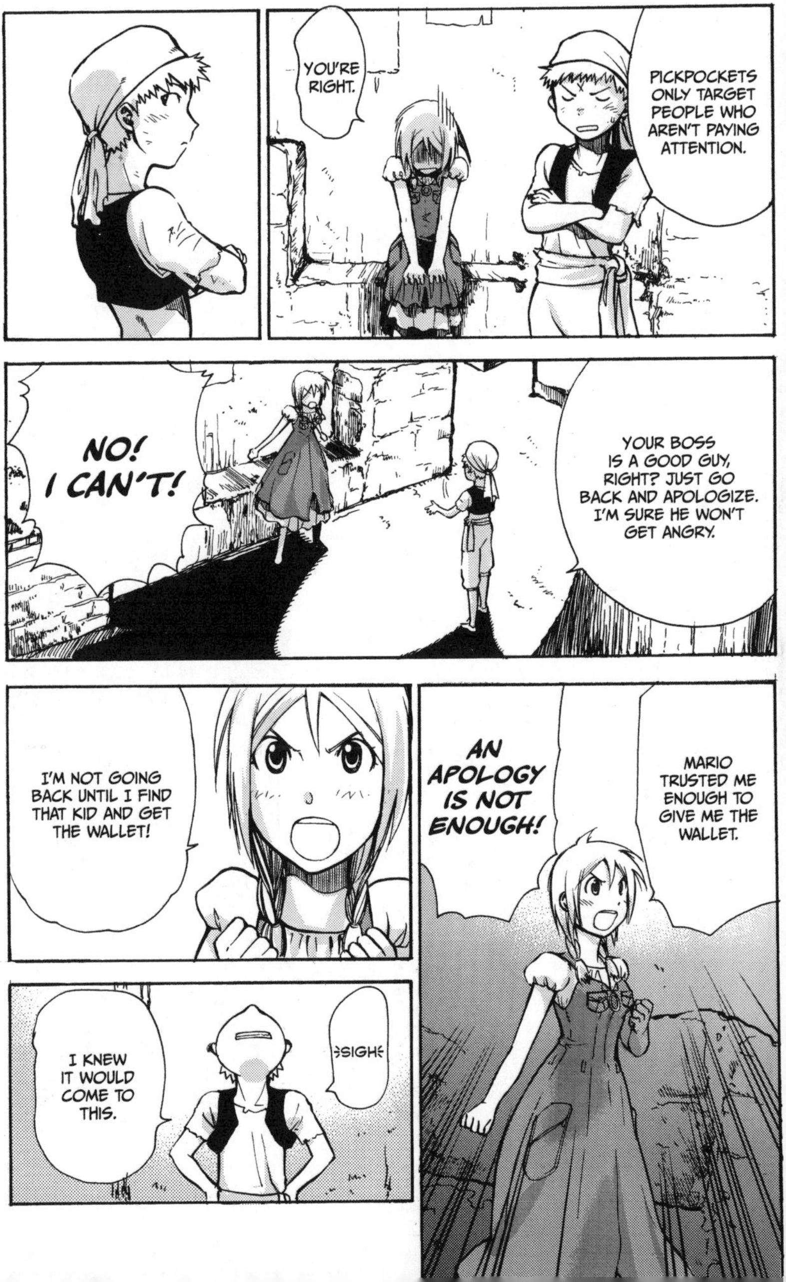
PICKPOCKETS ONLY TARGET PEOPLE WHO AREN'T PAYING ATTENTION.
YOU'RE RIGHT.
YOUR BOSS IS A GOOD GUY, RIGHT? JUST GO BACK AND APOLOGIZE. I'M SURE HE WON'T GET ANGRY.
NO! I CAN'T!
MARIO TRUSTED ME ENOUGH TO GIVE ME THE WALLET.
AN APOLOGY IS NOT ENOUGH!
I'M NOT GOING BACK UNTIL I FIND THAT KID AND GET THE WALLET!
SIGH
I KNEW IT WOULD COME TO THIS.

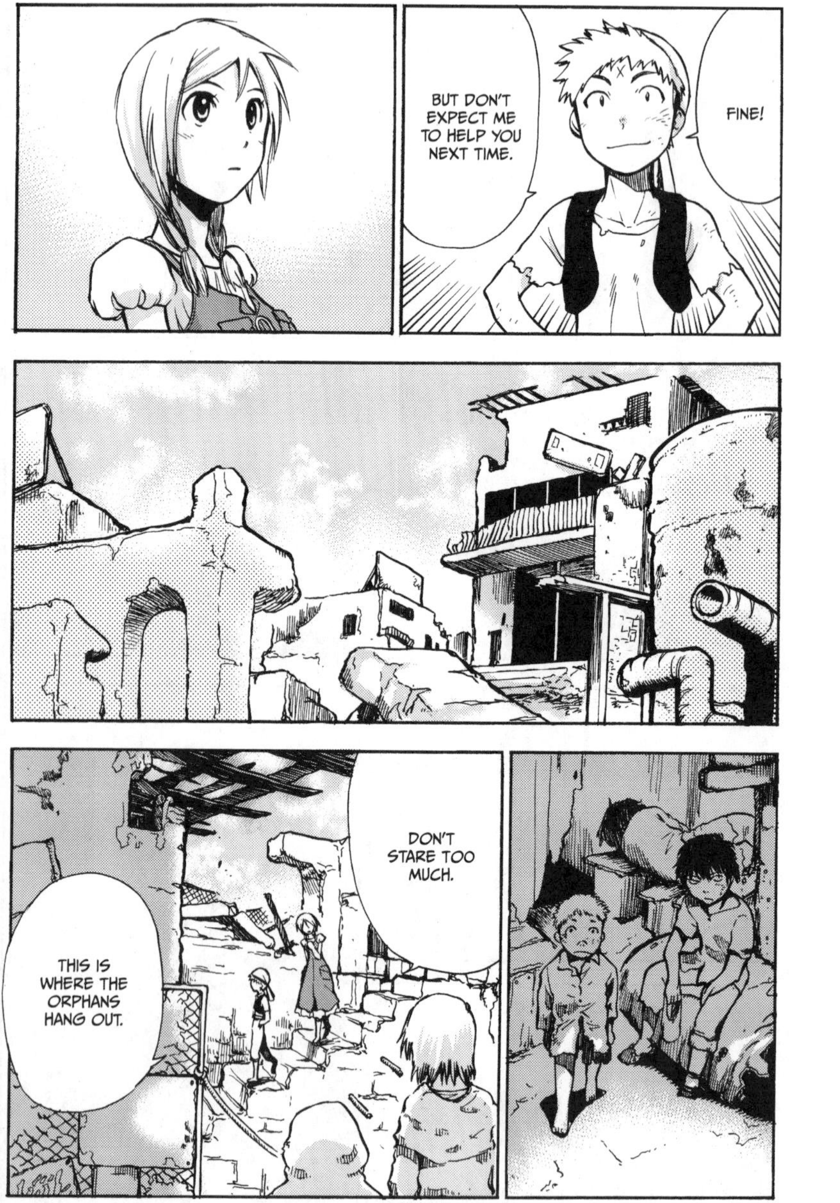
FINE!
BUT DON'T EXPECT ME TO HELP YOU NEXT TIME.
DON'T STARE TOO MUCH.
THIS IS WHERE THE ORPHANS HANG OUT.

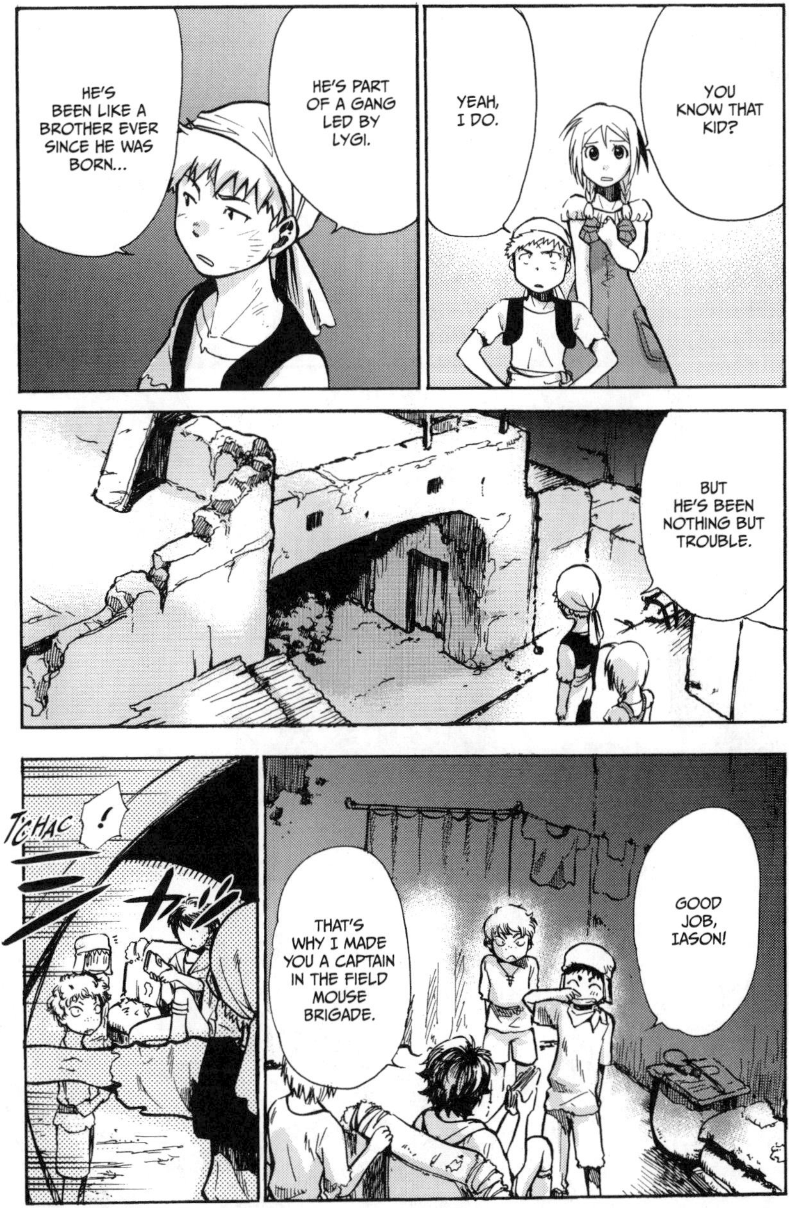
YOU KNOW THAT KID?
YEAH, I DO.
HE'S PART OF A GANG LED BY LYGI.
HE'S BEEN LIKE A BROTHER EVER SINCE HE WAS BORN...
BUT HE'S BEEN NOTHING BUT TROUBLE.
GOOD JOB, IASON!
THAT'S WHY I MADE YOU A CAPTAIN IN THE FIELD MOUSE BRIGADE.
TCHAC
!

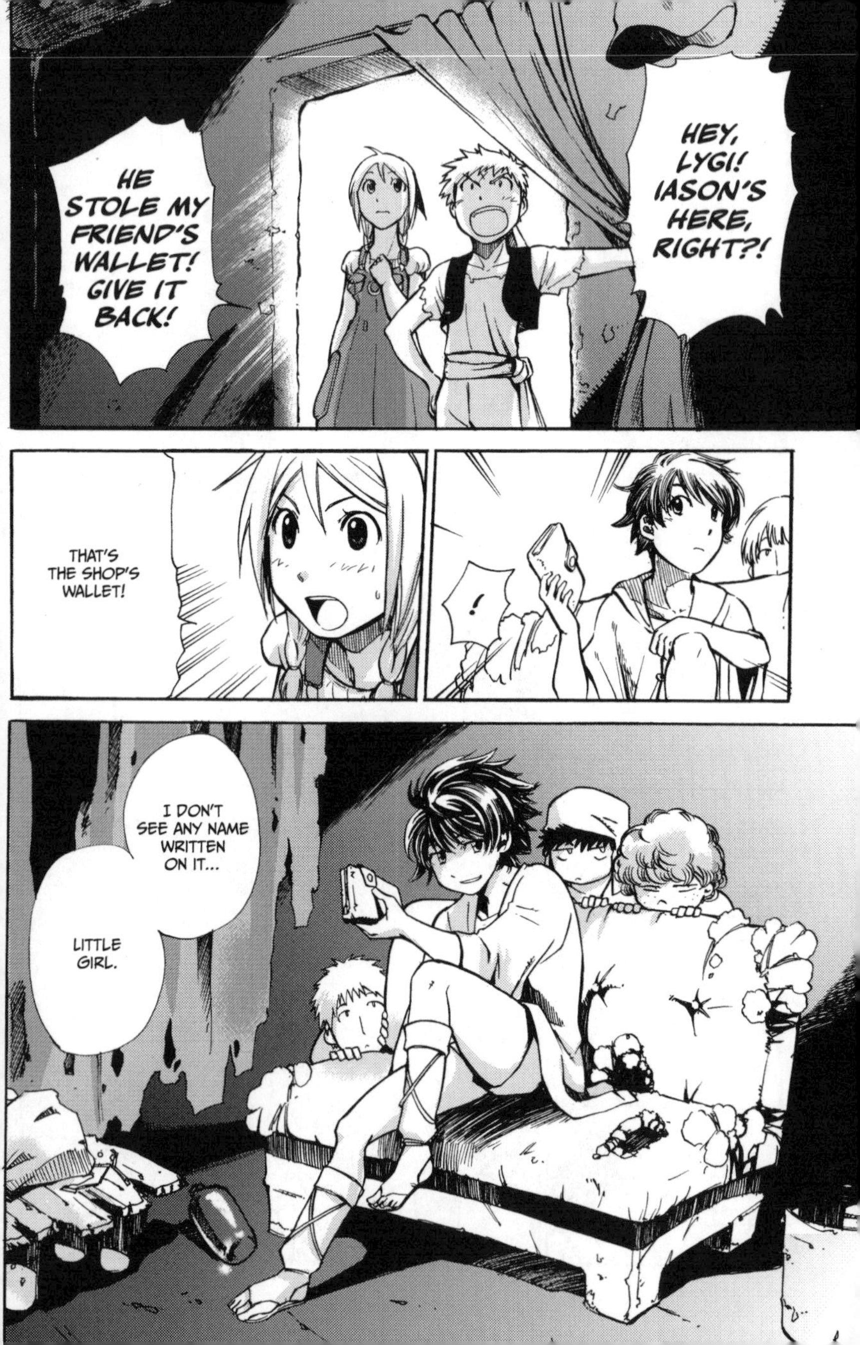
HEY, LYGI! IASON'S HERE, RIGHT?!
HE STOLE MY FRIEND'S WALLET! GIVE IT BACK!
!
THAT'S THE SHOP'S WALLET!
I DON'T SEE ANY NAME WRITTEN ON IT...
LITTLE GIRL.

[CHAPTER 5]

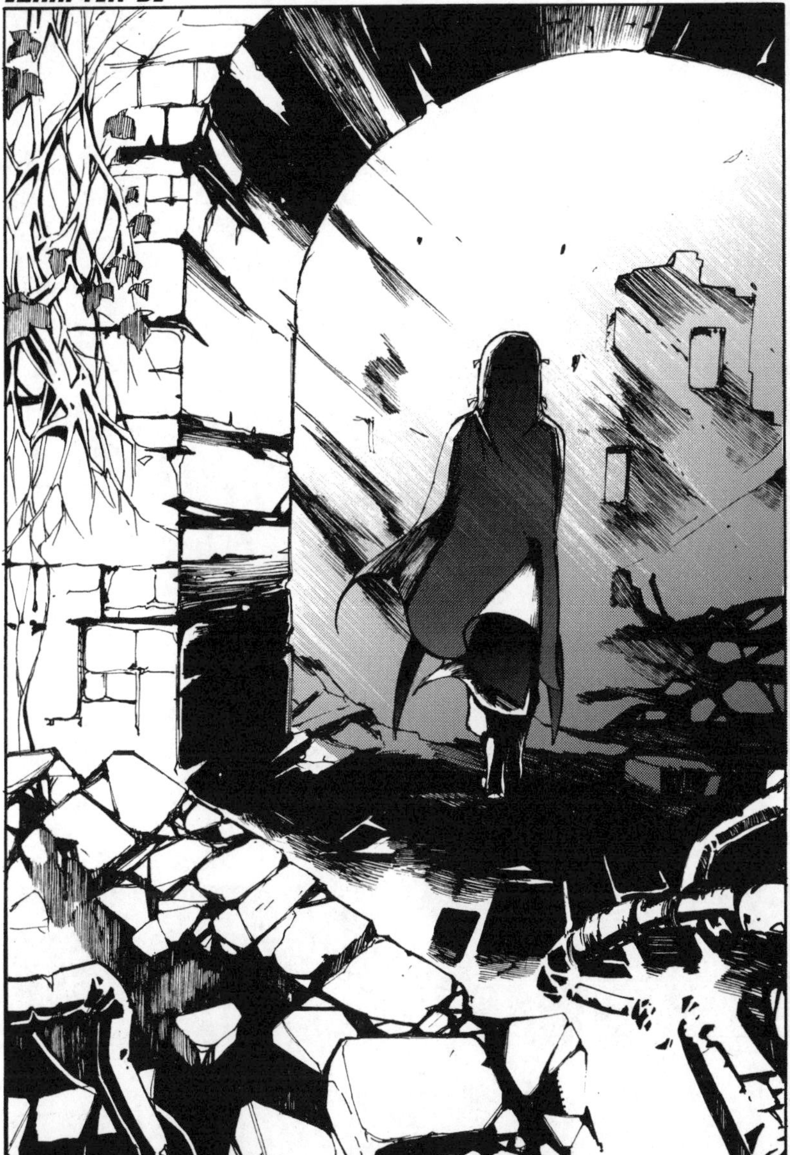

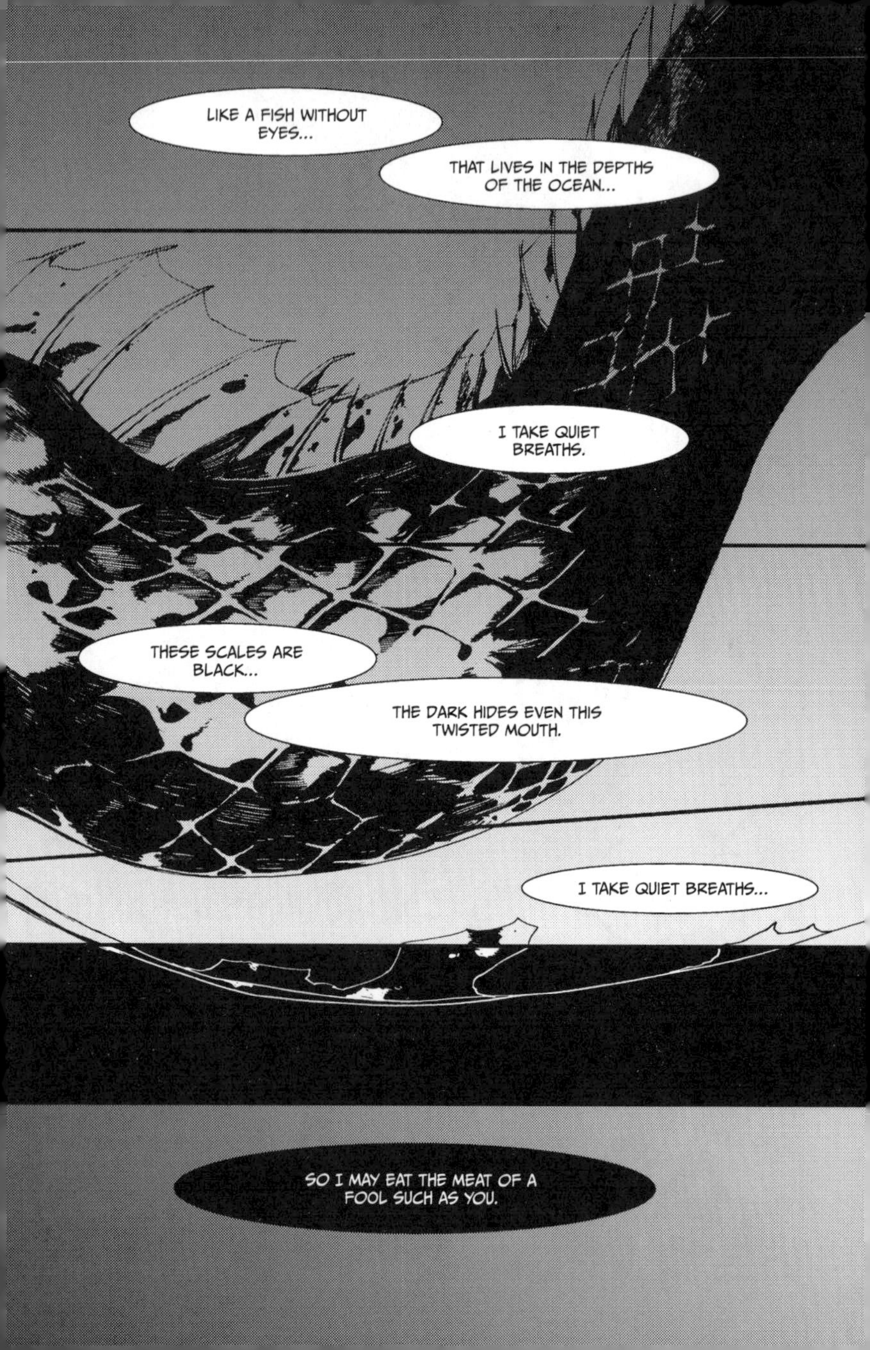
LIKE A FISH WITHOUT EYES...
THAT LIVES IN THE DEPTHS OF THE OCEAN...
I TAKE QUIET BREATHS.
THESE SCALES ARE BLACK...
THE DARK HIDES EVEN THIS TWISTED MOUTH.
I TAKE QUIET BREATHS...
SO I MAY EAT THE MEAT OF A FOOL SUCH AS YOU.

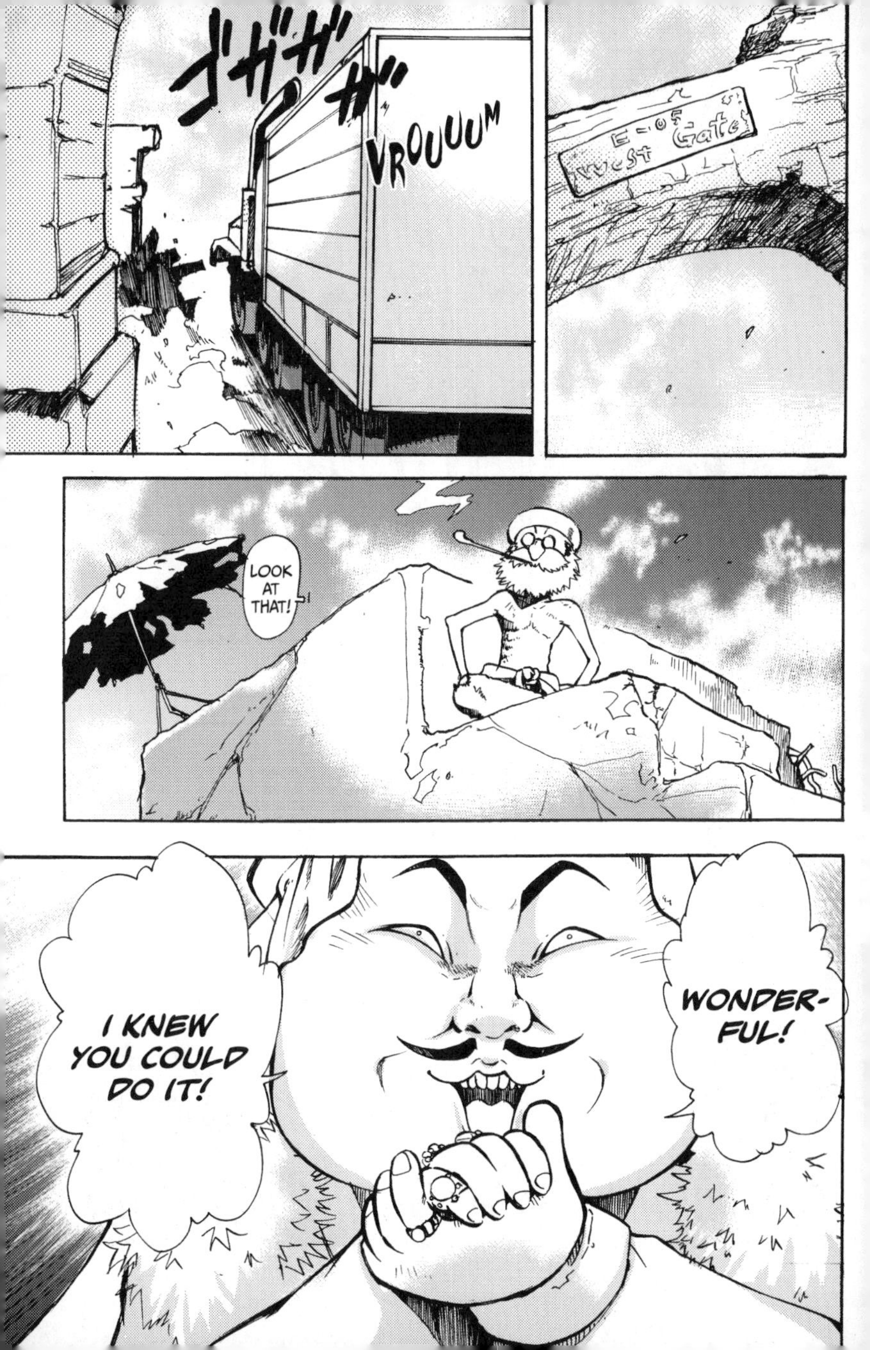
West Gate
ゴガガガ
VROUUUM
LOOK AT THAT!
WONDER-FUL!
I KNEW YOU COULD DO IT!

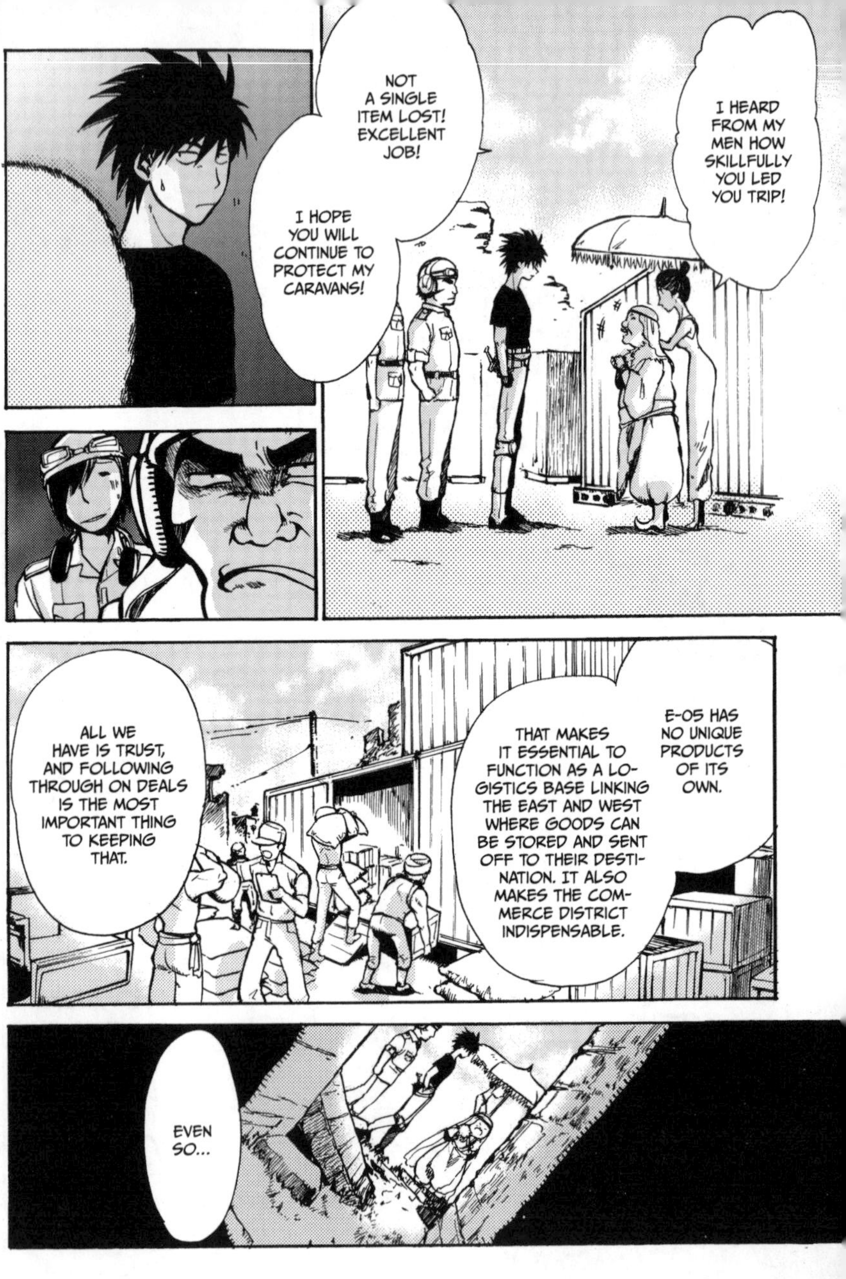
I HEARD FROM MY MEN HOW SKILLFULLY YOU LED YOU TRIP!
NOT A SINGLE ITEM LOST! EXCELLENT JOB!
I HOPE YOU WILL CONTINUE TO PROTECT MY CARAVANS!
E-05 HAS NO UNIQUE PRODUCTS OF ITS OWN.
THAT MAKES IT ESSENTIAL TO FUNCTION AS A LO-GISTICS BASE LINKING THE EAST AND WEST WHERE GOODS CAN BE STORED AND SENT OFF TO THEIR DESTI-NATION. IT ALSO MAKES THE COM-MERCE DISTRICT INDISPENSABLE.
ALL WE HAVE IS TRUST, AND FOLLOWING THROUGH ON DEALS IS THE MOST IMPORTANT THING TO KEEPING THAT.
EVEN SO...

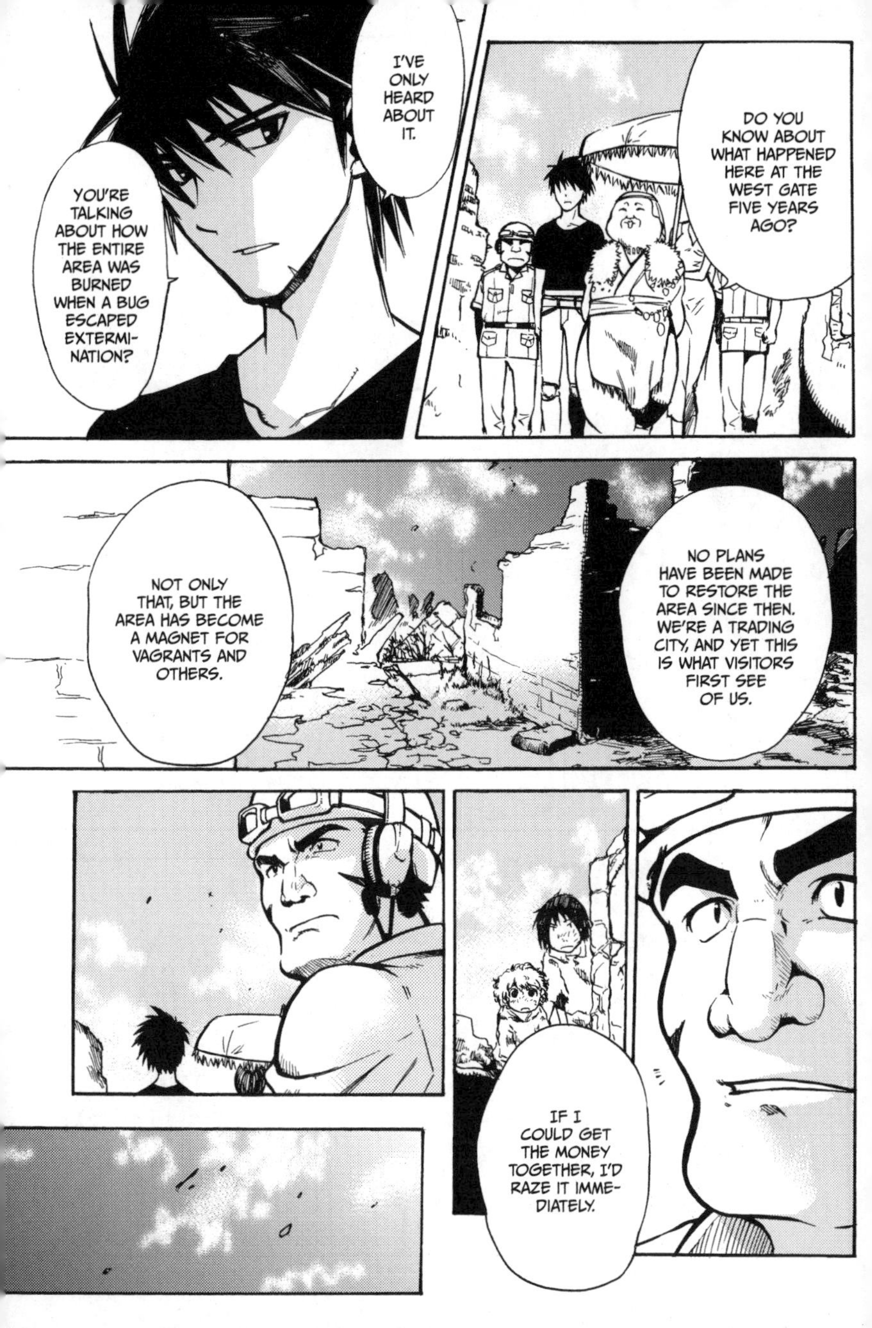
DO YOU KNOW ABOUT WHAT HAPPENED HERE AT THE WEST GATE FIVE YEARS AGO?
I'VE ONLY HEARD ABOUT IT.
YOU'RE TALKING ABOUT HOW THE ENTIRE AREA WAS BURNED WHEN A BUG ESCAPED EXTERMI-NATION?
NO PLANS HAVE BEEN MADE TO RESTORE THE AREA SINCE THEN. WE'RE A TRADING CITY, AND YET THIS IS WHAT VISITORS FIRST SEE OF US.
NOT ONLY THAT, BUT THE AREA HAS BECOME A MAGNET FOR VAGRANTS AND OTHERS.
IF I COULD GET THE MONEY TOGETHER, I'D RAZE IT IMME-DIATELY.

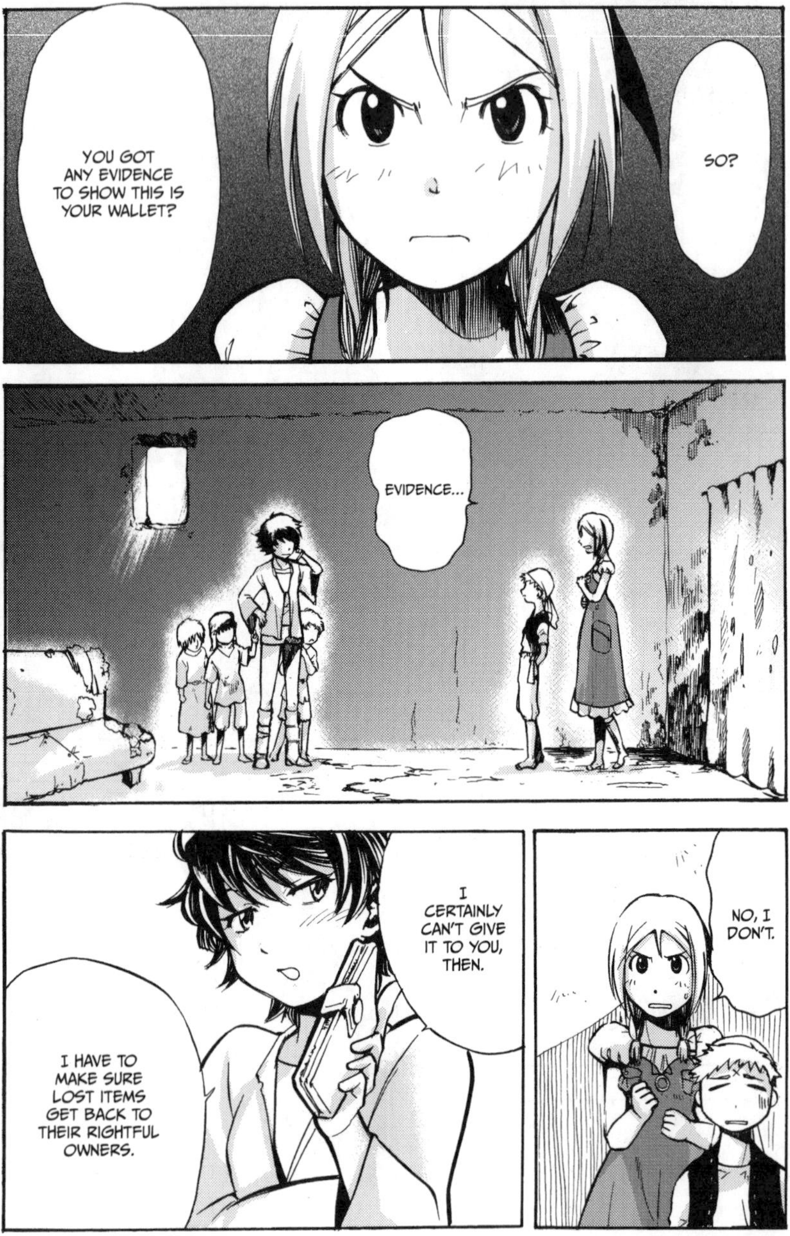
SO?
YOU GOT ANY EVIDENCE TO SHOW THIS IS YOUR WALLET?
EVIDENCE...
NO, I DON'T.
I CERTAINLY CAN'T GIVE IT TO YOU, THEN.
I HAVE TO MAKE SURE LOST ITEMS GET BACK TO THEIR RIGHTFUL OWNERS.

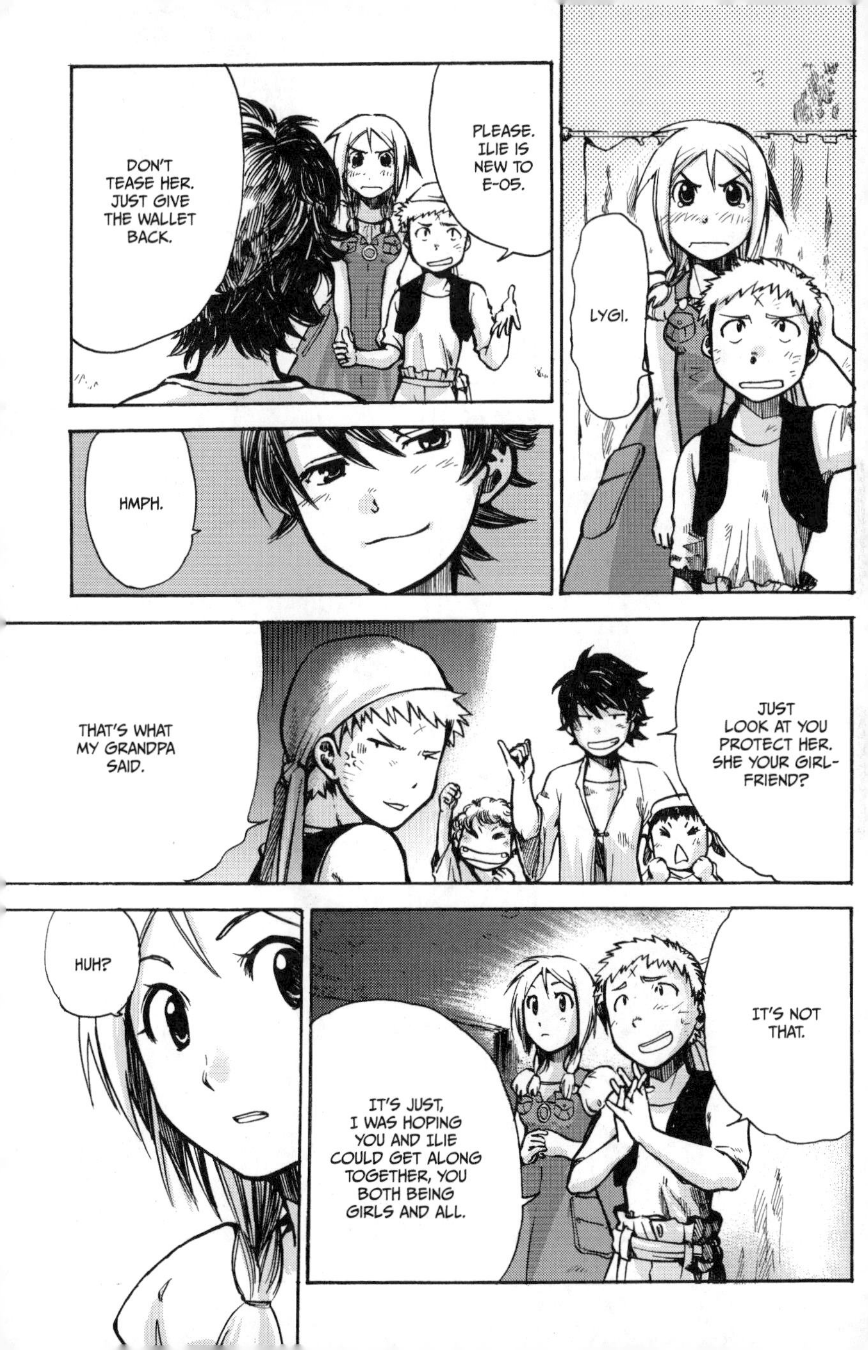
LYGI.
PLEASE. ILIE IS NEW TO E-05.
DON'T TEASE HER. JUST GIVE THE WALLET BACK.
HMPH.
JUST LOOK AT YOU PROTECT HER. SHE YOUR GIRL-FRIEND?
THAT'S WHAT MY GRANDPA SAID.
IT'S NOT THAT.
IT'S JUST, I WAS HOPING YOU AND ILIE COULD GET ALONG TOGETHER, YOU BOTH BEING GIRLS AND ALL.
HUH?

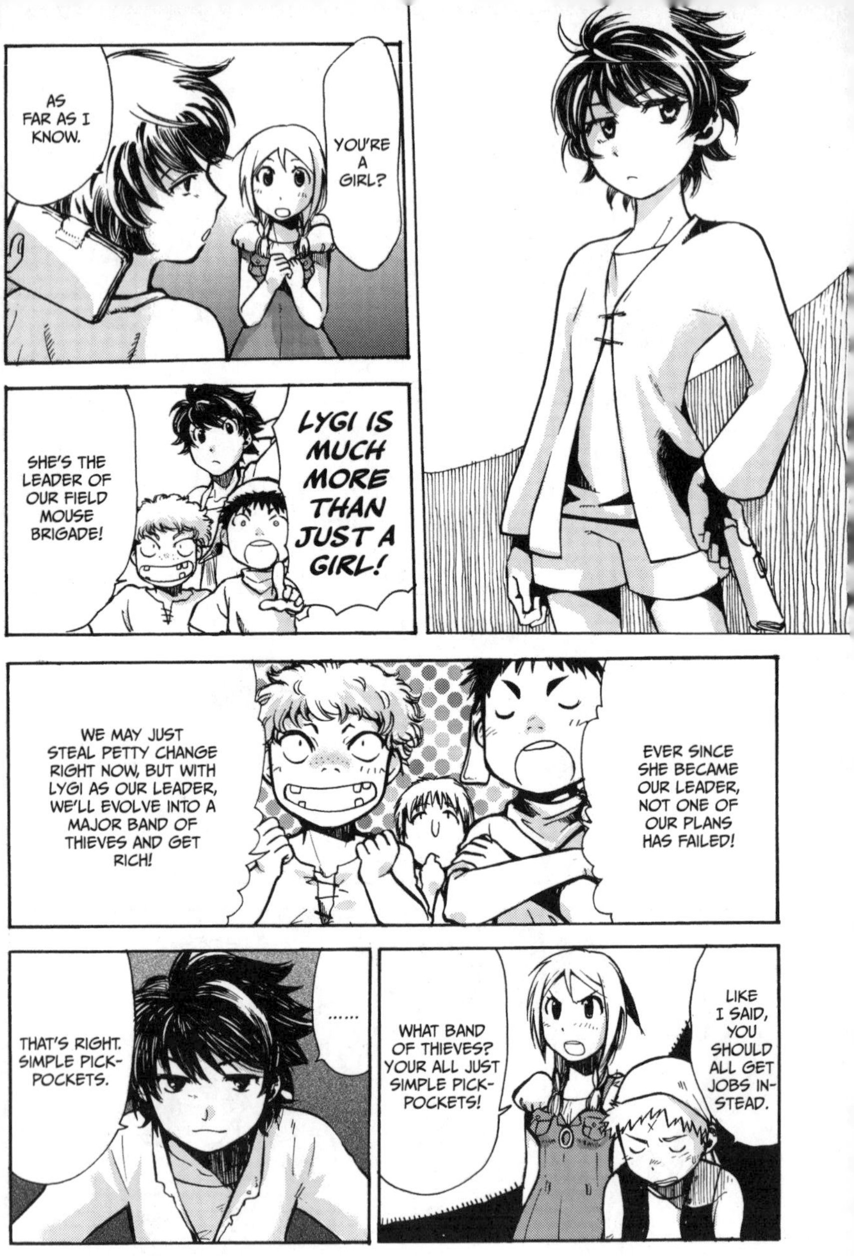
YOU'RE A GIRL?
AS FAR AS I KNOW.
LYGI IS MUCH MORE THAN JUST A GIRL!
SHE'S THE LEADER OF OUR FIELD MOUSE BRIGADE!
EVER SINCE SHE BECAME OUR LEADER, NOT ONE OF OUR PLANS HAS FAILED!
WE MAY JUST STEAL PETTY CHANGE RIGHT NOW, BUT WITH LYGI AS OUR LEADER, WE'LL EVOLVE INTO A MAJOR BAND OF THIEVES AND GET RICH!
LIKE I SAID, YOU SHOULD ALL GET JOBS IN-STEAD.
WHAT BAND OF THIEVES? YOUR ALL JUST SIMPLE PICK-POCKETS!
......
THAT'S RIGHT. SIMPLE PICK-POCKETS.

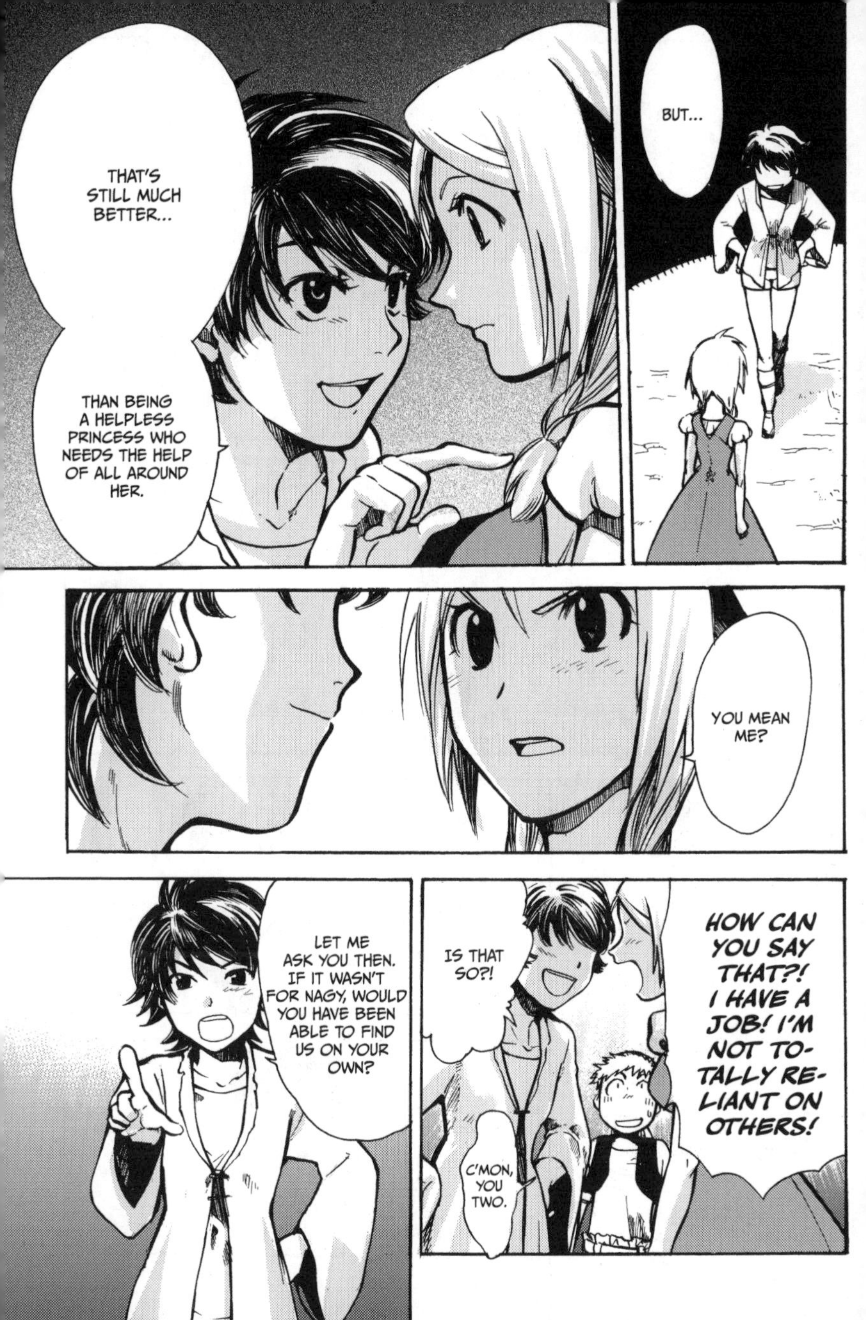
BUT...
THAT'S STILL MUCH BETTER...
THAN BEING A HELPLESS PRINCESS WHO NEEDS THE HELP OF ALL AROUND HER.
YOU MEAN ME?
HOW CAN YOU SAY THAT?! I HAVE A JOB! I'M NOT TO-TALLY RE-LIANT ON OTHERS!
IS THAT SO?!
C'MON, YOU TWO.
LET ME ASK YOU THEN. IF IT WASN'T FOR NAGY, WOULD YOU HAVE BEEN ABLE TO FIND US ON YOUR OWN?

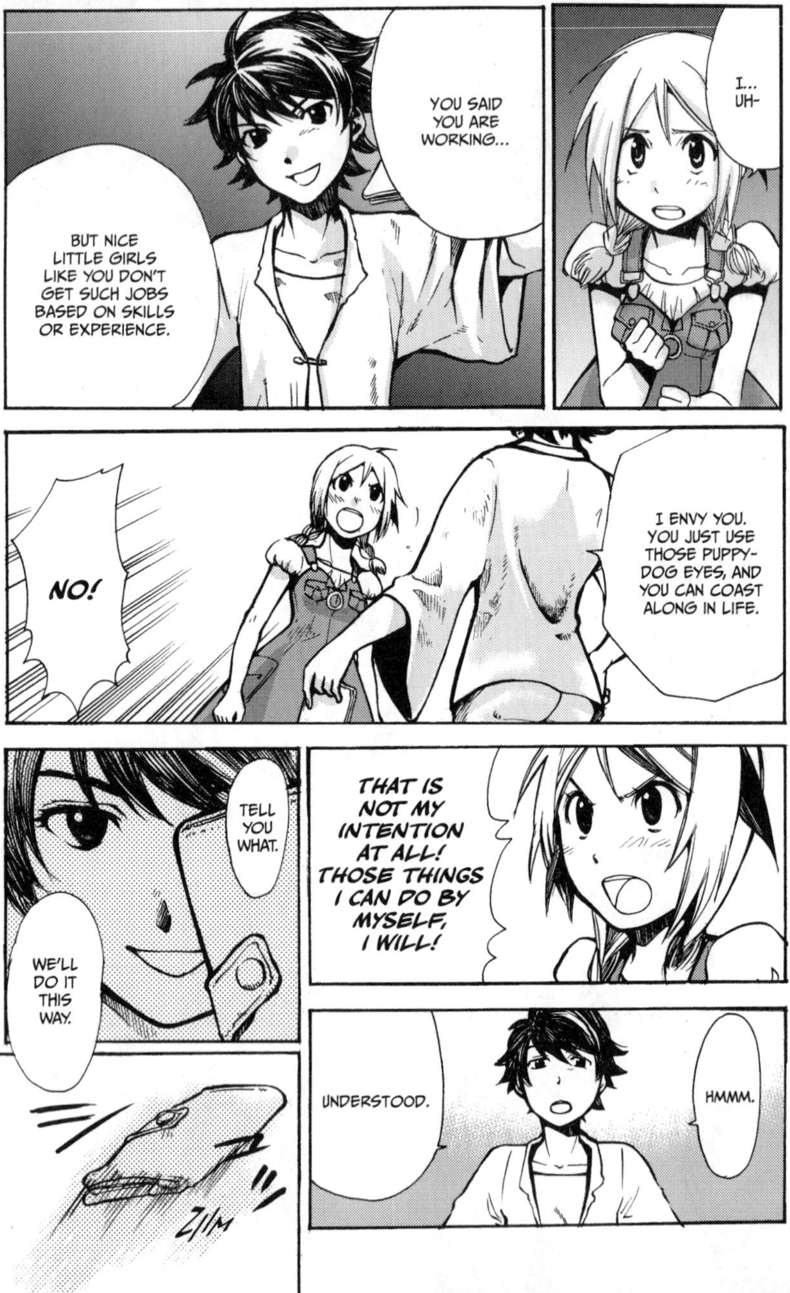
I... UH-
YOU SAID YOU ARE WORKING...
BUT NICE LITTLE GIRLS LIKE YOU DON'T GET SUCH JOBS BASED ON SKILLS OR EXPERIENCE.
I ENVY YOU. YOU JUST USE THOSE PUPPY-DOG EYES, AND YOU CAN COAST ALONG IN LIFE.
NO!
THAT IS NOT MY INTENTION AT ALL! THOSE THINGS I CAN DO BY MYSELF, I WILL!
TELL YOU WHAT.
WE'LL DO IT THIS WAY.
HMMM.
UNDERSTOOD.
ZIM

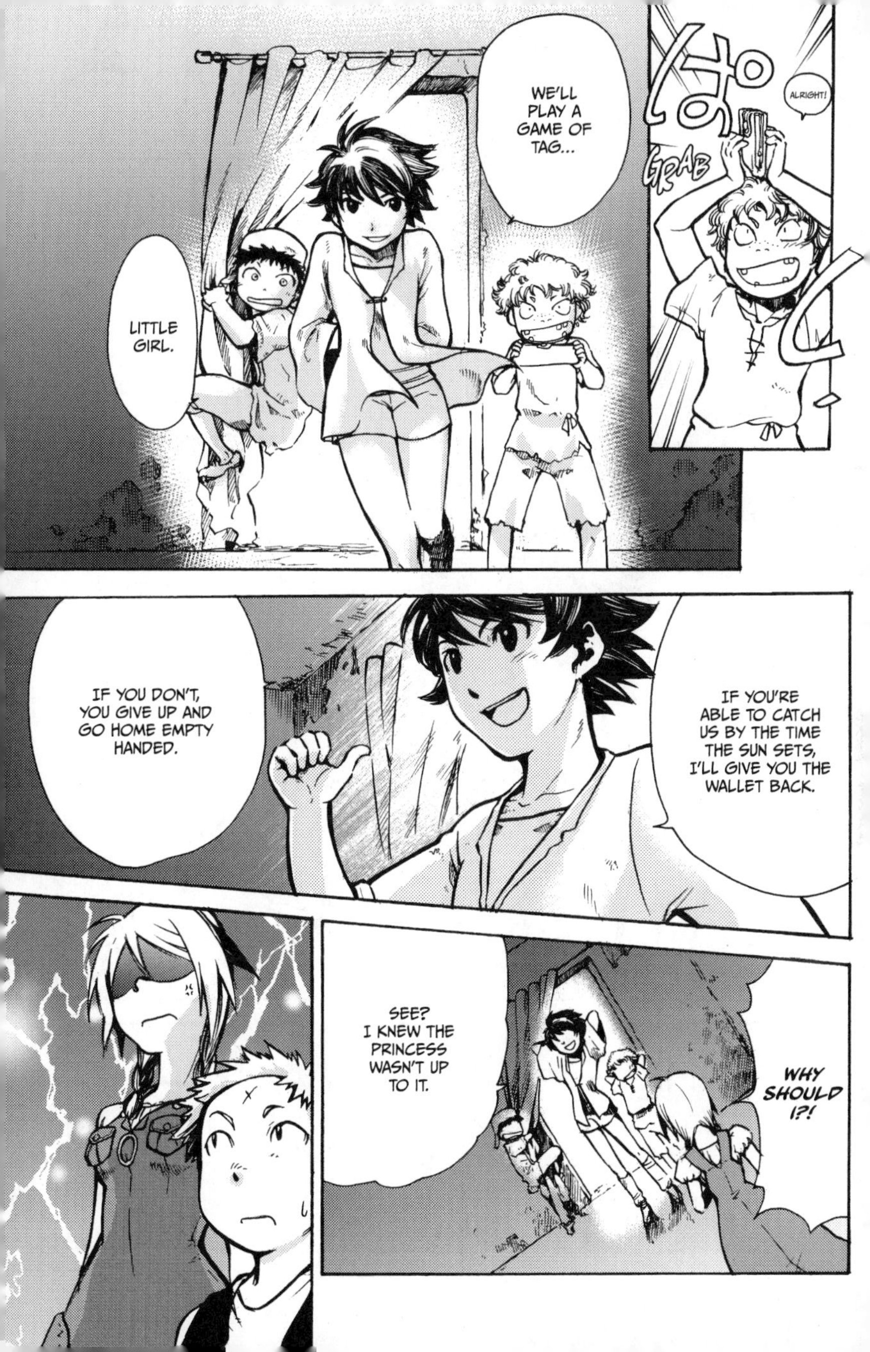
GRAB
ALRIGHT!
WE'LL PLAY A GAME OF TAG...
LITTLE GIRL.
IF YOU'RE ABLE TO CATCH US BY THE TIME THE SUN SETS, I'LL GIVE YOU THE WALLET BACK.
IF YOU DON'T, YOU GIVE UP AND GO HOME EMPTY HANDED.
WHY SHOULD I?!
SEE? I KNEW THE PRINCESS WASN'T UP TO IT.

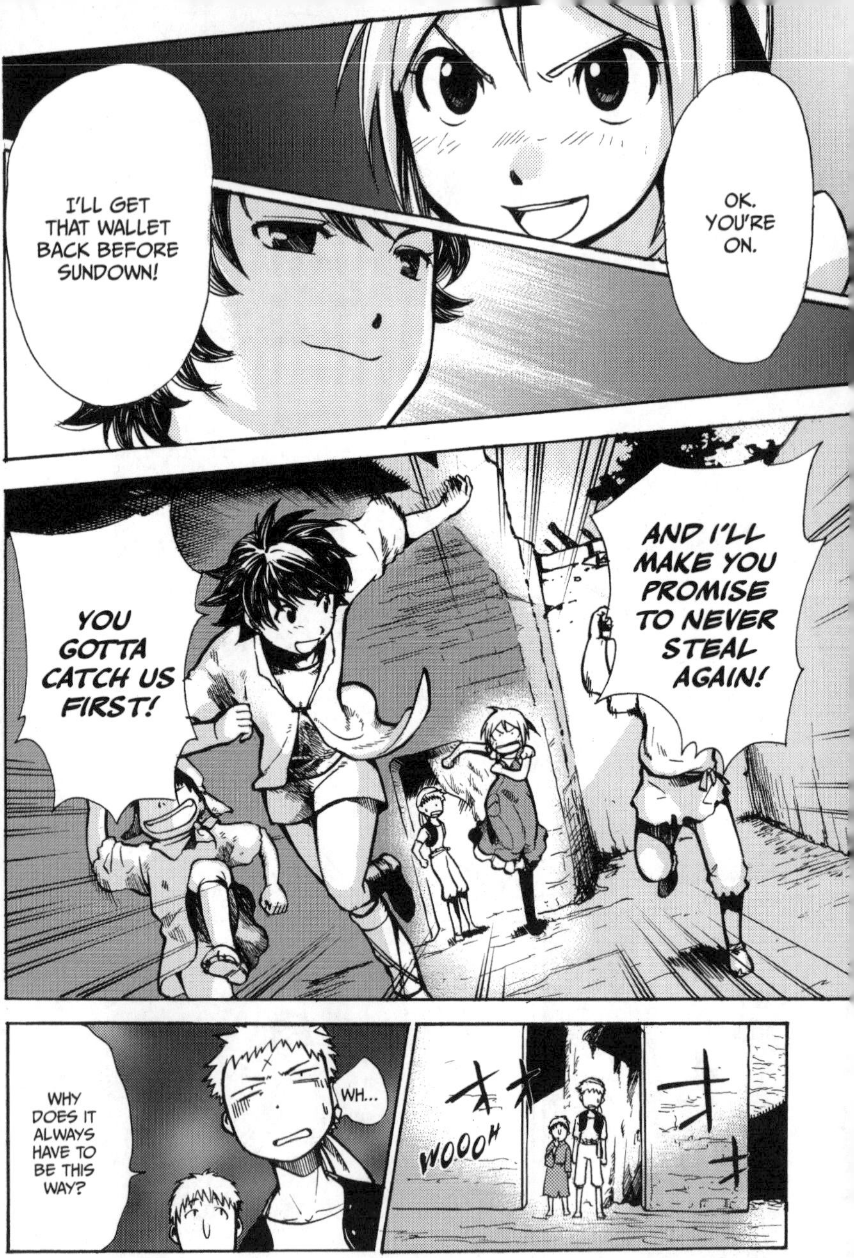
OK. YOU'RE ON.
I'LL GET THAT WALLET BACK BEFORE SUNDOWN!
AND I'LL MAKE YOU PROMISE TO NEVER STEAL AGAIN!
YOU GOTTA CATCH US FIRST!
WOOOH
WH...
WHY DOES IT ALWAYS HAVE TO BE THIS WAY?

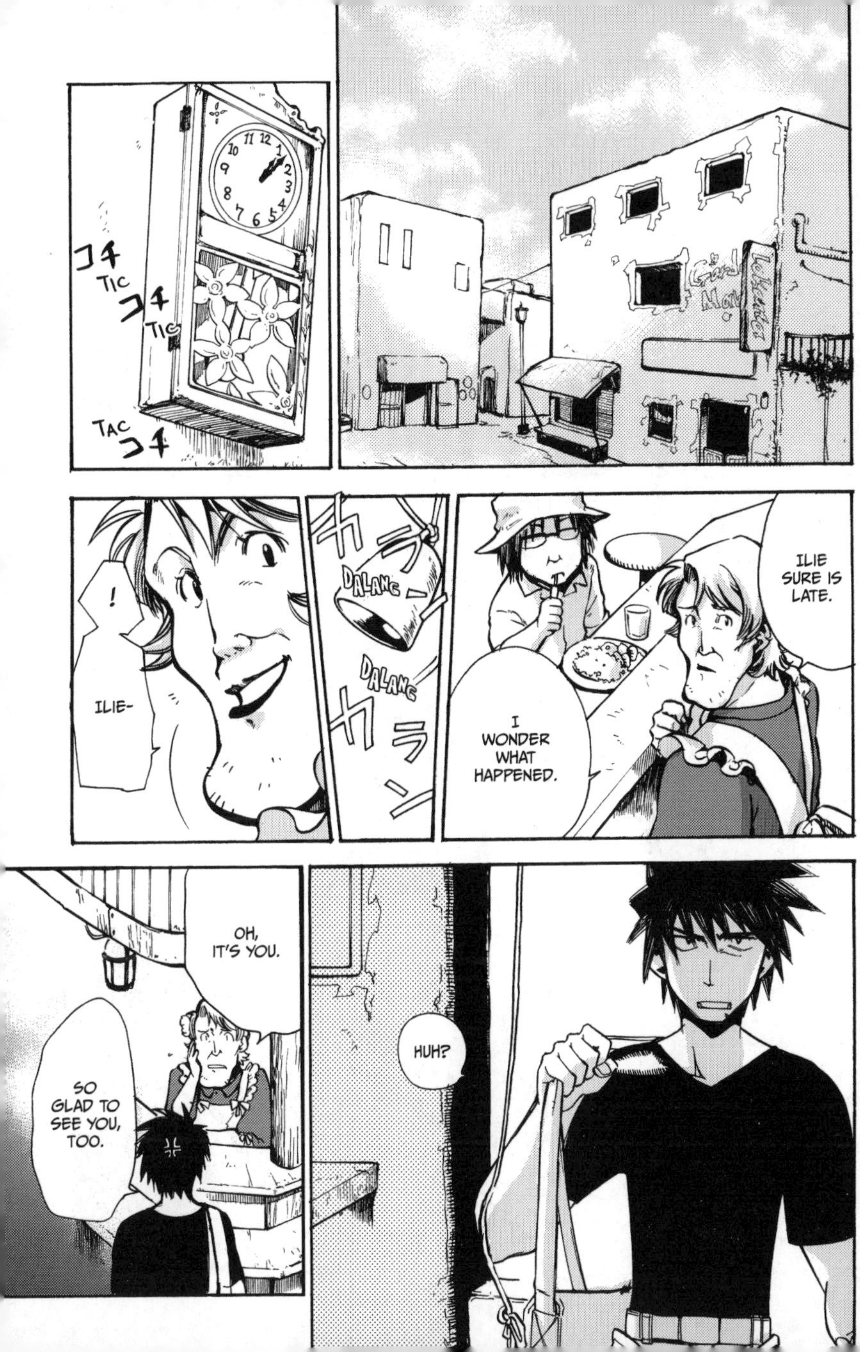
コチ
TIC
コチ
TIC
TAC
コチ
ILIE SURE IS LATE.
I WONDER WHAT HAPPENED.
カラ
DALANG
DALANG
カラン
!
ILIE-
HUH?
OH, IT'S YOU.
SO GLAD TO SEE YOU, TOO.

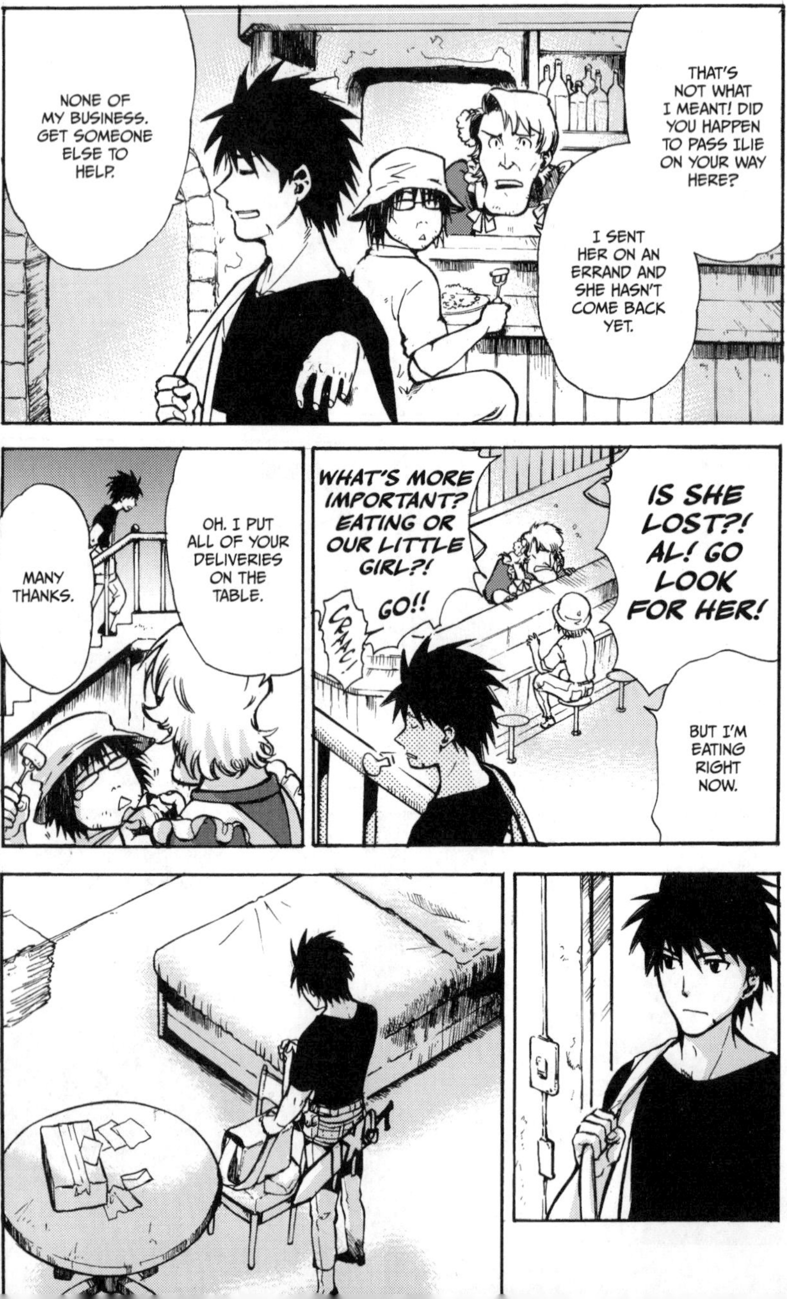
THAT'S NOT WHAT I MEANT! DID YOU HAPPEN TO PASS ILIE ON YOUR WAY HERE?
I SENT HER ON AN ERRAND AND SHE HASN'T COME BACK YET.
NONE OF MY BUSINESS. GET SOMEONE ELSE TO HELP.
IS SHE LOST?! AL! GO LOOK FOR HER!
BUT I'M EATING RIGHT NOW.
WHAT'S MORE IMPORTANT? EATING OR OUR LITTLE GIRL?!
GO!!
CRAAC!
OH. I PUT ALL OF YOUR DELIVERIES ON THE TABLE.
MANY THANKS.

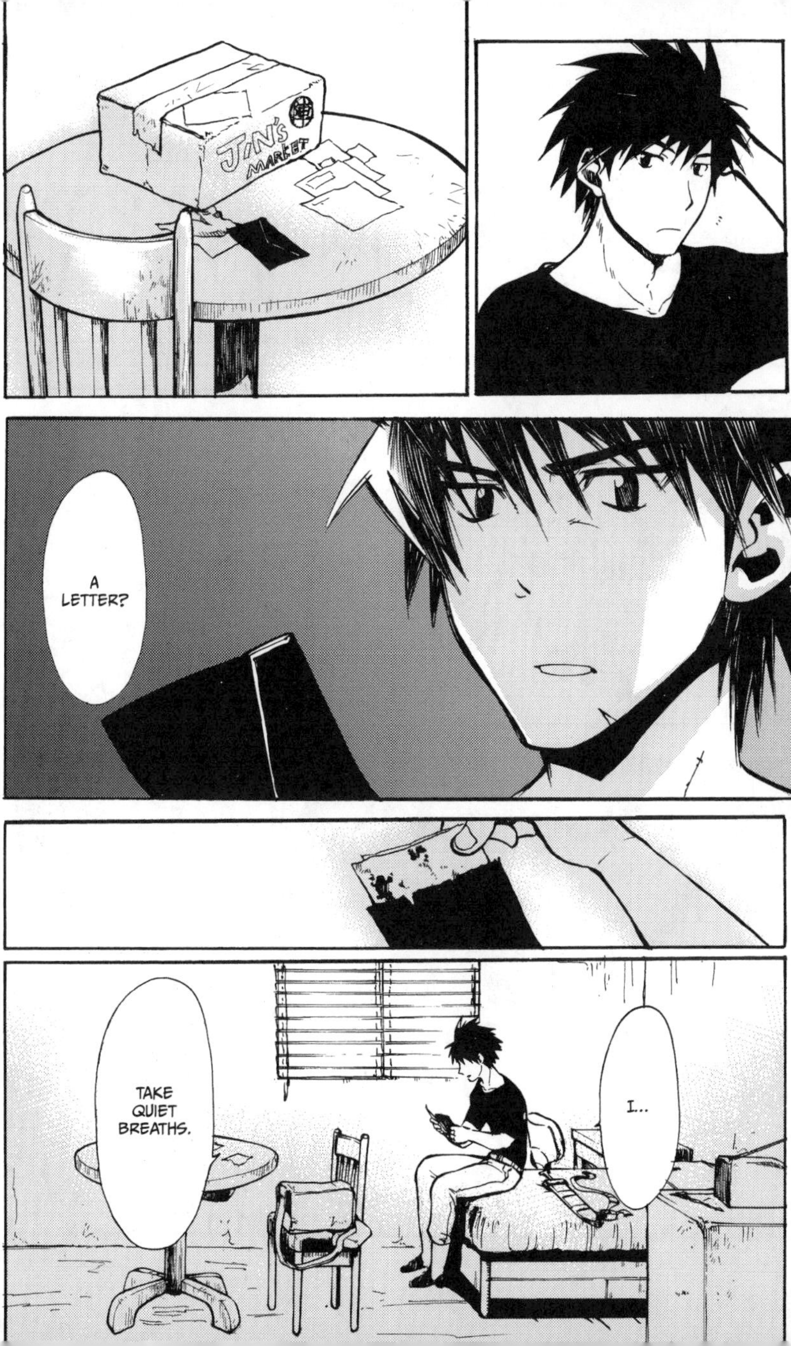
JIN'S MARKET
A LETTER?
I...
TAKE QUIET BREATHS.

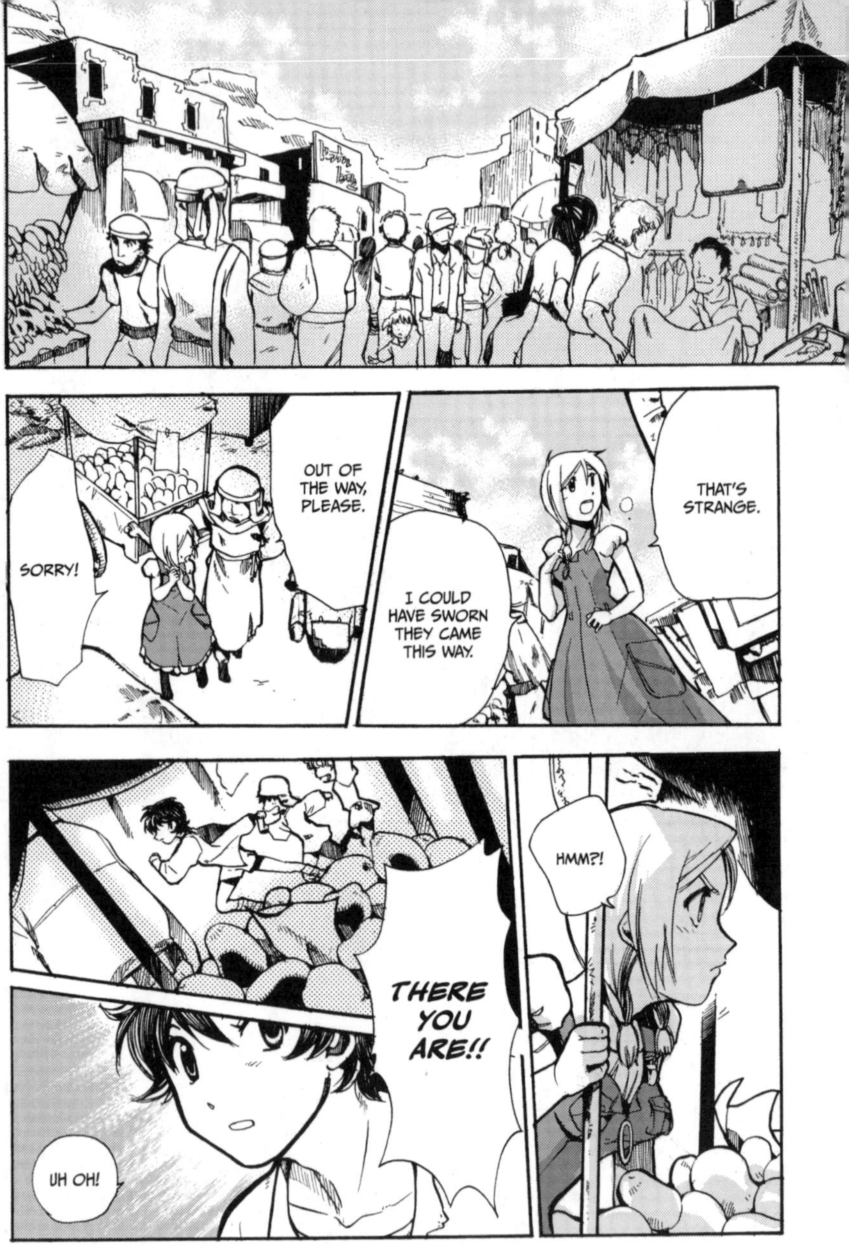
THAT'S STRANGE.
I COULD HAVE SWORN THEY CAME THIS WAY.
OUT OF THE WAY, PLEASE.
SORRY!
HMM?!
THERE YOU ARE!!
UH OH!

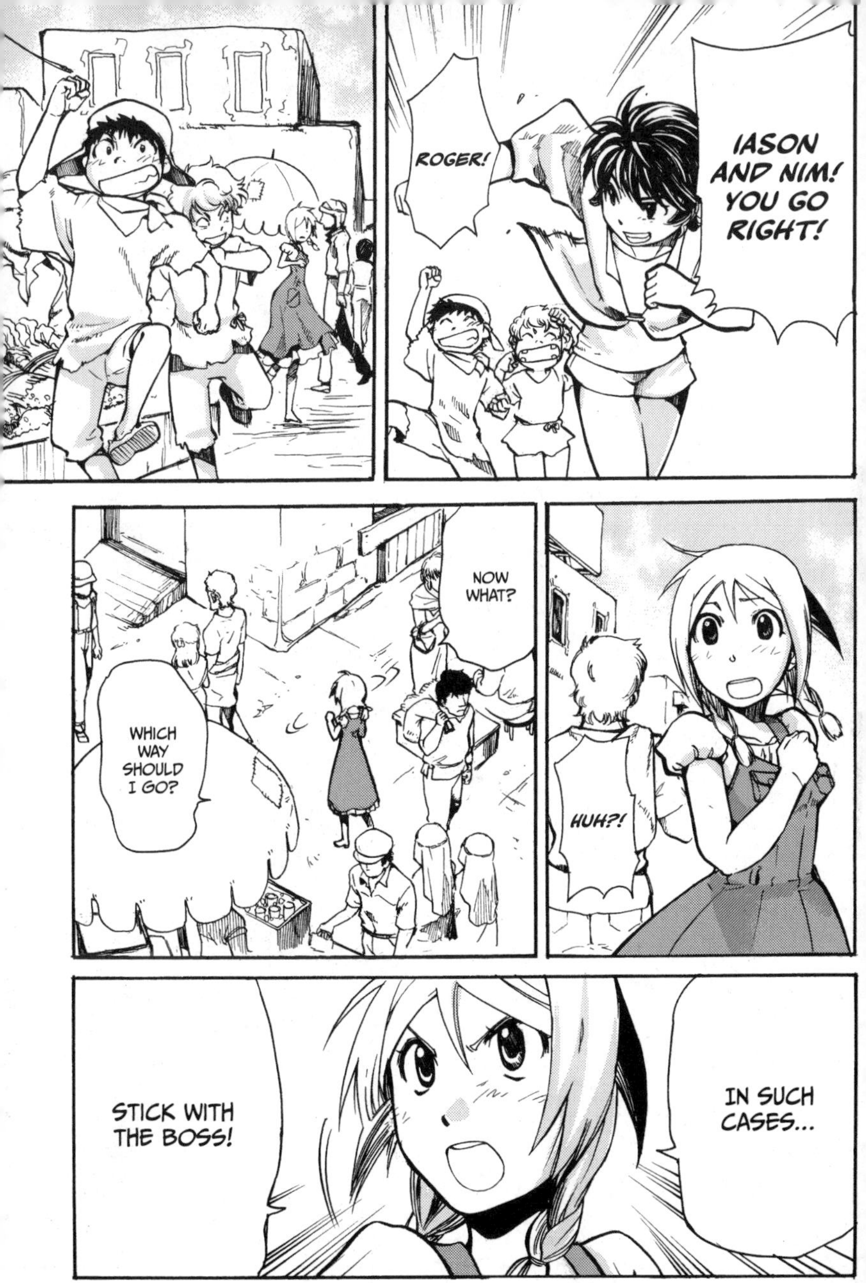
IASON AND NIM! YOU GO RIGHT!
ROGER!
HUH?!
NOW WHAT?
WHICH WAY SHOULD I GO?
IN SUCH CASES...
STICK WITH THE BOSS!

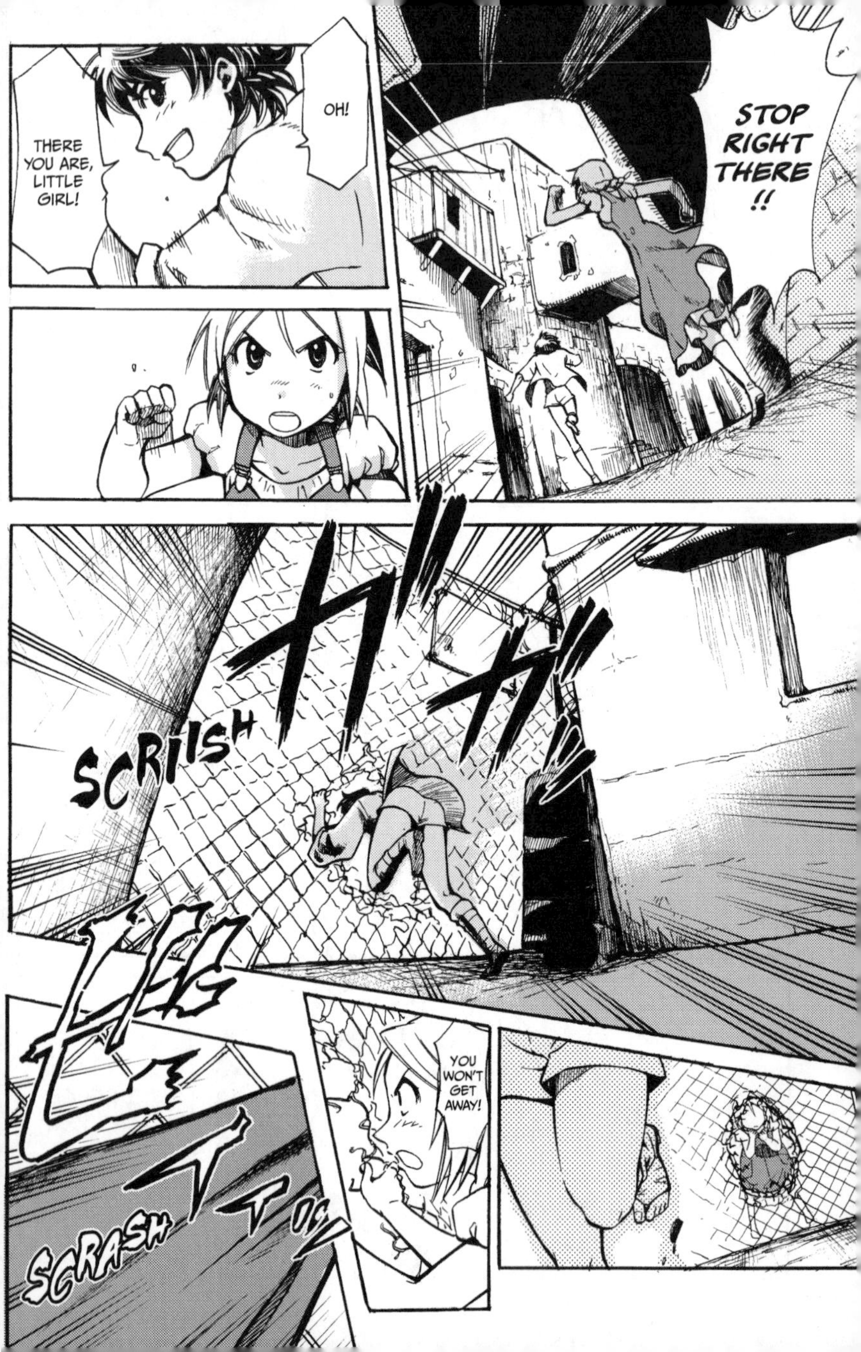
STOP RIGHT THERE !!
OH!
THERE YOU ARE, LITTLE GIRL!
SCRIISH
YOU WON'T GET AWAY!
SCRASH

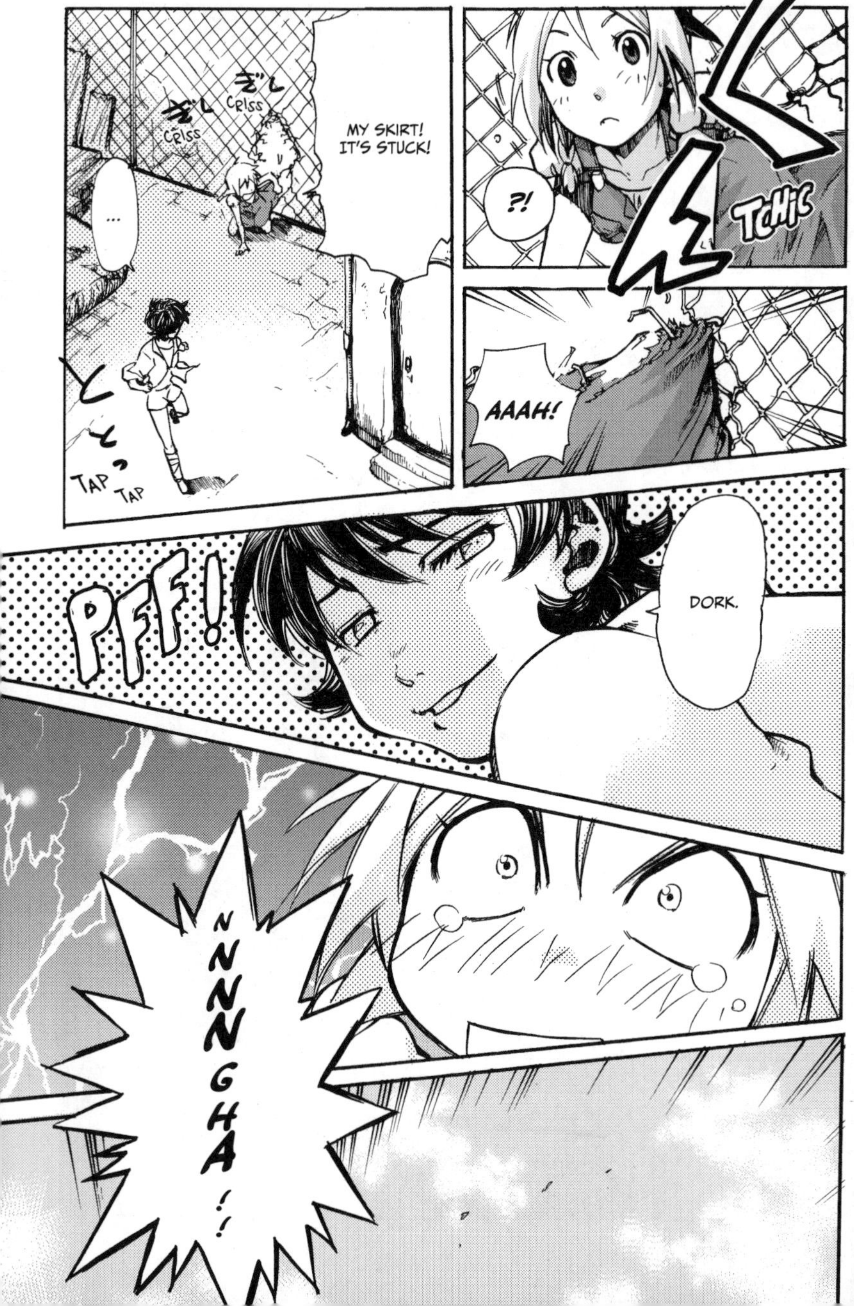

?!
TCHIC
AAAH!
ぎし ぎし
CRISS CRISS
MY SKIRT! IT'S STUCK!
...
TAP TAP
DORK.
PFF!
NNNNGHA!!

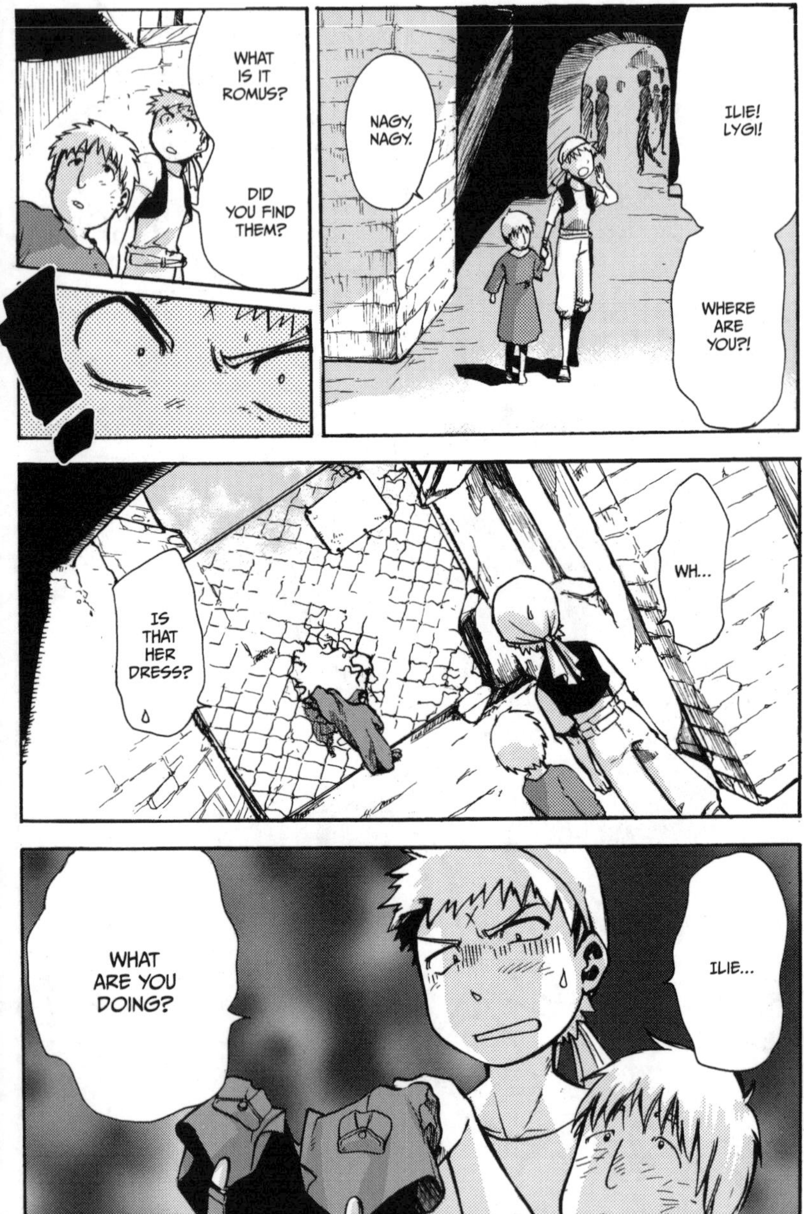
ILIE! LYGI! WHERE ARE YOU?!
NAGY, NAGY.
WHAT IS IT ROMUS? DID YOU FIND THEM?
WH...
IS THAT HER DRESS?
ILIE...
WHAT ARE YOU DOING?

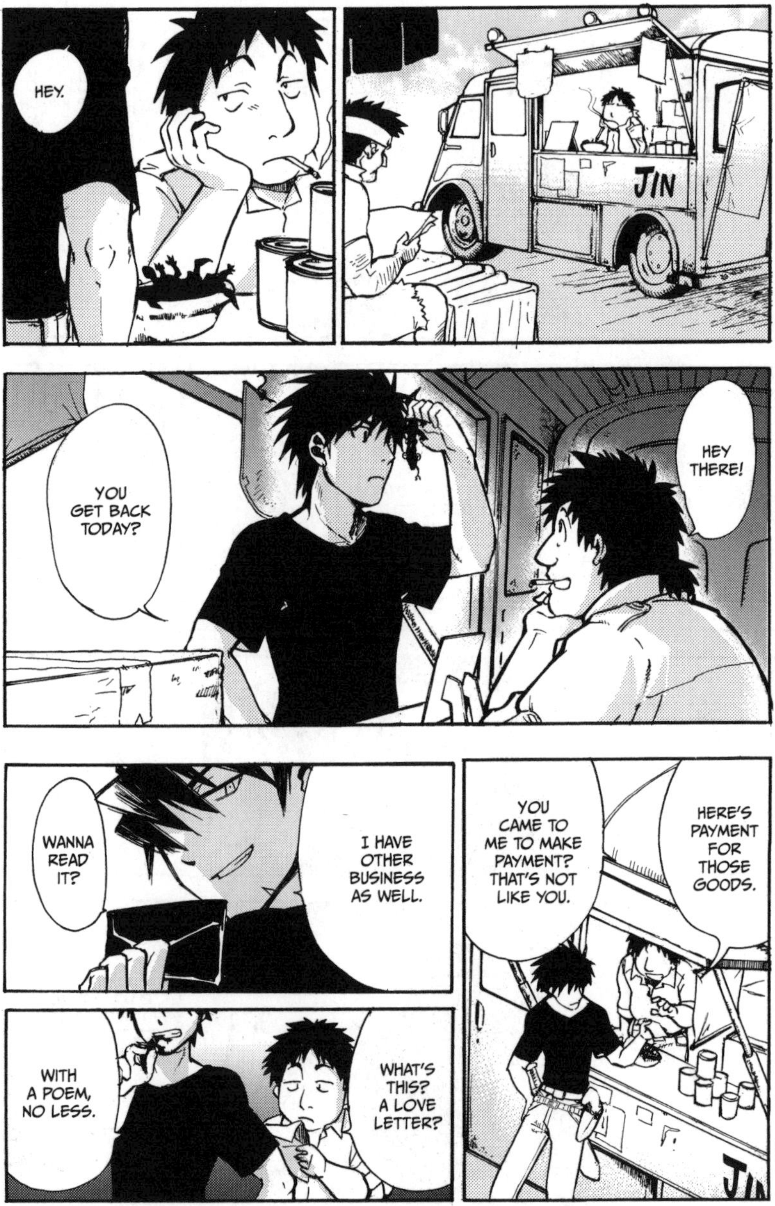
JIN
HEY.
HEY THERE!
YOU GET BACK TODAY?
HERE'S PAYMENT FOR THOSE GOODS.
YOU CAME TO ME TO MAKE PAYMENT? THAT'S NOT LIKE YOU.
JIN
I HAVE OTHER BUSINESS AS WELL.
WANNA READ IT?
WHAT'S THIS? A LOVE LETTER?
WITH A POEM, NO LESS.

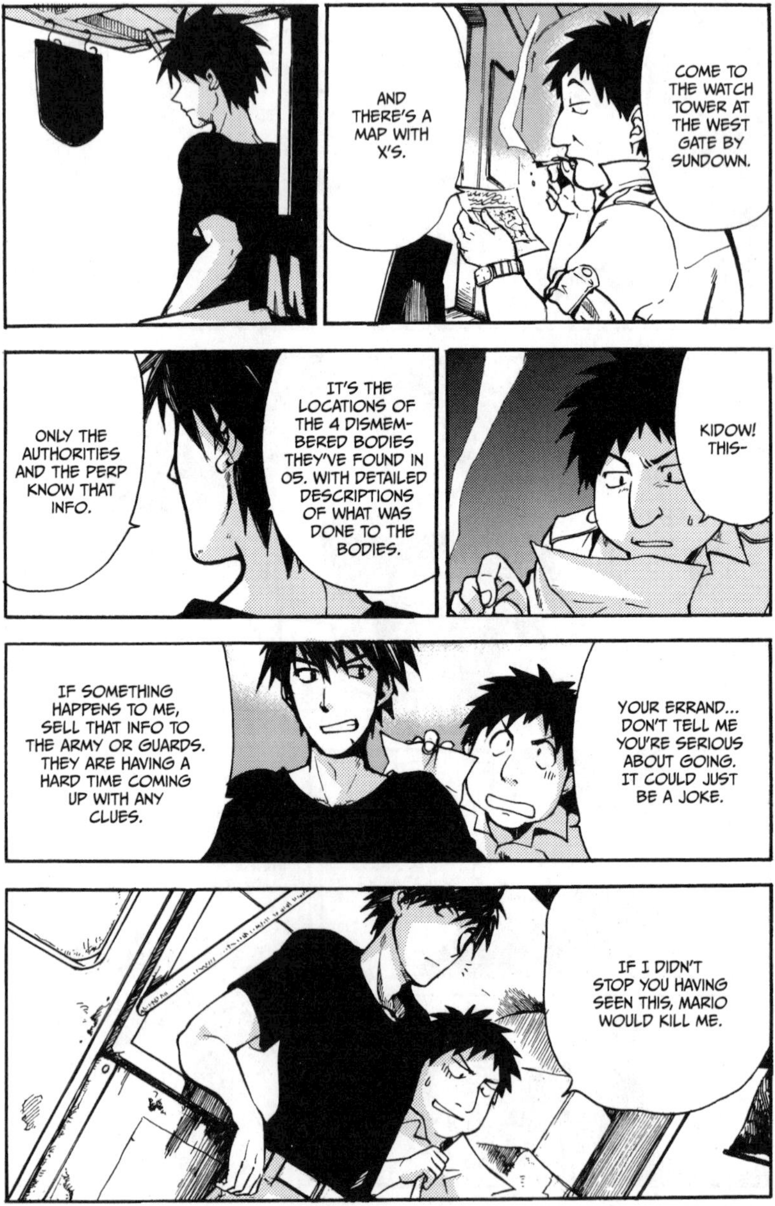
COME TO THE WATCH TOWER AT THE WEST GATE BY SUNDOWN.
AND THERE'S A MAP WITH X'S.
KIDOW! THIS-
IT'S THE LOCATIONS OF THE 4 DISMEM-BERED BODIES THEY'VE FOUND IN O5. WITH DETAILED DESCRIPTIONS OF WHAT WAS DONE TO THE BODIES.
ONLY THE AUTHORITIES AND THE PERP KNOW THAT INFO.
YOUR ERRAND... DON'T TELL ME YOU'RE SERIOUS ABOUT GOING. IT COULD JUST BE A JOKE.
IF SOMETHING HAPPENS TO ME, SELL THAT INFO TO THE ARMY OR GUARDS. THEY ARE HAVING A HARD TIME COMING UP WITH ANY CLUES.
IF I DIDN'T STOP YOU HAVING SEEN THIS, MARIO WOULD KILL ME.

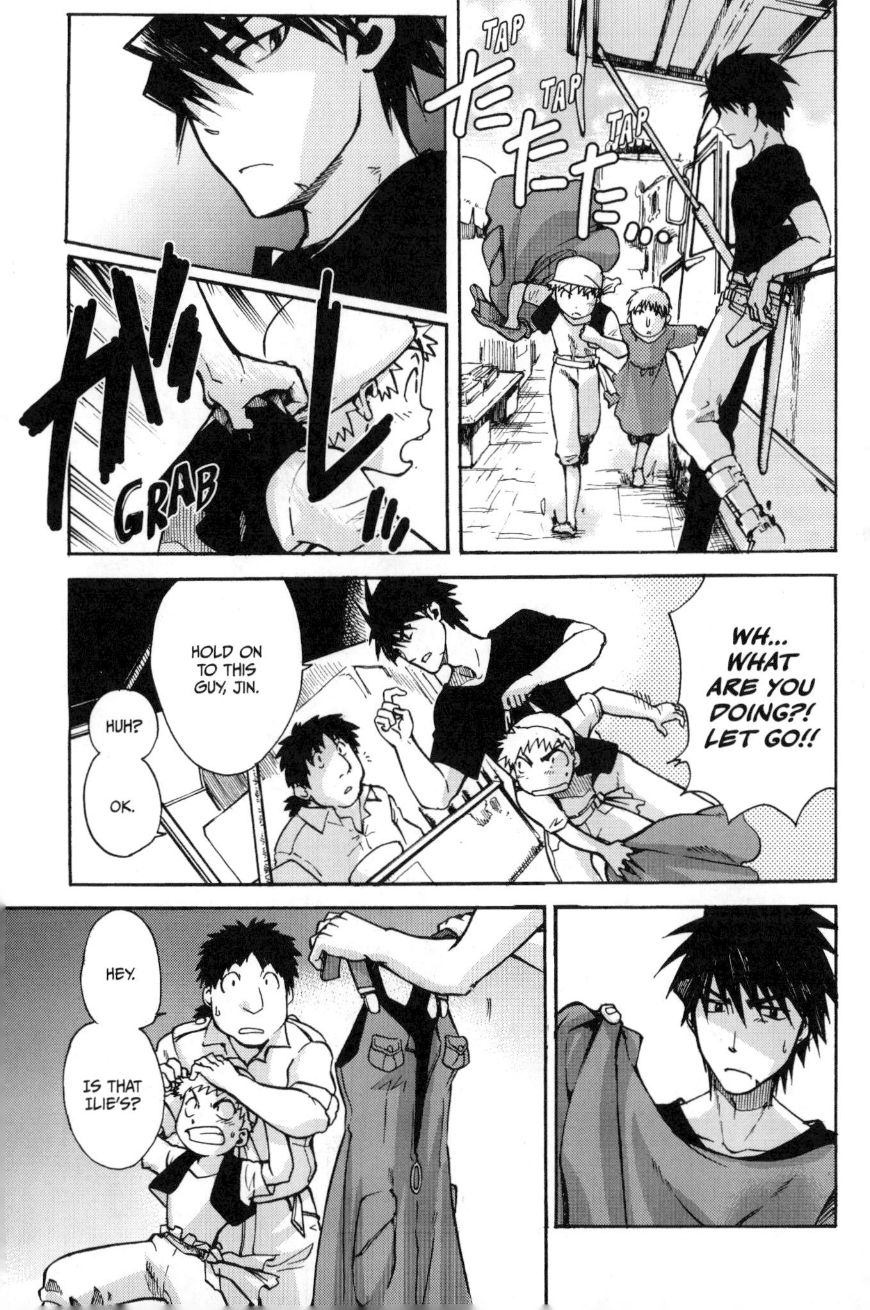
TAP
TAP
TAP
GRAB
WH... WHAT ARE YOU DOING?! LET GO!!
HOLD ON TO THIS GUY, JIN.
HUH?
OK.
HEY.
IS THAT ILIE'S?

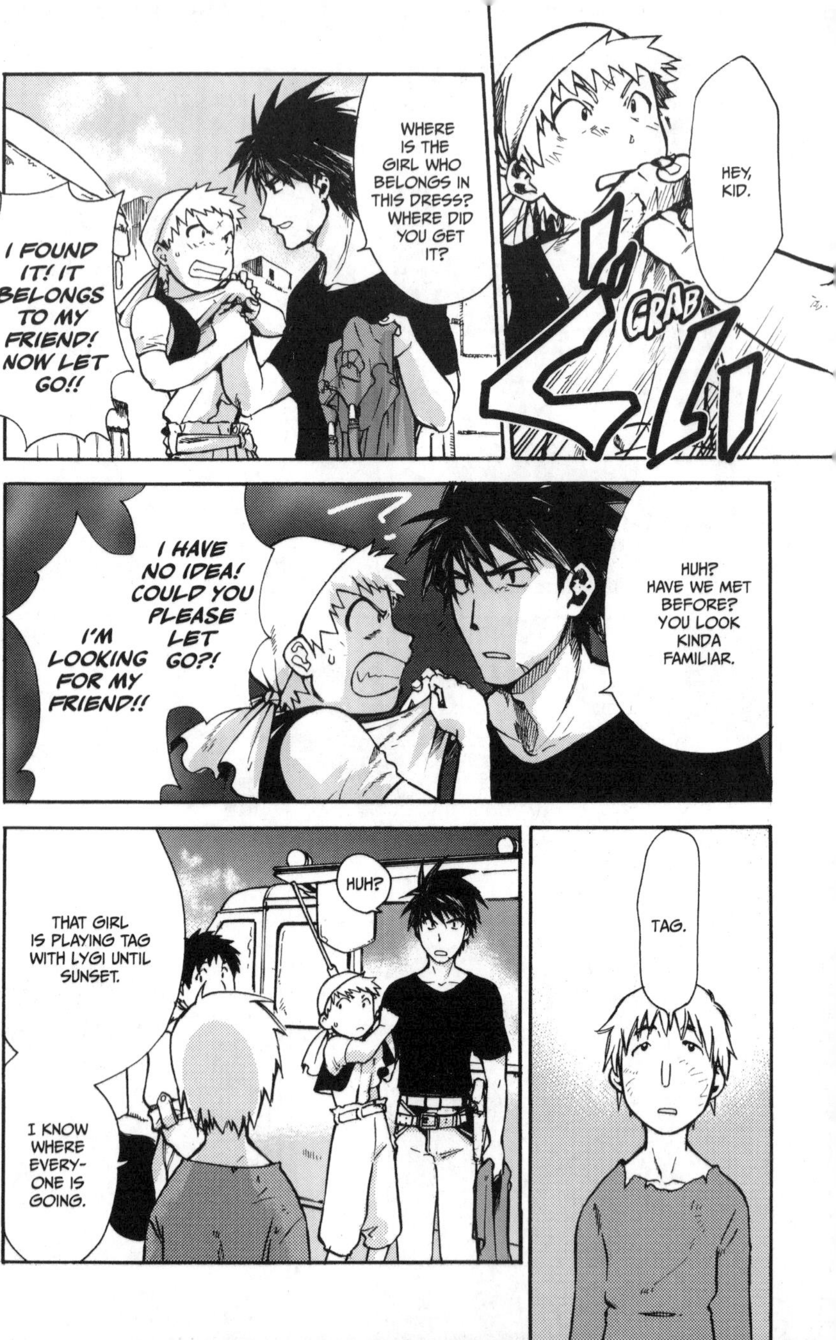
HEY, KID.
GRAB
WHERE IS THE GIRL WHO BELONGS IN THIS DRESS? WHERE DID YOU GET IT?
I FOUND IT! IT BELONGS TO MY FRIEND! NOW LET GO!!
HUH? HAVE WE MET BEFORE? YOU LOOK KINDA FAMILIAR.
I HAVE NO IDEA! COULD YOU PLEASE LET GO?!
I'M LOOKING FOR MY FRIEND!!
TAG.
THAT GIRL IS PLAYING TAG WITH LYGI UNTIL SUNSET.
HUH?
I KNOW WHERE EVERY-ONE IS GOING.

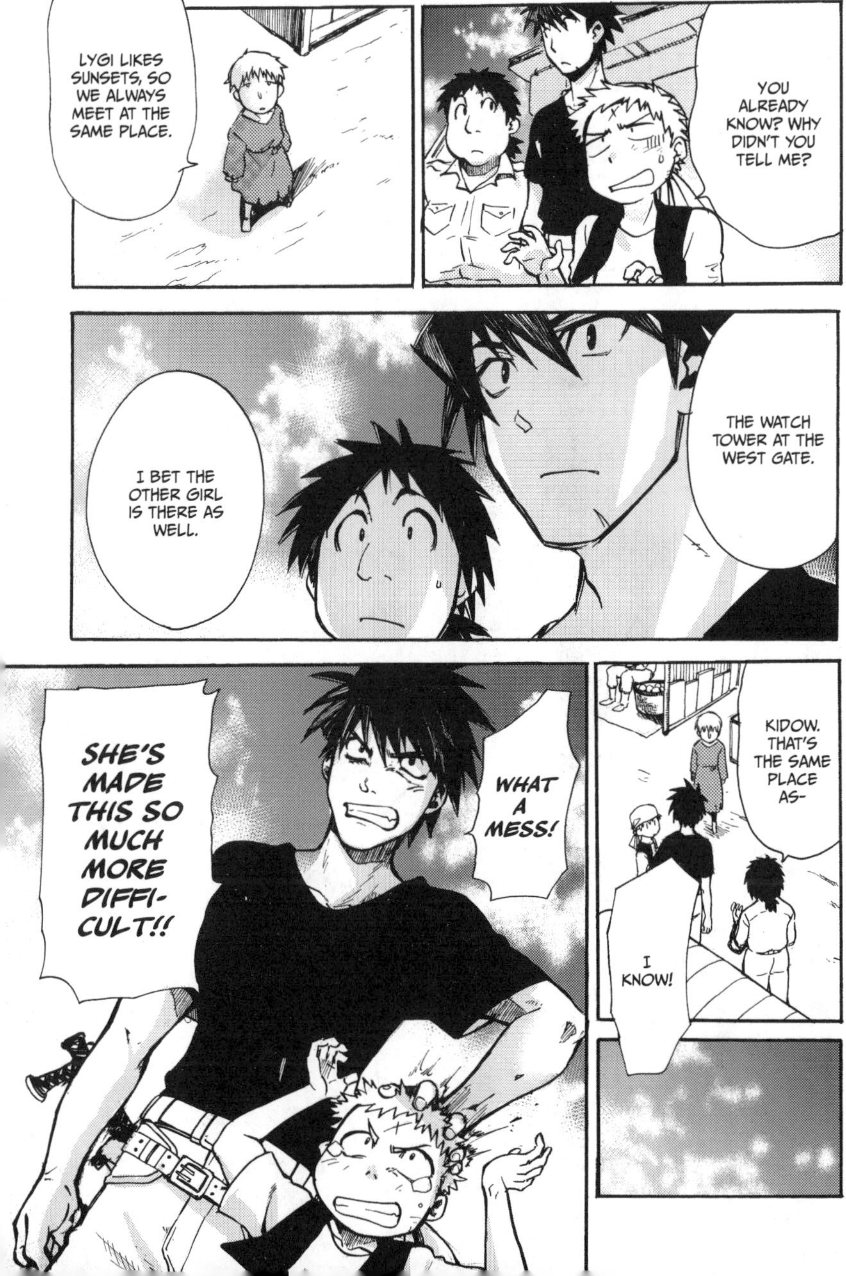
YOU ALREADY KNOW? WHY DIDN'T YOU TELL ME?
LYGI LIKES SUNSETS, SO WE ALWAYS MEET AT THE SAME PLACE.
THE WATCH TOWER AT THE WEST GATE.
I BET THE OTHER GIRL IS THERE AS WELL.
KIDOW. THAT'S THE SAME PLACE AS-
I KNOW!
WHAT A MESS!
SHE'S MADE THIS SO MUCH MORE DIFFI-CULT!!

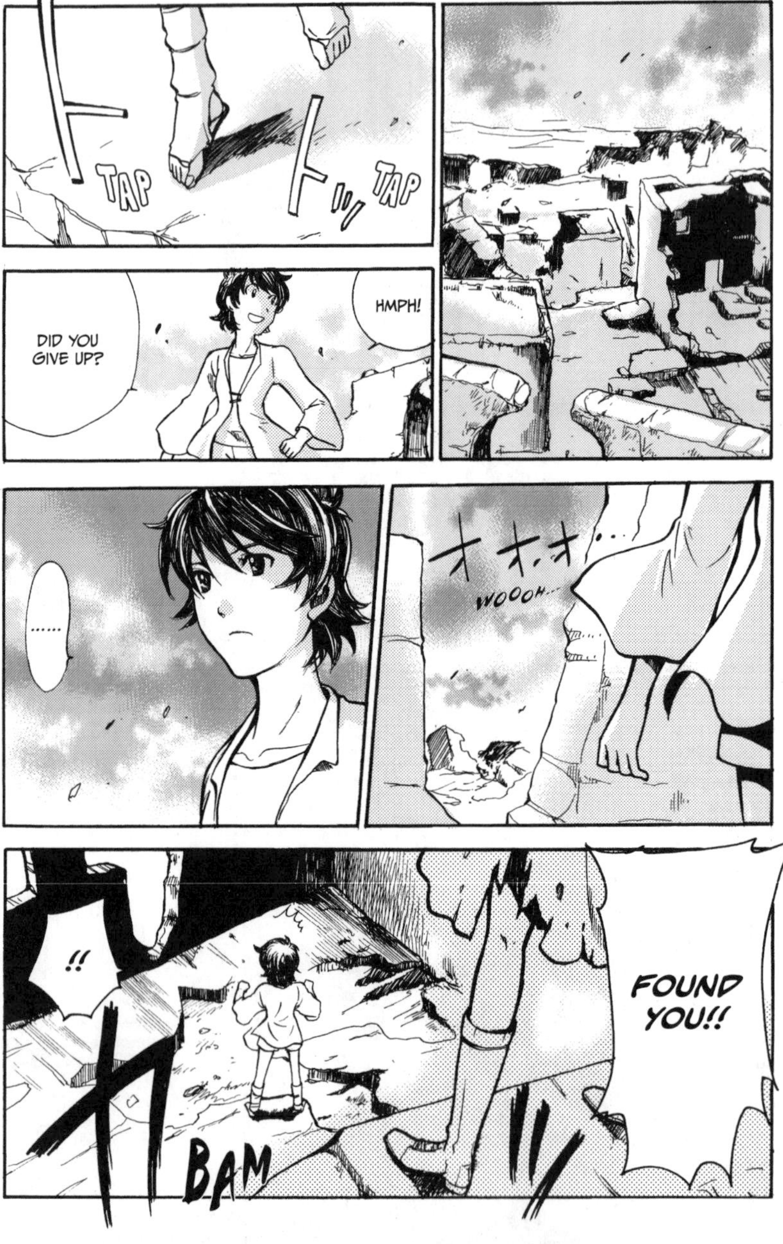
TAP
TAP
HMPH!
DID YOU GIVE UP?
WOOOH...
......
FOUND YOU!!
!!
BAM

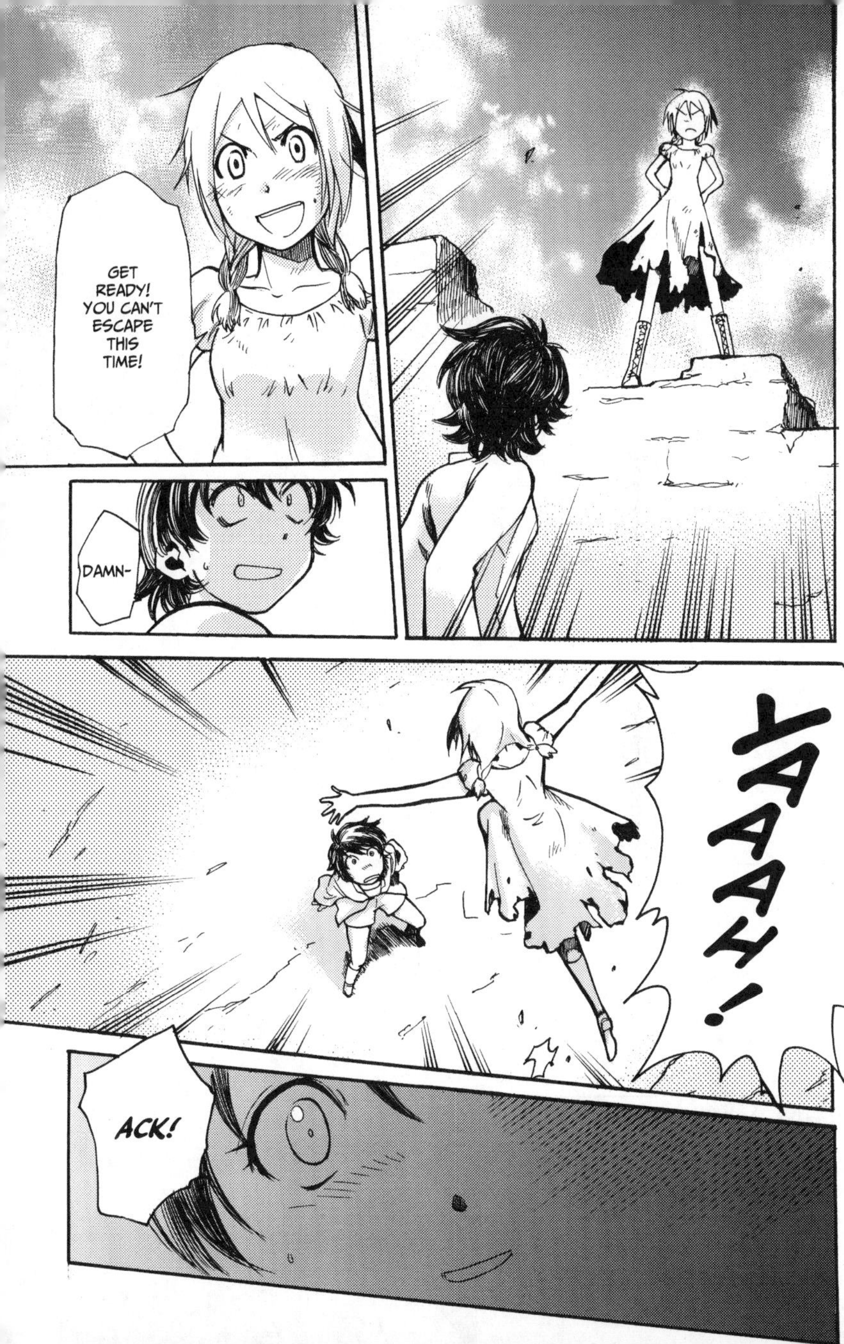
GET READY! YOU CAN'T ESCAPE THIS TIME!
DAMN-
HAAAH!
ACK!

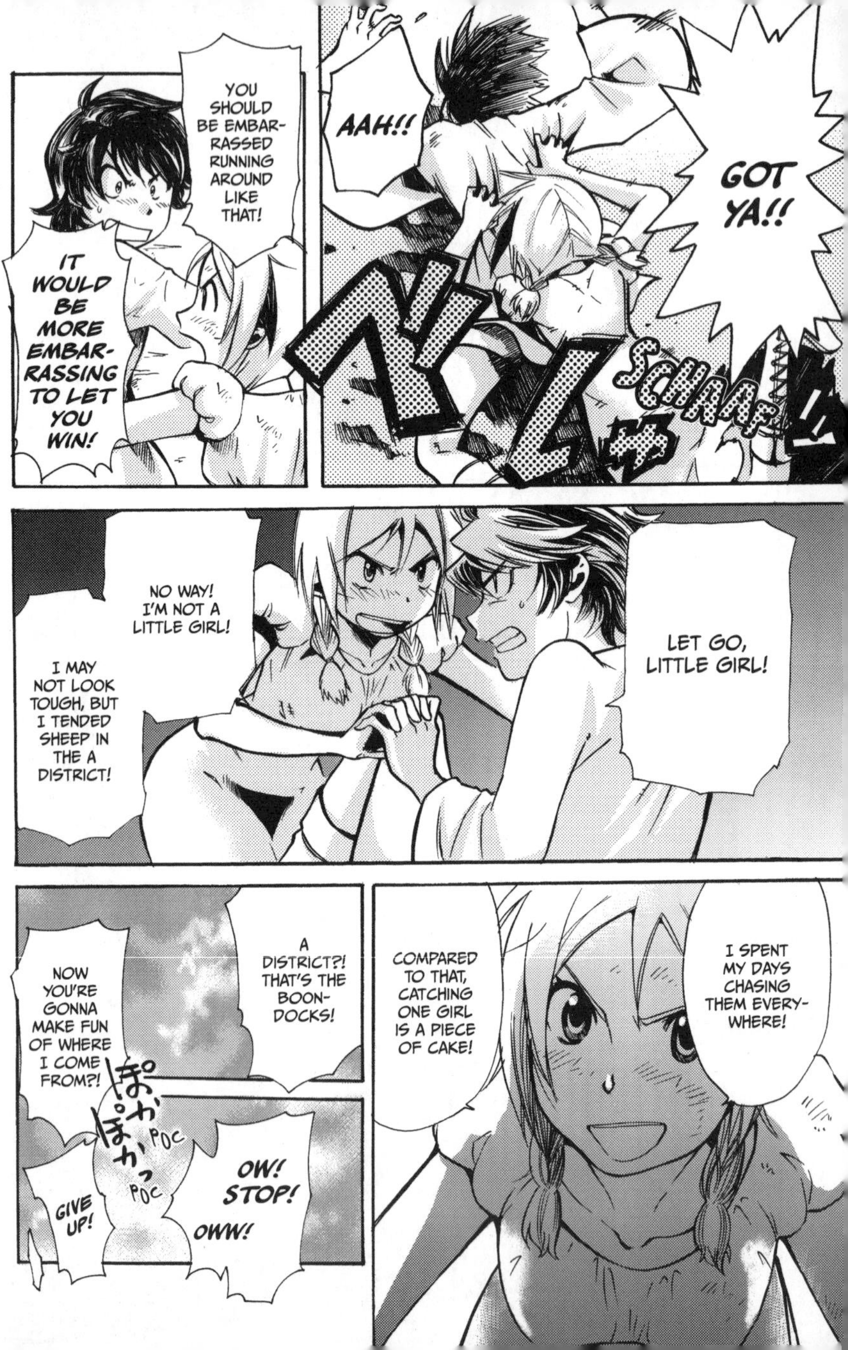
GOT YA!!
AAH!!
SCHAAF!
YOU SHOULD BE EMBAR-RASSED RUNNING AROUND LIKE THAT!
IT WOULD BE MORE EMBAR-RASSING TO LET YOU WIN!
LET GO, LITTLE GIRL!
NO WAY! I'M NOT A LITTLE GIRL!
I MAY NOT LOOK TOUGH, BUT I TENDED SHEEP IN THE A DISTRICT!
I SPENT MY DAYS CHASING THEM EVERY-WHERE!
COMPARED TO THAT, CATCHING ONE GIRL IS A PIECE OF CAKE!
A DISTRICT?! THAT'S THE BOON-DOCKS!
NOW YOU'RE GONNA MAKE FUN OF WHERE I COME FROM?!
OW! STOP!
POC
POC
OWW!
GIVE UP!

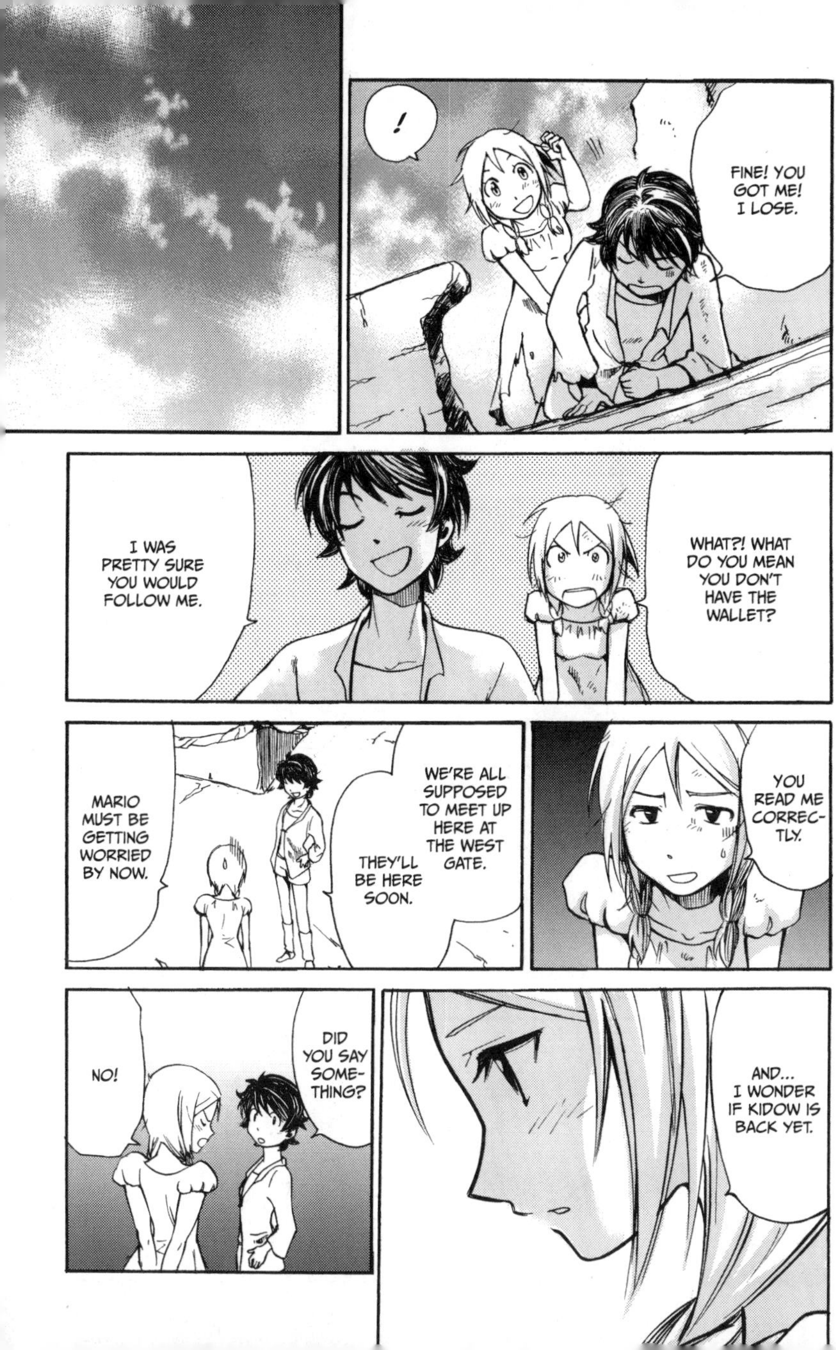
FINE! YOU GOT ME! I LOSE.
!
WHAT?! WHAT DO YOU MEAN YOU DON'T HAVE THE WALLET?
I WAS PRETTY SURE YOU WOULD FOLLOW ME.
YOU READ ME CORRECT-TLY.
WE'RE ALL SUPPOSED TO MEET UP HERE AT THE WEST GATE.
THEY'LL BE HERE SOON.
MARIO MUST BE GETTING WORRIED BY NOW.
AND... I WONDER IF KIDOW IS BACK YET.
DID YOU SAY SOME-THING?
NO!

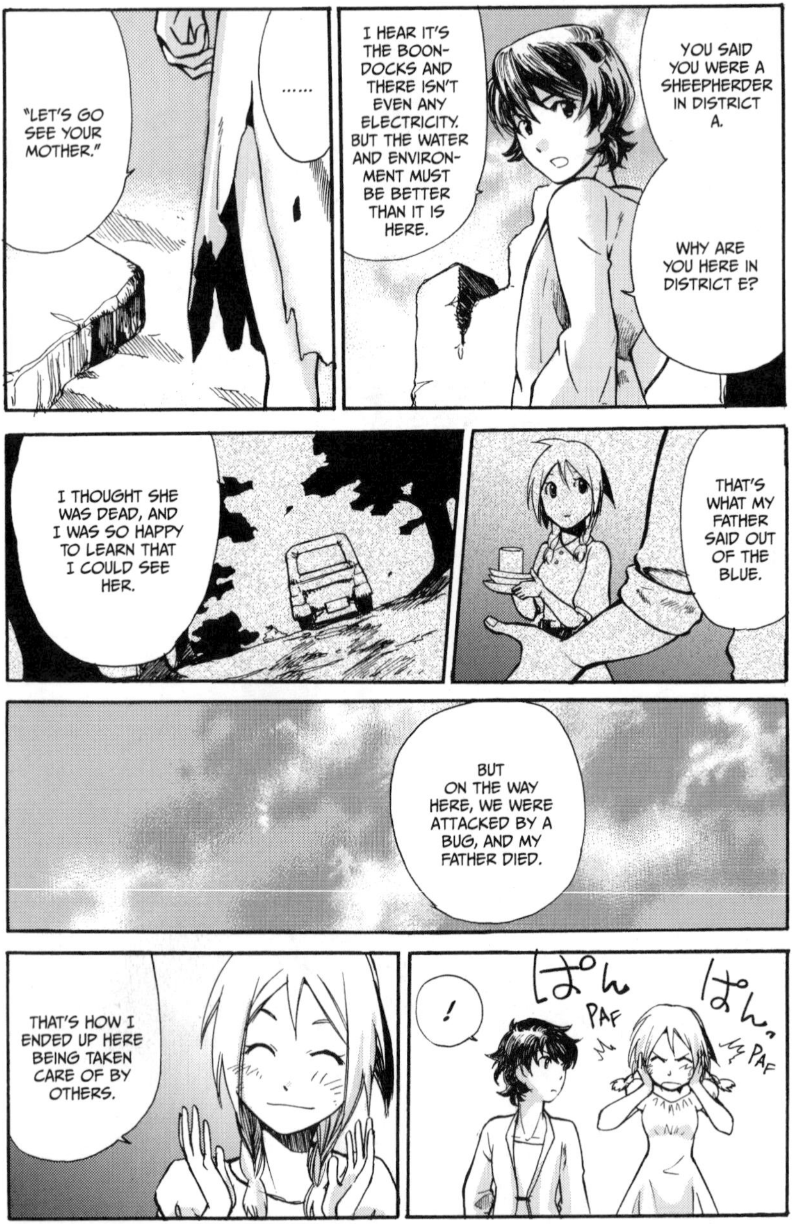
YOU SAID YOU WERE A SHEEPHERDER IN DISTRICT A.
WHY ARE YOU HERE IN DISTRICT E?
I HEAR IT'S THE BOON-DOCKS AND THERE ISN'T EVEN ANY ELECTRICITY. BUT THE WATER AND ENVIRON-MENT MUST BE BETTER THAN IT IS HERE.
......
"LET'S GO SEE YOUR MOTHER."
THAT'S WHAT MY FATHER SAID OUT OF THE BLUE.
I THOUGHT SHE WAS DEAD, AND I WAS SO HAPPY TO LEARN THAT I COULD SEE HER.
BUT ON THE WAY HERE, WE WERE ATTACKED BY A BUG, AND MY FATHER DIED.
ぱん ぱん。
PAF
PAF
!
THAT'S HOW I ENDED UP HERE BEING TAKEN CARE OF BY OTHERS.

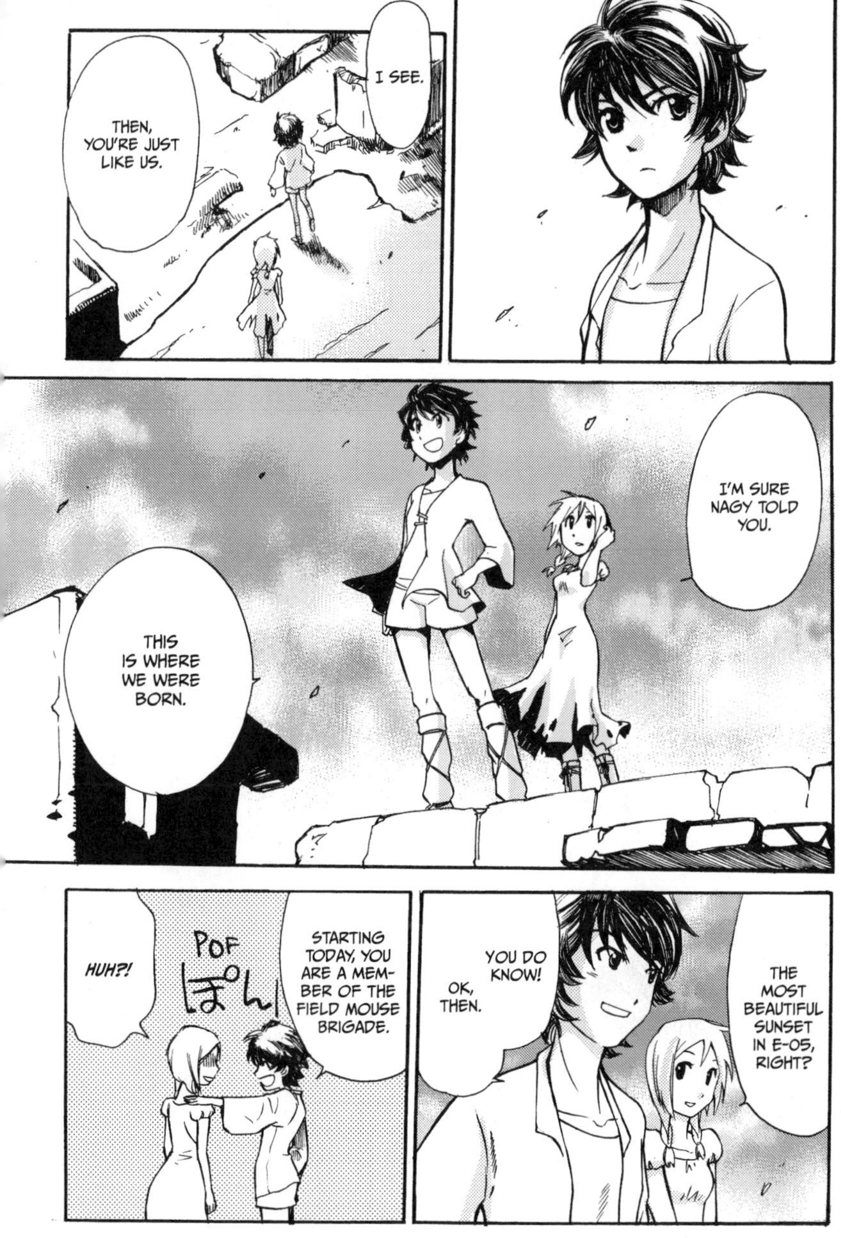
I SEE.
THEN, YOU'RE JUST LIKE US.
I'M SURE NAGY TOLD YOU.
THIS IS WHERE WE WERE BORN.
THE MOST BEAUTIFUL SUNSET IN E-05, RIGHT?
YOU DO KNOW!
OK, THEN.
STARTING TODAY, YOU ARE A MEM-BER OF THE FIELD MOUSE BRIGADE.
POF
ぽん
HUH?!

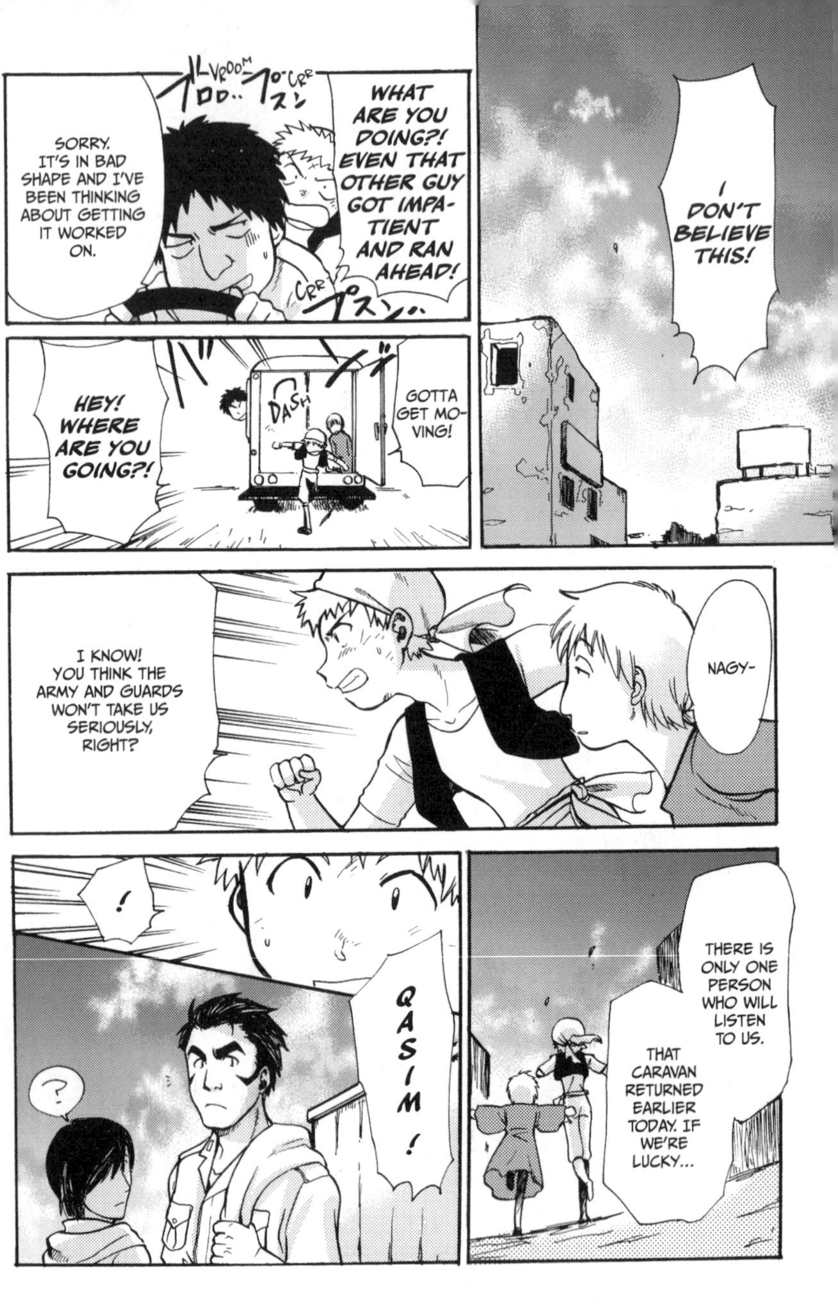
I DON'T BELIEVE THIS!
CRR
WHAT ARE YOU DOING?! EVEN THAT OTHER GUY GOT IMPATIENT AND RAN AHEAD!
VROOM
SORRY. IT'S IN BAD SHAPE AND I'VE BEEN THINKING ABOUT GETTING IT WORKED ON.
CRR
GOTTA GET MOVING!
DASH
HEY! WHERE ARE YOU GOING?!
NAGY-
I KNOW! YOU THINK THE ARMY AND GUARDS WON'T TAKE US SERIOUSLY, RIGHT?
THERE IS ONLY ONE PERSON WHO WILL LISTEN TO US.
THAT CARAVAN RETURNED EARLIER TODAY. IF WE'RE LUCKY...
!
QASIM!
?

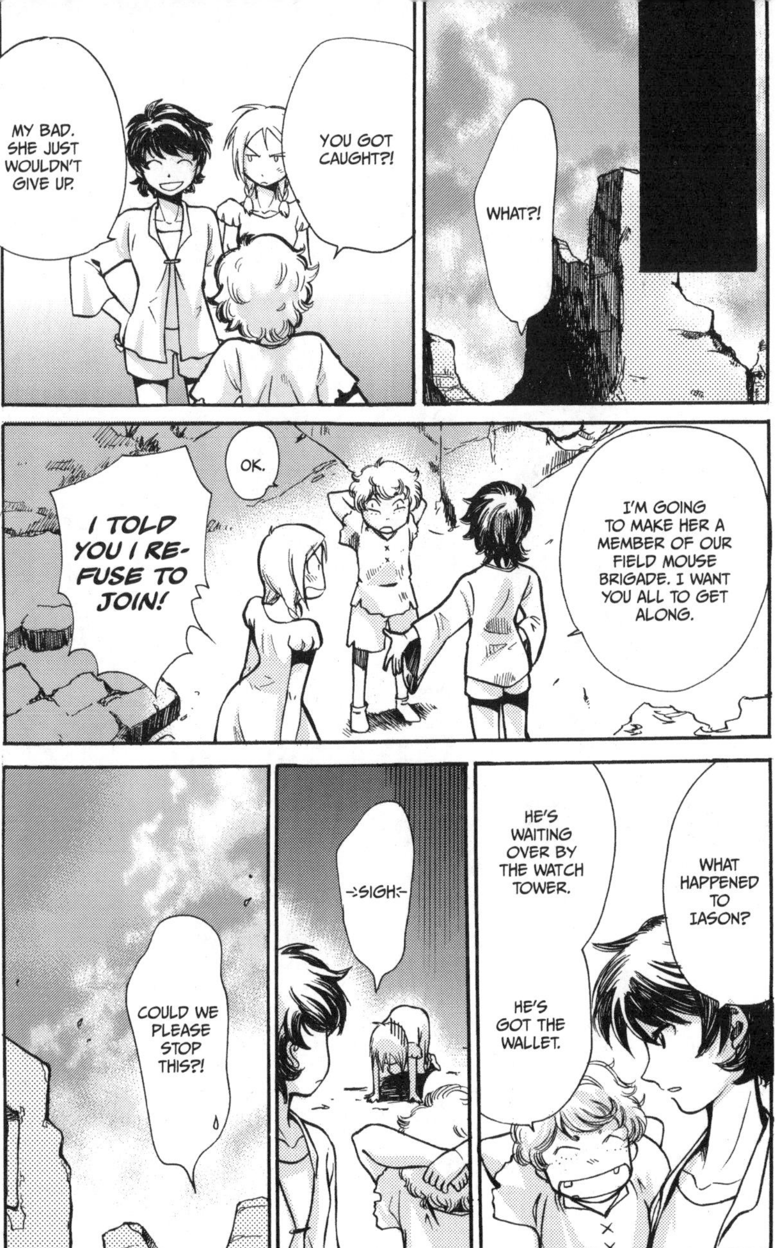
WHAT?!
YOU GOT CAUGHT?!
MY BAD. SHE JUST WOULDN'T GIVE UP.
I'M GOING TO MAKE HER A MEMBER OF OUR FIELD MOUSE BRIGADE. I WANT YOU ALL TO GET ALONG.
OK.
I TOLD YOU I RE-FUSE TO JOIN!
WHAT HAPPENED TO IASON?
HE'S WAITING OVER BY THE WATCH TOWER.
HE'S GOT THE WALLET.
-SIGH-
COULD WE PLEASE STOP THIS?!

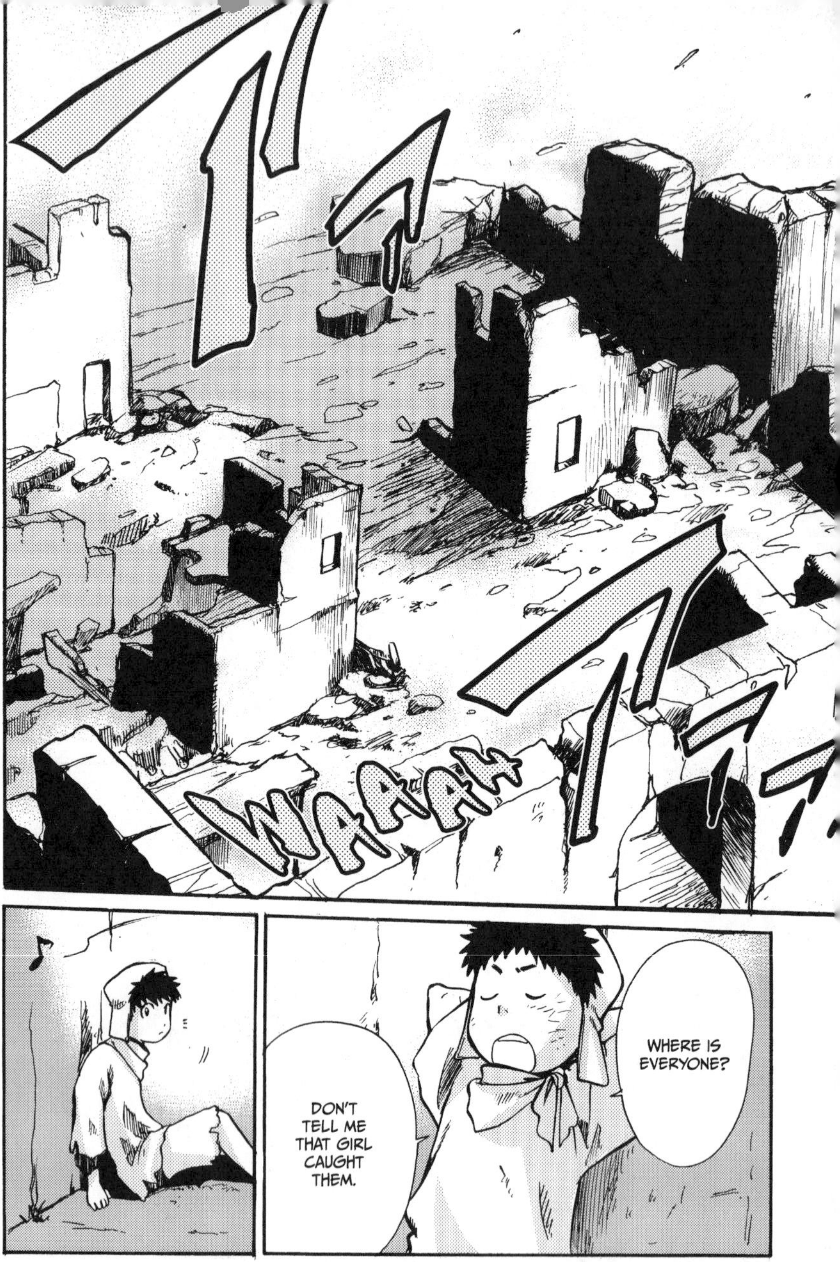
WAAAH
WHERE IS EVERYONE?
DON'T TELL ME THAT GIRL CAUGHT THEM.

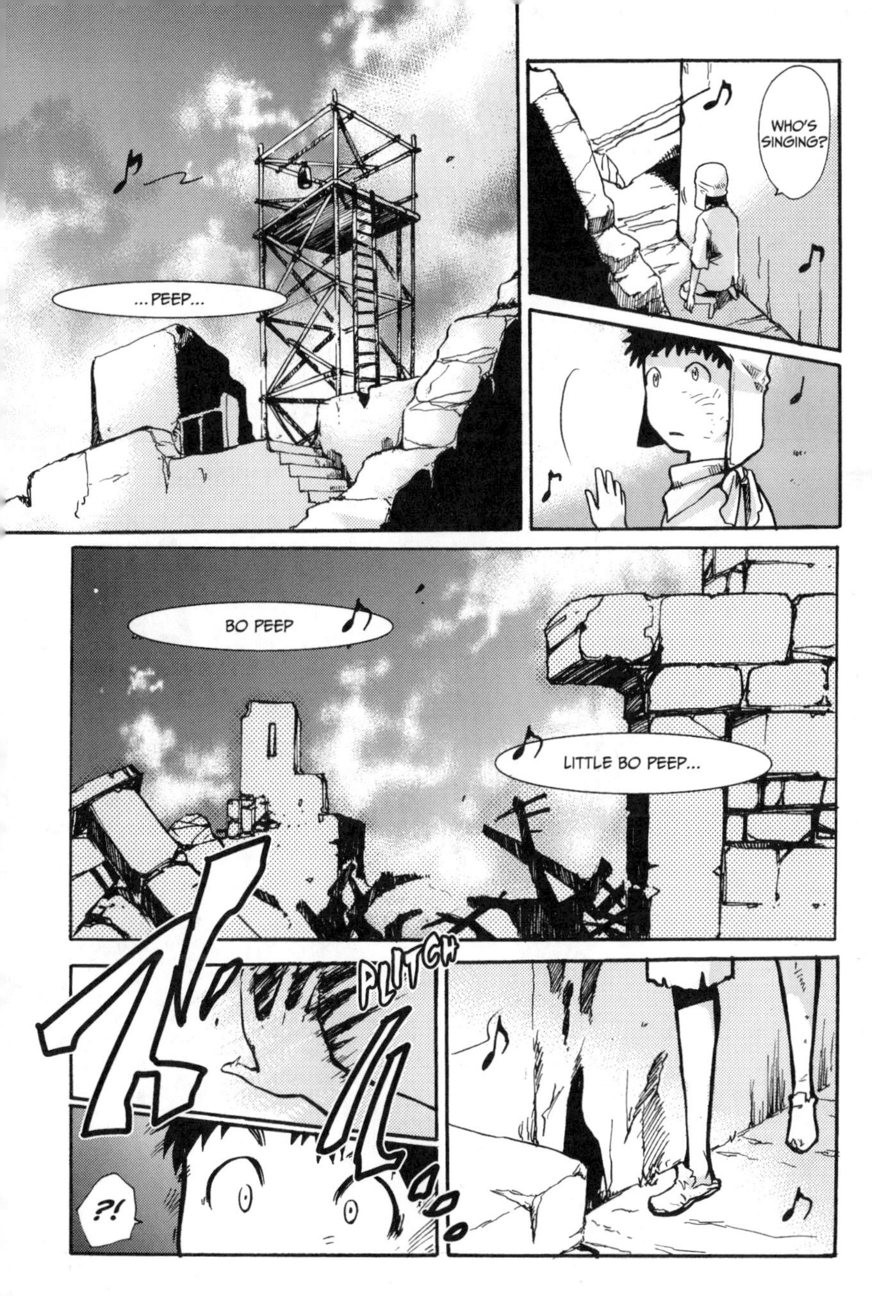

WHO'S SINGING?
...PEEP...
BO PEEP
LITTLE BO PEEP...
PLITCH
?!

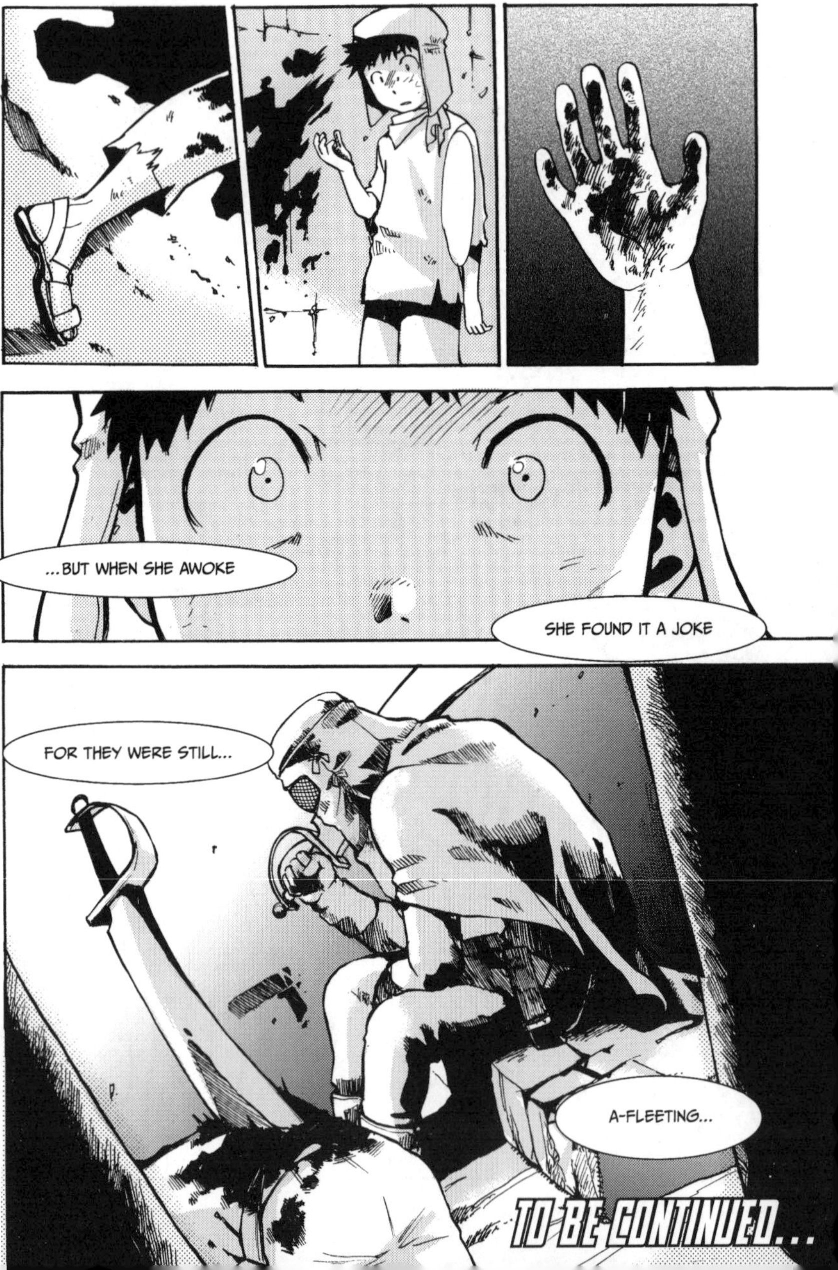
...BUT WHEN SHE AWOKE
SHE FOUND IT A JOKE
FOR THEY WERE STILL...
A-FLEETING...
TO BE CONTINUED...

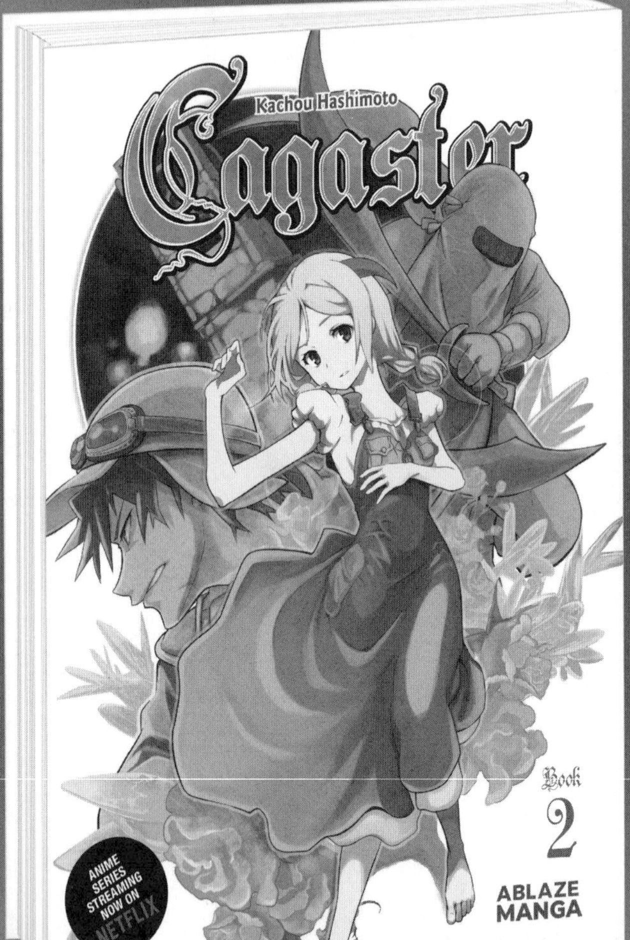

Kachou Hashimoto
Cagaster
Book
2
ABLAZE
MANGA
ANIME
SERIES
STREAMING
NOW ON
NETFLIX

# Cagaster

## Book
## 2

## Coming soon!

Complete series in 6 volumes

**ABLAZE MANGA**

# CAGASTER
## by Kachou Hashimoto

Translation: Matthew Johnson
Lettering: Studio Makma
Editor: Rich Young
Designer: Rodolfo Muraguchi

---

CAGASTER, VOLUME 1. First printing. Published by Ablaze Publishing, 11222 SE Main
St. #22906 Portland, OR 97269. CAGASTER © Editions Glénat 2014-2016 – ALL RIGHTS
RESERVED. Ablaze and its logo TM & © 2020 Ablaze, LLC. All Rights Reserved. All names,
characters, events, and locales in this publication are entirely fictional. Any resemblance
to actual persons (living or dead), events or places, without satiric intent is coincidental.
No portion of this book may be reproduced by any means (digital or print) without the
written permission of Ablaze Publishing except for review purposes. Printed in China.

For advertising and licensing email: info@ablazepublishing.com

---

**Publisher's Cataloging-in-Publication Data**
Names: Hashimoto, Kachou, author.
Title: Cagaster, Volume 1 / Kachou Hashimoto.
Description: Portland, OR: Ablaze Publishing, 2020.
Identifiers: ISBN 978-1-950912-07-0
Subjects: LCSH Mutation (Biology)–Fiction.
Cannibalism–Fiction. | Dystopias. | Fantasy fiction. | Science fiction.
Adventure and adventurers–Fiction. | Graphic novels.
BISAC COMICS & GRAPHIC NOVELS / Manga / Dystopian
COMICS & GRAPHIC NOVELS / Manga / Fantasy
COMICS & GRAPHIC NOVELS / Manga / Science Fiction
Classification: LCC PN6790.J33 .H372 v. 1 2020 | DDC 741.5–dc23

---

/ablazepub  @AblazePub  @AblazePub
**ablazepublishing.com**

**To find a comics shop in your area go to:
www.comicshoplocator.com**

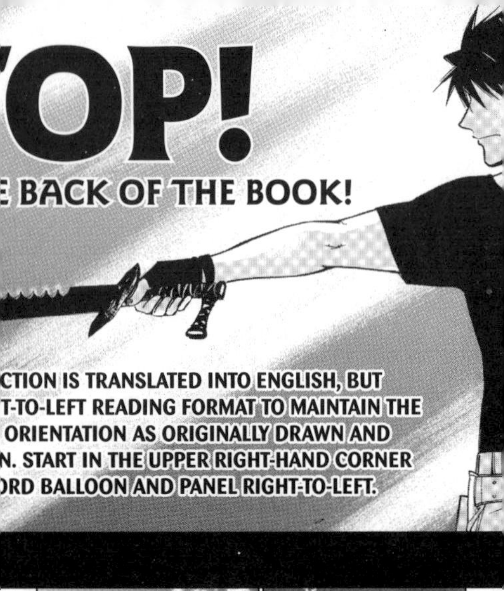
OP!
E BACK OF THE BOOK!
CTION IS TRANSLATED INTO ENGLISH, BUT
T-TO-LEFT READING FORMAT TO MAINTAIN THE
ORIENTATION AS ORIGINALLY DRAWN AND
N. START IN THE UPPER RIGHT-HAND CORNER
ORD BALLOON AND PANEL RIGHT-TO-LEFT.

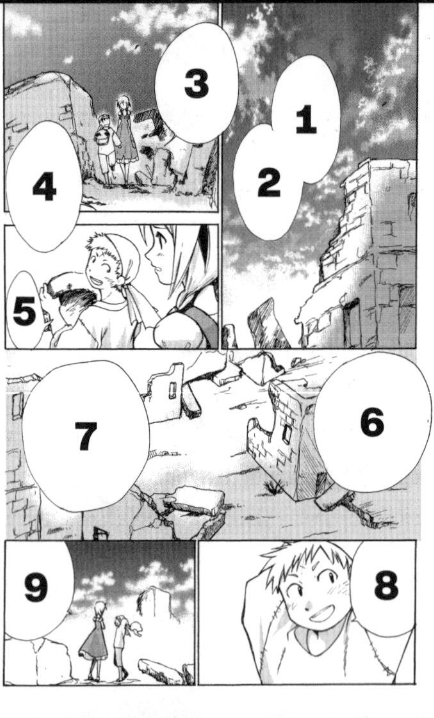
1
2
3
4
5
6
7
8
9